I0738998

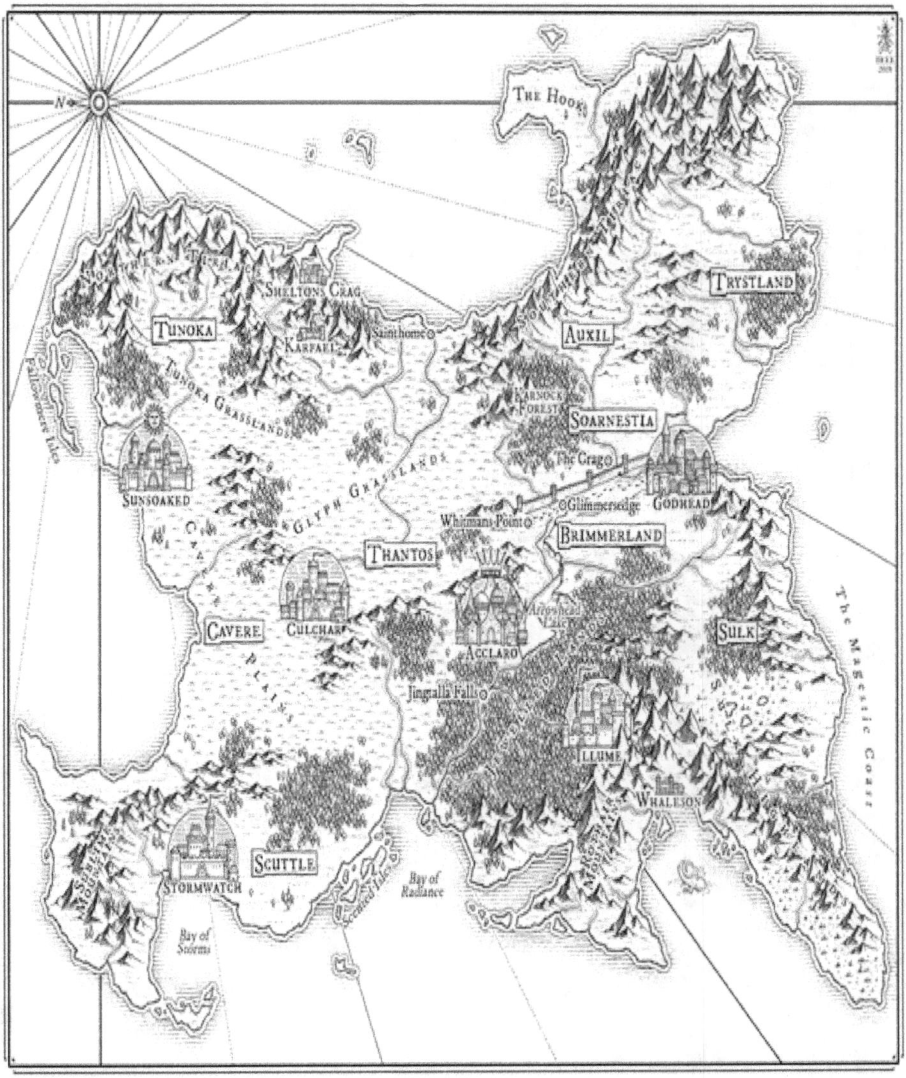

N
THE HOOK
TRYSTLAND
AUXIL
SOARNESTIA
KARNOCK FOREST
The Grag
Glimmersedge
GODREAD
BRIMMERLAND
SULK
TUNOKA
SHELTONS CRAG
KARFAEL
Sainthome
Tunoka Grasslands
GLYPH GRASSLANDS
SUNSOAKED
Falconberry Lake
Whitmans Point
THANTOS
ACCLARO
Arrowhead Lake
CAVERE
CULCHAR
PLAINS
Jingralla Falls
ILLUME
WHALESON
SCUTTLE
STORMWATCH
Bay of Radiance
Bay of Storms
The Majestic Coast

Pariah

Troy Church

Pariah by Troy Church
Published by T.A Church Perth Australia 6111

© 2019 Troy Church

Cover by Justin Randall.
Print ISBN: 978-0-6483115-2-2
Ebook ISBN: 978-0-6483115-3-9

Contents

CHAPTER 1...1
CHAPTER 2...7
CHAPTER 3..14
CHAPTER 4..22
CHAPTER 5..27
CHAPTER 6..30
CHAPTER 7..37
CHAPTER 8..40
CHAPTER 9 48
CHAPTER 10 54
CHAPTER 11 61
CHAPTER 12 69
CHAPTER 13 75
CHAPTER 14 78
CHAPTER 15 87
CHAPTER 16 95
CHAPTER 17 103
CHAPTER 18 108
CHAPTER 19 113
CHAPTER 20 120
CHAPTER 21 124
CHAPTER 22 131
CHAPTER 23 136
CHAPTER 24 141
CHAPTER 25 147
CHAPTER 26 152
CHAPTER 27 159
CHAPTER 28 165
CHAPTER 29 172

CHAPTER 30 178
CHAPTER 31 185
CHAPTER 32 200
CHAPTER 33 206
CHAPTER 34 217
CHAPTER 35 229
CHAPTER 36 233
CHAPTER 37 238
CHAPTER 38 244
CHAPTER 39 247
CHAPTER 40 251
CHAPTER 41 257
CHAPTER 42 261
CHAPTER 43 265
CHAPTER 44 270
CHAPTER 45 281
CHAPTER 46 286
CHAPTER 47 291
CHAPTER 48 297
CHAPTER 49 300
CHAPTER 50 307
CHAPTER 51 310
CHAPTER 52 318
CHAPTER 53 321
CHAPTER 54 325
CHAPTER 55 328
CHAPTER 56 335
CHAPTER 57 341
CHAPTER 58 347
CHAPTER 59 352
CHAPTER 60 355
CHAPTER 61 359
CHAPTER 62 364
CHAPTER 63 366
CHAPTER 64 370
CHAPTER 65 375

Chapter 1

When morning came to the capital of Thantos, Acclaro had become a reflection of the Infernal realms that the new inhabitants longed to return to. Houses burned and bodies littered the streets while packs of monstrosities searched through buildings, rooting out any survivors. The Infernals wouldn't make the same mistake as the humans had done in the great cleansing; they would purify this place completely.

Rapture basked in the blood of his slain. It had been too long since he had truly let himself participate in such carnage. Now, finally sated, he left the menial chores to the lesser Infernals and headed back to the castle. The Lady of Whispers would be happy now she had her prize and would be unveiled as the queen of the city. Rapture grinned and licked the blood from the back of a clawed hand. This was just the beginning, and now they had a stranglehold on the city to use as a base they could plan the assault on the rest of this loathsome world.

At first Rapture had been hesitant to leave the Lady of Whispers alone in the castle; however, she had insisted he lead the assault with his elite and even hinted at a promotion once the city had fallen. Already he had achieved the highly sought position of fiend and was given control over the lady's personal guard. Rapture had served the lady since before the Severing, and the separation from his homeland had nearly broken him like it had many others. The Lady had shown him how they would return to their home and shared her knowledge of what truly had happened to cause the Severing to take place. Soon the power he had been severed from would return and the gate to the Infernal lands once again would open for his homecoming.

Rapture had expected the throne room to be empty since the Lady of Whispers preferred the tower room and its long balcony, but the torches burnt brightly in the throne room, ruining his night vision, and he could just make out figures about the throne itself. He paused and the only sound was the jeering and laughter of the elite warriors who had followed him. Surrounded now with his exultant warriors, Rapture bent his knee at the base of the stairs leading to the throne.

'Lady, I return with news of your victory. Acclaro is yours.'

Rapture flinched as something was flung down the stairs towards him. It was a body, the lady's body, with her neck torn open and a gaping hole in her chest where the rose of spite had sat.

'The Lady of Whispers is dead and you have a new lord now. The Bone Lord.'

Behind Rapture mutters of confusion and discontent could be heard, and then the shadows about the throne were dispersed by torches held by two warriors wearing white tabards emblazoned with a flame.

'What foolishness is this?' Rapture drew his great, jagged sword and as it was echoed by the many blades of his warriors, tension thrummed through his body. Upon the throne sat a hideously deformed Infernal with features twisted from scar tissue that turned his smile into a sneer. In places bone could be seen where the skin from what looked like severe burns had failed to heal. Just behind his left shoulder, an old snowy-haired human stood grinning, and Rapture ached to stave in his skull. A human child sat chained to the old man's wrist, cowering at his feet and around the throne stood eight other warriors of the flame looking determined and spoiling for a fight.

'You have no authority here,' growled Rapture as he began ascending the stairs.

'No authority, you say,' said the broken figure on the throne. 'And yet surely you remember these.' The scarred impostor stood holding the ornate rod of an infernal lord up for Rapture and his warriors to see.

'And this.' He let his tunic fall open to show the dark metal shaped in the design of a rose where it sat embedded in his chest. It was the rose of spite

'You should count your blessings that I am in high spirits and need powerful warriors such as you and your elite. Now bend to the bone lord and report the status of our city.'

The door to her latest prison opened, and Dalwyn Trevlon pushed Nina inside. He looked scornfully down at her then closed the door, leaving her in darkness at the foot of the stairs. She listened to the key turn in the lock then began to trudge up the long, winding staircase. Nina knew Dalwyn tired of her presence, but since she was the only way he could gain any control over Zacriel, he kept her here with him. Often Nina had wondered exactly why Zacriel didn't kill the evil old man and why he let Dalwyn push him around when he tolerated no such thing from anybody else. She guessed that he really must know something Zacriel needed, something very important.

Zacriel had decided he would keep her and show her the true path to power and refused to listen when she told him she didn't even want power. Nina just wanted to have a life of her own where she wasn't something to be used against others. Since Zacriel had claimed her she had not thought things could get any worse, and yet they had. Her family's killer, Ezekiel Perdomo had almost killed her too when the Illume blades destroyed Slumsville, and it had been the hideous Zacriel who had come to Nina's rescue, and shown her a way out of the pain and back to hope.

The time spent flying from Illume City to Acclaro had allowed Nina to see Zacriel in a different light, one opposite the monster she knew so well. He had nursed her back to health, coaxing her out of her anguish with kindness and allowing her the space to emerge from the fear that had almost broken her head. Surprisingly she had learnt that Zacriel had been just like her once. As Nina climbed the stairs past the chamber where Dalwyn's men bunked, she wondered what had become of Cinerus and if he had survived the failed attack on Illume.

Since they had entered the city and Nina had watched Dalwyn torture Ishmael's sister and her husband, Nina had been given little time to see Zacriel. In a strange way she missed him; he was the only one who had showed her kindness even though he also gave her pain and mocked her for being weak. There was a nice person deep down somewhere in him, she often thought, but then he would do something so terrible that she would change her mind. Nina had cried as Dalwyn made her watch Zacriel kill Manu who was a celestial travelling with Zahra and the monk Ishmael. Nina had never seen a celestial and he had been beautiful, surrounded by soft white light… but he was dead now. Nina reached the chamber at the top that she shared with Dalwyn and made her way to the stained glass window that opened out onto a ledge. This was her favourite place now, a place of her own where she could sit and feel the wind play with her hair. From here Nina could see out over the city and away over the Glyph grasslands. If she went to the window at the other end of the chamber she could sit looking down at Arrowhead Lake.

Far below her the castle drawbridge was winding down to let the infernals into the city to play with their slaves. Each night the cries of terror haunted Nina, and tonight she closed the window, opting to find some other way to amuse herself. A package sat on the bed with her name scribbled on it, and she carefully unwrapped it in case it was a trick. Inside was a doll that almost looked like Deidre her old doll, except it still had both eyes.

Nina threw it on the floor. She was too old for dolls now and would rather read a book. Her eyes spotted the large book on the table that Dalwyn would often sit reading. Nina walked over to it and ran her hand over the large, leather-bound book; usually it was locked, but today the brass clasp lay open and the small lock on the table beside it. The book was called-The Astral Conundrum. Nina didn't know what a conundrum was, but she had heard about the astral world. Where was it and what happened there? Nina sat at the table and uncovered the glass bowl so the glow from the sun-shrooms lit the chamber with their yellow orange glow, and she began to read.

Dalwyn drained his mug of wine then threw it against the wall. One of his men moved to retrieve it, but at the glare Dalwyn fixed on him thought better of it and stayed where he was. 'Leave it and leave me, you can wait outside,' Dalwyn said.

He paced over to where Nina sat on the window ledge looking down at the lake, unperturbed by his foul mood. The girl turned as he stopped beside her, looking up with wide eyes that also held a hint of iron, a barely restrained challenge. Dalwyn thought about pushing Nina from the ledge but instead turned and paced back to the table. Unfortunately he still needed the girl for a time to try and control Zacriel.

Dalwyn knew it was being trapped in this damn castle that accounted for his foul mood, and each day here in this infernal nest made him more uneasy. He wanted to leave Acclaro, but doing so without the information regarding the destination of the coterie of the heart would be only a distraction. The monk Ishmael and his sentinel, Zahra, had escaped the trap Dalwyn had set and now could be anywhere from the rolling plains of Cavere to the Road of Seekers in Brimmerland. To make matters worse, none of the agents he hired had returned with any other members of the coterie of the heart; he had heard nothing from them.

Dalwyn was all too aware of the passing of time. It seemed as if in these moments of inaction he could almost hear the soft sifting of sand through a time glass that reflected the precious yet diminishing life he had left. He slumped into a chair then regretted that action as his lower back twinged with muscle spasms. The back problem had continued to haunt him since the visit to a healer in Culchar, which of course added to his foul temper. These days he couldn't escape the signs of his age, the spots that dotted the backs of his hands, the crinkle of crow's feet at the corner of eyes once clear that had begun to lose their visual acuity, and more recently the popping of his knee joints when walking or standing after a period of rest.

It was due to the debilitating effects of age that he had begun to enjoy immensely the time he spent in the strong astral body formed by chimes of meditation and exercises that cleared his energy centers. During the long nights Dalwyn lost himself in beginning the first steps of exploring that strange realm that the sorcerers of old had put so much importance on. Baby steps were what he was taking, and yet the chimes flew by while he was in that mediative state.

Zacriel had been little help to Dalwyn lately and was still simmering with anger at Dalwyn's insistence that Nina stay with him. The infernal was something of an enigma to Dalwyn, and he knew if the roles were reversed he would have used his elite warriors to kill Zacriel even if that risked Nina dying. For reasons unexplained though, Zacriel allowed Dalwyn to control him through Nina. How much longer before he stopped caring for the girl or whether she lived or died? Zacriel was an infernal lord now and commanded an army that was swelling the city daily, and yet he allowed this upstart urchin to hold him back. Why? What did Zacriel see in Nina?

Dalwyn pulled the tome he had been studying across the table, noticing it was unlocked which was unusual, since there was no sign of the small padlock or his chain with the key on it. He chose not to let it worry him though since he was sure Nina couldn't read or even if she did, what could she do with the knowledge it contained?

Chapter 2

In the semi- darkness of the morning, Ishmael fumbled his way around the hay loft, retrieving his clothes as he watched Zahra sleep. He had wanted to tell her about the powdered life stealer-flower he had slipped into her wine before they had coupled, but his words had been washed away by her skilful hands and lips, denying him the chance to explain what he had done. It also had most likely saved his life.

Ishmael knew he had to leave Zahra, his feelings for her had become complicated, and more so since last night. He couldn't get the heady scent of her hair and skin out of his head. It wasn't just the sexual feelings though that scared him but the joy when she smiled at him or the cheeky wink she gave him when fooling around. Ishmael suspected he was falling in love with Zahra, which bought all sorts of problems to his mind regarding his vows to Illume. Last night Zahra had said his vows no longer mattered, but to him they did; they were all he had known for most of his life, and when he had needed to be strong he had slipped to the basest of pleasures.

There was enough blood on his hands without putting Zahra in unnecessary danger as he travelled to the Godhead. The holy vows of Illume he had sworn demanded he be solely focused on this pilgrimage like those of old who before him had traced the same path along the Seekers road. As Ishmael saw it, there was no choice. Zahra had to be left behind or else she would try to stop him following his heart on his spiritual journey.

When they fled Acclaro last night they had headed South East towards Brimmerland and the direction of Whitman's Point where the Seekers Road began and ran all the way to the coast in Trystland. By traversing the Seekers Road, pilgrims could personally petition the gods who all had an aspect of themselves at the end of this road in the form of a great, multifaceted, crystal prism that held an aspect of each god on all its surfaces. It was told that the Godhead would spin and one aspect would stop facing outward to reflect the deity who had deigned to favour the masses with their wisdom. From countless chimes spent in the monastery library, Ishmael had learnt all he could about the gods, and whether they still existed like his masters had taught. Now he was determined to find out the truth that only the visit to the Godhead would give him. In the vision he had received from the Mother there had been no mention regarding the death of the gods. He had seen their fall from grace when they became trapped in the world of man just like the infernals and celestials had, but not their deaths. So where were they?

Ishmael peered into his saddlebag where the two crystals, one given by the harlequin and the other stolen from castle Acclaro, sat wrapped in leather. The fleeting remnants of a dream echoed in his mind regarding how the five crystals that the coterie gathered would be instrumental in the return of magic. With his family lost to him and his connection to the divine deeply divided, Ishmael knew he needed to learn to control the surges of magic that the two crystals awoke within him. Returning to the simple lessons of his monastic life seemed to Ishmael the best choice of action as he searched for answers not just outside, but also within himself. With Zahra's plan to meet the rest of the coterie at the safe house, Ishmael wasn't content just to follow her and leave that one big question regarding the gods unanswered, even though it seemed the safest course of action.

This line of thought reminded Ishmael of the story Manu had shared with him where he had supposedly witnessed the remains of Shae, the lady of Illume in her temple and that, like all the gods, she was dead. Ishmael couldn't believe that. So many times he had followed the words of others, let them decide his actions, even though they offered no proof to their claims. This pilgrimage would prove the gods who were meant to be above all else except the Mother still lived, and proof of their continued existence would be a deciding factor in his next choice of action.

With a last, long look at Zahra, Ishmael left the mill before his conscience could stop him. Looking back at the city of Acclaro, Ishmael watched winged forms dive down into the billowing smoke only to reappear carrying some unfortunate that was then dropped to their deaths. The infernals were at their play now, torturing what survivors they found, and once again Ishmael felt a pang of guilt when he thought of leaving Zahra in danger. The dose he gave her should only keep her asleep for another chime or two; he prayed it would be sufficient time for her to flee the area.

The two louts chittered as he approached them, their antennae whirling. Ishmael sprinkled water upon their heads again to bond them, then he tied the spare lout to the other's saddle before securing his gear and mounting up. He would need to head south east through Whitman's Point before turning south onto the Seekers Road. He set a slow pace, not wanting to tire the beasts too early but needing to put distance between himself and Zahra. The sun sparkled, and yet a devilish wind skimmed off Acclaro Lake across the plains here. Soon the days would begin getting colder with the coming winter month of Iktar, but for now the days were pleasant, and Ishmael enjoyed the sights and sounds around him.

For the first time in his life, Ishmael felt free. If it wasn't for the burning capital and scent of smoke, he could get used to this. No rules to follow or chores to complete, now his destiny was in his own hands and he was responsible only to himself. He could still feel the thread of connection he had with the Mother through the Earth tree and had tried to follow it back to its source like he had when he first connected in his dream. Since then something had changed, and his attempts at communion with the Mother were now blocked.

Ishmael's choice to travel the Seekers Road had become clear to him the night before when he had raced up the tower to retrieve the blue crystal. At that moment after showing the rest of the coterie what had befallen Acclaro, Ishmael had walled them off in his mind, forcing them away so he didn't have to deal with their attempts to turn him away from this choice. Exhaustion had also been a factor in blocking any further communication between him and the coterie, and now rested, Ishmael hoped they would one day understand the need he had to verify his god's existence. The land began to change slowly now, turning stonier as he rode, and there was now only sparse vegetation in the small developing hills here. Ahead the spires of Whitman's Point called to him with the promises of answers.

When Ishmael came to the cobblestone road he knew he was near to the outpost. He marked it to be three chimes since he left the mill and Zahra. Taking only the supplies he needed, Ishmael released the two louts from harness and saddles, allowing them to jump away; there would be no need for them from this point on. That done, Ishmael watched the two free creatures disappear back into the grasslands before he climbed down the small cliff to stand on the road.

The road soon began a steep incline up towards the town that stood upon the highest hill in the area. This path was made more difficult with the defences built into the side of the hill and the meandering route anyone approaching the town from the north would be forced to take. When Ishmael made it to the statue of Wilhelm, the priest who had built the town he was breathing heavily and stopped to rest. From this high vantage point Ishmael could see a long train of people fleeing the capital on the main route that he had intercepted. They were at least a chime behind him, so Ishmael started off again to the gate, as he had no wish to get caught up in the rush that would soon follow and he planned to be on the road before midday. At the huge, tarred, wooden gates a side door opened to let out four guards while two with bows sat in a tower regarding him closely.

'Morning,' Ishmael said. 'Is the point still open to travellers?'

'That it is, sir; may I ask your reason for entry, and do you know what has befallen the capital?'

'I am a brother of Illume travelling to the Godhead and hoping to be on the road by noon. I have crossed the Glyph yet don't know what has befallen Acclaro. Farther back a large group is headed this way. Maybe they can tell you what you wish to know. May Shae illuminate your soul.'

'You travel light, brother, and yet emerged from the Glyph. Are you sure you didn't come from the capital?'

Ishmael forced himself to meet the man's gaze. He hated the fact he was forced to lie, however the thought of being trapped here in Whitman's Point was something he could not let come to pass.

'I have few needs in my chosen life, and everything I require is in this pack.' Ishmael passed his pack to one of the men, who lazily looked through the clothes and other small items on the top with little interest. Ishmael was relieved that he didn't dig deeper to the two crystals and relaxed when the guard thrust his pack back to him.

'On you go, brother, and may Shae guide you on your journey.'

Once in the gate Ishmael wasted no time. He only stopped briefly to ask where the path of prayers was before continuing down the famous steps that led pilgrims away from the ego and down to their most basic self before setting out on the Seekers Road. Ignoring the temples on the stairs that were just opening, Ishmael hurried down to where the gate to the road stood open.

Some scholars had suggested the gods themselves had crafted this road to allow mortals the chance to have direct communication with them, but no one really knew anymore. In his mind, Ishmael had pictured a dilapidated lonely road winding away into the distance. With the magic that was built into it long gone, it should have fallen into disrepair, but the sight before him was totally alien to his expectations. The road was magnificent, cut from cobblestones of multiple colours, which weaved beautiful patterns each side of two centre lines of onyx and pearl. Furthermore, the start of the road was flanked on each side by huge statues of the gods in all their magnificence. The morning sun had glazed the road copper with its rays, which appeared to lend even more significance to this special moment for Ishmael.

He estimated the statues each stood at least fifty feet high, and the sight took his breath away before he was bought back to reality. To Ishmael this seemed a pivotal moment; as he stood there, it had seemed the world stopped. There was no wind blowing along the road stirring up dust. Someone had kept the road here clean and well maintained as well as the statues; at some point Ishmael knew he would likely meet them. The road ahead winding below the gods seemed ominous, to Ishmael and the first thoughts of regret pushed themselves into his mind. He puffed out his cheeks then expelled the air out in a slow breath and stepped forward, fully aware of the towering gods casting judgement down upon him as he walked through their shadow. He was reminded of the vast cavern entrances under the mountain in Illume. With the total silence accompanying his every step he felt like he had arrived at the halls of the dead. He walked beneath the kindly gaze of Irdalar the goddess of water and then into the shadow of Aril the great slumberer, god of rivers in his half man half fish body. Even from here he could tell the stone work was sublime and appeared that the sands of time had done little to wear away the fine features that almost appeared lifelike. Ishmael kept walking, feeling the weight on him growing as he passed each of the major gods that lined the road; some known to him, others never seen before.

Ishmael felt utterly out of place here, acutely aware that this was the first time he would have no one to fall back on. He had chosen this, and now it was time to stand up and be counted, to make his father and the abbot proud. Before long Ishmael fell into that meditative state long walks bring as his mind turned inwards, counting his steps in a silent mantra. He became aware of Selene, Jona, and Raul as he walked, but rather than converse he followed the thin strands of those links to ensure they remained walled off like he had done yesterday in the castle tower. It had been Raul who had first gained this knowledge, and though he had never shared it with the coterie, Ishmael suspected that maybe the coterie shared a collective consciousness that could draw on the knowledge of the others as they learned skills. Before blocking the coterie off he had sent a brief thought message to them all explaining he was okay and had escaped the city of Acclaro but for reasons he couldn't share would be uncontactable for the foreseen future in order to complete an important task that wouldn't wait. The emptiness following his severing of the coterie was unnerving at first as he realized how accustomed he had become to their presence in the back of his mind. For the first time in many cycles since his father died, Ishmael felt truly alone.

Chapter 3

It took just over a chime for Ishmael to pass from beneath the shadow of the gods. The warm sun bathed the road in golden light that sent shimmering mirages ahead along with figures walking just in sight that vanished when he got closer. So when the houses that lined the cliff faces alongside the Seekers Road came into view, he immediately thought they also were products of his mind along with tricks of the sun. The noises proved otherwise.

A hammering had started up from somewhere above him off to the right, followed by a low, melodic singing. Now as he stopped to stare at the small town perched above the road he realized it was obvious that a quarry was needed in order to repair the Seekers Road. Rope bridges allowed access over the road to the other side, and from stained glass windows he saw faces peering down at him suspiciously as children swung on ropes between houses and even across the road with whoops of laughter. The whole cliff community was a bustle of activity with varied folk of all sorts haggling loudly, exchanging goods with smiles and curses. All the while the Road stood below, clean enough to eat from and unused as if the inhabitants of this strange place feared what might happen if they set foot upon it. Now that he was looking closely he also noticed a few narrow guard towers that ended in shaded lookout platforms each with a sentry standing there with some sort of tube that was attached to a pole that swivelled around. Ishmael caught the nearest one peering down that tube towards him, instantly putting him on his guard. What was it, some type of crossbow maybe?

Ishmael extended his arms out with the palms facing up to show he was unarmed. From the tower came a jingling of bells along with animated arm waving from the tower guard. Up ahead where a rope bridge crossed over the road a man shimmied down a rope to land in front of Ishmael. The man grinned broadly; a tobacco stain ran from his right lip up to the eyebrow, a brown stain against the reddish leathery skin. His well-worn, patched, dusty, white trousers were held up with a rope showing from beneath the green stylish vest that fit a little too snugly around the chest. He combed his grey-flecked hair back with a silver comb which he then placed in a pouch on his hip before slowly walked over to Ishmael.

'Tis a long road to travel alone, stranger.'

'I enjoy my own company, but yes, you are right. However, this is a necessity for my journey.'

'You a pilgrim?'

Ishmael pulled a water skin from his belt, drinking slowly, then offered it to the man, who waved it a way.

'Might be, who's asking?'

'I am Diego. There are four zones that cover the road to the coast. Each of these zones has a monitor who is responsible for the care of all pilgrims who are on their way to the gods' realm, and I am the monitor for this first zone.'

Up ahead from where Ishmael and the man talked, three other guards had arrived on the bridge with crossbows, which they leaned on the bridge supports sighting down at Ishmael.

'Strange kind of care you offer, my friend, with all these crossbows aimed at me. I bring no trouble with me. I just want to be on my way.'

Diego threw both hands into the air. 'For the sake of the gods, man, this is just a precaution against those who may wish to do us harm. I'm only asking you so we can give you the proper information to aid you along the road through the stages of wonderment where you will learn the correct way to approach the gods.'

'I have no desire to wait here when my time can be spent moving onwards, 'Ishmael replied, as politely as he could. 'Surely petitioning the gods can also be solo task for each of us when we stand before them. Of course that is if they truly are still alive.'

'So you're one of those non-believers then?' Diego shrugged. 'Well each to their own, but remember like all those before you what you see treading this road will change your mind.'

'No! I'm a believer. I am a brother of Illume come to see for myself if the gods truly still live. I would be in your debt if you can merely show this pilgrim how to get to the Godhead.'

'The children of Shae are welcome here; the collectors will be out this way in less than a chime to transport all who wish to the Godhead.'

'And if I choose to travel the road alone?'

'Not a great idea, my friend, the road is a dangerous place from here on in. For a man all alone, well… it would be hard for me to help people such as you avoid any unexpected trouble. My suggestion is that you spend the time slaking your thirst in my tavern where other travellers await the collector's arrival.'

Ishmael could see the sense in that, but he didn't trust this man at all, especially with his three cronies pointing their weapons at him.

'Unfortunately, friend, I have no wish to stay in your tavern, though this town does seem to have an appeal about it. I will take my chances waiting for this transport you speak off. It would be too bad if I got stuck in my cups and missed the ride.'

The monitor spat, scratched his head, and then stepped out of Ishmael's way.

'What, you think I will rob you, leave you lying in a pool of blood once parted from your valuables? Sometimes you need to trust others, my friend, especially when all alone,' He emphasized the last statement in a way that an adult would explain to a child.

'That is the precise reason I don't trust anyone. You see, it is because of my current situation.'

With another glance at the crossbow men on the bridge, Ishmael walked onwards. He got to the shelter that sat in the shadow of the buildings that flanked the road, sitting on a well-worn bench. Although the day had not been too hot until now, Ishmael felt shattered, he drank slowly from his water aware that the monitor still stared at him with a crooked sneer. When Ishmael turned to look back at him the man kicked a puff of dirt in his direction then shimmied easily back up the rope ladder to the bridge. Maybe he was rude, thought Ishmael, but he just couldn't shake the feeling that the man intended to help him not one little bit.

Ishmael sat quietly listening to a heart-catching tune that someone somewhere above was masterfully coaxing out of what sounded like a lute. The noise of the town had quieted, making him wonder if they all listened too or if everyone had simply vanished.

Soon after the song died away a steady stream of people began descending a ramp that was lowered down from a building by a winch that two huge men operated. A small crowd soon gathered around where Ishmael sat. He saw a couple clothed in white robes with golden torcs around their necks, showing they were followers of Illume like himself. There were dark-skinned followers of the River God with silver scales tattooed all over one side of their bodies. An unsavoury, heavily pierced, red skinned man with gems along his forehead who sported several curved blades strapped across his bare, upper body talked loudly about the Jester of Death.

Not wanting to appear rude, Ishmael stopped his staring and concentrated on the upcoming journey, which brought up a tingly excitement deep inside him. The crowd was followed by peddlers, who were selling everything from small, beautifully painted images of the gods to warm meat dripping with spicy sauces and wrapped in leaves. Ishmael couldn't resist from buying two. He greedily scarfed one before giving the other to a skinny child who kept staring at his food. The child's mother dipped her head in his direction in thanks then refused to meet Ishmael's gaze. The food was terrific, but by now the peddler of those delights had melted away with the crowd.

All sorts of religious paraphernalia was on sale along with the food and drinks.

A steady excitement began to spread through those waiting as a faint vibration on the road slowly became stronger. The collectors were coming, someone muttered, and along with the others Ishmael strained to see over those in front. He was lucky that his height was above average so he could see easily. He watched with childlike anticipation.

From a dust cloud up ahead on the road, two rust-coloured, scaled heads emerged with gnashing teeth snapping at each other. Long, white whiskers hung off their bottom jaws, and golden eyes locked on the crowd then rolled away. Behind the heads of those fierce creatures sat a driver upon a saddle, and as Ishmael watched he saw the driver crack his whip to slow the beasts down. As the whole spectacle kept emerging from the dust cloud, Ishmael could now see that many carriages sat upon the segmented, centipede-like bodies with their many legs moving as one. The carriages, like the segmented bodies they were harnessed to, allowed the beasts to swivel to the sides if necessary. Ishmael stood staring; he had never expected something so interesting. The creatures stopped close to the crowd that surged forwards before the guards could get in place. One man strayed too close to the beasts and was torn to shreds. The driver wore bright clothes with a red, high necked, cloak and a tall hat that gave him the appearance of a show performer. He stood, removed his hat, and bowed to the eager crowd.

'Away from the sand whips if you want to see your god in the flesh, or you will meet your makers long before you wished to.'

From near the front of the carriage a door was flung open. A plume of smoke puffed out, followed by a short, hunched man in ochre robes holding a belt pouch that he jingled loudly.

'Come on, pilgrims, come to see the gods then, have you? A silver ketch per person and no need to rush, let's just have you one at a time in an orderly fashion. This will be the chance of a lifetime, and mark my words, the gods will remember those who travel to their holy abode in service to give to them so they might return to our maligned world that has become lawless, even broken, since their absence.'

As each person stopped beside the man they were given instructions as to which carriage to go to.

'Greeting, lad; which God do you follow?'

'I'm a disciple of Illume,' Ishmael told the man, who nodded.

'Third carriage down with the white flag then. Here is your ticket, and welcome to the Seekers Road.'

Ishmael moved off, following the man's directions. Each carriage had intricately painted each depicting a different god. He gave the guard at the carriage door the ticket, noticing the man's emblem of a shattering portal.

The inside of the carriage was freshly painted. It gold material trimmings around the door and windows. In the centre of the carriage was a statue of Shae the Goddess, arms held out imploringly while looking to the heavens lost in rapture. The couple Ishmael had seen in the robes with the torcs around their necks were seated on a bench. They looked up at his entrance, smiled, then turned back to one another talking in low voices.

Four long benches stretched the length of the carriage while the outward walls had slatted wooden windows that could slide open. Ishmael was surprised at how nice it was; someone with money had obviously made sure this unusual public transport was kept up to a high standard. Now his thoughts had brought him to money he wondered how the poor travelled. What did they do on their journeys to see the gods? Were the needs of the many taken care of by the wealth from the other petitioners? He thought not; there would be those who would aid someone without thinking twice, but in his experience so far exchanging of blessings in return for money while at the monastery had left him knowing many people would not offer any charity to the less fortunate.

Looking out the door Ishmael saw the man who called himself

Diego talking with the guard. He had a hand on the man's shoulder. The two men turned to look at Ishmael then quickly away when they saw he had caught them. Ishmael sat there a while as the other carriages filled up, but no new passengers came to his. Illume must not be popular here, he mused.

When they were finally on the way, the guard came in to sit at the rear-most bench. The movement of the sand whips that carried them was surprisingly smooth. Ishmael's excitement soon turned to boredom as the views were comprised mainly of the cliff walls, some painted with yet more images of the gods. A few times the road rose above the canyon walls and he saw glimpses of a sparsely wooded countryside where large pyres of strange timber sent thick ribbons of smoke into the sky.

Ishmael's confusion must have been obvious, for the robed man leaned over in his direction.

'They are soul pyres to allow the spirits of the dead who are always buried along this ridge of the section of road to materialize in order to fight off any would be unwanted travellers onto their lands.'

'I take it that they get few pilgrims trying to enter their lands then,' replied Ishmael.

He tried to doze, but each time he tried he started to slide off the seat, so he gave up instead focusing on what he would do next in his journey. He hoped the other coterie would not take offence to cutting them off, and he was sure he could show them why he felt the need to go his own way.

Zahra, however, would hold a grudge. By the hells, the last to cross her was Jayne of the river whom she had destroyed. How could he who had slept with her before drugging her expect any sort of forgiveness? He knew that he would be made to answer for breaking his vows when he finally looked upon the visage of the Lady of Illume from the Godhead.

They pulled into the next small town after he managed to find a comfortable position to drift off in. An even larger throng of people crowded around the carriages, hawkers patrolled the slatted windows offering all sorts of delicious goods. Ishmael purchased a bag of fresh water flavoured with lemon rinds and a large slice of roast fowl. The couple who had shared the carriage prayed before the statue of Shae then left with a nod in his direction.

'Travel with Shae's light brother,' they said in unison before departing.

Once again content, Ishmael sat back in the comforts he had rarely known with his eyes shut, hands on his belly. The sound of the carriage door opening meant nothing to him until something prodded his foot. Opening his eyes slowly Ishmael found the monitor standing above him flanked by two formidable looking men. Beside them the monitor ran his comb through his hair then looked down with contempt at Ishmael.

'Go back to sleep, princess,' said the monitor, then one of the men slammed a club into the side of his head, knocking him to the floor. As he lay there they began kicking him hard around the ribs. The statue of Shae his Goddess looked upwards away from his distress while the beating rained down on Ishmael.

He was dragged back to a sitting position. A hand was holding his face forwards by the chin, the wavering face of the monitor was so close to his bleeding nose to detect a concoction of spices while he was given a message.

'Normally I wouldn't hesitate to kill you for the disrespect you showed me back there, but it's obvious you are a stranger to our lands and customs. Next time someone offers you somewhere to rest remember it is an insult to refuse without giving a gift to the one who offers.'

Ishmael was turned, then a meaty arm slid beneath his chin choking him, easily fighting off his weak hits then clawing fingers as his struggle turned futile. He could hear the laughter of the men around him then he grew blissfully unaware of anything more.

Chapter 4

Haakon rose early to be by Latasha's bedside. He entered the chamber with a tray containing broth and fruits which he placed beside the bed before removing the cloth covering the bowl with sun blazer fish. He knew he shouldn't be here without the permission of Faustus, who had managed to keep Haakon away for the night.

Haakon looked down at Latasha as the green and blue hues played over her skin. The simple fact that Latasha had awoken was testament enough to the healing prowess of Faustus. Her silver hair had regrown since her stay here, hiding the scars that crisscrossed her skull. Nearly all her broken bones had healed well except the most horrific that ensured her legs would never move well again if at all. Now Latasha was recovering, Haakon was inpatient to start helping her back to health. The road back would take time as her mind and muscles healed. Time was now a dwindling commodity that slipped through Haakon's grasp. He needed Latasha's advice now, not later.

When he next looked at Latasha she was regarding him with those soulful eyes of hers that seemed to see right through him. When they had first met that gaze had unnerved him; now it thrilled him.

'Morning to you, Latasha, it is so good to see you awake. I feared for so long that you… ah never mind. It's just really good to have you back with us.'

Latasha's mouth opened as if to speak then shut again, then she pointed to her throat with one wavering hand, and Haakon gently

22

tilted her head so she could drink some water. She had soiled the bed, and so as he had been doing since she had been bought here broken and twisted, he gently replaced the dirty linens with fresh ones then bathed her body before dressing her in a clean shift. As he worked he talked tirelessly about whatever came to mind since this seemed the only way he could stave off the nervousness that fluttered in his stomach under those eyes that saw through his act of bravado.

Haakon braced Latasha's back with extra pillows so she was sitting, and then he fed her the broth as he prepared to tell her of his dilemma regarding the coterie.

'I must tell you news regarding the coterie. Brianna Dusk is dead, murdered.' It took all of Haakon's resolve to utter those words that indicated he had failed to protect all the coterie like he had sworn to do. 'The remaining coterie are all alive and on their way to a designated safe house. Your warning came too late to stop the attacks on some of them, but they survived, which is all that matters. My energetic body was almost damaged beyond repair when fleeing your home, so now it is too dangerous for me to ride the astral winds.'

The words were so softly Haakon nearly missed them. He paused with the spoon of broth between them.

'Did you say something, Latasha?'

In a voice as soft as a new winter's snow she repeated her first words since she had fallen into a coma.

'They need us.'

'You are of course right; however, with your current situation…'

Latasha's frail arm came up, knocking the spoon aside, and her bright eyes fixed on him.

'There is little time left for us to help the coterie, and without us everything we have worked for is lost.' The talking was visibly difficult for Latasha, and she lay back on the bed breathing deeply then started to weep softly.

Haakon tried to settle her down as she started to rock side to side in the bed, her face awash with tears. He put the broth down and embraced her, stopping the rocking of her upper body. She resisted him at first but then relaxed as he soothed her until the sobs subsided and she was calm again.

He removed the pillows so she could sleep again, and as he pried her fingers from his she spoke again.

'Thank you, my heart, for being there for me.' Haakon knew it hurt Latasha to show weakness even to him since her kind were so proud and independent. She continued to clasp his hand, pulling him closer.

'Time is short, my heart. We must go to them.' Then Latasha lay back breathing hard and closed her eyes. He removed the food when he left then decided to shave as he tried to process his troubled thoughts and Latasha's words.

The rasp of the wooden door catching on the warped floorboard alerted Haakon to a visitor. He paused in his shaving, his face still half covered with stubble, as the reflection of his old friend Faustus came into view behind him.

'You know, old friend, if you insist on visiting me while I'm bathing people will begin to talk?'

The old man's liver-spotted face curled into a smile, the age lines deepening at the corners of his eyes.

'Believe me, Haakon, you are hardly ideal for that kind of viewing, but it seems all the young ladies have either flown the coop or doubt my ability to perform in meeting their needs, so that leaves you.'

Haakon dried the foam from his face then turned to his oldest and closest advisor.

'Out with it then Faustus, how many did we lose last night?'

'We suffered a score of deserters last night, Haak, which means our food stores if nothing else remain formidable.'

'Was there anyone of note among them?'

From behind him Faustus snorted rudely.

'They were all of note Haakon. They are family to us, and to watch you dismiss them so easily pains me deeply as it should you.'

As he dressed, Haakon regarded Faustus. The toll of the last month was wearing the frail man down, but his eyes belied any frailty that might be mistaken for weakness as they gleamed with the intensity of his accusation.

'What would you have me do then, Faustus, lie to them?'

'Might have been better than simply strolling back into the camp drenched in gore just to show how big your balls are and what you are still capable of. In fact, my master, you did so well in slaughtering the ring leaders that the rest of your people fear they will be next, which would have been all right if you had left it at that, but then you go and tell the others that they are free to leave. The clan lies splintered, Haakon, pulled in two different directions between Latasha and the coterie, who we both know need you to be there with them at the safe house.'

'Those that wanted to leave have already gone, Faustus, and that is the only kindness I will offer them.'

Before he could continue, Faustus cut him off. 'But what of those that are left? They are left to mourn their friends and family and are wondering what is likely to become of them now. Haakon, my friend, you need to show them who have proved their loyalty by staying with you that they have made the right choice. They are highly trained so use them, I implore of you. Use your tools and stop trying to do everything yourself. It is time to let our people do what they know and what is in their blood; strike now at our enemies as they are gathering their might for the war to come and by being ruthless now you may just save thousands from dying unnecessary deaths.'

Haakon thought on his friend's words before answering.

'Whatever will I do when you are no longer by my side to correct my errors Faustus? Out of all my so called trusty advisors, you are the only one who has the guts to tell me how it is. Maybe you think I have neglected to think of all these points you raise, but I tell you these decisions weigh heavily on my conscience every moment of the day. This conversation only hastens my decisions so now let me tell you what we shall do. Call the clan to meet this evening and all but the necessary guards must be present. Then I will inform all of you together of what must be done. Haakon purposefully neglected to mention the new developments with Latasha.

When Faustus entered Latasha's chamber to check her, Haakon heard the old man's startled cry before he reappeared at Haakon's side.

'Hak, Latasha is awake! You knew, didn't you?' he accused.

'You should have called for me immediately.'

Haakon just stared at his old friend and shrugged his shoulders. 'I thought I had lost my mind, Faustus. After last night I no longer knew what was going on, what was real or imagined, and I thought I had imagined it until this morning.'

Faustus slapped Haakon on the back, laughing heartily. 'See, my friend, I told you she would come out from it. Now don't overwhelm her; I need to take her vitals.'

Haakon hardly heard the physician as he focused on meeting with the remainder of his clan. He felt a shake of his shoulder and turned to Faustus.

'Haakon, you need to let her rest. Now leave us so I can do my work.'

Haakon began to argue but the look Faustus gave him put an end to that, and so with a soft kiss to Latasha's forehead, he left. Haakon took a slow walk, which was the last thing he really wanted to do now Latasha was awake, but he knew his old physician was right. Latasha needed rest.

Chapter 5

Haakon couldn't help but notice the wary glances some of the clan directed his way as he stepped out from the shadows into the amphitheatre. The ascending benches lit by torchlight flickering in the wind normally would have been full of his clansmen, but with the recent exodus they sat only half full, bringing the reality of the situation alarmingly into focus. Haakon stood before his people, letting his eyes wander over them, meeting hard gazes taut with anger, fear, and loss. Haakon had expected a raucous welcome full of angry outbursts, but then again those who would have acted in such a way would likely have already left. These men and women before him were his stoutest supporters and they sat there patiently waiting for him to begin.

Haakon thumped his chest with a fist. 'We are Kenzu!' The answering shout was full of strength and passion and that more than anything gave Haakon hope for the clan. He indicated for quiet and then began.

'To be Kenzu means we share a bond stronger than blood, forged with love, strengthened with tragedy, and built around our craft of death. We are all hurting with the departure of those we called family, but trust me when I say the road ahead has no room for those who are questioning what it means to be Kenzu. I am the fifteenth clan master in our history and have been forced to deal with the clan's relocation to this sorry place. Our once Illustrious clan was betrayed by the very one we had called master, and due to his mistreatment of our order he left us bled dry and hunted from our ancestral home to this life, hiding like criminals and not the noble people we are.'

This last comment caused a ripple of laughter through the assembly.

'As the newest clan master my decision to cease our work of death has never been a popular one amongst us. However, the need to make sure the coterie were kept safe from harm had to take precedence, and now, with recent events, I feel my decision has been justified. I don't stand here pretending I have always made wise decisions, but I have always done my best for us all. By being here with me now you have revealed your choice, and so now I come clean and tell you what is next for us.'

One of the crowd stood then called down to Haakon.

'Haakon, you killed them, even young Alexis; surely there was another way.'

'Jurell, you were born to the Kenzu, so you know our history is written in blood, betrayal, and survival. We may have spent the last three hundred cycles free from dealing in contracts of death, but that doesn't mean we have abandoned death. It has its time and place, and in order for the clan to survive we must be ruled by the strongest. That for now is me, and when the ring leaders decided to usurp my rulership then I killed them by my own hand as it has been done for hundreds of cycles.' Haakon paused surveying the crowd again as whispered conversations broke out.

'Would you rather be ruled by weakness, Jurell?'

'Of course not clan master.'

'Would you like to challenge me for leadership Jurell?' asked Haakon, his voice taking on a low growl.

'No, clan master.'

Haakon turned slowly, meeting the eyes that bore down on him questioningly.

'Do any of you want to challenge me here and now for leadership of the clan?'

The silence was all the answer Haakon needed. He noticed Jurell sit down quickly.

'From this day on this dreary forest is no longer our home. It has served its purpose of helping us hide from our enemies, but we shall hide no more. One of the coterie is dead, as is their sentinel, and our enemies hunt the others as we speak. Most of you will be tasked with moving all we need from here to a safe house where we shall make a new start, the right way. Although this may be less dangerous than the other tasks I will talk about but make no mistake, it is just as important to our future. Strike teams will be formed to target our enemies where they are weakest. The time for peace is over and now the Kenzu will return to the path of blood. The magic stirs in the coterie and armies are manoeuvring for position in the struggle to come so we must act as promised to make sure the reshaping of our world is ushered back in by the coterie without them being in danger.'

Haakon raised a clenched fist to the sky. 'Kenzu!' and his cry was returned by his people.

'At dawn report for your orders, and good luck to all of you. Tomorrow I must leave for the safe house with Latasha and my personal guard. As you perform your allotted tasks you are writing a new chapter in the clan's history, so do the Kenzu proud.'

Haakon stayed until the last of his people filed away. He clasped hands with those that sought him out, muttered encouraging words, and noted the renewed vigour his speech had given his people, who seemed eager to be about their tasks. When the amphitheatre was empty he heard solitary clapping from behind him as Faustus approached.

'Bravo, clan master. By uniting the clan with a common cause you may have just saved the Kenzu from falling apart.'

Haakon nodded; he was weary now. Tomorrow was another day, a new start and time to set things right again.

Chapter 6

Zahra awoke to the blaring of horns carrying on the wind along with the assorted stench that a burning city brought with it. She lifted her head, which somehow had obtained the heaviness of a stone. In the back of her throat Zahra recognized the bitter taste of life stealer-flower, which could only mean one thing: Ishmael had actually drugged her. Life-stealer flower was a useful powder she always carried with her; he must have obtained it from her pouches then mixed it with the wine. Now Zahra wished she had of taken more notice when he had spoken of his herbalism skills. She had underestimated Ishmael, and the real question was why he had done this, but that musing would have to wait.

Trying to shrug off the remnants of the drug, Zahra pulled her sandals on then searched through her backpack noticing that Ishmael had left her a share of the food and water rations. She laughed out loud at his thoughtfulness. After slaking her thirst, Zahra was ready to leave the mill. The two louts were missing, which was no surprise, since Ishmael had obviously decided he didn't want Zahra catching back up to him.

Zahra stood for a while slowly chewing some bark that would help remove the lingering effects of the life-stealer powder as she stared at the capital from which smoke and screams still escaped. The city was lost to the Infernals, which in itself would bring war since no neighbouring nation could afford to let the Infernals create a power base. Things were heating up, the coterie were being hunted, countries were mobilising at the news of magic returning to the world, and soon everything would come to a head for better or worse.

Zahra set out from the mill once she was sure it was safe. She easily picked up the lout tracks that headed first back towards the Jewelled Lands then abruptly changed towards Whitman Point. Zahra suspected Ishmael was battling mightily with the guilt over the breaking of his vows even though he had put that life behind him. His faith was paramount at this time when once again his family had forsaken him, and his monastic life had been ripped apart by the Infernals.

Faith was the only thing Ishmael had left, which Zahra believed was why she now found herself hunting the very man whom only the night before had bedded her.

This fact didn't bother her so much, a fuck was a fuck and they would come and go; however, Ishmael was a man whom the very world depended on. Haakon himself had given her the duty to keep him safe, and Zahra owed the clan master everything. Soon a reckoning would come and Zahra would not be found wanting in the role she had been chosen to fulfil. She would rather die than disappoint Haakon.

The obvious place Ishmael would go to was the Godhead at the end of the Seekers Road where he would be one of the many pilgrims hoping to commune with their deity. Zahra followed the river to where it met the cliffs of Brimmerland then cut east across the hills to the south of the Glyph grasslands towards the small town and a Thantosian military outpost that was Wilhelm's Point. The town was built at the beginning of the Seekers road. It had been the scene of devastating riots following the Severing, when pilgrims swarmed to find out from their deities what was happening while unaware that the gods had fallen from their celestial thrones to become no better than their mortal followers.

Zahra pitied Ishmael's need to cling to his religion. Hers had never been a religious family, and the only experience with religion had been offerings to the gods for a bountiful harvest or hastily drawn symbols of protection. Even that hadn't saved her family when the townsfolk had come to stop the plague that her mother had caught. When her family tried to stop the villagers, they were also trapped within their burning home, and it was some miracle Zahra had survived to be found by Haakon. Haakon had recruited her to the Kenzu clan, and Zahra had learned about all the gods and religions of the world as all the recruits do. Then Haakon taught them to use that knowledge without becoming ensnared in the restrictive dogma of religion. He taught them to trust in their own skills and that of their clansmen, nothing else.

The power of the gods was a thing of the past. If by some chance they did return to their lofty positions, then it would be through some other life-changing event as disruptive as the Severing had been. Rather than trust in something that might not exist anymore, they had been taught to put that trust into honing their own abilities.

The last time Zahra had passed this way, Wilhelm's Point was in a state of disrepair and all but abandoned except for the garrison. The village that Zahra had outlived was only a few days travel east from here through the pastoral land called Brimmerland, which was where Zahra had been raised. She had never returned since the plague. As children Zahra and the other kids used to sneak away with any delicious treats they could pilfer then make their way past patrols of soldiers to the Seekers Road and its high walls. They would climb atop the wall to watch the long lines of pilgrims walking along it or maybe catch sight of the dangerous sand whips that carried the carriages upon their backs. Lost in those good memories, Zahra made her way slowly towards Wilhelm's Point.

Ishmael's problem, she mused, was that he was very inexperienced when it came to life outside of the monastery, especially when dealing with different cultures. Furthermore, he would be one of thousands travelling to the Godhead, and locating him would be very difficult. Asking around after a monk of Illume would bring too much attention to both Ishmael and herself.

The only possible way to avoid such an arduous process was by the astral plane. Zahra knew Ishmael well enough to hold an image of him in her mind then scry the astral for him, but such a technique would have to be done at night somewhere where she could hide her body without being vulnerable to attack. The thought made Zahra shiver. The astral was dangerous, especially to someone yet to master many of its techniques, but this might be her only chance to find him.

As the day wore on, Zahra noticed when farms behind her closer to Acclaro had been put to the torch. The only reason the Infernals would do that, she thought, was to cut off any food supplies to the armies that would gather or travel through these lands in the advent of war. Zahra stopped to rest briefly at the top of a hill, wincing at the blisters that were rubbing on her sandals.

Zahra knew she was not alone when a slight crack of a twig came from somewhere behind her. She rolled to the side, snatching her blade from beside her on the grass and came to her feet blade ready. Facing Zahra were a band of soldiers in the grey leather of Thantos. There were eight of them, all lightly armed and armoured, scouts maybe if they had managed to sneak up on her. Two hand crossbows were aimed at her chest while the others stood in a semi-circle facing her with their own blades bared.

With a grin Zahra sheathed her blade then lay it at her feet. There was no need to get killed against these hard soldiers.

One of the men, most likely the leader even though they all wore the same uniform without any signs of rank, stepped forward to kick her blade away from her.

'It's a dangerous time to be travelling. Where are you headed?'

'Anywhere but back to Acclaro. The infernals have taken the city.'

The leader was clean shaven and moved with the ease of a well-trained soldier. He squatted where he was and indicated that Zahra should be at ease.

'You were there then, in Acclaro?'

'Yes, when it fell. The infernals just continued to pour out of the castle, slaughtering as they went. The man I am employed to bodyguard managed to escape with me but since has disappeared. It seemed the best option for me was to head for Wilhelm's Point, which is the nearest place of safety this side of the Seekers Road.'

Some of the soldiers sniggered to one another at Zahra's words, and she heard the mention of *deserter* before the steely gaze of their leader fell on them.

'What of the city guard; did they fare well?'

'They fought valiantly from what I saw, but most of my time was spent heading away from any fighting in order to get my employer to safety. I will gladly share any information that may help when I reach the Point.'

The leader rose and pulled aside two of the soldiers, to whom he spoke quietly with before turning back to Zahra. 'Two of my men will escort you to Wilhelm's Point where you will be questioned on whatever knowledge you can give us on the situation of Acclaro. You are not a prisoner, but you will be held under escort until such vital information is passed on to my superiors. I would advise you not to run from my men; we are not enemies, but should they feel you have deceived us then they will not hesitate to kill you.'

The two escorts were stone faced like their leader and insisted that Zahra turn her blade over to them.

'Look at this Gunter. I never seen a blade like this before.'

'What's it made of, crystal?'

'It appears so. Where you find this, lass?'

'It was a gift from one of the harlequin.'

The gathered soldiers looked at her then each other before breaking into laughter.

'You sure you aren't a storyteller instead of a bodyguard?'

Zahra felt herself starting to bristle at the disbelieving comments.

'Enough! Leave her alone; she is not our enemy, and we have ill work ahead. Gunter, get away with you then and take the lass to the general with this message.'

The leader handed Gunter a small parchment that was quickly tucked away, and then at the leader's signal the soldiers melted away into the grass. The one named Gunter tilted his head to indicate Zahra should walk in front of them.

After a short time they came to a small hill where five cular mounts waited, basking in the mid-morning sun. Thankfully the pace of the lizards was much faster. Being waylaid in her search for Ishmael was one thing Zahra needed to avoid, but in this she had little choice. Warning whomever she could about the infernals' attack was paramount to the future of Acclaro if not the whole empire of Thantos, even the world.

They slowed again to a walk when they met the cobbled road to the front of Whitman's Point. Approaching the town at the top of a hill forced any who came that way to trudge a winding path interspersed with rock ledges built into the hillside which slowed their approach. Once past this twisting path the road opened to the outpost, where a stone statue of Wilhelm stood gazing to the east where the sun would rise. Wilhelm was the priest who had built the town for the pilgrims and his statue was considered a sacred site for many. Zahra watched her two escorts touch the foot of the statue as they passed, offering a prayer for luck and safety. They stopped beneath as they waited for the gates to swing open enough to allow them entry. The high timber gates had been tarred and sanded to protect against possible fire damage while the rest of the town walls appeared to be stone that was expertly fitted together, hardly leaving any seams visible. Above them on the wall soldiers were gathered looking back towards Acclaro City. As quickly as the gates were wheeled open to admit them they were winched shut again.

Once in they were met with a red-faced officer.

'Sergeant Holt bid us to return with this woman to see the general. She claims to have survived the night in Acclaro,' Gunter told the sergeant.

The man sighed loudly and looked as if he would explode at any moment. 'As if I don't have enough to do. Come along then, lass, I'm a busy man.'

Zahra was whisked away by the two escorts, who hurried after the sergeant and away from the questioning glances of soldiers watching on so no panic could spread before she was questioned.

Chapter 7

The barracks at the top of this hill were built up around a large house where the general lived. Zahra was taken by stairs up to a covered viewing area furnished as if for gatherings around a large table. Zahra found herself lost in the beautiful view, only turning away when her eyes again found Acclaro. Also from here she saw the famous path of prayer, a steep set of steps that wound down to the Seekers Road. Temples to the gods crowded the edges of those stairs where eager priests listened to the last prayers of the pilgrims hoping to gain blessings before starting their spiritual journey. The pilgrim's fresh in their belief with raised hopes, would step onto the road properly anointed in the holy oils and carrying holy trinkets.

The general, it appeared, had been eating his evening meal with his family when they had arrived and he was most unhappy at this interruption when they entered the house.

'Please accept my apology, General Caldro,' the guard said, bowing his head profusely as he passed the scroll to the general who sat chewing the haunch of some animal noisily.

His wife, stern faced with a pursed mouth, chewed lightly, rolling her eyes at the intrusion. If not for the look as if someone had punched her, Zahra thought she would have been beautiful.

'Not again! Monte, I long for the day when I can have the luxury of our family sharing a meal together alone without any interruption.'

The other two occupants at the table were two boys maybe around five or six cycles old who ran over to Zahra, wanting to see her sword. She pulled the blade free and laughed at the cries of delight from the boys as they inspected it.

'Do you think you could move the blade away from my children? I have no desire to see them injured. Monte, make the woman put it away; it is not for children to…'

'Oh, shut up, woman, can't you just give me some peace? I'm trying to read here.' His voice lowered as did the parchment he was reading, and a kind look came over his face as he reached out a hand to sit on his wife's. 'Soon you are going to have to allow the boys to study warfare. I won't have them raised as weaklings just so you can protect them. Now take the boys and go inside. I have urgent business to attend to.'

The woman slid her chair back noisily then sauntered over to her sons, guiding them away without a backward glance.

Monte bade them all take a seat then sent an attendant to fetch food for them all as he poured them both chilled wine.

'You have to excuse my wife, she has no patience for military matters when they encroach on family time. Now, young lady,' he said, once they were all seated and their gaze was on him.

'You bring dire news of the happenings at Acclaro?'

'Yes, general. I barely managed to escape the city last night and since then have lain low in hiding. I was forced to flee again when I realized the Infernals were now targeting all the farms on the glyph around the city. I think they aim to destroy any crops that could be used to help fight against them.'

'What of the king?'

'I'm sorry to bring more bad news, general, but he died in the throne room where he has been the tool and prisoner of one of the infernal lords. I saw him die with my own eyes, and though it may not seem so, it was a mercy. Now the city is in the control of a new infernal that calls himself Zacriel the bone lord, and he is in league with a former lord of the Tiariacs by the name of Dalwyn Trevlon.'

For the remainder of the day general Caldro questioned Zahra about everything she had seen in Acclaro before regretfully allowing her some rest. She was led to a bedroom where she locked and barred the door before checking all the windows were also secured. A meal waited on the table for her that she hardly tasted as she thought about Ishmael. Had he come this way? Could it be she was wrong about him and he never even chose this route? Tiredness soon crept over her and she slipped away.

Chapter 8

A strange buzzing came to Ishmael, circling near his ear. Ishmael managed to blink one eye open, which took a moment to clear; his lips were swollen with dried remnants of blood and dust. He explored his face with his hands, finding abrasions and more swelling. Groaning, he pulled himself up into a sitting position, noticing at once the metal band like a collar that had been fastened around his throat and led to an iron ring embedded deep in the tree trunk. A road angled down past him into a town where he could hear a number of dogs barking. By the position of the sun it looked to be late afternoon. He scanned around for his backpack but there was no sign of it. The bastards had taken his backpack with the crystals, he must find them, but how could he when he was chained to this tree like an animal?

'Help me!'

The words felt strange with his swollen jaw, and he spat out a mouthful of blood then slowly stood. Pain lanced through his back as he did so. He struggled to pull the chain free for a while, growing more frustrated then angry at the way he had been treated.

With not a lot else possible, Ishmael sat back down to ease the pain from his throbbing head. Could it be the monitor that had chained him here, and if so, for what reason?

Somehow he dozed and sometime later became aware of a man squatting beside him. It was the monitor!

'I see that the rude one has awoken.'

'Water, please,' Ishmael pleaded in a raw voice.

'Not yet, Yucca. First we talk so you know my expectations, then you get water. From this day on you are mine to keep until I am happy you have repaid the debt to my honour. Until such time you learn to use your manners and how to treat others, you will be in my service.'

'I don't even know what I did wrong,' Ishmael blurted out.

With a quick tug of the chain the monitor sent Ishmael sprawling face down on the hard ground. 'You insulted me by refusing my help, which demands repayment, but you offered none like the barbarian you are. If you travel it is wise to know the customs of the lands you will be entering. Without learning to change your behaviour you will never pass through to the Godhead. Although you may feel aggrieved at your mistreatment, it would be wiser to see how it will shape you into an upright man of respect when you face your goddess.'

'You can't keep me here against my will!'

There came a rough tug of the chain again. 'Next time you speak out of turn I will beat you. As to your question, I can and I have. The laws here are quite clear since I have witnesses to your insult while you have no one to back up your story. In time you will be released, but only when I perceive your debt has been repaid sufficiently. Now come see your new home, Yucca.'

'My name is Ishmael, not Yucca. Take me to see whoever is the law here, and we can come to an amicable agreement. Please, I beg of you.'

True to his word, the monitor beat him for that outburst with savage kicks to the legs, leaving Ishmael shouting with pain.

'For the time you are indebted to me you no longer have a name but are known as Yucca, which means rude man. I am the law here. Now you have a choice to make, Yucca. You can leave this place with me or not at all. I have stoved in the skulls of others who refused to respect our ways at this very spot, so don't think I will hesitate to do the same to you.' The monitor unlocked Ishmael's chain, watching him warily.

Ishmael climbed to his feet. 'Since I have no choice I will come, but know this. What you are doing is wrong.'

The monitor just laughed then turned away.

Ishmael stumbled down the hill after the monitor, who led him by the chain like a dog. He thought about attacking him, but his newest set of wounds ached terribly while the monitor looked very capable of fighting Ishmael off. They rounded the small bend then headed down a street where a handful of small, thatched roof houses stood. Chickens wandered around pecking for food as stray dogs howled and barked as they passed. Farther along the road Ishmael could see the main part of the town ahead and the winding wall that bordered the Seekers Road. It would seem he had not left the first town after all. As he walked he tried to remember the name of the place. Glimmersedge.

The monitor opened a gate at a house, pulling Ishmael in, and chained him to a metal ring in one wall behind the house. A mottled brown- hound sat in the half shadows of the afternoon on the opposite side of the courtyard, also chained to a wall. The monitor looked Ishmael over as he ran his silver comb through his black greasy hair all the while dragging deeply on a pipe, then he went inside the house.

Ishmael slumped to the ground with his back against the stone wall. Beaded curtains covered the doorway the monitor had entered.

This must be his home, Ishmael decided, but the realization did little to improve his spirits and just heightened his fear. Looking back he could already see the mistake he made of telling the monitor he was travelling alone. It had seemed an innocent question that had been used to confirm he was easy prey.

Ishmael could make out three voices from within the home. At least one child as well as a soft feminine voice. For what he was sure wouldn't be the last time in this journey he regretfully thought of leaving Zahra. She would have known the culture here, known how to avoid becoming a victim. This was his first test since leaving

Zahra, and Ishmael was still determined to get out of this then back on with his life by himself. The crystals were gone along with his other possessions, maybe already sold by the monitor for a tidy profit without knowing their true value. Now he must get through this alone without needing someone to always look after him.

He studied the area around him; the iron ring was deeply imbedded in the stone, and there was another one about five feet along from where he was now. To dig it out of the stone would be close to impossible, not to mention he would need some type of tool to achieve that. The yard had the one exit through the gate and was encircled by clay walls reinforced with timber. From one corner a rank stench carried from a barrel, which he assumed was where the family dumped their waste to be burned.

The hound lazily got to its feet then walked along the wall to urinate, its chain clinking softly as it went, then it sat back down watching Ishmael watching it in return. He was able to see its criss-cross of scars that covered its body as well as the half missing ear. It looked old, maybe an ex-hunting or fighting hound now just the family pet. When it stood or lay down a low moan accompanied the movements.

Ishmael tried to judge whether the hound's chain could reach him on his side of the courtyard; it certainly looked long enough. Standing then moving to the full length of the chain he could just see into the first room through a window with beaded curtains tied back to let in the light and air. The room was lit by candles that showed a dining room table low to the ground surrounded by cushions. At first he thought the room was empty, but then a small figure sat up from beside the table. The child turned, allowing Ishmael a quick glimpse of light-brown skin with dark hair. As if sensing he was being watched, large eyes fixed on Ishmael. The boy's mouth opened in a small gasp, then he was gone.

The night had closed in now with the only respite being the candles of the dining room through the window. Music played inside the house accompanied by loud jovial singing. Ishmael saw no sign of anyone else that first night. He could only sit with his back to the wall or stand peering into the dimly lit room as the delectable smells of food wafted out to him along with the festive singing. On the far side of the courtyard the grizzled hound sat with its head resting on its paws, its ears flicking up at any other noises.

The language the monitor and his people spoke was unknown to Ishmael. He briefly thought of communicating with Selene or Jona but he was determined to sort out this problem himself rather than having to continuously rely on others to save his skin.

Sometime in the early morning the crows of nearby roosters had Ishmael awake long before the sun started its long journey across the sky. Thankfully it was still some time before the cold month of Iktar and the walls sheltered him from the wind. His throat was still parched and coated with dust while his stomach had now begun gurgling again. Ishmael thought long and hard about his situation and where the crystals might be now, which bought him that queasy feeling of anxiety deep within.

Not knowing what else to do, he took up the kneeling meditation pose his body knew so well then began breathing in a four- time sequence that would still his chattering mind to quiet. After gaining some semblance of composure, Ishmael began his breathing exercises that the monks had taught him to us in order to keep the power of the magic rushing up from within and consuming him. Distantly a part of him realized that his life in the monastery was like a strange fading dream that had been better than the one he now found himself immersed in now.

It wasn't until well after dawn that someone emerged from the house into the courtyard, and Ishmael was only alerted to someone's presence when the hound stood, ears perked up with its tail wagging slowly as the boy he had seen last night walked out holding a large bowl of food. He placed it in the middle of the courtyard between the hound and Ishmael. It was full of roasted meat. The hound sat licking its lips, looking from the boy to the food then back again. Ishmael felt himself beginning to drool at the smell, and then he was crawling towards the bowl unable to stop himself as the need to eat overcame him.

He got to the bowl at the same time as the hound who came at a rush, lips peeled back, hackles on end and its teeth latched onto Ishmael's extended arm just below the elbow, puncturing through his shirt as well as the skin. The hound shook its head from side to side, tearing the wounds deeper. Ishmael punched the beast twice to the face to make it let go of his arm, but it held on so he gathered the slack of the chain in his free hand then smashed it into the hound's shoulder, making it grunt and let go of him.

Ishmael scampered backwards, putting all his weight on his injured arm as he did so; it gave away, causing him to fall with a cry. The hound now stood braced over the bowl, paws planted firmly watching him with a fierce growl, and then it began to wolf the food down. From the side the boy was laughing as he walked over to the hound that was now licking the bowl. It nuzzled the boy as he patted its grizzled head.

'Good boy, Chill, you still got it old boy, eh?'

'Hey, boy, can I have some food too?' asked Ishmael, cradling his injured arm.

The boy kept scratching the dogs face as he turned to look disdainfully at Ishmael.

'You are a no better than this hound, so from now on if you want to eat you must compete for it. My father told me it is my duty to look after you as if I have nothing else to do. You are a waste of my time and I really don't care if you die here. Ha! Some man you call yourself. You let a hound take your food, and now he knows you are inferior to him.'

The boy laughed again as he collected the bowl, then he re-entered the house leaving Ishmael lost for words and the hound eyeballing him, a soft growl in its throat.

Ishmael went hungry that day, but worse was the thirst. It had been over a day since he had drunk anything. There was water in a bowl but that was over by the hound and he was in no condition to confront it.

It was hard to keep the dirt out of his wounds but harder still to keep the flies off them. The wounds didn't look good and needed medical attention, maybe stitches. That afternoon in the heat of the sun the fever started. Ishmael thought nothing of it due to the weather, but as the afternoon wore on he began to feel stiffness in the arm close to the bite wounds, then it spread to the jaw and neck in the long night that followed. Ishmael repeatedly tried to open his mouth as well as stretching his neck muscles. He didn't remember falling on his side, but he came to amidst a series of muscle spasms. Ishmael stayed in that strange state of delirium through the next night until the boy came again in the morning. He placed a bowl of water next to Ishmael and another bowl between him and the hound with food in it. Then he stood to the side eagerly awaiting the upcoming confrontation. Ishmael hardly moved; he just lay there, for the moment free of spasms, but racked by fever that muddled his mind with confusion. Ishmael dragged himself to the water and managed to slurp some down. What was happening to him? Why wasn't the earth tree healing his wounds like it had before?

His throat was desert dry, the muscles of his jaw almost locked while weakness immobilized his limbs. At the boy's signal the hound rushed in then began wolfing down the food while watching Ishmael out of the corner of its eye. Ishmael heard the boy approach from the soft crunch of this sandals. He stopped next to Ishmael, looking down at him as if he was a bug and he wanted to tear his wings or legs off. A sandal poked Ishmael in the thigh hard enough to cause him to emit a dry grunt; unsatisfied with such a little reaction, he, did it again harder.

'C'mon, move rude man, you a coward or something? You must be the runt of whatever litter you come from I bet. Well next time you better fight for your food or you will go hungry again.'

Without warning he booted Ishmael harder, this time in the stomach, which rolled Ishmael onto his back. Ishmael felt the tremors start again as his muscles seized along his back, chest then up his neck to the jaw. He tasted blood as his teeth bit down, catching his lip. The last thing he saw before thankfully falling unconscious was the widening of the boy's eyes in surprise as he ran back into the house.

Zahra hardly slept in that strange room as noises she was unaccustomed to kept her awake. When she finally did sleep, Zahra had a nightmare that left her sitting up, lathered in sweat and breathing hard. The time was maybe two chimes after midnight when she rose and dressed. She unlatched the door then padded bare- foot out along the hallway then up the stairs to the balcony where they had supped the evening before. As she walked out she saw the general Caldro was standing there staring out towards Acclaro.

Monte turned towards her. 'Couldn't sleep either?'

'If I rest too long my mind is drawn to things I have no wish to dwell on.'

'Will you stay and fight, if it comes to that?'

'I will stay for a day, two at the most. I need to find my employer and get him to safety, and I'm sure he will have taken the Seekers Road.'

'Much the pity then; I could use a lass like you. While you slept a patrol returned stating much that you have already told us. They also bought news of more people fleeing the city towards us here for sanctuary. If it's going to be a fight tomorrow we all need to be rested. Good night to you, Zahra. While you are here at my outpost be sure you are ready to fight for its defence; otherwise be gone by dawn and may the gods, wherever they are, smile upon you in the coming days.'

The most recent stream of refugees began to trickle in before dawn broke the horizon. Word had spread through the Point, and women and men of all faiths gathered together to help bring in those of need to the halls of the pious for food, sleep, and medical attention. Zahra wanted to stay and help the defence of the outpost and those refugees in need, but Ishmael needed her more. She gathered her belongings then started the long descent of the stairs looking for the chapel of the Death Jester where someone could help her. The holy attendants of the temples were scurrying about setting up their wares for the day. Pilgrims seemingly unaware of the chaos to come burnt masses of incense or herbs as they uttered prayers.

It took half a chime to locate the temple of the Death Jester, which was pressed between two of the more opulent houses of faith. The building was run down and the handle on the tall narrow door came away in Zahra's hand when she went to announce herself. She let herself in and stepped into a corridor lit by nearly burnt out candles that weaved away into the darkness. Rats scurried across the floor as she watched, and water trickled down one wall to puddle below. Zahra sidled along the corridor, reaching up to take one of the half burned candles with her. She came to a door with a small chapel area off to its side. The chapel told a distinctly different story than the entry of the temple, and it had been kept immaculate with an altar bearing the items of death all set in the correct manner. Long black candles burned here, releasing the faint scent of anise.

Zahra dipped her fingers into a shallow bowl that contained the oil of the after- world. She dabbed it between her eyebrows, at the base of her throat, on both wrists where the heart's beat could be found and finally removed her shirt to dab more of the mixture along her sternum between her breasts.

The items on the altar would now need to be arranged to announce her real reason for visiting this temple of death. They were a skeletal hand, vial of blood supposedly from the Jester himself, a sacrificial knife, and a vial of the most noxious poison ever developed. It had been sometime since Zahra had needed help from the Jester, and she paused to remember the ritual. The hand placed in such a way as the thumb and forefinger made a circle with the palm up on which the vial of poison sat. With the knife she slashed a thin cut to her thumb letting the blood pool on the blade which then rested facing west, the direction where the sun went to die each day. With that complete Zahra buttoned her shirt back up then retreated to a pew to wait.

The priest didn't keep her waiting long. He emerged from the door in a stitched robe of many skins made from previous head priests of this temple as was the custom. The bones sewn into the full length jacket rattled against each other as he approached the altar, a rectangular box in hand. The deep cowl of the coat hid the priest's face but Zahra knew beneath it he would be masked. The priest lay the box on the altar careful not to disturb the items there.

'Who comes in search of death?'

Zahra rose and moved to the opposite side of the altar.

'One who strives to meet him daily and does his bidding.'

'Who comes to stand in death's home without fear?'

'One who has been spoken for.'

'Who speaks for the one who comes?'

'I have been touched by death, who speaks for me.'

The next line they spoke together

'The time glass will shatter, then death will gather the remnants of all.'

The priest opened the vial of blood then used the knife to drip Zahra's blood into that already collected. Then he reached his arms out over the altar to Zahra, who kissed the palms lightly. She stepped back, arranging her hands in front of her, the left hand with index finger pointing to the heavens in front of her face and the right with the index finger pointing down in front of the abdomen.

'I see you are of the Kenzu. You seek our aid in your search for something that is lost. Let us put such arduous ritual aside so we may speak freely in this house.'

The priest placed the items on the altar into the rectangular box then retreated to the door, where he ushered Zahra in before locking the door behind him. He removed the long coat and the mask that showed a peaceful semblance of death. Beneath it a man well into his middle age was revealed with gaunt cheeks, and a large brow set above dilated brown eyes that Zahra refused to look at for more than a moment. He carefully placed the items within a wardrobe at the back of the chamber whose walls were cluttered with relics of death. It appeared to be the priest's private quarters, furnished well with lavish rugs and even a large bed against one wall.

'Take a seat, I will pour us refreshments. You may call me Klaus, and who may you be?'

'Zahra, a chosen of the Kenzu clan.'

He returned with two goblets.

'I hope you don't mind cider. I make it from the offerings of fruit the worshippers place here daily, otherwise it rots then stinks the temple out. After a few days the stench truly becomes hard to stomach, not to mention a pain to clean up.'

'Cider is fine, thank you.'

'Now tell me, do we still have the same clan lord?'

Zahra thought the question was strange since all Kenzu would know by now if a new clan lord had taken Haakon's place. She sipped the cider again before answering and forced herself to stay calm.

'Haakon still rules far as I am aware, though I have not returned to the clan house for some cycles now.' Zahra noticed her words put Klaus at ease and she felt as if she had passed some unspoken test.

'Haakon was here when I first took up the post as a novice and I tried to forbid him entry.' Klaus sipped his drink then chucked heartily. 'He threatened to drag me by the hair all the way down the Path of prayer then back up, you know?'

'Yes that does sound like Haakon all right,' replied Zahra. Klaus, I need to find a certain somebody that has eluded me. It is imperative he is found before he comes to harm. This person is very important to Haakon and the clan.'

'What name does he go by?'

'Ishmael. He will be travelling as a monk of Illume and is intent on discovering the fate of the gods. Ishmael has never travelled these lands or the Seekers Road, and he is in such terrible danger that if he isn't found soon then I fear what will happen.'

'He is one of the coterie, isn't he?'

The priest noticed her pause. He pulled his tunic open to reveal a raised scar at the base of the sternum that she recognized as Kenzu.

Zahra relaxed. She was with a fellow brother at last and couldn't remember the last time she had spent time in one's company.

'Yes, he is and since you know that then you will recall Haakon's instructions to us that we are to aid our brethren in any way to be sure the coterie are kept safe. The time is nearing when magic may be ready to return and the coterie need to be kept safe and together. I was trying to take Ishmael to unite him with the rest of the coterie, but the stubborn ass drugged me then left after we fled Acclaro City ahead of the Infernals.'

'Drugged you? Ha, sounds like you have your hands full with this one.'

'Tell me, Klaus, do you have any news of the clan?'

'In fact I do but none of it is good. Haakon was gravely injured while in the astral and only the quick thinking of his men saved him from the fade. He was investigating the disappearance of Latasha and walked right into a trap. Latasha herself was found in such a state that she is comatose and it's thought that the secrets around the coterie were wrung from her poor body by.'

Before he could say anything more Zahra blurted the name out.

'Dalwyn Trevlon.'

'Well, yes, you are right.'

Zahra refilled her cider. 'Dalwyn has tried to take Ishmael from me and was waiting for us in Acclaro, where he still might be.'

They shared two more drinks of the cider Klaus was so proud of then Zahra outlined what she would need. She managed to stagger from the temple barely before noon a little unsteady from the cider and lack of food to hold it down. Her purse was now filled with gold and a list of contacts along the road that were also agents of the Kenzu as well as a letter penned by Klaus himself ordering that Zahra be treated with the deference her title deserved.

Chapter 10

Ishmael awoke to someone prising his eyelids open. Then his mouth was forced open slightly before cool water slipped down his throat only for him to choke it back up.

'Fausto, you were given one thing to do; make sure the man is watered then fed every day as well as look after him so he becomes strong for work, and you can't even do that right. Your father will shear the skin from your back if he finds out. You are just lucky he is gone to the Godhead for the next three days.'

'I did nothing to him,' replied the boy petulantly.

'Well you got that right, nothing at all it seems. Look at these bites! From Chill, I assume. They have begun to fester, and see here where his the jaw muscles have almost seized from infection. The fever has him cooking from within, Fausto! Get me fresh water with my herbs so I can try to save him.'

Ishmael was dragged inside the house to a pallet where his clothes were removed by the woman who checked his body for more injuries. She talked as she worked, but Ishmael had no way of seeing if someone was there with her, as his head was too heavy to hold up. This must be the monitor's wife he realized.

The woman gasped when she removed Ishmael's shirt. 'Look at all these scars. For one so young, you seem to have managed to get yourself into a lot of trouble.'

He was bathed, had an awful liquid forced down his throat, then his forearm wounds were covered in salves before being dressed.

After it all Ishmael dozed with the fever still burning through him.

'Faustus? Faustus, come here!'

'Why do I have to do everything? I have other chores that I am to do.'

Ishmael heard a slap then a cry of protest come from the next room.

'You think you will only get a slap when your father comes back? If he was here you wouldn't dare question him, now do as I ask since you were the one charged with his care.'

That began the next stage of Ishmael's relationship with the boy Fausto. He was always disappointed when the boy visited instead of his mother. Fausto would bathe Ishmael daily in water too cold or too hot then roughly dress him in fresh clothes as well as hand feed him. Twice in those three days he spent in that room he caught Fausto spitting in his food or noticed dead bugs mixed in with his poor meals.

If Ishmael happened to be sleeping and his mother was not around when Fausto came then he would slap Ishmael or pinch his skin. Within two days the fever was reduced considerably.

The woman, who he now knew was called Fajira, came to see him. 'You heal fast, Yucca. Your fever is nearly gone.' They both regarded each other silently for a moment before Fajira realized that Ishmael wasn't going to react to her words.

'What is your real name?'

'Ishmael, I am from Illume.'

'Yes the style of your clothes told me that when Diego bought you here. He will be expecting you to work when he returns from the Godhead, so we need to get you strong again. At least the fever is gone. Do you feel any different?'

'I no longer feel as if my skin is roasting, but tell me why am I being kept here with you?'

'My husband won't tolerate insults; he is a prideful man.'

'I had no idea that my actions had insulted him. As a stranger to these lands how was I meant to know your customs?'

'It is unusual for one of our people to take a stranger to task over perceived insults, but it seems my husband has taken a personal dislike to you, Ishmael.'

On the third morning in that small stuffy room that was in truth little better than the courtyard, Ishmael awoke to a commotion deeper in the house where yelling was coming from. The monitor was home. The voices carried easily to where Ishmael rested, still chained but slightly more rested and feeling better. He pushed himself to a sitting position, straining to hear the conversation.

'I do remember telling you that Yucca was to stay chained in the yard. Now I return home to find that you have moved Yucca into our home against my wishes. You go too far, woman!'

'Go on, do it, strike me down, Diego. But be warned if you do lay one finger on me then be sure to kill me. If you don't then watch your back and don't sleep or eat because I will be there to poison your food or cut your throat in your sleep. This is one battle you won't win.'

'Then tell me why you insist on defying me Fajira?'

'Because, you stupid man, if I had left him there he would be dead now. Old Chill nearly tore his arm off over a bowl of meat, and I only found out once the wounds were already infected. It is lucky for us I got to him before he could die, you know that to have a stranger die in our home would beset our house with bad luck. We know nothing of this man, Diego. Maybe his family or friends know he is on the road and will coming searching for him. I have talked to him, husband, he knows nothing of our customs yet you take his freedom for an insult he could have never known he had caused.'

'It's my right to keep him here, and until my honour is restored he will do my bidding. Where is he now?'

The voices came closer, then the monitor was standing in the doorway pushing his way past his wife and through the beaded curtain into the room. He strode over to the bed.

Ishmael raised his hands up before his face defensively. He could see Fajira hovering behind her husband, her face creased with worry.

'He looks fine to me, woman.'

The monitor beckoned to Ishmael. 'Can you work?'

Ishmael glared at the man. He would not allow this man to treat him badly any more. The monitor balled his fists stepping forward but Fajira stepped between him and the bed. 'Stop it, Diego, he is unwell, and if you won't allow him time to recover then he will be no use to you.'

Diego puffed out his cheeks, his face now flushed red, eyes crinkling with anger.

'Two days, then you work for me, Yucca. Until then you sleep outside in the yard again. I will not have the man who insults me stay under my roof.'

Despite Fajira's protests Diego unchained Ishmael then led him back into the courtyard where he was chained up again. Chill was still there; he trotted over with a low growl only to be kicked away by Diego.

'Fausto? Fausto? Where is that damn boy?'

Fausto came at a run. Ishmael could see the fear in the boy's eyes; he kept glancing at his mother but didn't dare meet his father's glare. Ishmael enjoyed seeing his tormentor experiencing some of his own medicine. Ishmael thought that the fear that Diego held over his son Fausto was something he could exploit over the boy if he continued to antagonize him. Fajira brought out a thin pallet with blankets for Ishmael, much to Diego's disgust.

When he was alone again, Ishmael took hope in that he was feeling much better again. Despite the boy's mistreatment, strength was returning to his limbs. The muscle spasms had stopped and his wounds, now stitched and bandaged, were healing well. It would seem that once again his connection with the earth tree had helped him recover from deadly wounds once again, but how many times could it do that? Thinking of the earth tree made Ishmael remember his near death experience after the attack in Illume. Since then he had dreamed many times of the Mother beckoning him to join the coterie and if he continued to ignore the Mother would she in turn stop helping him? Recalling the dreams again cast a heaviness over Ishmael as he struggled to find any positive meaning from them.

Another thing Ishmael had noticed was that he now had more control over the surges of the magic that would rise up through his body. Throughout the ordeal with the hound the magic had stayed coiled at the base of his spine. Could it be that finally he was learning how to control it? A number of times he felt the attentions of Selene or Jona as they tried to pass his walls and communicate with him. He wondered about Raul and what the bullish man was doing. Raul had never tried to contact Ishmael or the others as far as Ishmael knew. He knew that the coterie deserved an explanation, but he was cautious about dragging them into his problem. It would only cause more worry and danger for them.

The next morning when Fausto returned he brought food for both Chill as well as Ishmael, wincing in pain as he bent to place Ishmael's bowl of food on the ground.

'Thank you, Fausto, for your kindness.'

He received a nod in return, and as Fausto walked slowly back into the house Ishmael could see thin strips of crimson through the back of his shirt. Diego had whipped him.

Later that morning both Diego and Fausto came to the courtyard. Each one carried a gourd. They took Chill without acknowledging Ishmael at all. Though he was stronger now Ishmael had begun acting weak and lethargic in order for the monitor to stay unaware of his near- full recovery. Now alone, he decided to put his body through the series of exercises that he used to hate doing each morning while living in the monastery, but they would help him loosen the heaviness from tight muscles as well as clear his energy centers.

Earlier that morning he had once again experienced the queasiness deep in his stomach followed by a hot burning at the base of his spine that was the warning signs of the magic starting its rise up through his body. Now no longer in the monastery, Ishmael knew he couldn't rely on others to help him stay safe. Ishmael began the movements that would ease his energy centers and keep them from opening. The chain around the left ankle made it harder than usual, but he managed to manoeuvre around it anyway. It felt good to return to this routine, his tight inflexible muscles warmed ever so slowly, especially the muscles of his legs from days of being bedridden. He turned slowly, breathing deeply, flowed into a lunging position, back bent with his chest and chin thrust forward, arms pulled back as the mountain greets the day with the roaring wind at its back. In front of him leaning against the wall stood Fajira watching him with interest. Ishmael straightened up, unable to speak since his breath was coming hard.

'What is that dance?' she asked, twisting her skirts between her legs then squatting down.

'It is the dance of creation that the monks of Illume do every day to keep the body hard in order to train the mind as well as allowing us to acknowledge the mystery of life.'

'Well, no wonder I am unfamiliar with it. I study dancing. In fact, it has been my obsession since being a small girl, but rarely have I seen a dance performed with such beauty and joy.'

Ishmael flushed at the compliment, keeping his gaze away from her, not really sure what to make of this woman.

'It pleases me that you liked it.'

'I came to dress your wounds, but it's obvious that you are feeling much better if you can exercise so vigorously. For one so ill only five days ago, your recovery is remarkable.'

Ishmael used his shirt to wipe away the sweat on his face.

'I heal fast, always have.'

She smiled at that.

'My mother taught me medicine at an early age so that when I was older I could assist her with her field medicine and battlefield surgery. Both my parents worked for the Cavere army for some cycles before they got homesick and returned here to make a life. In all those cycles, Ishmael, never have I seen someone heal so quickly.

Ishmael allowed Fajira to see his wounds, which were now little more than raised scabs. She shook her head in wonder at the results.

'If I had not seen this with my own eyes, I would say to heal so quickly was impossible. You are a very mysterious person, Ishmael; first you appear from nowhere, insult my husband, who holds you as prisoner of his honour, then your wounds mysteriously heal. I am not sure what to make of you.'

'I am a simple man who has lost his family not once but twice. I came here to discover if the gods are still alive or not, because no one can tell me for sure. I have an important task before me and who better to consult than my Lady Shail of Illume.'

'What is this task is that burdens you so?'

Ishmael looked up meeting Fajira's eyes. 'Until I am a free man again I shall share nothing. For whatever reason I can only guess at I have been bought here to learn a lesson, but since very little that happens to me now is mine, I shall keep my secrets close to my heart.'

Chapter 11

Zacriel lay slumped on the throne with one leg thrown over the arm rest as he twirled the infernal rod across his fingers. He had often dreamt of power and now he found himself wondering what all the fuss of being an infernal lord was about. Yes, he had an army now and could order the death of anyone he chose that resided in the city, but then what? At first Zacriel had enjoyed having everything done for him by his human slaves which left him to deal with more important problems within the city. This feeling had now worn off as his days were filled with more problems as his growing army became harder to control, and the many factions within it began to squabble over areas of the city. He would be lucky to even have a city left if the crazed infernal horde didn't stop destroying it. Worse still, news had come that the three other infernal lords were on their way here to see this new upstart lord that had destroyed the Lady of Whispers, and it did nothing to improve his mood. It was rumoured that the other three lords were not happy at losing her since her death had spoiled their plans put in place earlier.

Although Zacriel hated to admit it, he missed Nina who had become a companion to him even if it was against her will. Now the girl was trapped with Dalwyn who had taken residence in one of the other castle towers and held Nina there as a hostage. The old man was close to pushing him too far, but with Dalwyn's vast network of contacts Zacriel knew he couldn't afford to kill the man until this business with the other infernal lords was settled, it would be foolish to act now.

The book was much different from what Nina had expected it to be. It sounded boring in an adult serious way and many of the words were beyond her reading ability. She loved the many colourful pictures that helped her understand what she thought the words were explaining. Nina became immersed in exploring the meaning and locations of the nine energy centers, or vortices, as the text called them. These vortices are in every person's energy field and funnel out from the front and back of the body and act as intake organs for energy flow between the person and the base energy that makes up everything. If the vortices were weak, too strong, or damaged they could cause disease or at least imbalance in a person's life. What many people didn't know was that the vortices had another use. Once you had learned to form your energy body through exercises you could enter the astral world through any of the nine vortices, and each would add a different type of experience based on what they represented and the state of the traveller's energy body.

The first vortex was the lowest and was one of the earth vortices. The main function was to ground yourself to the earth and connect to her feminine energy, which would keep your astral body connected while travelling. To become disconnected from this vortex while in the astral would have devastating effects on the traveller.

Nina heard Dalwyn returning; though he said nothing, it was the scuffing way he walked that she recognized along with the stamp of boots from the two guards outside the chamber door. She quickly closed the book, making sure to leave everything as it had been, and went to sit at the window. Tonight, she would begin to create her energy body through exercises designed to strengthen the vortices. Nina did a little jig then and could hardly stop grinning. She finally had something of her own and a way to escape her prison.

When Dalwyn awoke, nearly half the day had already passed. Nina sat at her usual spot on the window ledge, noisily eating shiny cherries and melon slices. At the sight of food Dalwyn's stomach rumbled, and his wandering eyes settled on the covered platter left on the table. Meat! He wanted meat. Now his astral work was progressing steadily and he could enter the astral through his first three earth vortices, but this consumed a lot of energy and he seemed always hungry and needed to sleep for longer periods after those sessions. The thought of travelling the astral to find the coterie of the heart had once excited him, but now he was fast developing a respect for the dangers of that strange realm.

Swinging himself up and out of the bed, he sat at the table in his loincloth and uncovered the platter that was spilling over with meats and vegetables. Nina had already claimed the fruit, but this would be ample for now.

As he tore into the meat, juice dripped down his chin, the flavour divine. Soft footsteps padded on the stone as Nina came to sit opposite him. She held out the bowl of cherries.

'I saved you some, Dalwyn, they're so yummy.'

He just nodded and continued eating as Nina watched with a look that spoke of disgust but fascination.

'Wow, you are really hungry all the time now. Why is that?'

'Go away and let me eat,' growled Dalwyn as he slurped from the water jug. 'You wouldn't understand.'

'I'm not stupid you know. I might be a child but that doesn't make it so you have to be mean to me.' After another bite of the meat he threw the bone at Nina who dodged easily and annoyingly kept sitting opposite him. 'What do you want, Nina?'

'Books? There is a great library in the city, or so my da used to say. I was thinking we could visit there and get some books for me to read.'

'No, not going to happen. If you think we can just go down into the city while our kind are at the top of the Infernals' menu then you are crazy. Anyway, you can't even read.'

'I'm sure Zacriel will give us an escort, especially if you take me, and you can get some books too like the one you are reading to help your studies.'

'I will think on it. Now go away and leave me in peace,' growled Dalwyn as he tried a cherry. Nina was right, they were delicious.

The longer Dalwyn thought about Nina's idea to visit the library the more it sounded like a good one. Any more information he could gather regarding the astral world would be invaluable, and he could add it to his collection of texts back home. Dalwyn had sent word back to his family in the Tiariacs and was still awaiting a reply. He needed more soldiers and felt his life was only hanging by a thread in this city due to the perseverance of Zacriel. To survive he would need to make sure he stayed useful and even allow the bone lord enough access to Nina to maintain the current situation.

Zacriel tried to appear attentive as Rapture rumbled on with his report.

'We sent a squad out to scour the Glyph plains between here and Wilhelm's Point with no sign of the monk or his bodyguard. The fields and granaries have been set to the torch, and the outpost at Wilhelm's Point has mobilized, ready to fight and protect the farmers and refugees from the city that are fleeing there. I have a winged squadron ready at your command. Reports farther afield say Illume is in the throes of war with those beneath the mountain, and even stranger tidings from the Jewelled lands along the Devouring River state that thick crystal now covers the river like ice and passage through the forest is to dangerous due to patrols of harlequin warriors. That is all, my lord,' the infernal bowed low then retreated slowly back down the steps before turning and leaving the throne room.

Finally, some time alone, thought Zacriel just as two figures entered the throne room from the side and his guards moved to intercept them.

'Move aside, scum, we are here to see Zacriel, not kill him!'

Zacriel's ears perked up at that; it was Dalwyn and he had said we. Did he mean Nina?

'Let them through, then wait outside so I may speak alone with them.'

He saw the heavily muscled monstrosity with gnarled bark skin huffing and flexing its muscles and then it signalled to the other guards and left with a snarl.

Zacriel stood as Dalwyn and Nina moved to sit by the throne.

'No, let's go to the tower balcony, I need some fresh air away from the unbearable stench of my guards in here.'

'Looks to me, Zacriel, that your guards are barely kept in check by your authority,' stated Dalwyn as they climbed the steps slowly with Nina skipping ahead of them.

'They don't trust you, Dalwyn, and for that matter neither do I. However, we are in this together for now and so they will not harm either you or your men.'

'Well I guess that's something if not totally comforting. How long do you plan to sit here in your city doing nothing, anyway?'

'Nothing? Bah, old man you have no idea of how things are progressing.'

'So, you have found Ishmael and that pest assassin of his then?'

'Not yet, but I will, and then they will pay!'

'I don't believe you Zacriel,' Dalwyn said. You forget they have escaped you twice now and you are the puppet on the throne with a city boiling over with chaos. Is it true the other infernal lords are coming here?'

'Unfortunately. At least one, and if you hadn't tried to betray me and have Knuckles kill me then Ishmael would never have escaped, so the blame lies with you, Dalwyn. Why is Nina so happy? I would have thought your company would make her leap from the tower by now.'

'She would be doing me a favour. She wants to go to the library, but due to the hatred your kind harbour towards us we need an escort.'

'It's not just for me, Zacriel, Dalwyn also wants to go there to get books on the astral world,' called Nina's voice from farther up the stairs.'

Zacriel laughed aloud and raised his eyebrows. 'Seems like Nina is getting the better of you Dalwyn, getting soft in your old age hmmm?'

They reached the balcony and for maybe the first time since the city had fallen it wasn't billowing smoke and reeking of death. From Zacriel's instructions his infernal army had begun the unenviable task of clearing the dead and debris to restore the place to some proper semblance of a city.

Zacriel had the servants bring wine for himself and Dalwyn and apple juice for Nina who came and sat beside him as he talked with Dalwyn.

'Zac, how is midnight?' asked Nina.

Midnight was the name Nina had given the lunar mount he had been given by Cinerus back in Illume.

'He is well, Nina. I don't get to ride him often these days, but he sleeps on the wall in my chamber.'

'When can I ride him again, Zac?'

'I'm not sure. With all the running of the city it leaves me with precious little time to do anything.'

'Then let's leave and fly away from here, or if you don't want to go, let me go. The castle is so boring and Dalwyn doesn't let me do anything, that's why I want to go to the library to get some books.'

Zacriel sipped the wine, rolling the oak flavours over his tongue. Below he could see a commotion as a small band of Infernals led two humans up into the castle. His interest was piqued now; who could that be?

They found out soon enough as Rapture swept out onto the balcony, his long cloak swirling behind him.

'Bone lord, we have important news. My soldiers have detained two infiltrators to the city. They were found trying to swim in from the lake gate.'

Both Dalwyn and Zacriel were on their feet now.

'Who are they?'

'They say that they will only reveal details of themselves to Dalwyn Trevlon or the Bone lord.'

'Bring them here then.'

'I wouldn't recommend that, lord,' Rapture replied. For all we know they could be assassins here to kill you both.'

'Well if you and your men have done their jobs properly I won't have to worry about them harbouring weapons, will I?' snapped Zacriel as the fearsome Infernal started back down the stairs.

The elite guards brought the two intruders up to the balcony. The man was young, maybe twenty cycles old. He was well-muscled with shoulder length, sandy hair. He stood there with his arms crossed and an arrogant glare plastered on his face. The woman was nothing short of beautiful. Tall with long brown tresses, golden skin, and a shapely body. Most telling though was that she seemed unperturbed by their predicament.

Zacriel studied them awhile as he finished his wine.

'Rapture, take Nina back to her room.'

Nina stamped her foot in frustration. 'I don't want to go back there, Zac. Let me stay and I promise to behave.'

'Not now, Nina, this is no place for a child!'

'No place for a child? And being the slave to a deformed creature and crazy old man is?'

Rapture grasped Nina by the arm and began leading her away.

'Zacriel, it's not fair, what about the library?'

Trying to regain his composure, Zacriel ignored her and turned to the two intruders.

'It's hardly a wise decision to try and sneak into Acclaro these days.'

He had expected the man to answer, but it was the woman who spoke.

'Is that what they told you? We let ourselves be caught, and this was our destination from the start.'

Dalwyn placed a hand on Zacriel's shoulder and pulled him close. We must allow them to rest here Zacriel. I believe they have important knowledge we can benefit from.'

'What? Do you know either of them, Dalwyn?'

'I am not sure yet. I will explain it all to you soon, Zacriel.'

As Zacriel turned to regard the newcomers again the man collapsed, his head smacking against the stone with a sickening thud.

'Oh, not again,' said the woman, kneeling beside him. 'He is so exhausted and has been suffering these seizures due to neglecting himself. She looked over at Dalwyn beside her and Zacriel behind him.

'He needs rest and we need to talk, Dalwyn.'

Chapter 12

A steady stream of pilgrims hurried past the temples not bothering to stop as they descended the steps of the path of prayers. Zahra reached out to one as he went by.

'What's the news, brother? I have been sleeping, why is everyone in such a hurry?'

'War has come; refugees are at the gate from Acclaro, which still burns on the horizon. There is talk that the road may close and so I am determined not to be trapped here when the Infernals arrive to slaughter us just like they did at Acclaro.'

He pulled free from her grip then continued pushing past people. Zahra took the steps two at a time as she fought against the crowd to make the top of the stairs then up to the general's house.

When Zahra had first arrived here the day before she had taken little notice of the defences of Wilhelm's Point. Now faced with the possibility of battle she scanned the defences which seemed up to standard at least at ground level. Soldiers manned the walls of the town where great cauldrons of oil were burning in preparation to pour on any enemies foolish enough to scale the defences, and three ballista towers stood manned at the possibility of aerial threats. One thing became glaringly obvious as Zahra surveyed the area. Even with the three ballista the town was ill equipped to defend an attack especially from the skies. Once the ballista's fell and it would not take long to destroy the main gates. When the Infernals came the only question would be how long the defenders could hold out before the town fell. Zahra continued up to the general's home, the soldiers there ushered her up when they saw her.

'General Caldro has been looking for you everywhere. He's up on the observation deck now.'

'Up on the deck soldiers busily placed spears in defensive rows along the walls and the house roof to help deter attacks from the air, barrels of arrows had been rolled up to stand with two rows of archers and containers of all sizes stood filled with water in the case of fires.

'Zahra there you are! I need you to help protect the house while we attempt to get the rest of the refugees through the gates. A force of infernals is closely pursuing the stragglers that lie still maybe a mile or two from the gate. Up here I am a target and am needed down at ground level to organize the defence. This rooftop is now yours to command.'

Zahra started to say she had decided not to stay, but she couldn't just abandon the men here. The look of steely determination the general gave her helped her decide to help him. At least she would now have a chance to fight back against this enemy. If things went bad she would be forced to flee, but for now the blood had begun to pump in her temples. She took the time to drink some cold water, checked her armour was intact, and then began to organize the soldiers she had been left in charge of.

Out on the hills before Whitman's Point the scene began to play itself out. The defenders watched as the scurrying pilgrims pushed themselves harder to make the gate. Some fell to be left behind, and it was each person for themselves down there. The pursuers came into clear view now amid howls and screams of madness as the fastest of them and some mounted tore into the flagging lines of the fleeing refugees. Many of the attackers were barely more than beasts with little if any human semblance. The horns sounded and slowly the gates began to close while many of the refugees had yet to reach the sanctuary of Wilhelm's Point. Those trapped outside would be slaughtered, but Zahra knew that to leave them open any longer would risk losing the town straight away. If the town was to repel this first half-hearted attack, then they must hold the gates.

Zahra stood at the rail of the observation deck silently willing the fleeing pilgrims onwards to safety. The defenders above the gatehouse were stretched too thin and must be shored up before any attack came. It seemed useless to Zahra to have as many archers up here as she did, some should help with the gatehouse defence. She turned to the archer next to her to give the order when he was snatched from his feet from above by a multi-coloured, feathered creature that sped out over the courtyard below, dropping the archer, he struck the ground with a cry and lay still.

'Ware the skies! Archers, make each shot count,' yelled Zahra.

Above her, Zahra could see dozens of the flying infernals diving from high within the thermal winds above the town snatching defenders from their posts to fling down onto the ground far below. Many of the defenders around her broke as they watched their brethren die. A few fired quickly into the air, dropping some of the attackers that screamed manically as they pursued more victims, but the majority of the archers dropped their bows and fled in terror.

Zahra grabbed a fallen bow, fired three arrows in quick succession at a feathered warrior who shredded the face of a defender with a mighty slash of its terrible claws. Two of the three struck the creature in the chest as it pushed past the screaming man then half ran at Zahra, laughing gleefully. She notched the next arrow, sighted down it, held her breath, and then released the arrow as the Infernal reached for her. The arrow tore through its face and out the back of its skull.

Its weight knocked Zahra from her feet, effectively saving her from the outstretched claws of another winged monstrosity seeking to dash her to the ground far below.

A group of citizens arrived then to help fight off the creatures. Among them Zahra could see two burly priests of war singing loud taunts at the attackers as they set about themselves with bladed flails in dizzying patterns, striking down any they came in contact with. At least those who called Wilhelm's Point home would have the chance to defend themselves, unlike the poor souls of Acclaro.

As the last of the wave of aerial attackers was shot from the sky above the general's home, Zahra glanced down to see how the defenders there were faring. It didn't look good. A group of grey-skinned, reptilian Infernals had scaled the wall and were tearing savagely into the defenders along the top. As Zahra watched, one of them grasped the edge of a boiling pot and sent it and the oil plunging down upon a group of soldiers fighting to keep the gate closed. It howled as its skin burned, which merged with the screaming of the soldiers below.

This was a disaster, the gates were nearly lost and the ballista destroyed already. Zahra had the remaining archers around her take down the reptilian leader, who was trying to douse its burnt arms in a water barrel. Its face became riddled with arrows and it swayed before falling head over heels to the courtyard. Miraculously the gate still held, and Zahra could see the general leading from the front as they fought off the attackers on the wall managing to keep the gate closed.

As quick as they came the attackers retreated, leaving the outpost in flames. Two of the guard towers had been destroyed, leaving only one still functional. The cries of pain pulled Zahra out of the battle fury she was feeling. They had barely fought the Infernals off, and next time would be worse

'Don't just stand there,' she told the remaining archers, 'collect any arrows that can be reused.'

The two war monks took up positions at the edge of the stairs leading down to the courtyard while a group of terrified women moved amongst the fallen offering water and first aid to those injured. Outside back on the plain the attackers below had regrouped as if waiting, but for what? They had the defenders outnumbered maybe five to one.

For now it seemed the attackers were happy to stay out of distance of the defenders. The whole town was on edge, the defenders were now rattled as below the force of infernals grew steadily. Mid-afternoon came and went as the remaining defenders worked beneath the glaring sun to rebuild defences where they could. The fact that the infernals had been fought off once already filled the defenders with hope, but this was washed away two chimes from dusk.

When the cries went up around the town Zahra roused herself from a quick nap to see what was happening. From the direction of Acclaro a dark mass was moving through the sky towards Wilhelm's Point. They would make the Point within the chime, and it was obvious to Zahra that such a force was unstoppable. It was wise for the enemy to totally destroy the town, which was the closest of the military outposts that served the outlying fringes of the Thantosian border with Brimmerland at the start of the Seekers Road. Already defenders were fleeing their posts as the sight of the new force.

Zahra collected her pack along with a spare bow and a quiver of arrows then headed for the path of prayer. There was a time to fight and that was gone now; it would serve no one if she was dashed to the rocks below by an Infernal now. She turned to the men next to her.

'Flee now if you value your lives, there is no way to fight off that many enemies. The Point is lost.'

As she left Zahra could hear the general trying desperately to rally his men. It seemed futile since they would die pointless deaths buying time for those fleeing but what purpose would that bring, the Point was lost? General Caldro caught her attention, distraught as he rushed up the stairs to her.

'Zahra, someone needs to warn the other nations what has happened here and in Acclaro before the infernals can gain more of a foothold in the region. I know you have important duties of your own, but I will forever be indebted to you if you would deliver these scrolls to Glimmersedge, Cabre and the Godhead. Messengers should have been sent earlier and would have if I had not failed to take your warning seriously.' He thrust the scrolls into her arms. 'Go now, Zahra, and may the gods smile on you.'

Chapter 13

The frantic rush of fleeing civilians choked the path of prayers; Zahra saw a man punch a woman who tried to struggle past him. The woman fell to the ground as the crowd rolled over her, ignoring her screams as she was trampled. These acts of violence were happening all around Zahra, who copped an elbow to the mouth, cutting her lips as she fought not just to escape but to remain standing amongst the heaving crowd. Someone grabbed Zahra from behind on the neck and without thinking she drew her dagger from the waist and stabbed backwards over her shoulder; the hand fell away then she was pushed forward again feeling sickened as she stumbled with the others over bodies on the stairs.

It seemed an eternity before Zahra reached the base of the stairs bleeding from several cuts to the face and a burning pain across where her neck had been wrenched. Zahra stumbled along breathing heavily as she staggered out onto the road where the crowd was able to spread out between the statues of the gods that had been carved into the canyon walls that flanked the road. Rather than looking kind and benign, they had the sombre look of detachment and resignation as if the imminent deaths of the fleeing citizens from Wilhelm's point had already been decided.

The momentary relief of leaving the dangerous stairs was short lived as up ahead a score of infernals hurtled out of the sky to fly straight towards the fleeing citizens. They turned back straight into the path of those who swarmed after them. In moments the infernals were amongst them, whooping and howling as they fell upon the people.

Zahra threw herself to the side with her back against a pillar as a flying infernal dropped a creature with bullish shoulders and yellowish tusks to the ground nearby. It ducked its head then charged into a group of screaming people, knocking a score of them flat then falling upon them with vicious thrusts of its horns. Zahra followed the brute as it rushed past, then when it was busy killing those it had knocked down she tore its throat out with her blade from behind as it raised its bloodied snout in a war cry.

Now the crowd pressed from both directions, pushing Zahra once again, this time back up the stairs. She pulled a little girl who was knocked down back to her feet before losing the grip on her arm, and the crowd tore her away. Keeping as close as she could now to the walls of the temples, Zahra knew if she was knocked back into the crowd she would be dead. Her breathing came in ragged gasps and all she could do was stagger upwards with her sword held in front of her. More of the hellish infernals were now landing directly upon the crowd on the stairs; some fought back from necessity, but they were mainly merchants or families and were cut down fast.

Exhausted beyond comprehension, Zahra rested against a wall with her sword held low, its point on the ground as she rested weary arms. Passage below and above were both blocked by the press of bodies. The noise was horrendous, filled with screams of pain, and the howling of the infernals adding to the madness as the bodies piled up. A woman jumped from the stairs above to land near Zahra; she was covered in gore, but the eyes that turned upon Zahra were dilated with pleasure. Her smile one of ecstasy; she wasn't injured she was one of them. Zahra snapped up a kick into her stomach sending the creature back against the crowd, a thrust from her blade impaled the creature, and it fell to the ground where it began to be slowly crushed. Zahra managed to climb another set of stairs as a gap in the crowd appeared, then she forced herself to the side again.

From above her she thought she heard her name called and looked around, noticing that she had almost made it as far as the Death Jester's temple. Klaus stood at the temple door beckoning her onwards. He looked a fearsome figure in blood-spotted bone armour with an axe in one arm and a pile of corpses around him.

Zahra ducked and weaved through the throng of screaming people descending the stairs who now realized their escape was cut off and were trying to turn to make their way upwards like Zahra was. Then she was pulled from the carnage by Klaus who held her close while hacking about him with the axe as he slowly retreated to the temple door, closing it behind him.

They both stood with their backs to the door, chests heaving as Klaus wiped blood from his eyes with his sleeve.

'It appears, Zahra, that you have the misfortune of my company for some time yet. We can either go up or down to our deaths, or we can go mocking the gods with our joy and baring our asses in the face of destruction. Come, Zahra, we need to prepare the defences for when the infernals come.'

Chapter 14

The sounds of raucous singing woke Ishmael long before the squeal of the gate opened as Diego and Fausto returned from their day trip. Fausto assisted Diego through the gate, half dragging him across the courtyard. There was no hound following behind them, which confused Ishmael. Fausto steered Diego past Ishmael, who pulled his legs in close to get out of the way of the staggering pair.

'Stop 'ere a moment, Fausto. Hey, Yucca, why so worried? I'm not going to beat you.' Diego's words were barely understandable through his thick slurring, his heavy eyelids were almost closed as he puffed from the thin pipe tucked in the corner of his mouth.

Raising a small bottle to his lips, Diego drank deeply then smacked his lips together before regarding Ishmael quizzically with a tilt of his head. 'I bet Yucca wants a drink; what do you think, Fausto?'

The boy looked weary as he stood there bearing his father's weight with a grimace on his face. Blood soaked the boy's shirt around the side, and Ishmael remembered that he had been whipped the day before.

'I don't think Yucca deserves to drink with you, father. After all, he did insult you by questioning your honour.'

With a belch Diego attempted to stand straighter.

'Yes, son, you're right, he gets what he deserves: nothing.'

Diego attempted to intimidate Ishmael with a stern glare, but in the process he and Fausto nearly toppled over. Fortunately Ishmael was able to keep a straight face. To anger Diego in this state could bring terrible consequences.

'Come, Fausto. Take me inside, I have tired of this wretch. Rest up, Yucca, for tomorrow you work!'

As they passed Fausto managed to kick sand in Ishmael's face.

'That's for Chill. Mother had us kill him because of you.'

Great, thought Ishmael, now another thing that's been blamed on me. He knew Fausto loved Chill, so if what he had said was true and they had killed the beast, then it just gave Fausto one more reason to despise Ishmael.

Ishmael noticed the gate was still wide open. From where he sat he could see out to the street that led into the town proper. Being that close to freedom was difficult, but with nothing else to do Ishmael again tested his restraints. The iron ring that his chain was padlocked to was deeply imbedded into the stone wall of the house. There was no give when he tried to turn it or force it from side to side. For any chance of escape he would need a sharp tool that he could gradually chip away with, but even then the location of the pin mid-way up the wall meant that any success would soon be found by Diego or his family. He just needed patience, which was in short supply. A chance would come, he was sure of it. Anyway, he mused as he tested his restraints again. With Diego being one of the monitors Ishmael knew that if he escaped he would never be safe while on the Seekers Road. From conversations he had overheard it seemed Diego was a major player in this group called the Vorm with a lot of resources at his command.

Maybe it was the thoughts of escape or the soft wind that carried through the gate brushing him with its playful touch that found him drifting off, but not to sleep. Ishmael found himself in the strange amber realm of the astral.

He was standing on a dark plain that emitted a faint glow from beneath him. The diffusing light gave the land a translucent tinge. The plain stretched out in all directions, and the sun was low, near the horizon where it appeared to melt into the plains.

How had he come here? Usually he needed to be severely fatigued or having completed the series of exercises that would allow him to travel here. Neither of these had happened. When Ishmael felt a familiar presence he realized he had been summoned.

Far off in the distance Ishmael could make out a shadowy city that swirled away into nothing before coalescing once again. Seemingly from that city a single figure walked towards him. Even from a distance he knew it was Selene. She was struggling mightily against a sandstorm where chunks of amber rained down around her huddled form; their focus seemed to be coming from him. When Ishmael realized that, he focused inwardly, visualizing the storm abating, the wind flowing away.

Free from the wind now, Selene strode towards him, jumping forwards in bursts over the long distance. Then Ishmael stood face to face with Selene whose eyes were ablaze with hollow light.

'You came?' she said, and her words seemed to float into his mind.

'You somehow summoned me, Selene. One moment I was dozing off then I found myself here.'

'I called you because you have been closed to us. My sentinel was to come, but his anger was too great, so I came. You know you can trust me.

'Ishmael, for the first time in the history of the coterie we need to band together for our safety as well as the future of this world. We are like a coven of mages with flourishing abilities that need to be shared and learnt together in order to be able to protect ourselves from the enemy. If we are to do the Mother's bidding then it must be as one, not separated where we are easy pickings for those who hunt us. This is no time for our own agendas, Ishmael. Things are getting real serious now.'

'It's not like that Selene. I need to get away from those I care for,' Ishmael said. 'Death is all around me, and before I can meet the rest of you there is something that must be done. My spirit demands it. It is naught to do with anyone but myself, and until I find what I seek then there can be no reunion for us. Something is wrong. I am drawn away from the rest of you for the moment, but believe me, I will meet you at the safe house. This is merely a path of solitude to the same destination.'

'We need to know where you are, Ishmael,' Selene argued. 'Both Jona and I have tried to get through your walls to find you, but you have shut us out. What are we meant to think? First Raul blocks the three of us out and is still an unknown variable, then you disappear after showing us what's happening in Acclaro. Selene's form took on a more solid, threatening form as she spoke, a direct reflection of the anger she was expressing, then she faded away.

The next morning came too quickly. Ishmael awoke to something snuffling around his legs. In that half world between sleep and awakening he thought it was that old grizzled dog of Fausto's until he remembered it had been killed. He scuttled up out of his pallet in alarm to see something small with silver fur darting away out of the gate. There was a flash of bright eyes in the darkness as it glanced back at him, then it was gone. A stray hound, supposed Ishmael as he settled back down. He was wide awake now, shaking from the pre-dawn cold, so he took the time to stretch his body thoroughly. With Diego's threat to work him hard today fresh in his mind, Ishmael intended to meet the challenge head on without backing down. He had done nothing wrong besides misunderstanding another's customs, and he once again silently vowed to never allow Diego to break him. The dawn brought the ravens along with the sounds of the awakening town but still no sign of Diego or Fausto come to take him to work. He found himself looking forward to escaping from the small courtyard. The work would help make him stronger as well as giving him a chance to escape Diego.

It was mid-morning by the time a dishevelled Diego stumbled out of the house followed by a torrent of abuse from Fajira.

'Diego, the day is half over, and you have important meetings today. If you think the Vorm won't replace you because you're family you are sadly mistaken, and I won't suffer due to your moronic, drunken laziness.'

Diego just stood there adjusting to the light then stumbled to the garden to urinate. When he finished relieving himself he unlocked the chain from the wall, keeping Ishmael's leg irons on as the only restraints.

'Yucca, maybe you are thinking this is the chance to escape, but I'm telling you just this once it is pointless even if I am still drunk like this. You see, Yucca, everybody here now knows about the rude monk from Illume that is in my debt and under my tutelage.'

'Is this what it is then, an apprenticeship?'

Diego looked as if he would be sick then but just belched loudly then leant against the wall.

'In a sense, yes. It is until you have a total understanding of how you wronged me, that you will once again be a free man.'

'What of my possessions? There were important and valuable items that I carried on my person, when do I get them back?'

'That is a matter for another day, Yucca. This is about honour not thievery.'

Diego chained Ishmael to a cart out the front of his home then he climbed up beside him, whistled, and the huge beetle began to plod along. Diego elbowed Ishmael in the ribs, and he looked up to see Diego stood holding out a chunk of bread. 'Eat, you will need your strength.'

Expecting a trick, Ishmael was hesitant, but at Diego's insistent gesturing he took the bread and enjoyed every last stale piece as he chewed it slowly.

Several times as they slowly walked down into the town Diego stopped to vomit onto the rocky ground.

'We could stop for a while if you like,' said Ishmael, trying to be helpful.

Diego wiped his mouth with the back of a hand, his eyes crinkling as he looked at Ishmael. 'Yucca, you can never try to tell me what to do. If you do so in public or defy me, then any witnesses will demand the satisfaction of seeing me beat you. If I failed to do that then I would be laughing stock of the whole town. Now stay quiet, I don't want to hear you until we get to the warehouse.'

They trundled down into the main street of the little town where a line of carts were being unloaded before a great warehouse made of timber and stone. There were a number of tradesmen plying their skills, including a smithy and a carpenter who laboured beneath the hot sun stripped to the waist. A crowd of labourers struggled to remove heavy boxes from the carts to stack them within the warehouse.

'Monitor, stand still, I have been looking for you everywhere.' A hunched man limped up to them. He walked with a lopsided twist every time he stepped forward. From the look of it his hips were misaligned as well as his shoulders: the left sat higher than the right. Greasy hair was tied back into a single ponytail, baring his face, which was heavy with stubble. His wide, crooked nose obviously had been broken many times, and as he talked to the monitor he avoided meeting Diego's eyes as if he were afraid of making contact.

'Monitor, the goods from the camp in the hills are here earlier than expected, just like you said they would be. They sent all the fine cloth and, grain along with a small fortune of liquor. In return they request armour along with the mining tools the smithies are making. Rumour has it that a great vein of the fever stone has been found, which could make the hills men very wealthy.'

Diego packed his pipe with a mixture of sweet herbs. 'Ramiro, it seems that our neighbours' luck is changing, which is a good thing since it will bring also fortune to us. In ten days' time we shall send all we have back to the hills along with a trusted negotiator. I need you to find a good man who can be trusted to also find out what else is happening there. I think for us to trust them would be a grave mistake. At present we are also useful to them, but if this vein of fever stone exists they may well decide we are surplus to their needs.'

Diego pushed Ishmael forward between the two men. 'This here is Yucca, whom you have heard about. He is to work in the warehouse like everybody else until I am satisfied his debt has been repaid. Be sure to work him until he drops or it is you who will take his place on the morrow.'

The foreman turned to regard Ishmael in his sweat-stained clothes with his hair and new beard matted with dust. He waddled over to Ishmael with his thumbs tucked into the front of his trousers.

'Doesn't look like much of a man, does he? The next thing I know is that you will be giving me women or children to complete my tasks for you. What happened to his arm?'

Diego grinned then clapped the foreman on the shoulder. 'Tried to take Chill's food.' Then he walked off down the street.

'My name is Ramiro but you call me foreman or boss. That talk I just had with the monitor that you were intently listening to means that you are mine, you do everything when I tell you to that means eating, shitting even talking. This job is simple; you move stock from these carts that come along all day into the warehouse. When they stop coming you get to stop too. If I have to ask you to do something more than once or if you don't pull your weight you get this.' He indicated a length of timber that hung from his belt.

'Any questions, Yucca?'

Ishmael just stood there looking at his feet. He wasn't prepared to say anything because that would give the foreman the chance to inflict pain on him, so he stood silently.

Ramiro stepped right up to Ishmael from the side, then he slammed a fist into Ishmael's stomach, which dropped him to the ground with a gasp. As he lay there, Ramiro knelt beside him. 'You are here to work, Yucca, not stand about all day.' Then he patted Ishmael on the head like a dog before walking off.

Ishmael climbed to his feet. Now he had two people to concentrate on repaying for his mistreatment. He had known Ramiro less than a chime and already he hated the man.

Throughout the long morning and well into the afternoon the carts laden with crates of food stuffs, medical, and military supplies kept rolling in. There seemed to be no respite for the labourers. The other workers knew better than to talk with Ishmael, for Ramiro was never far away. There were twenty two labourers, all without an ounce of fat on any of them, but they all had that wiry strength that comes with hard manual labour.

When a meal break finally came they were all too tired to waste energy with conversation, and most ignored the food, instead choosing to cover their faces with the wide-brimmed hats they wore as protection from the sun as they lay in the shade resting. As hungry as he felt, Ishmael refused to eat the gritty gruel paste that was served with stale bread that the cook put before him. He spent the time observing his surroundings. The warehouse was little more than huge timber poles among stone walls with a roof of clay tiles. Within the warehouse there were wooden partitions to store the various stock such as beautifully coloured cloths, herbs, and fancy condiments that Ishmael had never seen as well as bags of grain, medical, and military supplies.

In one corner of the warehouse there was an office area where the foreman would sit looking out at the workers to make sure they did his bidding. In Ishmael's first few days Ramiro was constantly on his back pushing him harder or letting everyone break for food except him. On the third day the monitor disappeared inside the office with the foreman, and Ishmael had his first chance to talk to the workers beside him.

'Hey, I am Ishmael,' he said pointing to his chest. The other workers all looked at him then away again but for one who was maybe Ishmael's age who smiled shyly but said nothing.

'Just answer me this, friend, are you all here too for insulting the honour of the monitor?'

The shy one looked over at the office, but there was no sign of either the foreman or the monitor.

'Not the monitor. Mostly for insulting or going against the Vorm.'

'Who are the Vorm?' asked Ishmael.

'They are the family that run the Godhead, and they guide the pilgrims along the road as they petition the gods. Diego is married to the daughter of the Vorm lord.'

Later that day as Ishmael helped unload crates with the other workers he once again tried to make conversation.

'Diego has made me his slave until his honour is regained, do you also have to regain your honour from working like a slave?'

'We are paid as are you, Ishmael. Even though you have slighted Diego's honour the strange system they live by in Brimmerland demands he pay you; that money will be held by Diego until such a time as your debt is repaid.'

'Diego or Ramiro never mentioned it to me.'

An older man sneered at Ishmael then. 'That is because they take you for a fool. The monitor and foreman take your pay and divide it between them while working you harder and harder until maybe you die. Then they get some other unfortunate soul and repeat the manoeuvre.'

Another man hissed through his teeth at the three of them.

'Ramiro is coming.'

Ishmael doubled his efforts as he moved crates of tools into the warehouse. He felt disgusted at learning how the two men who controlled his fate manipulated the labourers for their own purpose, but what could be done about it?

Chapter 15

Zahra helped Klaus blockade the passage with an upturned table, and any other furniture they could move, then they lathered the corridor to the front door with oil, and prepared a rack of spears within easy reach. She kept expecting the sound of the door busting open to be heard, but no attackers came, yet.

Zahra took watch duty as Klaus searched his stores for anything that would aid them. He returned to her side as she intently watched the corridor where she thought she had sensed some movement.

'Don't light the oil until we are sure that many are within the corridor.' He pushed something soft into her hand, covering it with her fingers.

'Take this, Zahra, it will bring the battle lust upon you. If we are to meet our deaths this night, let's give these Infernals something to remember. Just place it beneath your tongue to dissolve while we wait.'

'Is there any other way of escape from the temple, Klaus?'

'None,' he said, slurping heavily from a clay mug. 'Here, drink some wine, it will help you put up with the awful taste.'

Zahra placed the ball of paste under her tongue. Klaus was right about the taste, but it didn't bother her too much since she had used this drug before. The two of them sat behind the barricade, waiting, while outside the sounds of killing continued. As the drug began working it made her sight and hearing keener so she felt as her body vibrated with a sense of urgency making it hard to stay still, she found herself eager to fight.

'I will die here tonight!' said Klaus as he sharpened his axe blade with a smooth stone.

Zahra looked over at Klaus, who stared back at her calmly.

'We will escape here. Death won't touch us, my friend.'

The priest grasped her arm and leant in close.

'I know I will die tonight because I have already seen it. When I was outside the temple fighting I saw his shadow; he stood there watching me and I knew then as I do now. They told me as a priest of the death jester that I would know when it was my turn to fall. I am telling you this not from fear, but because it surprises me. I want to die, Zahra. For so long I have helped others understand death's role in life and now that my time is nearly done I will meet it with a song in my heart.'

In the torchlight Zahra noticed he was silently weeping what appeared to be tears of joy.

'I will be honoured to stand by your side in this last battle, and should I be so lucky to survive then I will tell of your work and deeds here, Klaus.'

They clasped wrists then both turned back to the corridor, waiting. The waiting was always the worst. Zahra knew she had little patience and it felt that waiting for someone to come kill you was foolish, but she also knew that to be outside with the other poor souls that called Wilhelm's Point their home would be suicide right now. This way at least she had a chance and so did Ishmael.

They heard the door to the temple being smashed long before the first shadows of movement spilled across the corridor in the torchlight, Zahra was grateful the waiting was over. She pulled the mask up over her face, allowing the shadow within her to rise. A long-legged creature of bone and scarlet flesh silently rounded the corner staying close to the wall. When it saw the barricade it lurched forward, keening loudly in a feminine voice.

Klaus launched a spear at the infernal, which struck the wall beside it before skittering away. Zahra's spear didn't miss but impaled the creature through the torso as the corridor behind it came alive with bodies screeching, clawing, and biting to get to them in an obscene wall of flesh.

She threw the torch which ignited the oil, turning the corridor into an inferno. Some of the burning infernals reached the barricade but Zahra cut them down easily before they could set the barricade on fire. Then it was silent again with now the smoke and stench of burnt bodies to fight against.

The next attackers were more careful than their predecessors, and two stout creatures came forward with long shields that they hooked together to form a small wall. Klaus launched another javelin, which struck one of the shields as the two infernals crept forwards, using the shields to protect those coming behind. When they made it halfway down the corridor, the shield bearers charged. One of them dipped his shield too low, and Klaus skewered the creature with another javelin while Zahra stood and drew her blade as the second infernal tossed the shield onto the barricade then tried to leap over the table only to slip and leave Zahra an easy kill. The next wave of attackers crashed into the heavy table, knocking it backwards.

Zahra and Klaus barely managed to avoid being knocked from their feet as the battle engulfed them. Klaus fought beside Zahra like a man possessed. He hacked with his axe, chortling deeply in his chest as if this were the funniest thing he had seen.

Zahra moved about him, slashing and stabbing at foes that Klaus knocked from her path. She fought her way to the side of Klaus, caught up fully now in the euphoria of battle, exhaustion washed away with the drug and banishing anything but the need to fight, to kill those who would seek to harm her. The thought that there was no room for pity here in the house of death came to her, making her laugh, and that received an answering hacking bark from Klaus. They braced themselves side by side together in the face of the Infernals that were tearing each other apart to get to the two of them.

Sometime later, which in reality may have been naught but a few moments but seemed like chimes, the rush of enemies stopped. The lust for battle seemed to loosen its grip on them, and Klaus pulled a clump of the paste from a pouch breaking it in two. Popping half inside his mouth and chewing furiously, he offered the other half to Zahra who took it but placed it into a pocket when Klaus wasn't looking. The drug would seriously take its toll on her when it wore off, and she had decided to take no more unless forced to. Klaus had decided he would die this day and this was his final battle, but she knew she would need all her energy to leave here if she lived. There was a gracefulness that defied the raw horror of the situation, and she sensed something like a gathering of power within the rush of the drug that drove her on. Klaus turned to her with a feverish grin then motioned her forward ignoring her hand that she placed on his shoulder to warn of exactly this danger.

'C'mon we have them now, let's drive these abominations back to the holes they crept from.'

This left Zahra with no choice but to follow him as the next surge of energy poured into her, sending her scamping after him with the a grin at the prospect of more battle. They made it around the corner and half-way along the corridor to the temple entrance when a figure stepped into the frame of the door, blocking their way.

It was a hound of sorts, all red and grey sinew with sickly, green eyes balefully glaring upon them. Its lips peeled back in a hiss, showing jagged discoloured canines, and it arched its back and crouched on strong back haunches ready to spring at them. Klaus roared and shot forward swinging his axe about him as he ran at it. Somehow at the last moment the beast ducked away from the blade as it chopped down but the move was part of the feint and Klaus turned with the creature's movement, redirecting the axe to crash into its side; its ribcage splintering as the axe buried itself in its abdomen.

Klaus was now off balance and fell awkwardly near the entrance. The eerie cries of pain in the hound's death throes were deafening, and it's flailing kept Zahra back out of range of the sharp claws and snapping jaws. When the creature slumped into silence, Zahra moved forward to help Klaus up to his feet, but he waved her hand away so she pulled his battle-axe free then passed it back to him with a grin.

'Hope you don't think you're done yet priest, there are more notches for your blade yet to be cut. Klaus looked at the blade she had returned to him then up at her.

'This weapon has served its purpose now I need my hammer. Klaus marched back to his temple room and pulled a long hammer from the brackets that held it to the wall.

'He's here now, I can feel him,' he whispered to Zahra.

'Feel who?'

'Death Jester. I told you before, this is my last battle. Zahra.'

The calmness Klaus showed even after taking so much of the paste had a telling effect on Zahra and she felt the hairs rise on her arms and neck as Klaus turned then stepped out of the temple onto the path of prayers. Zahra followed him out to where he stood on the landing outside his temple where the staircase that was covered with broken bodies of the dead and dying. In the afternoon light swarms of flies had converged for the feast as she and Klaus stood there with the wind mussing their clothes. Klaus stood looking across the stairs. Zahra couldn't see any danger there, but the intenseness of his gaze kept her looking anyway.

Klaus laughed to himself then clapped Zahra on the back heartily.

'He is coming now, my death is upon me. Be my witness, Zahra.'

Across the stairs a figure emerged from the burnt remnants of a shop front. It was dressed in black armour fitted with wicked spikes. Strange fleshy tubes connected from a bulbous lump on the warrior's back to his helmet of twisted metal where a set of burning orbs watched them. The creature's deep laugh carried to them.

'I have been searching this damn excuse of a town for a challenge, and so far all have been found wanting. You however seem different, priest, could it be that I have finally found a worthy adversary?'

'If you're going to stand there all day boring me with your coward's words then I fear you will never find out,' taunted Klaus.

Zahra scanned the area for more enemies, but this dark warrior was the only one around. She noticed a large, feathered corpse crashed through a shop window. A body slumped from a heavy saddle on its back. Soarnestian raven warriors. Whitman's Point had been helped by allies after all, but where were they now?

The hulking Infernal met Klaus on the nearest platform, it hefted a chained flail rusty and coated in blood while in its other hand rested a long shield that was almost split in two but still held together.

Zahra squatted on her heels intent on the duel before her. She had been asked by a valiant warrior priest to bear witness to his death duel, and for his honour she would.

Klaus whooped as he sent the hammer spinning around his head twice, then moving with the momentum, he turned tightly, bringing the heavy weapon down in an overhead strike.

The dark warrior stepped in towards Klaus, its shield in catching the blow easily which he then thrust against the chest of Klaus, pushing him back. The dark warrior's shield was now completely split, and it threw the remnants of it at Klaus who ducked at the last moment and it clattered away.

The warrior came swiftly at Klaus with a series of furious strikes, making Klaus parry twice before he tripped on a step, throwing an arm out for balance as he fell. He rolled away from the kick that the warrior followed up with, but his hammer was met with another downward blow of the warrior's flail, sending it flying from his grasp as it smashed the fingers of his hand.

They circled one another now, Klaus clutching his injured hand and now armed only with a slender dagger in his other hand that he had pulled from his belt. The warrior attacked silently. It forced Klaus backwards again towards the stairs, and as Klaus snaked in with the dagger, trying desperately to duck under those lethal chains. The warrior bull-rushed Klaus, smashing into his shoulder.

Somehow Klaus managed to stay on his feet. He caught the flail arm of his opponent above his head, stopping the killing blow as the long chains of the flail still smashed into his forehead. The flail crashed into the helmet he was wearing, knocking it from his head. Klaus pushed the arm to the side then rammed the dagger at the neck joint of the foul black armour. He must have caught something important for as his dagger sunk between the breastplates and helmet the warriors knees buckled. Klaus jammed the blade deeper then tore up on the visor trying to rip off the warrior's helmet. The warrior desperately hugged Klaus, pulling him in close where his armoured spikes punctured through the bone armour and into the priest.

Klaus roared then tore away the helmet from the creature's face. Blood and clear liquid spurted from the neck of the armour as a wrinkled, slimy head was revealed. Its mouth opened and closed as if it were trying to breathe, and with a final effort the black warrior crushed Klaus to him snapping up to a standing position as he did. There came a sharp crack, and Klaus screamed then the two of them collapsed to the ground. The dagger was still deep within the warrior's neck and it lay there gasping as the orange eyes faded and it was still.

Among the silence once more the wind seemed to come from nowhere sweeping across the devastation that had been Whitman's Point. A vortex of debris raced around the stair platform, then with a sigh of the wind it collapsed. Zahra remembered the words of Haakon from long ago:

'Within us rests the knowledge of our final battle, and whether we realize it or not we can shape that encounter and truly make it an act of power that the whole world witnesses. The final fight of a warrior is truly a spectacle to behold. Stay true to the path and let your power build, then that knowledge will rise deep within you allowing you an insight that few beings are ever given.'

Zahra made sure the warrior was dead before she tried to move Klaus. She noticed liquid still flowed from the tubes that had been torn free from the helmet. The strange warrior appeared to need lubrication, and its skin was slimy at close inspection. Zahra managed to pry Klaus out of the warrior's death grip. His back had been broken while three of the spikes on the armour had punctured through his chest and abdomen. It was tiring after the ordeal of the last two days, but she managed to drag Klaus back into the temple of the Death Jester.

Since darkness was falling, Zahra knew she must stay out of the night, there would be too many dangers. She locked and barricaded the temple door as best as possible then dragged Klaus onto the altar so she could cut away his clothing and wash the signs of death from him. Zahra left him there afterwards dressed in the finest clothes she could find from his cupboards. Zahra then refreshed herself with fruit and warm water then locked herself in the private chamber of Klaus to sleep away the fog of exhaustion.

When she awoke the candles had burned low. Zahra rushed around gathering useful healing supplies as well as food and clean water. When she left the temple she paid a final visit to Klaus who for all appearances looked like he was sleeping. With the temple key Zahra locked the innermost temple door. One lock had been busted off, but a second larger one was unused. The key she would pass back to Haakon so the sacred items could be retrieved at a later date. Finally she made sure the list of contacts Klaus had given her was safely packed away. The still pre-dawn night was quiet now with only the twisted corpse's evidence of the suffering that had occurred here. From up towards the general's house Zahra heard some muffled coughing and detected what might be the soft glow of a fire. It was time to be gone from here.

~

Chapter 16

The excruciating pain after each day of back breaking work that was less an ordeal for Ishmael now his strength was returning, Ishmael was lonely. The nights were the worst when he was left alone without food which he could deal with, but to sit hungry and listen to Diego and his family eat was the purest agony. He realized now, as a prisoner, that one of the most basic pleasures was the sharing of a simple meal with another. Ishmael even wished for the return of Chill just to know the comfort of another being close by during the dead of night.

The boy, Fausto brought him food like he was meant to, but would sit and glare at Ishmael until he grew bored, then he would toss Ishmael's meal over the fence for the scavengers. He often heard Fajira within the house, but Ishmael rarely saw her now since he left before first light to work and only returned again after dark.

As it had many times before, Ishmael's knowledge of meditation served him well. His body suffered however, he still had the power to steel his mind and plan for that chance to escape when it came.

Ramiro gave Ishmael a new job the next day. He seemed unhappy that Ishmael had been able to keep up his work rate without complaining or falling behind.

Ramiro pointed out a large pile of rocks to the side of the warehouse away from its shelter in the raw sun. 'Yucca, those rocks must be moved over by the warehouse wall to there to make way for the new extensions.' The place Ramiro indicated was about thirty feet away.

'Get to it now.'

The shy man Chilo moved to go with Ishmael, but Ramiro smacked him across the legs with his stick. 'Not you, idiot, now get to it, Yucca. You can work through lunch today for not pulling your weight this morning. You truly are a worthless piece of dung.'

Once Ishmael had moved the rocks that he was able to carry, he needed to dig out the larger ones, which was nearly impossible in his weakened condition. He called over the foreman who swaggered over to him while drinking from a water skin. Ishmael longed for some of that water. He was dehydrated and starving and his muscles had started to shake from the exertion.

'Ramiro, I can't move these rocks without one of the pick axes, they are too heavy for me, and I need food and water.'

In answer Ramiro spat on the ground then took another long drink before pouring the remaining water over his head.

'Aaaah, nothing better than cool water, eh, Yucca? If you can't do the work required of you then what good are you to the monitor or me? When hounds or beasts of burden are no longer useful we kill them and replace them. Let me think about this a moment.'

Ramiro squatted beside where Ishmael sat on a rock stripped to the waist. 'Is that what you are saying Yucca, that you are no longer useful and have become a liability to us?' Ishmael looked the Ramiro in the eyes holding his gaze.

'What I am saying is that if you continue to try killing me even while knowing that out of all these men I am the most productive, then you are only cheating yourself and the monitor. How can I make money for you if you refuse to keep me strong, or do you wish to kill me?'

'You have a debt to repay, and this is how Diego chooses you to do it. It has nothing to do with me, so don't make it personal, Yucca,

I am just doing my job,' replied Ramiro.

Ishmael chuckled; his blood was boiling and he had to unclench his fists. Now was not the time to settle this dispute.

'I apologize for my outburst, foreman, I just desire to repay my debt in the best way. For that I need to be strong.'

The foreman looked warily at Ishmael's change of tone then rose to his feet, stalking away. 'Get the pick axe and some water, Yucca, then back to work.'

Ishmael smiled in satisfaction. It was only a minor victory, but he had appealed to the man's greed and won. When the others stopped for the noon day meal, Ishmael stayed where he was, slowly digging out a sizeable boulder from the rocky soil. Rather than focus on his painfully empty stomach, he kept at the labour; the repetitive striking of his pickaxe against the boulders had become similar to the moving meditations that he had practiced in the monastery.

Two chimes into the afternoon Ishmael heard a cry from behind him. One of the workers was on the ground curled into a ball holding his abdomen. Ramiro ran over with his cane, which he used to start giving the old man a series of whips across his legs. Even with the help of the other workers the man couldn't go on. He began vomiting, so the other workers carried him to the shade of the warehouse.

As the afternoon wore on, more of the workers began to collapse into fits of vomiting. Ramiro ran to and fro, trying to make them return to work, but to Ishmael it became evident that Ramiro too was starting to fall ill. Soon the foreman sat slumped against the wall of the warehouse, glazed in perspiration and breathing heavily. Without being asked to help, Ishmael made sure all those affected were out of the sun, then he served them cool water. In talking with them he found out they had all eaten the meal of gruel this time mixed with chicken. He found the cook at the back of the warehouse near the office. The man was in quite a state.

'They will kill me for this, Yucca. I swear I never knew the meat was bad.'

'It's going to be fine. I am sure they will understand it's just the inferior food they supply us here,' said Ishmael.

'You don't understand, Yucca. I must go; they only kept me here because I am the only one that can cook.' With that the man ran off without looking back.

Ishmael walked over to the cooking station. The fire pit was down to the embers beside a large slab of timber made for the table and chopping block where the remains of chicken still sat amongst other food scraps and cooking utensils. The table was crawling with flies and ants. The area stunk of rotten food, and the utensils were thick with dried food that had not been cleaned off for a long time. Ishmael did not consider himself an accomplished cook, but he had been taught the basics of cooking during the rostered kitchen duties within the monastery. It was easy for him to recognize that the cook had managed to poison them all due to cross- contamination in the preparation area. The gruel still stood in a large pot alongside the fire pit, and Ishmael used a knife to pull out a large piece of the chicken that he cut to check if the meat had been cooked thoroughly. It wasn't.

Diego was to return at the end of the day's work, but that was still three chimes away. Until then Ishmael used the time to have a break from the pickaxe and tend to the sick workers. He made sure he kept good care of the foreman especially, reassuring him it would be fine and that he had found where the problem lay. He busied himself when he wasn't tending the others by first of all cleaning the thick food that was stuck to the pots and utensils. Then he scrubbed the cooking table and threw out any contaminated food he found.

When Diego returned late that day he was surprised to find Ishmael tending to the workers, whose symptoms had worsened. Ramiro was delirious by now with fever.

'Yucca, what is going on?'

'Food poisoning, monitor. The cook had very little use for hygiene, and because of this everyone is now sick.'

Diego's eyes narrowed. 'If that is so then why are you not sick?'

'The foreman refused to let me eat, as he does most days. I was one of the few besides the cook who did not fall ill.'

'Where is the cook now? I will flay the skin from his shoulders for this.'

'He ran away, fearing for his life.'

'Get the men into the wagons there while I get some of the rouge beetles ready. We will have to drop them off to the quarters on the way home.' Diego was in no mood to converse since he was now expecting at least a few days before the workers would be well enough to work again. Now he would have to hire free men to help, which was going to cost a lot more than he was accustomed to paying.

By the time they made it back to Diego's home, Ishmael was stumbling with fatigue. Fajira met them in the courtyard. 'Good evening husband,' she said as well as nodding her head to Ishmael.

'Fausto is setting the table. It is good you are back so we can eat as a family.'

Diego motioned Ishmael over to the wall then refastened the metal collar to the wall.

'Not now, woman, I need to organize workers for tomorrow since now they are all sick with poisoning from the food.'

'Can't you just come eat, Diego? I'm sure this business can wait for a chime or two.'

Diego seemed to think on it a moment then pushed past her to the gate.

'No, this cannot wait!' The gate was closed, then it was just Ishmael and Fajira standing there in an awkward silence.

'Well, my husband won't eat with his wife and son, so you will, Ishmael.' Fajira moved to unlock the metal clasp with a key she had tucked on a thong around her neck. With a click it sprang open, leaving him free again. If he had such a mind he could have fled then, but Ishmael still had no idea where the two crystal pieces were and without them fleeing was not an option.

Fajira took his arm to pull him into the house, the anger evident on her face, and she looked about to burst into tears. He gently resisted her, pulling free of her grip then stepping away. 'Fajira, I cannot enter your home without Diego's blessing. It is not my place.'

'He is your master and I his wife, I can make things very hard if you displease me. Now come so we can eat.'

Ishmael picked up the chain then fastened it around his neck again. 'As much as I would like to have a meal in the comfort of your home, Fajira, I will not anger Diego further even with your threats. It would be wrong of me to do so.'

'Don't you want to get back at him?' said Fajira as she moved to Ishmael, pulling him close and stroking a finger down his shoulder.

'Yes, I do, but not like this.'

'You call yourself a man? You are nothing but a cowardly dog who won't even run when his chain is removed.' Fajira spat at the ground near Ishmael then rushed off into the house with her hand covering her mouth.

Ishmael sat with a sigh, if he wasn't so tired he would have cared more about what had happened, but weariness overcame him and he slept. He awoke to the light of the morning, not the pre-dawn, and realized he had slept through. His body was stiff from the digging the previous day, and it was good he had been allowed the extra rest. Where was Diego?

Fausto came out later with food for Ishmael, who expected the boy to toss it over the fence. Instead he was surprised when Fausto handed him a covered loaf of bread with a bowl of meat soaked in gravy. He took the food, trying to eat slowly and savouring it as Fausto watched.

'Yucca, I heard what happened last night between you and my mother,'

Ishmael stopped chewing and looked up to the boy. 'I just wanted to say thank you for not doing what my mother asked. She wasn't herself last night. Also you have no work today, but father said you will go with him tomorrow.' Then Fausto left without another word.

Later that day Fajira bought out a two buckets of water, one hot and one cold for him to bathe in. She also bought towels for him to dry off with. Before she could leave this time, he spoke. 'Fajira, I just wanted to apologize to you for my behaviour last night…'

'You have nothing to apologize for, Ishmael, it is I who should be asking for forgiveness. More and more Diego is away from home. He comes to me with only food or sleep in mind, not his duty as a husband. I am starting to think he has another woman he favours, but that is no issue of yours and I was wrong to drag you into our dispute. I will go now so you can bathe in peace.'

'It's all right if you want to talk a while,' said Ishmael, getting to his feet. 'I am sure it's really nothing, Fajira. You are a beautiful woman who makes her husband proud. His job of controlling Glimmersedge and the road can't be easy. If he fails those responsibilities you will lose everything, and I know that he is afraid of disappointing your father, Lord Vorm.'

'How do you know of my family?'

'Workers talk, Fajira, and the stress Diego is under is no secret.'

'Even when Diego is here he is distant. He is away so often now,' said Fajira, gathering her skirts and squatting beside Ishmael. 'I am expected to sit and wait on his every whim, and yet he is able to do as he pleases. His love for me has cooled, but I would rather be dead that live this life of lies and guesses. My son needs his father. I need him too, dammit!'

'Maybe you could talk to him about it.'

Fajira wiped tears from her eyes. 'You of all people know Diego now, Ishmael, how his temper is a sudden storm. He won't listen to me. I have become like a plaything that he has grown tired of.'

Fajira grasped his shoulder, the intense need in her eyes pierced him keeping him still. 'Do something for me Ishmael.

Find out if he has someone else. Not knowing is killing me.'

Ishmael stood there staring back at Fajira, lost for words as she turned and left him alone. As he bathed he thought of just recently how she had stood up against Diego for him, nursed him to health when he lay dying from infection and tried her best to make his situation better than it was.

Chapter 17

Haakon rubbed his scalp irritably. The camp around him was a scene of chaos as the clan went about their new orders, laughing and singing amongst the work. As he watched he mused that even the most loyal soldier they had was sick of this ruined castle and forest. It was supposed to have been a temporary answer to their problem but had managed to become permanent. Over the time in which Latasha had lain comatose Haakon had arranged for a palanquin to be made that would carry Latasha now that she couldn't walk. He had never actually seen the palanquin once it was finished, and now he watched in wonder as it was carried out towards him.

It was made from oak and engraved with a detailed woodland scene that must have taken quite some time to craft. Latasha had been carved into the scene, and her hair wound down to form a silver lake made with real silver. The men carrying the palanquin stopped so Haakon could view it. He ran fingers over the well-crafted timber, and looked inside to see a comfortable complete with cushions and the other necessary items that would make Latasha's journey easier.

'This is much better than I expected you to make, Heath.'

'Haakon, carpentry was my old life, and I had to find something to do with all my spare time. Latasha is not just special to you. She is not despised by all of us like you might expect. We wanted to do something for her, and this is the end result. Do you think she will like it?'

'I know she will love it, Heath, and I insist you help me personally make her comfortable within it for the journey.'

When the cular mounts were fully packed with supplies and the warriors and Faustus were ready to leave, Haakon went to get Latasha. He carried her thin form out into the chill morning air, watching her inhale the fresh air greedily. Haakon had blindfolded her, insisting it was necessary. When he took the blindfold off to reveal the palanquin, Latasha sat still in his arms then began to weep.

Heath knelt before Haakon, looking distraught.

'My lady, I am sorry if it has offended or angered you, I just thought it fitting for you to travel in style.'

Latasha wiped her eyes slowly then smiled down at Heath.

'No, you haven't upset me, you silly man; I love it. The crafting is sublime, and I speak the truth when I say that even our best carvers would have had trouble creating a better piece of work than this. Thank you so much. My heart sings with the beauty of your gift.'

It was close to midday when they finally set out. Besides Latasha and Haakon, there was Faustus the physician and eight of Haakon's best. Travel, as expected, was slow with the large cular lizards and the palanquin, which four of the warriors carried. Haakon had hoped that they would be able to buy faster mounts once in the grasslands, but that just created the problem that the palanquin would fall too far behind, so he gritted his teeth and accepted that it would take some time. He knew he could take heart that at least they were on the road now. They emerged from the thick canopy of the forest, noticing at once the smoke-filled sky to the south, the direction of Acclaro.

Dalwyn called over Faustus.

'What do you make of that, old friend?'

'It seems we are not the only ones with big problems, so it might be a good choice to steer away from Acclaro altogether. Culchar is to the north, but our best course is to follow the river towards Sainthome, then swing south to the beginning of the Southern Tiriacs just north of Karnock Forest.'

'That was my thinking too. I had hoped to cross the Glyph grasslands closer to the city, but it may be a lot better to start out once we make it to the river. It must be only a chime away or close to that.'

Haakon called a halt so everyone could drink and rest once they made it to the river. Acclaro was submerged in its own smoke, and the road from the capital towards Culchar showed a straggling line of fleeing families. They passed a discarded cart with a broken axle where the grass opposite the cart had been trampled. Haakon drew his sword then indicated for one of his men to follow him along the path left by its maker.

They found a dead man not long after with his head a bloody mess. The trampled path continued, except now it was not so distinct. They managed to find the second body, this time a young boy, his face contorted in horror. There was bruising around his throat and face. Someone had murdered these two.

'Let's get back to the others, we need to change our route it seems.'

They hurried back to the others.

'There were two dead out there, a man and a boy, and they seemed to have been murdered,' Haakon reported. Heath, take one other and scout down towards Acclaro, but don't engage anyone if possible. We will head east until we reach where the river splits, do you know the one?'

'I am familiar with that area, Haakon, we will take one of the lighter cular's; otherwise you will be waiting too long for us to return.'

The two headed off through the grass with the cular mount huffing through its nose with excitement. Once they had gone from sight, Haakon gave the order to continue.

'Tek, you're up front. I don't like the look of that smoke over Acclaro, and I don't want to get caught up in whatever is happening there.'

They continued heading east across the grasslands, moving with more speed now. Just when Haakon started to think they would be able to make good time with the travel Tek motioned for them to halt, and for Haakon to come forward. Haakon crouched then moved to the scout's side.

'What do you see?' he asked.

'More refugees. In a short time this area will be crawling with people based on what I have seen. They are scattered all across the glyph and fleeing Acclaro.'

'Damn it! Go and see what if you can find out why, Tek.'

It wasn't long before Tek returned. 'The capital has fallen to the infernals and the king is dead!'

Haakon reeled at the news. 'Come on, Tek. This means we need to travel with even more haste now and could do with a clear run. Rest and get one of the men to scout along this side of the river.' Haakon shimmied forwards to a worn path. He poked his head out enough to see down it, but all he could make out was a dust cloud, and the sight of hurrying figures as well as laden carts heading towards them.

'As I see it, Haakon, we can pull back and wait but risk the chance of being found by whatever is pursuing these refugees, or we can hasten onwards and try to beat them to where the grasslands meet the Tiriacs.'

Haakon quickly gauged it would take between a day to two of travel if they were to head for the Tiriacs. It was too long.

'Tek, we keep going as fast as we can once we meet the ford, then we head straight for the mountains, and bypass the refugees heading north from Acclaro. Tonight we don't rest. We keep moving until we reach the Tiriacs, and anyone who needs rest can do so in the cart by rotation.'

'What about the scouts you sent off?' Tek asked.

'No time to wait for them, but they are no fools and will find us again.'

Haakon motioned for the others to follow him. He waited for the palanquin to get alongside him then looked in on Latasha. She was sleeping or maybe even travelling the astral so he didn't interfere. A chime and a half later they made the ford. It had appeared their route was out of the way of the fleeing refugees. As organized and since they were directly out of the way of trouble Haakon called them to stop and rest. He placed two guards then sat with the others to eat and drink. The small group jumped up as something was heard rushing through the long grass towards them from the south east. It was Heath and the other scout and. Haakon allowed them a moments respite to drink then pressed them for information.

'Haakon, those fleeing Acclaro are indeed its residents. They say the city has fallen to an army of infernals, who seized it from within. The infernals are systematically hunting down anyone they can find. We could hear the deaths of those who were closer to the city being pursued by the damned creatures.'

'What happened to your arm, Heath? You are wounded?'

'It's only minor, Haakon. Some of those fleeing were so desperate to escape they sought to deprive us of our cular mount, but as you can see we got through that. What do we do now, Haakon?'

We turn south until the Tiriacs, let the refugees head for Culchar and maybe that will be enough of a distraction to keep the infernals off our trail.'

Chapter 18

Haakon kept up a murderous pace now that they were out of direct danger and they had kept moving like this for most of the day now. The small plains encampments they had come across had stood deserted, fleeced of all valuables the small simple homes and storage granaries had been abandoned. It was in one of these camps they stopped to gather a few chimes of rest for the cular lizards.

'Get what rest you can, we will stay two chimes. Those who guard now sleep when we travel again. When it's your turn at guard, stay alert and no fires! The last thing we need is the infernals knowing where we are.'

Haakon was awoken a chime later for his turn at guard duty.

'What, already?' he grumbled.

'It should actually be Faustus's turn,' whispered Tek. 'He was limping when we made camp so we decided to let him rest.'

Earlier, Haakon had noticed the difficulty his old friend was having, but when he approached the physician his worry had been laughed away.

'It's going to take more than a sore leg to stop me Haakon?'

Haakon checked in on Latasha, who lay still within the palanquin as she had most of the day. He longed to reach over and gently awaken her, but if she was in the astral that could cause a number of problems. Even at night Acclaro was a beacon of flames and as he stood there staring at it a shrill cry came from the Palanquin. He raced towards pulling the curtain open where Latasha lay panting, her eyes wild and scared.

'Haakon, we must go, they will set the grasslands on fire. Those poor refugees will be decimated.'

Haakon didn't bother asking Latasha how she knew something like this was going to happen, because he knew she could often see glimpses of future events within the astral.

Within the chime they were moving as fast as they could,' but the palanquin bearers were flailing now after the gruelling days travel. Haakon allowed one of his men to ride a cular and took his place bearing the palanquin along with his personal guard, who knew better than to complain about taking their turn.

As they travelled through the long grass, the smell of smoke became increasingly apparent around them. The sight of the burning city far behind them was a grim reminder of what they faced if caught by the Infernals. As dawn creased the horizon, they had made it to the start of the Tiriacs and the long narrow winding path that took them along a steadily climbing path up along the mountain side parallel to the grasslands. Haakon had hoped to avoid using this dangerously narrow path that may prove to be their undoing while trying to move the palanquin. It was too late, now, though and they all needed rest.

'Let's stop,' he called out to his people. 'Running ourselves into the ground won't achieve anything now we are out of any immediate danger. There is plenty of food in the saddlebags so eat and drink then rest, and remember no fires. Yasmin and Lukai, you take first watch. Tek after you have some rest scout forward for a chime to see what's up ahead for us. I don't want any surprises.'

Tek, weary like the rest, looked over at Haakon and winked then spat from the cliff edge before heaving himself to his feet. Haakon had the palanquin placed so that with the curtain open it looked down over the grasslands and he could sit with Latasha to hopefully enjoy a moment's peace.

First Haakon checked on Faustus. The physician's knee was a swollen, angry red down to the ankle. He squatted beside Faustus, who grinned over at him despite his obvious discomfort.

'It doesn't look good, Faustus. In the morning you will travel on one of the cular mounts.'

Faustus opened his mouth to speak, but Haakon was having none of it.

'That's my final word, friend. You are too valuable to us all to let your injury get any worse.'

Haakon could tell Faustus wasn't happy, but he waited until the physician nodded, then he rose and headed over to the palanquin again, where he found Latasha sitting and looking down on the burning plains below them, eating slowly. He climbed in alongside her, noticing for the first time the track of tears down her pale cheeks.

'Latasha…'

She spoke without looking at him. 'It's such a waste of life. Such a waste of natural beauty, burnt away with no regard for the world or its people. The sort of thing we are seeing now is the very reason I decided to help bring the Severing to this world. It seems that even after the lessons of the Severing we never really changed. Man seems determined to destroy our beloved paradise anyway. They have no damn regard for the other races or even the future generations of their own.'

Haakon didn't know what to say to this and so he said nothing, just stroked her beautiful hair and wiped away her tears with his sleeve.

Latasha put down her food. Her arms shook with the effort of even that small action. She was still weak.

'I don't expect you to understand, Haakon, and I am not belittling you for being what you are. Being an Ancient means we are tied inexplicably to the land. We feel its triumphs and its tragedies, because we are the direct children of nature, created to protect and serve. The shorter-lived races like man have no idea that the Mother has consciousness, and if we the people forsake her, then she will fight back as you already know. Even after the Severing the people of our world are readying for war again at the merest hint of magic returning to these lands. I really wonder why we are bothering to bring it back at all.'

Haakon knew she didn't expect an answer, but one bubbled from his lips between the soft reassuring kisses he planted on her cheek.

'You must bring the magic back to our world, my love, because in doing so we will return hope to this world that so sorely lacks it. It may not seem like the Severing achieved what it was meant to, but I would argue that the races of our world now know more than any time in their history of the importance of looking after the Mother. They will be slow to forget these cycles and will pass down the lessons to future generations. There will always be good and evil, and if we stop fighting for what is right now, then we have lost. Who really knows what will happen if we manage to keep the coterie alive long enough to usher magic back to our world. To stop now and not try is just as bad as letting evil take its course. Latasha, we must do what we can and in the doing of that service others will rise to carry on our fight. I truly believe that.'

Latasha smiled at his words and lay her head on his shoulder.

'I'm so tired, Haakon. It feels like my long life has settled all its burdens upon me at one time. So what do we do from here?'

'We travel for a way, following this ridge path hopefully the path is still intact that leads to the Witness, a castle looking over the Glyph grasslands and Karnock forest.

'I have a long-time ally who will help us down past Karnock forest, which will save us a considerable journey. It will take the better part of another month to reach the safe house. Latasha, are you sure you will be fine with all of it?'

'No. I will have bed sores, headaches, and feelings of self-doubt due to my situation, but it would seem I have the easy job while you and your people have to lug me around. The one thing I can try to do is to unite the coterie together from the astral and rally them to us. I cannot say why, but it feels from my probing in the astral that there has been a split within the coterie. It's imperative that this rift is healed so I can help the coterie achieve their task.'

Chapter 19

The following day Diego shook Ishmael awake just before dawn. He must have returned late during the night. 'Yucca, come on, we have to start early. Today you have extra work to do.'

On arrival to the warehouse, Diego ushered Ishmael to the cooking area.

'Ramiro told me you looked after him and the other workers well. Then you spent chimes cleaning this area. Why would you do that?'

'I was made to take my turns in the kitchens at the monastery where I grew up. The main thing we were taught was proper food preparation as well as personal hygiene. By not cleaning properly, food can become contaminated, which allows for many sicknesses. Your men got sick because the cook didn't cook the chicken meat enough and he used dishes and utensils that were caked with old food. If I am to eat with the workers I want to know it is safe; otherwise this sort of incident will continue to occur.'

'It's settled then. Yucca, you are the new cook. Your mornings will be spent preparing the day's food for the workers then you shall labour the afternoons alongside the others. Those crates over there contain fresh vegetables as well as some meat, use what you need but do not disappoint me in this, Yucca, I will be watching you closer than ever.'

The other workers arrived by cart driven by Ramiro, who conversed with Diego for a time looking over at Ishmael as he searched through the crates Diego had pointed out to him. When Ishmael prised off the wooden cover of the crate, the smell of rotting food hit him right away. The vegetables were not fresh. The next crate was more chicken but one sniff told him it was inedible.

He stood looking around at the crates that were stocked up before him then realized each crate had a date scratched into its lid. He searched through them locating the ones from the previous day with a grin. When it was open the vegetables, fruits and herbs were still in good condition. He also found one with salted red meat that smelt fine although he had no idea what animal it had come from. He picked up the two crates to take to the preparation area as Ramiro walked over to him. 'Put them down, Yucca, those crates are for the inns along the road. The first ones you opened are for you workers.'

Ishmael replaced the crates on the ground. 'The monitor asked me to cook food for the workers. It was because of the state of the food that everyone fell ill.'

'Strange you should say that, Yucca. The monitor just mentioned to me that you told him the problem was lack of hygiene and proper food preparation.'

'Yes, that is correct, foreman. It is both of these things.'

The first hit of the cane struck Ishmael across the back of his neck with a loud thwack, then the blows rained down on his back dropping him to his knees, but Ishmael didn't cry out.

'You will use what we tell you to use. These decisions are no longer yours to make since you are no longer a free man.'

Ishmael carried the crates back to the preparation area then began to chop the produce up. Most of the vegetables were unsalvageable, but he managed to save the bones of the meat and made a bone broth soup with spices to go with steamed vegetables and charred chicken pieces. The smell wafted across the work area, bringing glances from the workers as the morning rose on. At meal time Ishmael made sure he put two heaped bowls of the food down for Diego and Ramiro before serving the other workers who looked famished and thanked him profusely for the food as he served it.

Ramiro and Diego took the food into the corner office area from where they returned the bowls without praise or acknowledgement, but he noticed with satisfaction the bowls were empty. The shy man who Ishmael now knew to be Chilo beamed at Ishmael. 'First decent food that isn't gruel since I came here. You have given us all a great gift this day, Ishmael.'

'Well you better get used it, Chilo 'because I am the new cook around here,' said Ishmael, pretending to brush dust from his shoulders. 'Some changes are coming.' They both burst into laughter then. The compliments continued over the afternoon, and as Ishmael once again scrubbed the food preparation area, Ramiro approached him. 'You cooked good food today, Yucca. I have spoken with Diego, and we both agree that you should continue with the cooking duties as well as the other work when time allows. You should also know that from tomorrow some new workers will arrive making the number of workers up to thirty, so allow for the extra mouths when you cook.'

'If that is so, Ramiro, then I shall need the extra time for preparation and cleaning as well. There is still a problem with the food. The produce we are given is of low standard while the good quality food goes to the inns or market. With good food I can get more out of the workers, which will raise production levels.'

Ramiro cracked his knuckles loudly. 'The inns along this section of the road pay good money for the best produce, so you will just have to make do with what food you are given.'

The foreman turned to walk away, but Ishmael reached out to touch his shoulder, releasing it under the stern glare of the man.

'Foreman! I understand your concern regarding the cost of the food,' Ishmael threw up his arms in exasperation. 'With better produce and more men the work will be finished faster, allowing more stock to turn over as well as more regular orders of perishable items to be delivered here to us for use before they rot. The one thing the monitor cannot afford is for the men to get sick again from food poisoning. The supply chain that you and the monitor have set up would be dealt a heavy blow if it happened again. I believe it is possible for all of the people here in the town to have fresh produce. The other day Diego was loudly complaining about the pressure on him to see more produce is sent from Brimmerland farmers. He worries it will turn into something he can't control since good workers are hard to find. He doesn't want the Vorm to intervene, but they will do so if they find out.'

The look Ramiro gave him was suspicious.

'What? Diego babbles all the way home about all his troubles.'

The afternoon heat drained the energy from Ishmael's arms as he repeatedly smashed the pickaxe down to break up a group of rocks. He was relieved when Ramiro's whistle cut through the air signalling the end of work. The ride home in the cart was silent, and Diego was distant with some inner distraction. He took Ishmael into the courtyard, put on the restraints, but left again through the gate down the road without going inside his home. It was becoming a regular thing for Diego not to stay in the house, Ishmael noticed.

The next morning Ishmael helped unload the carts of food before any others as usual. As he finished counting the stock of food crates, he turned to go and nearly ran into Diego.

'You asked for better food and the reasons you presented to Ramiro make sense to me, Yucca,' he said. No doubt you already noticed an extra crate with the green tag. There is now one crate of produce as well as one package of meat for you to use. I have brought with me the new workers, and you are no longer required to work the labour crew but as well as the cooking you will be required to deliver the food crates to the establishments in town, under guard escort of course. Now get to it.'

Ishmael turned away to hide his grin from the monitor. Already a plan was beginning to form in his mind.

As he worked he noticed two things. One, Ramiro was starting to swig whiskey from a bottle earlier in the day than he had previously, and now, while only mid-morning, he was half-asleep on a bench when he should be supervising the new workers. Two, the new workers were already being directed to the worst jobs by the twenty original labourers; it had not come to blows yet, but Ishmael could feel the tension rising.

When Ramiro whistled for lunch the men all crowded around the service area with much pushing and shoving.

'Move aside, we eat before you newcomers; now move.'

'Is that right? Well, then, I don't see anyone here capable of carrying that empty threat out?'

There came a chorus of approval. Ramiro blew his whistle, three sharp, short bursts, indicating the men to stop, but he was ignored. Ishmael grabbed two empty pot lids and started banging them together as he climbed on top of the bench, which got everybody's attention.

'In the kitchen where I learned my way around there was only one law, and that was the cook's law. Any man who lifts his hand against a work brother doesn't eat. This is a time of rest and camaraderie. I maybe a long way from that place, but this makeshift kitchen is my area, so if you choose to eat then line up orderly so we may begin, or if you choose to fight, then go out into the heat to spill your blood but know that when you come back there will be no food for you.'

As he uttered the words his heart thumped in his chest. Had he really just said that? But though the men continued grumbling they began to line up. He noticed at the back Ramiro stood whistle still in the corner of his mouth just staring at Ishmael. The man hated him, he knew, how long before he would try to remove Ishmael from his elevated position?

The meal was a simple, hearty one of minced pork and beans spiced with hot peppers. There were even some half-stale loaves of bread to share around. Once they had all been seen to, he noticed with satisfaction they had squatted to eat not in two distinct groups but together.

He filled two large bowls to take to the monitor and the foreman. Ramiro fell into step alongside him as he carried the food to the office. He stepped in front of Ishmael.

'So already you overstep your place, Yucca? You think to feed these useless scum before the monitor? If it happens again…'

The door flap to the office swung open, revealing Diego. 'You can berate him later Ramiro, I am hungry and we have to discuss this trip to the Godhead, which cannot wait.'

Ramiro let Ishmael past into the office. Ishmael gave the best bowl to the monitor then left. They were going to the Godhead again, which was where Ishmael needed to be. He had to escape this place so he could petition his goddess then get to the safe house. Time was passing by, and every day stuck here made his situation more precarious.

Ishmael was dropped off at the warehouse early the next morning to fulfil his new duties. Under the escort of Lew, a burly, serious soldier in the customary uniform of the Vorm, and a cart laden with supplies, Ishmael delivered the food to the inns of the town. At the second of the five inns which was a three-storied wooden manor called the Swinging Derriere. A rider flew past them on an animal that Ishmael had never seen before except from pictures on scrolls, and he remembered it was called a horse. It was the first time he had seen one of the creatures that were only found in the Cavere Grasslands and were highly prized as mounts for messengers or within battle.

Over the next ten days the mood of the workers at the warehouse improved considerably, partially due to the great cooking that Ishmael delivered day after day. It was well known around the town that the work was hard and whereas before Ramiro had trouble trying to recruit workers, word had got around that his workers now received food of a level that only the very wealthy or family members of the Vorm received.

Ishmael worked diligently at his cooking. He arrived at least a chime before the other workers in the morning to make a breakfast of pancakes or omelettes ready as they arrived. There was always a guard nearby watching Ishmael. It was usually Lew who accompanied him to the inns to deliver the supplies, and slowly he had begun to win the man over through the use of his cooking. The monitor was usually away, but one day Ishmael spotted him coming in through the office from the back of the warehouse with someone beside him. Ishmael only caught a glance of long skirts and an ornate fan held in front of the face before they both disappeared inside and out of sight. Could this be the woman that Fajira feared had stolen her husband?

Each night Diego just dropped Ishmael off, fixed the restraints, and then drove off with the cart. Diego's absence had begun to bother him since it was every night either Fausto or Fajira would come out with a look of expectation at his arrival only to be told by Ishmael he had already left. After about five days they stopped coming out to check. The house was so quiet at night as if empty, its occupants trapped in silence.

Chapter 20

Nina sat cross-legged, breathing in short huffing breaths that she had learnt about in the book. It was called the rising breath, and its benefit was the same as stretching but for the vortices of the energy body. The practice didn't take long since Nina could only access the first of her vortices, but as her practice grew stronger she would be able to use all nine vortices and perform amazing feats. Nina waited to feel energized by the breathing technique, then she adopted a deep, whooshing breath to draw the energy down into the earth until she felt a deepening connection.

Visualizing the first vortex locking closed, she waited for the steadying feeling in her belly that let her know her foundation vortex was open and locked in place, ready for her to venture out in her energy body. Next Nina took long slow breaths to draw the red flow of energy at the base of her spine upwards and with it her energy body from the dark chamber in the castle.

The red energy body pulsed faintly since her body was weak. Then the red energy reached the second vortex, the place of the self with the colour orange, Nina pushed her energy body through the spinning vortex into a world of orange and was floating, caught in a swirl of love so strong she feared it would engulf her. How easy it would be to let go and allow the strange wind to take her where it pleased. Images of her dream to see the highway beneath the mountain become a reality flashed before her, a life without pain and one in which her parents were with her. All thoughts of scarcity disappeared, and Nina knew what it was to be connected to everything. Then the shaking started from within her belly, and Nina felt the anger and sadness at the loss of her parents as around her the orange darkened as if burnt, leaving only darkness and fear all around her.

Nina let herself be pulled backwards as if being reeled in by a fishing pole. When she woke up her mouth was thick with her blood; she had bitten her tongue. That was, *too close*, she thought, lying there still with the cool stone comforting her. Nina could feel herself getting a headache, her stomach knotted with muscle spasms as she lay working through the feelings and fear, which became easier to control each time she travelled. A part of her also rejoiced at finally breaking through into the second vortex and its orange world, but like the book had warned she wanted to go again right now. Nina knew enough to remember the warnings of travelling too often without allowing the energy body time to heal. Elated and exhausted, she lay in the darkness imagining her next voyage.

Zacriel had watched with great interest when the two newcomers Lana and Nelson had been introduced to him and Dalwyn. The look that passed between the comely Lana and Dalwyn had told Zacriel one thing: they knew one another. When Nelson had first collapsed, Zacriel had been content to let Dalwyn's men place him under guard within his tower. Dalwyn had told him they would speak soon and he would share what he knew.

That had been a day ago and still Dalwyn had not bothered to report his findings. With a snarl, he called over Rapture from behind him.

'You and four of your strongest come with me now to Dalwyn's rooms. I have lost all patience with waiting for him in my own castle.'

Rapture returned with four brutish warriors with matted fur, tusks and hooves, and eyes burning with hatred. The door to Dalwyn's chamber was guarded by two flame warriors whose bravery was to be applauded if not their sheer stupidity at thinking they could stand against the infernals gathered before them.

'Move aside now!' snarled Zacriel.

'You know I can't do that, Zacriel. Either way I die.'

'Will be my pleasure then,' laughed Rapture, moving fast, grabbing the guard by the throat and slamming him against the door, which splintered.

The second guard tried to draw steel but was knocked from his feet by a head butt from one of the tusked warriors and slid down to the floor. They battered down the remains of the door to find Dalwyn and Lana sitting calmly watching them while Nina sat on a window ledge gawking at their spectacular entrance.

'Zacriel stood there raging from within. 'You promised me an explanation, Dalwyn!'

Dalwyn's face reddened. He leant forward, poured himself some water then sipped slowly before meeting Zacriel's gaze again.

'I am quickly losing patience with you, old man. Here in my city you are nothing.' Zacriel could feel the rage pulsing through him and realized his hands grasped the infernal rod with his full strength as Dalwyn and Lana looked on at him like he was a spoiled child.

'I want to know what is happening, Dalwyn!'

'And so, you shall, Zacriel. You are right to feel aggrieved, and I should have spoken to you earlier. Now sit here with us. Water?'

Zacriel nodded a yes to the water, his throat was parched and his breathing heavy and he felt like a huffing beast as he tried to control his anger. He noticed Nina watching him too and felt embarrassed at his childlike behaviour.

'Now, Lana, would you care to start from the beginning for our friend Zacriel?'

Zacriel knew he was being mocked by the old bastard. He had fallen for the old man's ploy by meeting Dalwyn on his terms, and he had ceded control to Dalwyn.

'Lana tell me how you know Dalwyn?' asked Zacriel.

Lana's eyes flicked to Dalwyn as if asking permission then back to him.

'I'm a mercenary and Dalwyn pays well; there is nothing more to say. I won't divulge what my task was to you or anybody, so don't ask.'

'Who are the both of you anyway? Nelson definitely isn't a mercenary.'

Dalwyn rose from the chair to stand in front of Zacriel. 'Get your pet here to take Nina from the tower while we explain to you some great news regarding the coterie.'

'Why do I always have to leave?' grumbled Nina as Rapture chased her to the stairs.

Dalwyn went to the large table in the chamber where he uncovered a map.

'Zacriel, come here so I can tell you the plan we need to follow. Lana has returned to me at the perfect time with the news we need to act.'

As Zacriel listened to Dalwyn enthusiastically pointing out locations on the map and their relevance, he began to think his luck might be changing after all.

Chapter 21

Haakon was only half dozing by Latasha's side when he caught sight of Tek returning from his scouting. He quietly slipped out of Latasha's embrace, covering her with his blanket before meeting his scout. Tek was sipping bitter moss wine, and checking the state of his boots which Haakon saw were in a sorry state.

'You better find another pair, Tek, they look about done.'

'Yeah, they are. I have another set so it's no trouble. Speaking of trouble…' He looked up at Haakon. 'At least half a chime up the path there is a lookout tower that seems to have been kept in use since it is fully supplied. No sign of anyone except an awful blood stain as if a group of people had been executed in that spot. I would guess the stain is weeks old but no more. I travelled on to where a steep path diverts down into a pass and where I saw an encampment below of many tents and fires. They had guards posted, but it didn't seem as if they were too concerned about attracting attention. There could easily have been close to two or three hundred warriors down there, but it's hard to see.'

'Warriors? Did they have any banner or emblems to show who they are?'

'There was no way I could even try to get closer, but I did hear a guard cough who happened to be maybe ten feet away behind a large rock. It was pure luck he didn't see me. I took care of him but had to kill the brute when he nearly overpowered me. He wore this.'

Tek passed Haakon a round disk on a heavy chain. The disk was gold and held a sky-blue stone in its centre.

Haakon sighed.

'Cloud Lords. This comes from a noble warrior of the Cloud Lord tribe. They rarely descend from their deep mountain fortresses that they build on the highest peaks they can find, hence their clan name. The big question is, what are they doing so far from home?'

'Cloud Lords huh? I always just thought they were stories where they believed themselves to be direct descendants of the rock god Melde and would raid down into the lowlands for slaves and wives to take back to their mountain homes,' Tek replied.

'Not just stories, my friend. Their prowess in battle and the harshness of mountain life makes them feared enemies. So now we have a dead guard to worry about. I would have thought that with your experience you would have left no trail to follow.'

Tek smiled then proffered the flask of bitter moss wine to Haakon.

'So we have come to the time, master where you doubt my abilities? Now before you insult me more you will be happy to know that the guard had ample wine with him; hence where I got this. I took the liberty of drenching his shirt in it and pouring some down his gob before I pushed him off the cliff near where I watched the army in the valley. They will assume the fool got too drunk and fell to his death.'

Haakon grinned then slapped Tek on his back. I must admit you had me worried there, and it's good to know that you still have the abilities we worked so hard to instil in you. Now get some rest. I will set a guard up the trail in case they decide to come wandering this way, and I will also go and survey them myself. You have done well, Tek, and I thank you.'

When he returned to the palanquin, Latasha was awake looking at him questioningly.

'There is a nearby watchtower up ahead that belongs to the Witness, that citadel I was talking about. The guards have been killed and an army of mountain warriors called the Cloud Lords are camped in the valley. If we try to go past we will be spotted, so we best find another route or send a messenger to the Witness in order to get help.'

'Can you be assured the citadel and your friend will aid us, Haakon?'

'That's the problem, isn't it, Latasha? I can't be sure my contact is even at the Witness anymore. The outpost owes allegiance to Brimmerland, but in its seclusion they really just stay to themselves. Unless we backtrack and go deeper into the mountains near where we entered them or retrace our steps then cut through the Karnock forest, we are stuck. I need to go and see this force myself, Latasha.'

'I don't think that would be wise, Haakon. Send your best men to check, but if you go and something happens to you…'

'If something happens to me, then you know this land well enough to guide the men to the safe house,' Haakon finished.

'Your men don't share your loyalty to me. It's only because of you that they even tolerate my presence since they will always fear me.'

'Yes, that's true, my love, but I also think you underestimate my clansmen. They know the importance of having you there when magic is returned to this world, and the clan honours its contracts to their end.'

'I'm sorry, Haakon, I'm not attacking your honour or that of your clan. I'm afraid that after getting you back after so long that I will lose you again, this time forever.'

He kissed her deeply.

'I'm not getting close enough for a fight. It's just reconnaissance Latasha nothing more.'

Moving through the gloom, Haakon tapped three men on their shoulders to wake them. He chose two who were highly skilled with the bow and the third a veteran of war who he knew itched to be among the thick of it but could be trusted to give good advice. Kneeling down with them he gave them the details, then they all moved away silently into the night.

It was as Tek had said. The Cloud Lords numbered at least two hundred, but as most were still camped in large tents there was no way to be sure. What he could see was that they were well armed with large hammers, wickedly jagged swords, and long bone javelins. It appeared that the guard Tek had disposed of had been found and replaced by two others who sat quietly talking as they drank. Haakon motioned to his men to stay out of sight and wait. They conversed in a broken common dialect that allowed Haakon to understand most of what they said, and he lay there putting aside his uncomfortable position to see what information he could glean from the guards.

One of the men was huge and wore dark trousers partially hidden by the naked, obese folds of flesh that flowed down from above. He stood there guzzling from a wineskin undeterred by its dark greenish liquor running down his chin and over his chest.

'When we arrive at the moot then you shall see what I have learned, Racuth. Mock me now, my small friend, but when this upstart who claims to have been healed by the gods shows his face it will be I, Krowulf, who breaks his back with my bare hands before the assembly.'

The smaller man, whom Haakon could see was a lot older, sat eating something thoughtfully. He was clothed in grey leather that suited the mountain landscape and wore long braids that fell to his waist.

'Krowulf, they say this warrior is changed. He left his family to reside in the great city of dreams and struggled to find his place as one would expect of our kind. It was here that he was shown a vision as he lay dying and great lights came from the sky that healed his injuries and showed him what he must do to unite the many people and stop the second breaking of the world before it can happen.'

'Bah, that's bullshit and, you know it, Racuth so don't pretend you don't. I am sick of this waiting,' said Krowulf as he snatched the wine skin from Racuth. 'How many warriors must we need to show our enemies our strength when we have me and you? If I had the clan in my control I would go now to the moot and leave the stragglers to chase our heels,' growled Krowulf, tossing the now empty wine skin into the undergrowth.

'Yes, but, Krowulf, you don't have the clan's favour. Be done with these empty boasts and watch and learn when we go to the moot. My heart tells me there will plenty of chance to fight when we attack the low landers who gather amongst the sacred peaks. Then, brave Krowulf, you can take out your many problems on the kin of those responsible for the breaking of the world.'

Haakon had heard enough, and it seemed by some cursed luck that they had only crossed paths with a war band who was forming to fight a battle against others. With his eight warriors, Latasha and his old friend Faustus there was no way he could risk any trouble with the Cloud Lords. He motioned to Yasmin that they were leaving and carefully followed her route away from the two Cloud Lord warriors. When they arrived back at camp, the other scouts had already returned.

Haakon directed them to wake the others, and before long they were all gathered together, sharing blankets to keep warm.

'The route forward has hit a problem,' Haakon told them. A large one in the form of a Cloud Lord war party camped in a valley we need to pass through. I was hoping to make it to the Witness, but now that seems impossible unless we retreat down to the burning mess below and wait for these barbarians to pass, of which I have no intention of doing. Any suggestions?'

Haakon looked around at the best of his warriors he had bought with him, but they looked as perplexed as he as to a possible solution that didn't involve more danger.

'I know a way.'

It was Latasha, and her soft voice seemed to cut through their urgent talking while her palanquin was still facing the Glyph grasslands. Haakon had not bothered to wake her since he foolishly had thought she could offer no real advice for their situation and it would be better to let her rest. He felt the flush rise to his cheeks and the eyes of his warriors on him.

'It's dangerous, of course, and barely known to man since us ancients built it, but you have an advantage in this matter. You have me.'

Haakon motioned for two of the warriors to carry the palanquin in to where they sat. Latasha's eyes shone like a cat's in the dark, which seemed to unnerve the others, and Haakon knew that her assumptions of them should something happen to him were true. Without him they would leave her.

'Speak, Latasha, and accept my apology for any slight I may have aimed at you.'

'It is of no consequence, clan leader; sometimes it's easier to forget how long my race has lived and what knowledge we may hold. Maybe a half day's hard travel from here lies a hidden temple called Tinselthwain. It was a magical place for us once, but now like everything, is devoid of its true power. It offers a way to go down to the sky lake near the middle of Karnock forest close to the route you chose.'

Yasmin leant forward, her lean face scowling.

'No disrespect, Latasha, but all you have bought our clan is danger, and now you ask us to trust you again.'

'Yasmin,' cut in Tek.

'No, Tek, she is right and wise to question my judgement,' Latasha said. 'I am partially responsible for this situation and was one of those who chose to create the magic that caused the Severing. But without that intervention, none of us would even be having this conversation.

'The Kenzu were the only clan to agree and help me protect the coterie, and you have done incredibly well, even looking after my broken body to stop me dying when that was all I wished for. Now I simply offer you another way. It may be more dangerous, but as I see it there are no better options. Take it or leave it, but if you have no alternative to give then be silent.'

Haakon smiled when no one offered any more complaints to Latasha. When she wanted to, she could cut the tongues from the best.

'A show of hands then,' said Haakon.

'I for one side with Latasha; never has she left us to fend for ourselves,' he said raising a hand.

'Of course, you would,' muttered the gaunt Yasmin, but she too raised a hand. The others looked about at one another, then Tek shrugged.

'Be beaten to a pulp by Cloud warriors, burn to death on the Glyph, or be one of the only men to enter a temple of the ancients forgotten by time? I'm in.'

Once Tek was in the others followed suit, and Faustus's pained face was filled with a wide smile. 'I'm in, wouldn't miss this opportunity before I die.'

— ❧ —

Chapter 22

Zahra descended the stairs quickly, only stopping if something of value caught her eye. By the time she reached the start of the Seekers Road she had added a map of the road with information of all the towns between here and the Godhead as well as a spare change of clothing that she donned so she looked like a young maiden fleeing Whitman's Point and her family's death.

The dawn had brought with it the familiar moist heat that lathered her in a layer of dust and sweat, and Zahra was glad of the early start to try and avoid the worst of the weather. Two chimes later she found herself at the rear of a small group that had also been fleeing Whitman's Point. A few men at the front were calling up to the top of a makeshift barricade that had been erected across the road. A red-haired man was glaring down at them from above the barrier.

'Town's full already, you would be better served to move on to the city, Cabre and the Crag, on Soarnestian land.'

A man with a considerable paunch threw his hands in the air in disgust.

'We need supplies, I tell you. We lost our homes, some of our loved ones, can't you see that?'

'I know, but it's not safe here, so we will escort you to beyond our town where if you have coin the sand whips will carry you to the Crag or you will need to walk yourselves. This is the decree of the monitor who runs Glimmersedge.'

A door in the barricade opened, revealing a well-armed warrior who led the group through the area. Zahra followed and pulled the letter from her pocket that the General Caldro had bid her deliver if possible.

'Come on with yer, girl, we don't have all day.'

'Sir, I have an important letter…'

'Don't care about your letter, girl, you can send it later.'

'It's from General Monte Caldro, sir.'

'Ha, I'm sure it is,' He laughed then pushed her past him.

'I need to talk with the monitor. I have valuable information from Acclaro and Whitman's Point that can aid you all if battle comes here.'

Another guard came over when the first beckoned him.

'This one claims to have a letter from the general of Whitman's Point for the monitor.'

'That right, huh, where is it?'

'I will only give it to him personally.'

'Well at least produce it now so we can see the wax seal.'

They checked the seal between them.

'Seems to be genuine. Take the woman to Diego. Search her first and be sure she knows the law. '

'Yes, sir. Did you hear that? Drawing a blade in Glimmersedge is considered a crime, and the monitor is known for whipping culprits for it.'

Zahra was half dragged-half-pushed to where a ramp had been lowered to the road near the bridge overpass at the town of Glimmersedge. The guard who took Zahra squeezed her hard on the arse, making her jump. He rested a heavy arm around her as they walked up the ramp, trying to grope her breasts.

'How's about after you see the monitor you let me take you somewhere where we can get a drink and some alone time,' He waggled his eyebrows and flashed a set of fine teeth at her.

She giggled slightly at him then gave him a coy look.

'I suppose that could be a good idea. It's sure a lonely road for a woman, and after the terrible things I've seen... I just want to shut it all out and not be alone.'

He actually looked surprised at her answer.

'My name is Rin,' he stammered, momentarily off guard by her forwardness.

'Well, all right then, my shift will finish at the next chime, and then I'm on leave for a day.'

Zahra stepped to him, ran a finger down his chest, then pulled his long hair until he leant down so she could whisper in his ear.

'Don't be too long, soldier boy. I have quite the appetite today, so it's not a good idea to keep me waiting.'

The small shops front window was nothing but a large notice board upon which layers of notices had been added over old ones, giving the place a rather run down look, reducing the appeal of the neighbouring establishment. The door was ajar, and Zahra knocked three times then waited.

What could only be described as a grunt sounded from within the shop; so assuming it was an invitation Zahra went inside. The man behind the desk was shabbily dressed in a food-stained, grey shirt beneath a white vest. A pipe hung from his lips and smoke coiled up then swam around his face before dispersing. He swung his leather boots down off the table where they had been resting, made a pitiful attempt at cleaning the mess his boots had made, then indicated with a wave of a hand that Zahra should sit.

'Are you the monitor, Diego?'

'Sure as the sun rises, yep, what brings you to me?'

'I have misplaced a friend of mine, well that's not entirely true. I have lost my brother. We fought and well he ran away. It is very important I find him, and, well the last I saw of him was at Whitman's Point before the Infernals attacked. I was hoping you may have seen him or at least are aware if he is here in Glimmersedge.'

'This brother of yours, does he have a name?'

'Oh yes, sorry, I am weary beyond thoughts. His name is Ishmael. He is a brother of Illume. Have you seen him?'

'Well, yes I have seen him. Yet looking at you I would be assured in saying you are a native here in Brimmerland, am I right?'

'Yes, that is true, monitor.'

'So the question that begs to be asked, my friend…'

'Zahra.'

'Zahra, the question I have is that if this Ishmael is the same man we are talking about, he is certainly not from Brimmerland, so how could he be your brother?'

Zahra felt her anger rising but pushed it away.

'Truth be told, Diego, Ishmael is my step-brother, and our parents have perished in Acclaro. We fought over some valuable possessions, and he left. I know he has always wanted to visit the Godhead, so I chose to start looking here first.'

'I have indeed seen this man you call, Ishmael but fleetingly. He declined my invitation to stay in Glimmersedge then moved on to I believe the Crag, but who can know. Maybe he is at the Godhead now, this brother of yours. These valuables you speak of, what were they? And did he steal them from you?'

Zahra feigned indifference at the last comment about the valuables. Why was he asking about them?

'No they were more family heirlooms than anything, but something he has no right to claim for himself. Are you sure he never stayed in Glimmersedge?'

'Zahra, you have my word on this. I saw him go myself. Will you be staying here long?'

'No. I am keen to catch up with Ishmael so one night in the inn next door and then I will be on my way.'

Zahra only stayed briefly to talk with Diego. She had wanted to turn the scroll over to someone who could genuinely use that knowledge to protect their people from the Infernals, and now after talking to Diego she realized he was not that person. The man was calculating and clever, and she didn't want to share any more information about herself than necessary. He couldn't be trusted even with the Vorm family crest on his coat that hung from a hook. That family crest made him nearly untouchable unless you wanted to attract a whole horde of strife upon yourself.

Next door in the Swinging Derriere, the delectable smells wafting from the kitchen even at this chime of the morning had Zahra's stomach rumbling. She had arranged for Rin the guard to come find her room there, and when she paid for the accommodation Zahra made sure they knew she was with him.

A bustling older woman with short hair took the order of two sweet cakes, a pot of tea with honey and some fresh melon. The same woman cleaned the dishes away from her table later and sat down opposite Zahra.

'The girls who work for me tell me you are with Rin; is this true?'

'For now as long as he meets my needs.'

'Be warned, he is far from a good man. He left the last girl he was with dead by the roadside.'

'Listen, I am grateful for your concern but…'

'He beats them. That's what excites Rin, you see. It's best to steer clear of him.'

'I said I will be fine.' She unwrapped her blade from her cloak to show the woman.

'I can look after myself, and thank you for the food, it was divine. Now I think I will go to my room.' She was awake when Rin tapped on the door, and she opened it naked.

'Thought you weren't coming,' Zahra sauntered back to the bed then lay there waiting for him as he undressed. He was rough, biting her flesh and even choking her as he searched for that sweetest relief.

Zahra didn't mind at all, the pain made her feel alive. The sting of his hand on her thigh or the crushing on her throat just enough to remind her she could still feel even after all that death that was Whitman's Point and Acclaro. The things she had seen would send most people mad. The love making was all over too fast, but soon she had convinced Rin for another round. She even repaid his bruises and bites with her own.

Afterwards they drank and Rin pulled out a bag of wraith flower powder, snorted a thumbnail full of the stuff before offering it to Zahra. This wraith flower was the new crop that Brimmerland was looking to capitalize on. Any long term effects were largely unknown so far with the only knowledge being that the powder sent you to the astral world where if you learnt to control your mind the strange world could be navigated just like the waking world. However, the storms that wracked that strange realm since the Severing made it dangerous for travellers to be trapped especially while under the influence of the strange plant.

Zahra took some wraith flower anyway; it would stop her exhausting her own energy, and she was too tired to access the astral naturally. The wraith flower offered her an opportunity to learn of Ishmael's whereabouts. Zahra snorted some of the powder then also poured some more into the mouth of the resting Rin before lying back beside him. She looked at him smiling strangely as his eyes lids flickered, and then the room about her soon became transparent as a faint pressure in her skull began building. When the pressure subsided, Zahra's energy body stood up, then she floated up out of the open window. Rin's astral cord was a sickly green colour that ran from his solar plexus then out into the sky beyond what she could see.

It was the first time in many cycles since she had accessed the astral during the day since it was harder to stay in that realm during the day. Zahra rose up with her thoughts higher until she was above Glimmersedge. She turned towards Acclaro noting that in the astral the twisted, dark visage of the far off city gave off an image of corruption that was bleeding away the amber light that surrounded it, replacing it with a dull, lifeless void of swirling energy.

Closing her eyes, Zahra could feel the thrum of the astral wind pulling at her as if to take her some place. When she bought her concentration back to herself by glancing at her hands and when her energy had settled, she sent forth the memory of the windmill where she had stayed with Ishmael. In her mind she perfected that place as well as she could from her memory then created an anchor point by attaching a thinner cord that emerged from her solar plexus to her memory of the windmill two days earlier, then she allowed her body to float down to stand on the road itself, which appeared as a rusty reddish path.

Next Zahra focused on Ishmael as she had seen him last when they fled Acclaro, and to this image she connected the third and smallest cord that emerged from her third eye vortex. She was ready for the last part now, and this was where one could easily be dragged into danger if not careful. The connection to Ishmael was an orange cord that brightened and disappeared as it traced Ishmael's movements. Zahra could feel the energy rushing from her solar plexus and hoped the wraith flower would last long enough. She accelerated the pull on the energy cords as she had been taught, which allowed her to speed up the time since she had been at the windmill. The glow of the orange trace moved along the Seekers Road to Glimmersedge, and Zahra saw the ghostly figure of Ishmael waiting with a large crowd. From the side of the image the huge sand whips emerged to stop before the people, and Zahra watched Ishmael climb aboard a carriage. She disconnected the anchor point to the windmill then followed the orange cord towards the carriage when she noticed the wind had grown considerably stronger, and she had no idea how long had passed.

Not willing to risk the dangers of an astral storm Zahra reluctantly severed the connection to Ishmael then relaxed as she allowed her sleeping body to call her back. When she flowed in from the window, a glowing Rin stood above his body looking panicked. With the powder Zahra had poured into his mouth added to his own dose, it had been too much, and it would be impossible for his energy body to re-enter his real body anytime soon.

When Rin saw her he turned on her in anger, attempting to strike her, but he had very little control in the astral and she easily avoided him. Next he pleaded for her to help him back into his body, but of course she couldn't do that and it was the same for her. The wraith flower had its hold on them both now, and until it wore off they were in danger.

When the storm struck the window imploded inwards; the floorboards and bed began to warp. Zahra knew this was only happening in the astral not the real world, but to die in this storm would mean someone would find their lifeless bodies the next day in their room. They both cowered in that room as the wind tore what it could and sucked it up into the storm. Another gust of wind threw the both of them against the wall, the bed slamming against the window then bending under the great force until it too was sucked out and away.

Rin screamed and grabbed at Zahra; his hand went straight through her and she saw now her form was fading which meant the drug had worn off now and would return to her body at any moment. Rin grabbed her shoulders urgently.

'You are fading. Don't leave me here, Zahra, I don't know what to do. Zahra? No!'

It was too late, and when Zahra opened her eyes she was still beside Rin on the bed. He moaned while his head turned from side to side, sweat beading his face and soaking his clothes. She waited by his side for some time wiping his forehead with a towel, and less than a chime passed before his body stiffened then went limp. There was no pulse. Now Zahra had a new problem, and worse still she realized that his death could very well be blamed on her. Adding the extra wraith powder had been stupid and now if questioned Zahra would have to explain that the idiot had killed himself. Many people had suffered the same horrible fate using the dangerous drug without the advantage of the astral training that she had received? As Zahra dressed she thought about covering the bruises that Rin had given her that now marred her face, but then just left them for all to see. Even though she was back in the physical realm she felt less than whole, vulnerable but infused with energy. She had paid for the room for two days but had no interest at sharing a room with a corpse. Gathering her pack, Zahra also pocketed the bag of wraith powder but left any valuables the man had.

At the front of the inn Zahra took in the knowing glances of the girl whom she approached. 'I paid two nights, so just tell your mistress that Rin will be staying the extra day. He has some type of drug, wraith flower I think he called it, and has been asleep since. Anyway, I won't be a target for any man if he is as incompetent in bed as he was, so I'm going.' Then she spun on her heel to leave but as an afterthought occurred to her, she turned back. 'He has consumed quite a large amount of the drug, so you may want to check on his wellbeing later.'

Chapter 24

Ishmael passed down a particularly heavy crate to Chilo as the two of them unloaded the most recent cart. The morning had been busier than most, and so Ishmael had jumped in to lend a hand. As he had worked, Ishmael kept an eye on Diego who paced about looking worried and distracted as the crates of fresh food were moved under his supervision. He hadn't even verbally abused any of the workers yet.

'Diego? Diego, I waited for you as you asked, but you didn't show up. I was so worried.' Both Ishmael and Diego turned to look at who was shouting to the monitor. It was a tall, slim woman with dark hair to the middle of her back, her face a pale heart shape with large eyes and lips. She was striding across the street, her long dress flowing out to drag through the dust behind her.

Diego cringed when he saw her but then composed himself quickly.

She approached pouting which only emphasized her beauty. 'Do you think you can ignore me?' Her hand raised to slap Diego, who easily caught it in one hand pulling her close to his side.

'I told you never to bother me at the warehouse, Lucinda. You cannot come here.'

'So you want to talk about what's right and wrong?' she answered with a narrowing of the eyes and her chin thrust forward.'

Diego turned to Ishmael and the other workers.

'What are you all staring at, haven't you seen a woman before?' Then he practically dragged her to the office.

Could this be the woman who had come between Fajira and Diego? Mused Ishmael as he worked. He had seen the woman before, of course. She had been the rider who had overtaken them when he was delivering the stock to the inns.

That afternoon at the end of the day's work Ramiro emerged from the office with a chest to pass out the wages for the past ten days. Ishmael had worked for nearly a month now at the warehouse and was yet to see a glimpse of the coin owed him. His job finished, he decided enough was enough and marched over to fall into line behind the other workers. From previous talks with the other workers he had found out they earned a silver ketch per day or one gold ceta per ten days to be paid at the end of the month.

Ramiro sat with the chest open and was just closing it when he looked up at Ishmael standing there.

'Yucca, what is it?'

'You know what I want,' breathed Ishmael from between clenched teeth.'

The chest shut with a catch of the lock and Ramiro stood hands on hips facing Ishmael.

'No, I don't know so, why don't you enlighten me.'

'I want what is my due since I have worked here for you and the monitor. I am a good worker being forced to work for you because of the rule of honour, but I know my rights in this, Ramiro. I am entitled to still earn pay that will be given to me at the end of my sentence.'

'There you go, Yucca, you said it yourself, at the end of your sentence, not before, so move along onto the cart.'

Ishmael stepped closer to Ramiro, causing a guard to step forward, jerking him away from Ramiro by the shoulder. He glared at the guard then at Ramiro before he continued.

'I know that both you and the monitor run a little scheme here at the warehouse. You trap people into debts of honour then force them to work for you all the while keeping their earnings to split between yourselves.'

Ramiro laughed. He wiped a hand across his mouth, then with a nod at the guard Ishmael was shoved to the ground face-first as the guard held him firmly there.

'Now, Yucca, we will only have this conversation once. You are not family, friend, or an honourable member of the Vorm, here you are nothing but a rude man. It is true that you earn money doing this work, and yes it's true that we take your earning then split it between us. My question to you is, what are you going to do about it? How will you prove this great crime against you?'

The next moment drops fell upon Ishmael's face and head as he realized that Ramiro was pissing on him. When he had finished, he gave Ishmael a toe kick to the genitals for good measure. He grasped Ishmael by the chin turning his face up to him. 'Can you believe, Yucca that you almost had me fooled. I was beginning to think you were a smart man, but now I know I was so wrong. Now Diego will have to be told. Do you think anyone here actually cares for you or what happens to you?'

'Ramiro!' The voice came from behind the foreman. 'Leave Yucca alone; he has done you no wrong.'

Ramiro stood and moved away from Ishmael, who rolled to his side, levering himself up into a sitting position. It was Seki, one of the original workers who had thanked him for the great meals, and now stood facing Ramiro and his guard, who now had a curved blade drawn.

'Seki, this is none of your business,' growled Ramiro. 'If I were you I would walk back to the cart and get on.'

'Yucca means more to you and the monitor than all of us, and it is was due to him and his cooking that this work camp has turned around. What do you think will happen if you take the one good thing away that this job gives us?'

'You dare…' Ramiro had gone a beet red colour, the veins of his neck standing out.

From his belt Ramiro drew his own sword as he advanced on Seki with the guard, but then a peculiar thing happened. Three more of the workers jumped from the cart to stand beside Seki, then more until ten of them stood facing the two armed men.

Seki's face split into a wide grin. The little man looked at his unexpected allies then at Ramiro.

'It's now the end of day, boss, do you really want to do this now?'

Ramiro sheathed his blade, nodding at the guard to do likewise. He turned to glare at Ishmael then back to the men grouped around Seki.

'Get on the cart, all of you. When Diego finds out then you will all pay for this insubordination.'

Seki walked over with his arm extended to help pull Ishmael to his feet.

'Thank you, Seki, but it was a stupid thing for you to do. You know he will make life hell for you now.'

'He is too weak for that Ishmael. He's a regular bully and we have no interest in losing you or you're cooking.'

'Thank you, I am proud to be able to call you friend,' replied Ishmael as the two grasped each other's forearm then ran to join the cart. Ishmael noticed that Diego was nowhere to be seen. They dropped off the workers to their quarters then headed off not towards home but instead stopping at the inn, The Swinging Derriere. Ishmael attempted to get the reason why they were here from the guard, but he was ignored and so he jumped into the back of the cart to sleep while they waited. He had no idea how long he had slept and was awakened once the cart lurched into motion this time with Diego on board. As the cart drew away from the inn Ishmael saw the long raven-haired woman standing at an upstairs window watching them leave. *So that's where he has been*, thought Ishmael. But why bother returning home now?

Later he sat there chained to his usual spot, chewing on a strip of meat he had hidden within his clothing to eat that night. It was rare for him to get food during the night unless Fajira brought it herself. Fausto still seemed to hate Ishmael but showed a grudging respect despite his dislike.

For the first time in many days there came the festive music and laughing from within the house. Listening to Diego and his family laughing brought back similar memories of such times he had shared with his family before his father's death. That family was gone now, and so was his second family that the monks at the monastery had become for him. Ishmael knew he needed to leave here soon. Selene and Jona kept testing his walls, but he wasn't ready to continue to the safe house yet.

That night Ishmael dreamt of Zahra. He sat on a large log by a fire from which sparks flew high above him. It was night outside, the fire glowing, and the sound of rustling beyond the firelight of whatever lay out there waiting for him. Ishmael stayed where he was though, he was safe here. A shadow hovered at the edge of his perception and seemed to bleed out of the night before him, and into his haven from the darkness. It was Zahra. She was dressed in the black clothing she usually favoured, smiling as she stopped five feet away from him. Zahra began to unbutton her tunic. Her eyes danced in the firelight as her tunic fell to the ground, baring her upper body, the light playing off her scar covered curves.

'Finally we can be together, Ish,' she purred, unlacing her trousers to bunch around her ankles. 'I have missed you so much since you left me. Let's fix that.'

As Zahra stepped forward to look down at Ishmael, he felt his lust as a fire that consumed him, his dry mouth aching for the relief of her lips. He rose to meet her, to take her in his arms, but behind her he saw the darkness fading to amber and he knew then this wasn't a dream, it was the astral.

Ishmael felt a strong sharp pain pierce his forehead area, then a glimpse of a dark candlelit chamber. He was seeing through Zahra's eyes; she was trying to force her way into his mind. He threw his walls up as he had to keep the coterie out and pushed away. Zahra's features betrayed her frustration; then she was gone altogether and he was sitting in the courtyard alone.

Ishmael had not thought much from that night that seemed so long ago, when Zahra had asked him to contact the sentinels of the other coterie members since she had lost her ability to reach the astral. Now he knew she had lied to him. Her control over the astral must be impeccable, and she had nearly totally fooled him into dropping his defences. He knew she would have had at least a moment like he had where she saw through his eyes. What would she find out from his surroundings? He regretted pushing her away again, and he knew Zahra would rather die than fail to protect him. Zahra had already told him that there was no way they could detour to the road because they needed to make it to the safe house and the coterie. The moment he had seen through her eyes had told him little except it was night and she was in a room, maybe an inn. She was looking for him and the hunt was on in earnest.

Chapter 25

They quickly dismantled the camp before dawn while in the glow provided by the marauding fires on the Glyph grasslands. The sentry they had left to watch the Cloud Lords drifted into camp as they were finishing packing.

'The brutes are only awakening now. It would be wise to get away now before they send any scouts forward,' said Liam as he wolfed down his ration of the cold food for breakfast.

With no visible route and following Latasha's insistent urging to keep them moving they reluctantly forged onwards. When they came to a cliff face, they pulled the palanquin, cular mounts and the injured Faustus up by ropes. Within two chimes they were exhausted and Haakon was forced to let them rest while they waited for the cular mounts to be taken around past the cliff face to reunite with the rest of them.

Battered, bruised, and disheartened, Haakon knew he had to act fast to stop the morale of the group diminishing any further. Dawn was upon the world, and though they had worked hard traversing the perilous route Haakon could see his men were cold.

'We will stop now that the immediate danger is behind us, and even the Cloud Lords will choose easier paths to follow. Tek, get a fire going for cooking. We will have hot food and some water for tea before continuing.'

Latasha called Haakon over to where she sat.

'Haakon, there is still danger about.' He stopped her with a finger to her lips.

'My people need hot food and drink, of which they have had neither for two days, and tension is building. Let us all fill our bellies with hot food before we continue.'

She smiled up at him, her silver hair catching the light.

'Come to think of it, I could do with something hot to chase away the chill myself.'

The rest of the morning they moved at a slow pace, picking their way along Latasha's route. They all sensed the change by late afternoon; it was as if an uneasy quiet descended on the area. No birds flew over them, no distant cries of mountain cats or signs of the shaggy goats up high watching them.

When they stopped for a break the next time, their supply of water had dwindled to three canteens. With the need to also water the cular mounts, they would need to find more fresh water soon.

Yasmin tipped back her water skin, barely receiving a mouthful, and threw it down in disgust. Haakon walked over to her, offering her a fresh one. 'Here, drink your fill. Latasha says we are close now and fresh water will be easy to find at our destination.'

'Do you feel the quiet? It's not natural? This place seems apart from reality, and it feels as if we are intruders here,' muttered Yasmin as Faustus returned from relieving himself and hobbled over to sit by the palanquin and Haakon.

'Wish we had something stronger to drink,' Faustus said, grimacing as he lowered himself onto a rock.

'In the pack at the end of my bed there is a flask of brandy, Faustus,' Latasha said. 'Pass it round. It seems we could all do with some. The absence of animals here that you noted, Yasmin, has never been explained. Once these areas were home to an abundance of animals, but as our race dwindled following the Severing the animals that also called these mountains home simply died or went away. Once the very stones would obey our commands to move and the path we have tried to follow would open to reveal a road for those who meant Tinselthwain or its people no harm.'

Haakon stretched his back, trying to unwind the tight muscles there. 'Can we expect your kin to welcome us when we arrive?'

Latasha drank from the brandy then handed it to Faustus. She paused, looking out at the route ahead before she answered. 'Sadly, no. There are few if any of my people alive now, and I would be surprised to encounter any living being when we make it.'

Tek had unwrapped some sausage and bread slathered with a sweet jam, and as they ate they joked with one another, trying to raise the mood.

Faustus turned to Latasha passing her some sausage in bread. 'You are the only ancient I have seen in my sixty-five cycles. Yet when I read the histories you were a thriving race before the Severing, so why are your numbers so few now?'

Haakon put a hand on her arm then clasped her hand. 'You don't have to answer this, dear one, I know it causes you pain.'

'Haakon, it's about time I stopped being so secretive with your people. If I want them to understand me, then I must tell them what happened to my people.' A chill ran over her body, or was it a tremble? Drawing her shawl tight around her shoulders, Latasha began.

'Like all the races, the ancients were to blame for the Severing. We were the world's sacred guardians, created to protect the Mother, so our betrayal of her was the worst out of all the races. Many of my kin lost sight of their sacred duties while chasing power, wealth, or whatever they came to desire. Our younger generations mixed with man and the celestials or Infernals, and they changed. They were no longer satisfied with defending nature and striving to maintain the balance of the world's powers.

When I helped unleash the Severing, there were nine of us magi. I was the only ancient present. I had approached my people many times to share with them our plans, and each time I was forbidden to go ahead on threat of being put to death. You see, the ancients are tied by magic to the world, and we need magic to procreate. Without it our race cannot continue. I have not set eyes on one of my kind since that day I damned my kin to possible extinction, but I made my choice: the world or my people, and I must live with that every day. The truth is I have no idea how many of my kin now live, but there is real possibility we will meet any survivors within Tinselthwain.'

The way onwards became easier as they descended a long, sloped trail that wound down into a ravine. When they camped at dusk that night they were in sight of a huge, rusted gate covered in what looked like fungus or lichen. The cular mounts refused to enter this area, hissing and slapping their tails. They were forced to unleash the beasts then send them off back the way they came, much to Haakon's disappointment since it meant more equipment would have to be discarded.

'That's far from reassuring if the beasts are set on edge in this place,' grumbled Yasmin as they watched them speed away.

The gate was built into the side of the mountain itself, and they all agreed to spend one more night here under the stars before entering this forgotten place. They set up camp amongst the white stone rubble.

Faustus and Haakon's other men bedded down, choosing to escape to their world of dreams rather than stay awake in this alien place and its oppressive silence. Latasha had reassured them that there would be no need to set a guard, which had left them even more on edge until Haakon suggested he wasn't tired and would stay awake to repair his equipment. He wanted to be able to watch over Latasha as she made the final preparations before she could enter this sacred place of her people.

He sat sharpening his sword as Latasha prayed over a bowl of water. He had removed her from the palanquin at her request, placing her on the hard ground before the gate. She removed her tunic and sat facing away from him with the firelight bathing her pale back. In flickering light as she moved her arms slowly above her head in a hypnotic pattern, he continued to watch the surreal scene that was unnerving but also had a beauty to it that truly spoke of her connection to this place. Haakon realized that very few men could say they had witnessed such a thing with their own eyes, and he felt at once humbled and honoured by just being present.

As the chimes passed and as his companions slept, Haakon began smoothing out the burrs to keen edges on his blades. He must have drifted off and later could only faintly remember Latasha pulling a blanket over him and curling up against his body.

Chapter 26

Dalwyn glided through the foundation vortex to bask in the red glow as he drove the connection deep into the earth, not waiting for the familiar feelings of connectedness to come over him. The deep meditation where he had spent over a chime had prepared him for the longer journey up through the earth vortices, and there was no space for the ego or thoughts of the self if this journey was to be a success.

He shot through the second vortex known as the home of identity as orange light blazed around his form, and in that moment his spirit soared free in the knowledge life owed him no debt and it was enough to exist free from expectation.

Next, he approached the glittering palace of the third vortex swirling in bright yellow, and unlike ever before it opened to his clarity and lack of ego, sending him surging through a glimmering tunnel and infusing him with energy, leaving him fearless and undeterred with obstacles.

His eyes cleared and settled on his first sight of the golden astral river that allowed travellers to be carried off to places in the past or present. Dalwyn was swept up in its flow, and it shot him forward towards a portal of green light, the fourth vortex named the unbound, which would give him the energy to traverse time and distance in the past or present. He lost sight of the green portal as the surge from the golden river of light washed over him again, and he was spinning away uncontrollably.

Dalwyn stood before the gates of Karfael. The city's spires rose majestically into the clouds, bands of energy flickered across the gates in front of him. Was this a phantasm or illusion, or had he managed to move into the past to stand here before the gates to his ancestral homeland? The gates opened inwards, revealing a road lined with people. His people, welcoming him back. A disc holding an ivory-skinned woman floated forward towards Dalwyn, and he knew her. Krell, an arch magi of his lineage.

The disc stopped to hover before Dalwyn as Krell looked him over. She was beautiful, with full lips, long eyelashes and copper hair that swirled about her face like snakes. The smell of sunflowers assaulted Dalwyn, and Krell's eyes drew his gaze to them even as he fought silently against it. He struggled to visualize the image of the third vortex, the palace of jewels. Something fell away from his form, leaving him free again to look where he wanted, which let him see the thing before him for what it truly was.

It wasn't Krell, his ancestor, but a thin, squatting creature with tendrils of darkness arching from its back and with screaming mouths on its skin all talking at once in a babble of languages, beckoning him with promises. Dalwyn pulled his energy back into him, allowing the scene before him to bleed back into his being; everything else collapsed and fell away. The impostor before him wailed then burst apart, and Dalwyn was back in the river allowing it to pull him back through to the orange of the self, soothing the troubled thoughts and then down slowly into red and his body again.

The journey had drained him considerably since this was the first time he had approached the fourth vortex and he was unable to rise from his meditative state for some time. When he did, the stiffness in his body took time to work out before he was able to walk again. Dalwyn had met his first psychic attacker in the astral, and even though he was heartened by the progress he had made he remained frustrated at falling short of the fifth vortex.

From her bed Nina watched Dalwyn's prone form foam at the mouth and shudder. She knew he was travelling and so his body was vulnerable, which just showed how complacent he had become with her being around. Nina rose and padded across the stone to his bed and reached down to grasp one of the plump pillows from the floor.

Kneeling on the bed beside Dalwyn, Nina felt the sweat on her palms and her dry mouth. He was nasty and more evil than Zacriel, and he hated her. If she wasn't so important to Zacriel, then Dalwyn would have killed her already. Except now she held Dalwyn's life in her hands and could end him. The pillow lowered, and Nina pushed down on it so it covered Dalwyn's head. There was less resistance than she had expected, and his body's movements began to slow.

With a cry, Nina pulled away the pillow from Dalwyn's face. She couldn't do it. She wanted to so much, but to take someone's life was wrong, and so just like when she had let Ezekiel Perdomo live, Nina let Dalwyn live.

This was what Zacriel had referred to as her weakness. Placing the pillow beneath Dalwyn's head, Nina pulled up the blankets around his still form, noticing how nice and kind he looked while sleeping.

From below Nina came the sound of footsteps on the stairs. She quickly moved away from the bed and stood by the table, watching the entrance. Muffled talking from below, and then the footsteps continued upwards. Whoever it was had been given the go ahead from Dalwyn's guards.

Rapture's huge form cast terrifying shadows as he entered the chamber. 'Come, Nina, the bone lord awaits.'

Nina took a last look at Dalwyn's resting form in the bed, grabbed her cloak and shoes, and then followed Rapture down past the guard room and into the castle. They continued down through the empty stone halls and past a busy kitchen to the stables where Zacriel sat looking out over Arrowhead Lake, one hand casually petting Midnight, his lunar mount.

Nina gave a squeal and ran forward to hug the beast, which turned to regard her, antennae whirling.

'Midnight! I have missed you so much! Have you missed me?'

The two regular saddles had been fitted as if ready for flight, and Nina turned expectantly to Zacriel and Rapture, who stood watching her.

'Where are we going, Zacriel?'

'Well that would ruin the surprise, Nina. You will see soon enough. Climb on and strap yourself in.'

With powerful strokes Midnight lifted and carried them up past the sky walk before dipping back downwards. As memories of that long flight from Illume to Acclaro with Zacriel flooded back, Nina's laughter bubbled out uncontrollably.

As the ground hurtled closer, Nina grasped Zacriel's waist tightly and could hear his exultant hoots. Their route carried them around the edge of the city with their appearance, causing shouts of alarm that turned to cheers as they went. When they circled down it was to a building Nina had never seen before but sat mostly intact from the city takeover.

Midnight landed in a courtyard with trees hung with soft lights and a grassy area with wooden seats. A door to the building stood open and an elderly man beckoned to her as she jumped down off the Lunar's back.

'Girl, follow me. I am Merilla the librarian, and this is my pride and joy. Your kind master has bid me to help you to find books you wish to read.'

Nina was so happy she let the comment about Zacriel being her master slip, and with a smile at Zacriel she jumped down and ran though the doorway leaving Merilla to catch up.

Nina scoured the hallways lined with bookshelves. She fell asleep while perusing a heavy volume about the denizens of the astral plane. Zacriel scooped her up in his arms, and in her sleep she turned and wrapped an arm around his neck before snuggling closer. *It feels good to have someone hold you*, he thought before realizing Merilla was smiling goofily at him.

'Looks like the child has a place in your heart, lord. Value that, my lord, it's a rare thing.'

Zacriel flicked through the volumes Nina had selected. He hadn't even known the child could read. There were some children's books of fantastical tales, but besides them many of the selected volumes had a common subject matter, the astral plane. Why would Nina even be interested in that? Then he remembered Nina mentioning Dalwyn wanted them.

'Merilla, have the books Nina selected bought up to the castle in the morning for her to read.'

Zacriel carried Nina back and strapped her into her saddle; as an added precaution he tied her wrists around his waist taking care not to burn her skin. Back at the castle Zacriel carried Nina to the tower himself. The guards let him in, and he quietly lay her in her bed before turning to leave.

'A midnight sortie with your toy?'

'It's not like that and you know it, old man. Heck, even you have taken a shine to her,' retorted Zacriel.

'The next time you enter my chambers uninvited, there will be problems,' Dalwyn's fists were clenched and a vein throbbed from his temple as he moved close to Zacriel.

Zacriel laughed. 'Even your men refuse to stop me, Dalwyn, and maybe you forget where you are. I will not let you keep Nina away from me any longer. Until we have the final piece of information we need then we are of use to each other, but don't make the mistake that I won't kill you if you push me!'

Dalwyn snorted then nodded at Zacriel. 'Fair point, Zacriel. It's my impatience coming through. I want to leave this city and can feel time slipping away, but you are right that I can't take it out on you or Nina. I awoke to an empty chamber and the guards told me you came for Nina, which made me wonder…'

'Wonder what, Dalwyn? Whether I had stolen the child from you, is that what you are implying? I may be a monster, but I won't tolerate or be accused of stealing a child that belongs to neither of us!'

Zacriel only realised he had been shouting when he heard Nina's sleepy voice.

'What's going on Zacriel? Dalwyn?'

'Nothing, Nina we were just talking and forgot you were trying to sleep. Lie back down. I was just leaving.'

Nina was still sleeping when late the next morning a knock came at the door and Dalwyn who was listening to the growing concerns of his men's safety in the city answered the door.

Three muscled brutes pushed past him and carried large bags up to the table in his and Nina's chamber.

'What is this?'

'Books that the young one chose to have bought up here for her reading. I will leave them here, Lord Dalwyn.'

Dalwyn nodded his approval, already leafing through the many books that now lay piled on the table. *Denizens of the astral, The astral lords and the river, Lessons of a magi, The Severing* and many more, but why would Nina choose these which were way beyond her childish intellect? He waded through the others and found all of them were on the astral world or the Severing. He stopped and turned to look at Nina regarding him from where she sat by the window. 'How do you know about these books Nina?'

'I don't. I just told the librarian to bring any books on the astral world which you talk about so much these days.'

Sitting down, Dalwyn began to peruse one of the volumes and was soon lost in the search for the one secret that would help his astral travelling. Nina sat on her usual spot of the window ledge watching silently, wanting nothing more than to run over and immerse herself as well. It would be a bad thing, she decided, if Dalwyn should find out her little secret, and so she padded over to the table and pretended to ruffle through the books before selecting one tome called *Landscape of the Vortices, a Guide to Astral Ascension* and hid it beneath her blankets for later while Dalwyn was preoccupied.

Chapter 27

The next day around mid-morning Ishmael looked up from his cooking to see Diego and the woman with the fan again. Her laugh told him it was indeed Lucinda, who had dared to visit Diego here at work a few days earlier. He began to notice a pattern of their meetings: every three days, coinciding with the night markets that took over the town. On those days Ishmael would be dropped off by a guard but Diego would stay at the warehouse. On this day Diego pulled on a jacket and took one of the wagons with Lucinda beside him and left the warehouse.

As Ishmael turned away he saw Ramiro berating Seki, who was sluggishly striking rocks with a pickaxe in exhaustion. The small man then grabbed a push barrow of the debris to take inside the warehouse. He looked about to fall over at any moment, but sheer determination kept him going. Ishmael found himself painfully grasping the handle of the knife he was holding as his temper rose.

He watched on as Seki dumped the debris where Ramiro indicated, then Ramiro motioned for Seki to follow him farther into the warehouse out of Ishmael's sight in one of the aisles amongst large stacks of crates.

Ishmael continued to glance in that direction as he cooked; he noticed some of the other workers also looked concerned. Once he finished the immediate work of cutting up vegetables, Ishmael motioned to the guard Churl, who watched him every day. He had gained Churl's favour with his cooking and small talk as he was taken back to Diego's house when the monitor wasn't returning home.

Ishmael cleaned the knife blade with a cloth then rolled the blade in the front of his apron, concealing it along the waist band of his pants. He approached the guard with a hot mug of cocoa that the man loved. 'Churl, I need to get supplies; you don't need to escort me as I will just be a moment.'

Churl seemed about to question him, but Ishmael didn't wait for him. He pushed the cup of cocoa into Churl's hands and hurried away in the direction Ramiro had taken Seki. He knew something was wrong; he could feel it in his gut and berated himself silently for not realizing that Ramiro might take swift revenge on Seki. Ishmael and Seki had humiliated him in front of the other workers, which was something Ramiro would not let happen again.

Ishmael turned the corner down an aisle where Ramiro had gone, but there was no one in sight. He stopped, even holding his breath as he listened. A faint thumping came from up ahead, and as he walked he dreaded what he might find.

He found both of them in front of a heavy stack of crates at the back of the warehouse. Both men were stripped to the waist shaping up to each other. Seki was easily the smaller man, gaunt next to the bulk of Ramiro, whose aging muscle was beginning to turn to flab. Seki had blood streaming from a cut above his left eye that had swollen almost shut while Ramiro shuffled around him, grinning.

'C'mon, Seki I thought this was what you wanted, to have a crack at me. I guess you're not so tough now, are you?'

'Leave him alone, Ramiro, your argument is with me, not him,' said Ishmael, stepping into the narrow area.

Seki glanced over at Ishmael's arrival but kept his fighting stance. 'I got this, Ishmael; just let me go at him. He's had it coming a long time now.'

Not liking it but wanting to respect Seki's decision, Ishmael watched from the side.

Seki weaved as he moved. He was quick of foot as he snapped out punches, keeping Ramiro at bay who was the more patient fighter. Seki nimbly jumped in, connecting with a series of strikes to Ramiro's jaw that turned the man's head but nothing more.

Seki jabbed again, but this time Ramiro stepped in, catching his hand in one of his own then twisting the arm downwards hard. Seki was pulled inwards easily, allowing the bigger man to scoop him up in a body hug. Then Ramiro ran at the stacked crates behind Seki, smashing the small man into them. Seki fell to the ground in a heap with a groan as Ramiro stood back, chest heaving.

'Seki, you're done here. Pick your sorry ass up and leave. From this point on there is nothing here for you.' Ramiro bent to pick up his discarded shirt. Slapping the dust from it, he pulled it on over his head.

Then Seki was up and grasping Ramiro's shoulders. 'No, you can't do this to me, Ramiro, my family relies on this money. How can I feed them without this job?'

'There is no place here for those who cause trouble, Seki. Now get away from me!'

Ishmael stepped between the two men. 'Surely we can work something out, Ramiro. It's not too late.'

'Stay out of it, Yucca, your turn is coming soon enough.'

Seki uttered a terrible, maddening scream, then rushed past Ishmael, he drove his shoulder into Ramiro's back, which sent the foreman crashing into the wall of crates.

Ramiro hit hard as he fell. Cursing, he began to rise to his feet as unknowingly the crates above him teetered off balance then fell.

'Ishmael, watched; time slowed as he somehow managed to pull Seki back out of harm's way. 'Ramiro, look out!'

With a thump the crates fell on Ramiro burying him beneath the crates, spilling their contents of iron sword blades and shields. A wall of dust fell over the area.

Still holding onto Seki, Ishmael stumbled from the dust cloud before they both fell to their knees, coughing.

Footsteps came running. Moments later it was Churl with his blade drawn who appeared.

'What's going on, Yucca?'

'The foreman, there has been a terrible accident, it's Ramiro.'

Churl vanished into the wall of dust, and moments later his voice emerged. Don't just stand there Yucca, go get the other workers. We need to get the crates off him before he dies.'

All the workers helped to free Ramiro from the wreckage, but it was too late for the man. His body lay partially crushed and submerged in the ground by the force of the fallen crates. Many of the men uttered prayers to their gods, and even Ishmael found himself reciting a prayer to speed on Ramiro's troubled soul. 'May the light of Illume or whatever god your worship speed your soul's journey to its final destination.'

The workers carried the body outside as Ishmael watched them alongside Churl. They tied his hands together in the position of prayer over his chest then pinned his eyes open so he could see his path to the next world. His lips they sewed shut so his spirit wouldn't talk its way out of its final journey. Ishmael watched the strange ritual as it unfolded. The men, even though they had all hated Ramiro, moved with a calm, respectful solemnity that touched Ishmael deeply, bringing with it a wistful yearning for his old monastic life.

'What do we do now, Churl? '

'We shut down work. Diego will need to be informed, and a priest will be needed to perform the rites otherwise this place will be haunted by Ramiro's spirit. No work can be done until the proper ritual has been observed. The monitor won't be happy, but even he will follow this.'

Ishmael turned to walk away but was stopped by Churl calling his name. He turned to the big man, who eyed him questioningly.

'Like I said before, it was a terrible accident,' said Ishmael wearily. 'Ramiro had asked us to help him retrieve some stock for him. We had mentioned how dangerous the stacking has been down those aisles, but nothing was done about it.'

'Do you think you can fool me, Yucca? How am I to explain this death to the monitor so he believes it?'

'Like I said, an accident in which Seki was injured trying to save the man. The monitor is aware as much as we all are of the dangers down the back of those aisles. Tell Diego what you must, Churl; after all it is he you are working for. I was there and I saw the accident occur, so no doubt Diego will question me also. You have nothing to fear. There was nothing untoward about the whole unfortunate event.'

Once Diego arrived he spoke for some time alone with Churl. Soon after his arrival, a priest of the death jester arrived. He wore a faceless bone mask beneath a colourful outfit of a jester. A mirrored time glass pendant hung from around his neck that reflected the energies of the living so that the priest who was death's consecrated servant would not gather their lives as well as that of the deceased. It was a strange reminder to Ishmael that though he had been here for the last two turns of the calendar that he really knew nothing of the customs here.

Churl was ordered by Diego to drop off the workers, and the day's events made for a sombre journey. As usual he dropped Ishmael off last, notifying Fausto, who happened to be out the front of the house when they arrived. Churl left him shackled in the courtyard. There were still a few chimes before nightfall, so Ishmael used the time to meditate on his next move. The death of Ramiro was unexpected but left him with an opportunity he could maybe take advantage of.

His short reverie was broken by the sound of footsteps, and when he opened his eyes, Fajira was standing there with a bowl of food.

'You are back early without warning; it is as if you are my husband now,' she laughed without vigour. 'I certainly see more of you than Diego these days.'

Ishmael stood accepting the bowl with a nod. 'There was a death. It was Ramiro. Diego is there now with the priest, and since no more work can be done today I am here.'

Fajira sat quietly while Ishmael ate. It was good, filled with cooked vegetables and even some chicken, but better than anything it was hot. He needed something to wipe the chill off his bones that he had been feeling since the accident.

She graciously waited for him to finish before she spoke again.

'Ishmael, I am slowly losing my mind over my husband's prolonged absences. Without you telling me anything I still know as a wife does that Diego has another woman in his life. Just tell me if it's true. I don't have to tell Diego it was you who told me.'

'Ishmael paused as he thought over how to respond to Fajira. He knew he had to get moving since already he had been here over a month and still was missing the two crystal orbs along with his freedom.

'Fajira your thinking is correct. Diego is seeing another woman whom I have heard him call Lucinda.' He looked away at her gasp and hands clenched over her mouth as her fear was vocalized. 'They meet at the warehouse every three days, and sometimes Diego goes to one of the inns to meet her. I can help you catch them, but I need something in return: my freedom!'

When Fajira looked up at him again she was sobbing, so he let her cry herself out then gently touched her shoulder.

'Fajira, I need my freedom. It is too dangerous for you and your family to have me here. I don't expect you to understand my situation, but you know I have done no wrong to Diego. Did you know he was stealing my pay then sharing half with Ramiro, and that's what they do to new workers they can trap like they did to me. I don't care about the money or other belonging, but I must have the two crystals in my pack and be allowed to go on my way.'

Fajira nodded. 'You shall have your freedom in return for telling me when they next will meet and where.'

'Then sit, Fajira, while I tell you what I know.'

✦

Chapter 28

Cabre would never be called a beautiful city. The castle, nicknamed the Crag, squatted above the Seekers Road. The fact that it was an obsidian monstrosity that spilt out from it in an impressive sprawl helped make sure that the visage of this militant city remained unnerving and unforgiving; the exact feel that the rulers of Soarnestia wished to show. Every wall and, tower reflected strength and order, which flowed down to the very capable people of Soarnestia, who since the Severing had been recruiting others to their cause in order to fight off the legions of the Infernals when they next rose up in power. And now that day had come.

Zahra reflected on her options during the long ride to the city of Cabre. Unfortunately, she already knew they were limited. Ishmael was gone, and he was no longer the green boy that she had saved from the monastery of Illume. He had learnt hard lessons, and now he had evaded her. She had guessed right that he would go to the Seekers road, and this was at least confirmed when she had ingested wraith flower with Rin at Glimmersedge. The risk she had undertaken was something Zahra normally would have avoided, and she had nearly paid dearly just like Rin had. Ishmael had come through Brimmerland and Glimmersedge, then he had boarded the sand whip train towards the Godhead, but did he go straight there? The festival of gods was maybe a month away, so he could very well be wanting to wait for that, but Zahra thought not. She would wager that Ishmael, who saw this as a holy pilgrimage, would travel lightly, trying to find out if his goddess was alive.

It was a question that raised a lot of debate amongst the peoples of the world even so long after the Severing. Were the gods dead or gone, leaving their followers to fend for themselves? Once Ishmael had resolved this need, Zahra knew he would aim to fulfil his duties as one of the coterie, but to do this he would need to survive. She had been the one chosen to make sure Ishmael lived in order to fulfil that duty. It seemed to her that she was doing a terrible job of it, but rather than focus on this Zahra silently resolved to find and remove Ishmael before something truly terrible could happen to him.

The sand whip train stopped beneath the great castle. A huge, iron portcullis dropped to contain the sand whips and their passengers at the station. Outside, Zahra could see large numbers of guards mobilizing along the length of the carriages. The loud cries of the sand whips carried even as far back as Zahra's carriage. They were skittish creatures in confined spaces, Zahra thought and was thankful she was nowhere near the beasts.

It took over a chime for the guards to empty the train of passengers, and tempers began to fray. Zahra had tried twice to tell the stern soldiers that she had vital information from Whitman's Point, only to be told to wait her turn. The line ahead of Zahra was still considerable, and so she forced herself to wait patiently.

It seemed the Soarnestian guards too were at the limits of their own patience; Zahra watched many people were denied entrance to Cabre. Currently three merchants squabbled with the soldiers, who blatantly stated they didn't really care if the grain rotted before thoughtfully remembering that all such foodstuffs would be likely seized by the king as stockpile for the perceived upcoming war. Zahra used the time in line to come up with a plan so she could gain entrance to the city. She needed to contact the Kenzu spy network here to enlist their help in finding Ishmael.

An old guard waved Zahra forward as the unhappy merchants were bundled back onto the train.

'City is closed, miss, unless you are a resident with correct papers and family living within Soarnestia.'

'I hail from Brimmerland, sir, but in the days leading up to the fall of Acclaro I worked as a messenger to the king there, who as you may have heard is believed dead now that the infernals have taken the city from him. Within this scroll is valuable information gathered by the general at Whitman's Point. It was rejected at Brimmerland, so I am forced by my word and duty to Chez the fallen king to make sure this information gets to the correct hands. And that, sir, I believe, is your king.'

The guard reached for the scroll, which Zahra nimbly pulled back.

'No offence, sir, but I swore to pass this directly to your king or to hands that I know can be trusted to willingly see it happen.'

The man looked taken aback by Zahra's insistence but recovered well.

'And your business following its safe delivery?'

'"To continue on to the Godhead, sir, to warn the leaders there. It is imperative that the Infernals be stopped before they have time to get organized.'

'Well at least we agree on one thing, miss.'

Zahra was held there and forced to undergo a personal search from the wiry guard, and she removed all her weapons for him. The knives in her boots as well as her sword wrapped like a staff was turned over. He failed to find the garrotte in the waistline of her trousers as she watched on in a resigned manner as he then went through all of her belongings. He held up Moonbite before giving a low whistle.

'I never seen a sword like this in all my days. Where did you get this?'

Zahra bit back a rude retort, not wanting to anger the guard but keen to be on the way to the palace.

'You would never believe me if I told you.'

He stopped then turned to face her with a curious look.

'There's something about you that doesn't quite fit the courier type,' he said, continuing to inspect the crystal blade.

'That's the whole point, sir, to blend in and not bring any undue attention to myself. You know how it goes.'

'Well, that sword's got you all the attention you can deal with now…'

His words trailed off as she spoke over him. 'I was gifted the blade when travelling from Illume to Acclaro, it was from the harlequin.'

'The harlequin?' he repeated.

'That's correct, I won the sword by not losing a duel to one of their warriors.'

'Well, I'll be damned. That's quite a story, don't you think?'

Zahra saw the man make eye contact with two of the nearby guards who began moving towards Zahra.

The game was up, and Zahra knew it. She stepped over to pick up her sword, and the old man stepped in front of her. Without thinking Zahra rabbit-punched the man in the throat, not causing any real damage but enough to incapacitate him. She snatched up her pack as the cries of other guards rang out.

Before she left Zahra quickly stuffed the sealed scroll in the old guard's belt; there was no way she was going to the castle now. Too many guards were between her and the ramp, so Zahra hurried over to where the sand whips still huffed great clouds of dust. The two creatures were still agitated, and one huge head rolled around to regard her with one copper eye.

'I'm sorry,' said Zahra as she pulled a small vial of oil from her belt. She unstoppered it then flung the liquid into that deeply gazing orb. The sand whip roared then pulled back its long neck and thrashed its head towards Zahra.

Zahra leapt and rolled to the side to evade the huge head and gnashing teeth then ran for the ramp with everyone else as the other sand whip smashed the nearest carriage against the wall sending people flying from within it and causing great cracks to spread across the stone.

The loud screaming only worked the sand whips up more as people panicked and those still unlucky enough to be in the carriages fought to get off without being flung away by the thrashing of the two creatures.

Zahra leaped up onto the ramp that the soldiers at the winch were frantically trying to close. She dodged past them, becoming caught up in the movement of the crowd that pushed her along with it. Guards were now rushing the crowd from the top of the ramp, pushing through with body-length shields to deflect any unlucky people in the way. Zahra surged with the people near her, careening into each other as the soldiers forced their way past.

For a moment Zahra came face to face with a girl who seemed the only one besides herself to not be screaming. The girl regarded her coldly as they pressed against each other before they were knocked to the side. Someone near them cried out, but their gazes stayed on each other's face. As the crowd pushed again, Zahra was sent crashing into the girl, and she used her hands to brace herself between them.

The girl slammed her head down at Zahra's face, catching her on the cheekbone with a thud. Zahra's left hand chopped around as she pulled back again, aiming for the girls unprotected neck but only striking her lower on the shoulder. Zahra could now see the girl's arms were caught by the crowd around her and leant in from the side to her face.

'Who are you?' she whispered, and in reply a wad of spit smacked into her face. As Zahra wiped the spittle off she was pushed away again in the crowd that now flowed towards the entrance easily now the guards were past them. Trying to look behind her to the girl, she only managed to catch sight of her a few times, and each time the girl was staring right back intensely.

At last Zahra was free of the throng of people. She could feel her cheek beginning to swell, but so far it wasn't interfering with her sight, so she took off at a run.

Trumpets blared and riders raced passed Zahra towards the ramp area as Zahra made her way down to a cluster of homes near a small park complete with a white bench surrounded by a grove of coloured blooms. The cobblestones were slick with water, and farther up the road she saw a team of workers scrubbing the road with long brooms. After turning down a side road she paused at the corner huddling against the wall and looked back behind her where now the platform area was swarming with Soarnestian guards. The girl was gone now, but the short violent, meeting had managed to unnerve Zahra.

Zahra hurried into the lanes that ran between housing districts here to put more distance between herself and the commotion she had left behind. She came across a textile shop yard where clothes hung on long lines fluttering in the wind. She pulled herself up over a wooden fence, narrowly avoiding crashing down the other side on her face. Soon afterwards from the opposite of the yard a young man emerged onto the street in the tan colours of a labourer with a grey coat and a limp, walking slowly with the aid of a cane and tapping his way deeper into the city.

Once Zahra was happy she had evaded any of the local guard she discarded all of her disguise but for plain, tan clothes. Now she wandered down the bustling inner streets of Soarnestia frequented by haggling merchants and crowds vying for the best deals. Food stalls cloaked the street in delicious smells. As Zahra moved through the crowd, all the talk was already about the earlier events at the Seekers Road station beneath the castle.

'Hundreds dead, smashed to pieces by the sand whips, and those who were lucky enough to escape were cut down by the guard. It was the work of assassins here to murder the king.'

Zahra grimaced at that news, happy that they had the wrong idea but annoyed that leaving the city and continuing to the Godhead would be that much harder now.

Unable to ignore the delightful scents any longer, Zahra made her way to one of the quieter roadside eateries where people sat devouring pastries and drinking tea. First she needed to acquire local currency; she stumbled to bump into a noble lady in a gown of orange with sequined arms hardly appropriate to the weather.

'Oh my, apologies to you, lady,' Zahra said, dipping her head in acquiescence. She steadied the lady and removed a considerable coin purse from her bag, which had been knocked from her hands when Zahra fell into her.

'These darn shoes! The heel you see is almost broken right away and…'

'The lady looked down at her and cringed at Zahra's touch.

'Remove your arm from mine; who knows what a bedraggled one like yourself might be infested with.'

And with that the woman brushed past Zahra, who meekly looked down at her feet until she was alone. A great deal richer now, Zahra purchased her food and sat with her back to a large tree draped with chimes and harbouring a great many birds along its large boughs. She sat eating chocolate and custard pastries with a spiced tea topped with grated glint root to boost her energy, and for a short while the world seemed a fine place.

Zahra pulled out the bloodstained note that Klaus had given her that had the address of a known safe house that the clans used. Personally Zahra had never been one for safe houses. She preferred to avoid others in her line of work, especially from other clans wherever possible. Since the Kenzu had forsaken all other contracts to protect the coterie, the other clans who knew nothing of this had mocked them. Zahra could take others mocking her but would never sit idle while they mocked clan lord Haakon, who had given her a life.

Chapter 29

The next morning it was Churl who came to take Ishmael to work. Churl was a quiet man who preferred silence to spouting incessant rubbish, which suited Ishmael well since it gave him another short nap before they arrived at the warehouse. He wondered as they rode when Diego would confront him over Ramiro's death. As if to reassure himself, Ishmaels, hand went to his pocket where he could feel the scroll. Ishmael knew it was just a matter of time. Today fresh caravans would arrive with the supplies for the town, which Ishmael would deliver to the inns along the main road. As it turned out, Diego was at the warehouse when they arrived.

Ishmael helped unload the heavy wagons, then he split the deliveries up amongst the inns before starting to reload the wagon they would drive into town. With a grunt he threw the last bag of potatoes onto the wagon, happy that it was the last of the heavy stock. As he finished wiping the sweat from his face, he drank deeply from a water skin. He saw Diego come from the office to motion him over.

The office was unusually messy with papers strewn across the room, and the monitor's clothes were stained with sweat and food. As Diego motioned for Ishmael to go inside, he could see the monitor's face was face creased with the strain he was under. Ishmael followed him into the office, where Diego slumped into the chair before regarding Ishmael standing quietly in front of him.

'Do you wish for me to clean up in here, monitor?'

'I didn't call you in here for that, Yucca. You already know what I want from you, don't you?'

Ishmael wiped his damp hair back off his forehead.

He reached into his pocket, retrieving the letter and held it out to Diego.

'Before I share my version of events, monitor, your wife wanted you to have this since you didn't return home last night.'

Diego read the letter silently, his head shaking slowly from side to side and his brow creasing.

'Damn this family. As if I don't have enough to do already. It would seem Yucca that our talk will have to wait even longer. Ramiro was a good man that will be hard to replace. Do your deliveries, then later we will talk.'

Ishmael hurried back to the wagon Seki was leaning against as Churl secured the cular's reins.

'What did he say, Ishmael?'

'We still haven't talked. Some important business has called him away for the rest of the morning.'

'He spoke to me, you know? Kept trying to trap me with his questions to see if you had killed Ramiro. I told him it was nobody's fault, but I know he has you pinned for the blame, so be careful, my friend.'

'Stop worrying, Seki, the monitor is going to have his hands very full soon.'

'What do you mean by that?' Seki called after him as he climbed into the wagon seat alongside Churl. The stocky guard handed Ishmael the reigns, regarding him suspiciously.

'What were you two taking about back there?'

'Is it a crime to talk now, Churl?'

'No crime, Ishmael, but I've been told to watch you to see if you are conspiring against the monitor, so from now on cut the whispered chats around me.'

Ishmael raised an eyebrow at the guard.

'So do you think I am planning something?' Before the man could answer Ishmael continued. 'Because I sure know easier ways to get at him.'

'Is that a threat, Yucca?'

Ishmael sighed then whistled to set the beasts off on the road with their long gurgling bleats. 'I am not threatening anybody just saying that for hell's sake I'm the man's cook so if my intention was to harm Diego I would have just poisoned him!'

The short drive took them first to a rowdy tavern called Elms Tankard with a colourful sign showing a buxom lady licking the side of a silver tankard. The tavern was open for business even at this early chime of the day. Ishmael had heard the other workers talk of the steady string of bards willing to play for their night's stay and a meal and that it was a favourite for the locals of Glimmersedge.

Churl banged the metal stopper hard enough that Ishmael expected the handle to break off. When the door opened, it was the owner's son who also doubled as the security for the establishment. He looked like he had been dragged from the grave and was none too happy about it.

'What, you again? You get earlier each time. I'm in a good mind to talk to Diego about this,' he said to a stone-faced Churl.

In response the large guard casually pushed the man aside. 'Not if you don't want your father to know about the early morning parties you throw with the whores. Now stay out of our way, we have work to do.'

After that initial delay the unloading took half a chime before they were off to a second classy establishment called The Swinging Derriere. Lucinda who Ishmael had seen at the warehouse with Diego was the owner of the place that was known to provide only the highest quality of food and wines. As on each day they delivered here, the servants were waiting for them to get the unloading done so they could finish their work for the morning.

Ishmael loaded his arms with a box of sweets that the late Ramiro received each month by a sweetheart. They were a fine, delicate collection that Ishmael ached to taste, but they were needed for this part of his plan to fall together. He took the sweets along with the scroll from his pocket then entered the busy kitchen, dodging through muttering cooks with silent apologies as he reached the stairs leading up to the main room.

Cook Delsa sat there seemingly oblivious to the frantic chaos below in her kitchens as she sat calmly having a pot of tea.

'There you are, dove face,' Ishmael crooned, moving to sit opposite her. 'I barely survived crossing your kitchen, you know?'

Delsa chuckled then sat her cup back down on the saucer. 'Stop, you idiot, you will make me spill my tea. Now what possesses you to disturb an old lady like this on her break?'

'Old lady. I bet you could outdo many of your younger workers. They seem to have extensive girths, unlike you. Why is that?'

'Well a lady has to stay trim, you know, since I am required to greet the customers.' She leaned forwards conspiratorially. 'The secret, young Ishmael, is simply to taste each dish once without ever going back to it.'

Ishmael removed a small wooden container the size of his palm from his jacket.

'Whatever have you got there?' she asked.

He removed the lid, revealing a pearly cream that smelt faintly of sage. 'This, Delsa, is a cream I learned to make while in Illume. I made it for your bad hip. It won't fix the problem you have, but it will give you more mobility and warm the joint up, allowing blood flow in.' He pushed the container across the table towards her.

Delsa ignored it, picked her cup up, and drank slowly before looking at him over the rim.

'So what do you want from me, then?'

'Just deliver these to Lucinda for me.' He held up the sweets box with the scroll tied to it. 'But she must not know who sent it, Delsa, all right?'

'If this is something to hurt Lucinda I will not do it. I owe her my life!'

'What kind of monster do you think I am? There is nothing to injure her. I give you my word, and you may just get a pleasant surprise from all this.'

'Sit then and tell me all the juicy bits.' Delsa motioned for him to sit again then poured tea for both of them as Churl stomped up to them, looking at Ishmael questioningly.

'We are only through two of the six inns, Yucca, and I find you here sipping tea like a lord?'

'Oh, get ya head out from your ass, Churl, I gave him no choice but to sit with me, now come with m.' Delsa rose smoothly, grasped Churl by the arm then escorted him back to the stairs shouting out in a deep voice as they went. 'Tess, get Churl here his favourite pastry and don't let him back up here. I have things to discuss with Ishmael.'

She sat opposite Ishmael with a wide grin that shook the cycles away, giving a hint of the beauty she had once been blessed with. 'Now where were we?'

When they resumed their deliveries, Churl turned on Ishmael who sat alongside him.

'You are well aware of the need for haste, so why do you have to cause me so much grief, Yucca?'

'I am sorry, Churl but she is forever trying to get me to stop and discuss life in Illume. Today she would not accept no for an answer. Anyhow you got a pastry, it's still caked around your mouth.'

The big man wiped his face with a sleeve then looked back at him.

'The pastry was very good, but no more delays today. We simply cannot afford it.'

The Sacred Veil was the next stop and a small place where secrecy of the patron's identities was top of the menu. Even the servants whom Ishmael had tried several times to converse with never offered small talk or could be baited into discussing anything about themselves or the Veil.

The fourth inn was a five floored house filled with dormitories called the Tinted Pickle complete with street food for those who dared brave the cheapest produce that they bought from Diego. They dumped the supplies by the entrance, which was usual, then set off for the quarter-chime drive to the next inn called The Vision, which Ishmael had to concede was the best of the lot.

The walls were white stone with a large, domed ceiling of glass brought in from Trystland where the Godhead was located. The place was a chapel devoted to all gods where no weapons were accepted or violence. Those who stayed beneath its starry rooftop were housed in small alcoves for sleeping. There always came songs of worship from all corners of the world, day and night, and Ishmael had often annoyed Churl until the man stopped to allow Ishmael to listen for a while in wonder. There was none of that this day since they were in a hurry.

The last delivery was to a the roadside inn called Gods' Home that creaked and strained under its wooden towers that swayed above the road while the bottom story was a tavern where the serving staff dressed as gods and goddesses.

They arrived back to the warehouse just over two chimes after they started. The large pot of stew he had left simmering now bubbled away, releasing its delicious aroma across the worksite. *How long do I have?* Ishmael thought, knowing this was all going to come down to timing. Lunch was served and all the while Ishmael mentally hurried the monitor to return. He had just finished cleaning the preparation area when Diego rode in on a beautiful horse with ash grey spots across its white flanks.

Ishmael had little knowledge of horses but enough to know that the steeds that were only naturally found in Cavere fetched a small fortune for their speed. The beast was magnificent as it stamped its hoofs and snorted at its new surroundings. Diego tied its reigns to a post, and Ishmael moved to his side to look the horse over.

'Diego, where did you find such a glorious beast?'

'A gift from me to Fajira. He is in his prime or so I'm told but I never expected it to be so tall.'

'He is a fine gift, Diego, where did you find it?'

'Diego was about to reply when behind them came a squeal of delight. They turned to see Lucinda struggling towards them in a cream dress that fanned out at the bottom, exposing pale legs. Diego's mouth actually fell open, though Ishmael suspected not at the sight of her fine body but at her untimely arrival.

'Oh, Diego, you know I love horses but I never guessed you would actually buy me one.'

She threw herself into his arms, kissing him deeply.

'Lucinda, what are you doing here?'

Lucinda laughed heartily then kissed him again.

'Don't be rude, Diego, we both know our little meetings here are seen by your men. So then why continue with the secrecy? Now what should I name him?'

'Lucinda! About the horse…, well… you see…'

'You don't need to explain yourself, silly man, just come with me.' She half dragged Diego into his office, leaving the horse with Ishmael who was smiling now that the first step had fallen into place.

He brought water for the horse along with some apples and carrots he found, then he went to work with the others who were doing maintenance on all the carts. Ishmael had barely raised a sweat when as he had previously organized, Fajira arrived dressed in pants with a bone corset beneath a snowy shawl over the top. She looked nothing like the mother whom he usually saw doing everyday chores. Churl, who stood nearby, hurried over to stand between Fajira and the door.

'Miss Fajira, your husband is currently unavailable and still attending to urgent business from this morning.'

Fajira rounded on him in anger.

'It's bad enough my husband treats me like a fool without you also doing it, Churl! My husband has sent for me to get my birthday gift you see which is why Diego had to rush off this morning, but I know he's here now and I want to surprise him.'

Churl groaned as she stalked past, and Ishmael felt sorry for the guard with whom he had become friends.

Fajira pushed through the bead curtain to disappear into Diego's office, leaving Ishmael and Churl standing there listening for her reaction at what they both knew she would find.

There was a curse then a crash as something broke, followed by screams then sobbing.

'Fajira, what are you doing here? Put the knife down, you have already cut her. Just put the knife down so we can talk about this.'

'Oh my god, she stabbed me, Diego! Stop her, she's crazy, I'm bleeding. You told me she never comes here, you asshole.'

'Come here, you bitch, Fajira screamed. Do you think I didn't know about the little meetings you two plan? I thought you of all people would be above this, Lucinda, considering all the help we gave you when your husband died of the fever last cycle. So this is how you repay the Vorm family's honour?'

'Wife, you overreact as usual. Lucinda is here to organize festivities for the merging of the moons late this month, nothing else.'

'So how does that explain her mouth on your dick, you stupid ass? I'm done, Diego, you can have your little bitch, but Fausto will be returning with me to the Vorm residence in the Godhead as soon as we can. You have thrown all we have away for this young whore. How can I even be near you anymore?'

More screaming, and then Lucinda half fell out of the door. Her dress was torn, leaving her bare to the waist, showing a cut across the right breast bleeding freely turning the dress a rusty red. She staggered to her feet as Fajira came out behind her, smashing a fist into Lucinda's stomach and doubling her over with a groan.

'Please, no more, Fajira, please,' wailed Lucinda as she lay curled on the ground.

Diego came out with his shirt undone. He grabbed Fajira by the shoulders as she went to kick Lucinda, and she turned on him.

'Don't you touch me ever again, Diego, you are dead to me. Dead, I say!'

Diego grabbed Fajira by the shoulders and shook her. 'Don't say that, Fajira. It was a mistake and will never happen again. I give you my word.'

'Your word means nothing to me,' she replied. 'Now at least I know who has been sharing your bed while your family sat home wondering where their husband and father were.' Fajira was crying now.

'On my birthday, you bastard. I hope you suffer from this.'

Diego held her by the shoulders now. 'I'm sorry, so sorry, Fajira. She means nothing to me. Here, let me show you your gift.' He started to lead his crying wife to the fine horse he had ridden in earlier.

'You said the horse was for me, Diego, not her you lying sack of shit! Screamed Lucinda. She rose to her feet, trying to hide her breasts with her arms from the gaze of all the workers.'

Diego turned slowly to face Lucinda. 'Of course it's not for you, Lucinda, I tried telling you that but you come here still expecting we can be together. Just leave, Lucinda, just go away.'

Lucinda covered her sobs with a hand. 'I was warned about your devilish ways, Diego, but I still chose to give you a chance, and you do this to me?'

Fajira turned back to Lucinda from where she stood near the stallion.

'He is your problem now, Lucinda, and mark my words everyone will know of your betrayal.'

Then Fajira beckoned to Ishmael who came to her side. 'Ishmael, help me up before I collapse.' He linked his hands for her to boost herself up onto the stallion's back.

'Fajira, don't leave we can sort this problem out, just don't do anything foolish,' called Diego after her.

In answer Fajira kicked her heel against the beast's flanks with a 'Yah!' and they raced out of the warehouse with Diego running after her in the cloud of dust.

He emerged a moment later looking defeated. Lucinda ran over to him. She had pulled her dress up to cover herself, and her hands were sticky with her own blood.

'Diego, I'm dying, I need help.'

'He turned on Lucinda, grasping her hands in his.

'You are not dying, you stupid whore, now leave and never come back. It's over now.' He turned to Churl. 'Churl, I need to go after Fajira to settle her down. You finish up here with the workers.'

Diego started off after Fajira on one of the empty wagons, turning haunted eyes on Ishmael as he drove away. That look told Ishmael that Diego had not forgotten him and the promised confrontation that was coming.

'Diego, Diego don't leave me here.' Lucinda collapsed to the ground, pulling at her hair and screaming, which then subsided into sobs.

Ishmael walked to the girl then helped her to her feet. She seemed to have entered a state of shock and allowed him to lead her to the office, where he sat Lucinda down.

'Lucinda, I need to check the cut to see if you are going to need a healer.' He gently tugged her dress down on the one side, showing where Fajira had cut the girl but not exposing her breast. The cut was clean and would need a stitch or two, so it was all he could do to bandage the injury as best as he could.

Churl came into the office, his brow furrowed in concern. He poured himself a measure of brandy from a decanter, offering it to Lucinda, who gulped it down with a cough. He offered one to Ishmael, who refused, so he chugged it down himself.

'Ishmael, you will come with me to return Lucinda to her home. I have left Seki in charge here until we come back. Go get the cart, the less anyone knows about this the better.'

They coaxed Lucinda up onto the cart seat as she still seemed to be in shock and stared ahead seeing something neither of them could.

The trip to The Swinging Derriere was uneventful. Lucinda stayed in her lost state, occasionally muttering: 'He said he loved me.'

Once there Ishmael escorted her inside, calling for Delsa. When the cook saw Lucinda her smile dropped away.

'My lady, what has happened to you?'

The arrival of her friend awoke Lucinda from her fugue state.

'Oh, Delsa, he lied to me. He doesn't love me. I know that now.'

Delsa took the girl in her arms. 'There, there, my girl, it's all going to be all right, you're safe now. Shelby, take Lucinda upstairs to the bathing room and send for the healer to come see her wound. I will be up shortly.'

When Lucinda had disappeared upstairs, the matronly woman turned on Ishmael poking one thick finger against his chest.

'You said she would come to no harm, Ishmael.'

'I gave you my word, Delsa, and I kept it. Fajira showed up at the warehouse and caught Lucinda with Diego, and as you can see Fajira didn't take it well. I think Lucinda may have learnt a hard lesson just now.'

'I will make sure she keeps clear of him, don't you worry about that. Now off with you,' said Delsa who was on the verge of tears at the state of her lady. 'I have to see to Lucinda.'

Back on the cart with Churl, Ishmael felt no joy at the success of the little plan he had hatched up with Fajira. They both had gotten what they needed, but the victory felt empty to him. He had wanted to see Diego get hurt for all the pain the man had caused him, but he should have foreseen the pain it would put Fajira and Lucinda through. It was just lucky that Fajira had only managed a shallow cut to Lucinda or this whole event could have led to murder.

When he arrived back at the warehouse the other workers were just finishing off their jobs for the night market, which was already being set up throughout the main street of town. No doubt the story of the events here today would spread throughout Glimmersedge like wildfire and all would know of the dishonour Diego had bought his family. There was one thing left for Ishmael to do now, and that was find the crystals then leave this place. Fajira had promised him that she would remove the debt he had to her family as one of the conditions she would force on Diego.

Seki wandered over to Ishmael as they were getting ready to close the warehouse up.

'I just had word from one of the street vendors that the town guard are looking for Fajira. Lucinda has decided to make her answerable to the assault on her. Just be aware that you may be in danger, Ishmael. Diego will be looking for someone to blame.'

Ishmael clapped the smaller man on the back. 'I will be fine, Seki. Soon I will leave this place to continue my journey to the Godhead. Diego has no reason to keep me here any longer, supposed debt of honour or not. I can no longer afford to be stuck here as Diego's whipping boy.'

They clasped hands, then both climbed onto the cart to head home. With the sun sinking, Ishmael momentarily shivered as they set off. Despite his optimistic words, he just couldn't shake the feeling that something was not right.

Chapter 31

After the strange pair of visitors arrived at the castle in Acclaro, Nina saw less of Dalwyn, who was up before dawn each day and back after dark. Now they were moving her to another tower to be guarded by Dalwyn's flame warriors. The only good thing about the change was she had a whole room at the top of the tower to herself without stupid old Dalwyn. Nina knew this had something to do with the two visitors. *Who were those people anyway?* Nina thought as she waited for the servants to bring all her things. Stuck all the way up here with no company meant that Nina must have the one thing she wouldn't go without. Books. It had been a magical experience to wander the wide halls of the library for chimes without rushing, and Nina had been very annoyed when Dalwyn refused to let her have any of the books she had returned with.

Nina followed the flame warriors through the barred gate at the tower's base and knew she was a prisoner now. Deep inside Nina knew Zacriel would never allow this, and so she concluded he didn't even know. The same stairs up past one chamber with two rooms for sleeping and then to a third at the tower's top, which was even higher than her previous room with Dalwyn. At the top Nina saw a large bed bundled with pillows and thick rugs. At its base sat a chest with a rolled canvas and scroll.

The note read; Nina here are new clothes and things I thought you may need. I will call upon you soon. I thought you might like this too.' Nina carefully unrolled the canvas, squealing in delight at the vibrantly painted picture of herself on Midnight. So Zacriel did know.

An old lady with a hump on her upper back hunched ambled into the chamber grimacing and stood before Nina. As she waited she stole, short nervous glances in the direction of the flame warrior near her.

'What is it?'

'What food do you want, Miss Nina?'

'The usual, thanks.'

'So nothing cooked then? You need meat, Miss Nina.'

'Meat makes me sick now and I don't know why, so just bread, fruit, and steamed vegetables, and maybe some marmalade. I do so love that.'

'As you wish, Miss Nina,' said the woman.

The day passed with no visitors, and the gurgle of her belly made Nina wonder what had become of her food. To pass the time Nina sat on the window ledge reciting the vortices names, functions, and how to strengthen or weaken each one. The droning words became like a meditation for her, and to Nina it seemed very important to learn all she could about the vortices now her access to the books had come to an abrupt end. Memories of her family seemed less clear now, and dreams of their deaths no longer kept her awake at night. These days she slept like a baby now that her astral work was strong enough to create an energetic base for her physical form, which was what one of Dalwyn's books said. All it meant to Nina was she could fly through another world that was exciting but very dangerous too, and so far Nina didn't dare try anything without making sure she knew what was going to happen. She did realize how strong her body here in the world was becoming now her astral body was stronger too. Amazing that people actually had two bodies but most of them didn't even know that or if they did, how to strengthen the astral one.

If the cooks had of been wondering why she demanded only fresh food pulled from the earth, no one had mentioned it. Maybe they were just used to her demands now. It had started to become a game for her now to ask for increasingly difficult things and wonder if the slaves or the Infernals could provide it for her.

The sound of the great wooden door opening into her chamber as it grated on the stone floor gave Nina long enough to climb off the ledge. Even though Nina had access only occasionally to bathing and clean clothes she smoothed her hair, hoping she looked good. Her ma had always said, 'No matter what, Nina, always do your best to look presentable.'

A girl dressed in the white servant livery entered with a stacked tray of food. She looked a little older than Nina and had jaggedly cut orange hair that framed her freckled face. Her eyes were sad and pale blue like faded sky.

'Lady Nina, here are some of the things you asked for.' She stopped to gather breath then continued. 'There sure are a lot of stairs to get here. Down the bottom of the stairs are writing implements and ink as well as your own scrolls and some books, too which I will bring up too in a moment. Sweat dappled the girl's face, and Nina felt sorry for her but elated that she was to get books after all.

'What is your name?'

'Trin, Lady Nina.'

'Trin, I am not a lady, I am younger than you, ten cycles but soon eleven.' She looked at Trin expectantly.

'I am twelve cycles, Nina.'

'Here, Trin have some water. It's yummy and has lemon and mint in it. Have you ever tried it?'

The girl shook her head no then smiled shyly when Nina offered her a glass.

'Thank you, Nina.

Wow! This is a big room. Why are you so special?'

'I'm not special, I'm just like you, but Zacriel wants to be my friend even if he does let mean old Dalwyn keep me locked away like a prisoner.'

'Zacriel, is he the horrible-looking infernal?'

'I guess so, but he doesn't look horrible to me anymore, and he tries to be nice to me,' said Nina taking Trin's hands in hers. 'I must be lucky because I have seen some bad things he has done to other people.'

'What, Trin, why are you sad?'

'They never let me have time to do anything or have books. I am a slave now that my parents are dead. Nobody cares what I think.'

My parents are dead too, so I know how terrible that is. I'm going to ask Zacriel if you can stay here with me and be my personal servant.' Nina looked around with wide eyes as if they might be being watched or listened to. 'We will just pretend you are my slave and when nobody is around we can be sisters. What do you think of that, Trin?'

'Sisters? I always wanted a sister, but maybe I will get in trouble if you ask about it, Nina, and I don't want that because if we are naughty or don't do what we are told they will feed us to the monsters.'

'I'm very important to Zacriel, which usually means I get what I want so maybe he will let it happen since this tower is too big just for me and I am so lonely.'

They dragged the heavy books up to the tower room, chatting as they did. Nina had no idea how much time had passed when a tall servant hurried into the chamber and saw Nina talking to Trin with both of them giggling. He cuffed a hand across the back of Trin's head, making her shy away from him with a scream.

'Back to work, girl,' you know not to talk to the young lady. It is forbidden.' Then the man grabbed Trin by the ear and pulled her towards the stairs.

'Hey, you,' shouted Nina, and the man turned to look at her.

'Yes, Lady Nina, what can I do for you?'

'You can leave Trin alone. She wasn't doing anything wrong, and it was me who started talking to her, and Trin didn't even want to in case she got in trouble. Please don't hurt her, and if I find out you did then Zacriel will know I'm unhappy.'

'Yes, Lady Nina, I understand.' they turned to leave, and Nina called out one more thing.

'Also from now on Trin is the only servant who can come up here, so tell everybody this new rule.'

'Lady Nina, that won't be possible.'

'Are you such a silly man that you think I can't get what I want? I can come with you now to Zacriel and tell him how difficult you are being if you want?'

'No, lady, that won't be necessary. I will notify the others.'

When they had disappeared down the stairs, Nina sat, rather pleased that she had found a friend. She poured herself water, pretending it was summer wine with sliced melon garnish, then began to go through the too few books that had been delivered.

Lately Nina had begun experimenting with her astral body in and around the castle. It took more energy to send the astral body out on its cord than to keep close, and the book she had been devouring through the last two nights explained how the traveller could access not only the dreams of those sleeping but also the minds of those awake. Nina had decided to give it a try. Once connected and comfortable, she let her astral body wander around her chamber little by little until she could move her astral body with a thought to anywhere in the chamber.

Session by session Nina became more daring. This night Nina allowed her body to float down the tower stairs to the bottom door. Pausing here Nina channelled the energy racing through her into a glowing sphere before her on the door. Then, although she was too weak to access the sky vortices, she had enough power to allow the vortex at her forehead to open enough for a thin band of indigo, tracing a star on the door; she stepped through. If there had of been an astral ward here no such thing would have been possible, but luckily there was nothing to stop her. Even with her constant worrying she would be found out, Nina was learning that very few people actually knew anything about the strange world so close to theirs.

She went down the stairs to the throne room where she saw Zacriel talking with Rapture, who turned her way sniffing like he had caught the smell of prey on the wind. Quickly she headed to the other tower door and its two flame warriors of Dalwyn's guard, who didn't even sense her as she pushed through and onto the stairs, jumping from one landing to the next until she stood outside her old chamber. This door had an astral ward on it, but someone had scratched through the symbol, which cancelled its power and made it useless.

Nina stepped into the old chamber; it had changed dramatically. Now the walls were lined with maps, and books and scrolls covered the table. Dalwyn stood talking with the mysterious woman visitor. The other stranger whom she called salt and pepper from the look of his hair was sitting up and looking much better since his collapse. He appeared to be asleep. Nina sat in her old position on the window ledge. She knew that by assuming a well-used spot in the waking world while in the astral deepened the connection, making it less draining on the traveller's energy.

Nina watched a servant bring tea for Dalwyn and the mystery woman, and she settled in to listen to their conversation.

'Can you be sure that all of the coterie will be there when we move in?'

'I can only go on what he knows, Dalwyn. They never had a strong relationship from the start, and he has been trying to mend that.'

'How many of them are there now?'

'Two. Which leaves only himself and Ishmael.'

Nina's ears pricked up at that. Did they mean Ishmael whom she had led with Zahra out from under the mountain?

'So the question is then, do we wait for this, Ishmael, or take action anyway?'

'Ishmael may have arrived by the time we get there. Transport will be arranged most likely by air since it is a long trip by land, and we need to be fresh.'

They are going somewhere, realized Nina, but where, and am I going?

Nina was so caught up listening to the conversation that she didn't notice salt and pepper standing there looking at her curiously. The same man was sitting in the chair behind him too, and then Nina realized that like her, this man was in his astral form. The realization surprised her so much that she was pulled back into her own body in a moment. As she lay allowing her body to recover, she had the feeling that salt and pepper could cause her a lot of problems. Maybe he didn't know who I was she was, but the man had been staring straight at her looking as surprised as she had.

In the time Nina had been trapped in this castle she never encountered anybody else in their astral form. Sometimes an Infernal would be seen in the astral, and they were easy to recognize because their astral bodies gave off what looked like sparks when they stayed still. Trying to ignore her headache, Nina got up to drink water and eat fruit to replace the energy she had burnt. Then she sat and waited since there was nothing else she could do but wait out her headache.

Nina stayed in her room all the next day reading and waiting for someone to drag her away for spying on Dalwyn. Whoever salt and pepper was maybe he didn't like Dalwyn either and that's why nobody had come for her. When Trin came to clear away the rubbish and deliver fresh linen, she bought her armful of belongings. She looked terrified, and the white flesh of her face made her freckles stand out even more as she practically sprinted away from Rapture who had led the girl up the tower. He stood there laughing as Trin cowered behind Nina.

'Leave her alone, you big oaf, you don't scare me, and Zacriel will have your head removed if you harm me or Trin.'

'I don't want to hear a peep from either of you. If you can't behave yourselves then this won't happen again.'

Then he turned and began stomping down the stairs.

They both looked at each other and screamed while jumping up and down.

'I still have to do chores, but I will sleep here and be your personal maid.'

'I don't need a maid, I need a best friend and a sister. We will have so much fun Trin, I promise.'

That night was simply the best night Nina had ever had. They had food bought up from the kitchen without any horrible vegetables and a whole chocolate cake along with juicy watermelon. They pretended to be princesses locked in the tower like the story books and then they played I Spy' from the window and imagined they would be saved from the infernals that infested the city by knights riding grand lunars sent on a secret mission to save them.

When the next day passed without anybody confronting Nina about what she had heard in Dalwyn's tower, Nina tried finding out everything about the lady and salt and pepper man but gave up when she realized nobody knew anything and didn't even know of the strange couple at all.

That night when Trin came back to their chamber with dinner it consisted of salted beef with thick brown bread, and a small bowl of soup made from vegetables. They were both talking hurriedly and eating when Nina realized how thirsty she was. 'Trin, did we get anything to drink, or are we truly prisoners left to die of thirst?

'The drinks weren't ready so they said it would be dropped off to us later.'

Later came and no drinks arrived. They both ran down the long, winding stairs to the door at the base then knocked loudly.

'Guards? Guards?'

'Is anyone there? We have no water or drinks. Hello, anyone?'

Nina lay on the floor which made Trin giggle. 'What are you doing Nina?'

'My brother showed me once that if you lay on the floor and look under you can see if anyone is there. And they are Trin; I can see the guard's boot.'

'Hello, guard, I know you are there. Answer me or when Zacriel finds out he might take your head.'

The guard refused to answer and the two girls who soon became bored and they both raced each other back up the long staircase. They sat watching the city from the balcony, which was quieter now the takeover was complete. There were few humans in Acclaro now, and they all worked in the castle seeing to Zacriel's and Dalwyn's comfort and managing the castle.

'What happened to your mummy and daddy, Trin?'

Trin climbed up beside Nina and sat there twirling her fingers through her hair. 'The I nfernals ate them and would have eaten me too, but I hid in our wine cellar in a barrel. Eventually I had to sneak outside to get food and they found me then decided I would work here in the castle.'

'That's so awful. My parents are dead too, they got murdered in Illume.'

After a long moment of silence Trin turned to Nina and took her hand in her own.

'Well at least we have each other. Sisters forever.'

'I always wanted a sister.'

The two of them sat there until they both were yawning and soon were both curled up alongside each other.

Nina found herself outside her body once again, except this time it felt different, as if something had dragged her out and she had little choice in it. Her astral cord still connected to her sleeping body, and yet she was so thirsty, which was strange since the needs of her real body were absent when she travelled the astral. This felt different. When she moved her actions felt jittery, and swallowing was painful. Nina tried to rise up through the vortices but found she couldn't do it, and yet she was in the amber realm which now tarnished her chamber a rust colour. Beside Nina's real body slept Trin, snoring softly with a relaxed smile on her face.

It was a ripple in the energy of the astral that alerted her to someone else's presence in the chamber, and when she turned the man with salt and pepper hair stood leaning against a wall at the top of the stairs. There was a wolfish feel to the wide smile that engulfed his face, and it unnerved her that he had snuck right up to her.

'Hello, Nina, don't mind me. I am just returning the visit that you made to my chambers three nights ago. I really wanted to speak with you, but you left before I had a chance to do so.'

'Go away, I don't want you here,' said Nina defiantly.

'You can't have your cake and eat it as well, child, you were spying on us and I want to know why.'

'I wasn't spying, well not on purpose. I just am new to this astral world and was experimenting. I am so thirsty.'

'Yes, you would be terribly thirsty since I ordered you to be fed salty foods without any liquids. The astral body will free itself from its physical body to search for water if dehydrated.'

'Dehydrated, what does that mean?'

'It means when you need water.'

'Oh, I didn't know that. I really am new and don't know much.'

'Someone must have taught you. I watched as you exited your body with no trouble at all while someone untrained wouldn't manage to disengage the energy vortices of their body.'

I only read lots of Dalwyn's books. He doesn't think I can read, but I'm not stupid like he thinks. Can I ask you a question?' Nina approached salt and pepper.

'Go ahead.'

'How come there are not many people in the astral world?'

'It's because there are many dangers in this world, Nina, like astral storms that will tear your astral cord free and you will be lost forever; or monsters trapped here will steal your body for themselves. Most people lack the energy to visit the astral realm and don't have the patience to learn how to clear the energy vortices. The more you try to ascend through the vortices, the more dangers will confront you.'

'What is going to happen to me now that you know what I can do?'

Salt and pepper shrugged. 'Maybe nothing. It depends on what you heard when spying on us.'

'Nothing, I heard nothing at all except maybe how you were all going to go somewhere.'

'Then you heard too much Nina,' he said, smiling and faster than she could pull away from him he grabbed her by the arm, then rapped her hard on the back of the head, which made her suddenly unable to move.

'Just relax; I am not going to hurt you. I just need to be sure you won't go around spying on us again. Salt and pepper closed his eyes, and when he opened them again they were now flecked with amber like the world around them. He reached out a finger and traced a star in front of Nina where the air rippled like water.

'Return to your body,' he said then blew through the star, and Nina was thrown back into her real body with Trin snoring softly beside her.

Outside it was raining and Nina quickly grabbed cups and bowls to put on the window ledge and collect something to drink. It was agonizingly slow before she had much to drink, and she sipped slowly so it lasted while the other containers filled.

Nina was still at the window when the wooden door rasped open at the base of the stairs and she heard the footsteps of more than one person. Not wanting to wake up Trin, Nina finished the water and waited at the top of the stairs.

Dalwyn, salt and pepper and his companion, followed by a handful of guards, emerged from the belly of the stairs.

'Hello, Nina, I think you know why we are here, don't you?' Dalwyn asked.

Nina was sure she knew they were here because of salt and pepper seeing her in the astral but didn't want to make it easy for the horrible old man, and so she shrugged her shoulders and stayed silent.

'You are a devious little thing and nearly had me fooled, but much has fallen into place now. The missing lock and key for my books and some of them going missing for days. I should have known you couldn't be trusted, and now I realize you can read and write there will be few opportunities for that in the future.'

The woman had moved to look around the room.

'Who is this other girl, Dalwyn?'

'She is Nina's personal servant that Zacriel approved to stay in the tower with her.'

'Please don't hurt her, Dalwyn she has done nothing wrong,' Nina pleaded.

'Why would I want to harm your friend, Nina, when all I came for was you?'

'Strong arms grabbed Nina from behind, lifting her from the floor as another hand covered her mouth, smothering her scream. Salt and pepper tied a strip of cloth over her mouth and then slipped a hood over her head. Nina felt herself being lowered to the floor and her legs were tied together. She began to panic with worry about Trin. Finally she had found a friend, and now they were taking her away from all this. Did Zacriel know what Dalwyn was doing? She knew he didn't because Zacriel would refuse to be separated from her.

In that moment though, Nina drew strength from knowing that they couldn't stop her from accessing the astral world or tie down that body. She would visit Trin at night in her friend's dreams and everything would be okay. Nina refused to cry or struggle and would show Dalwyn that she was beaten and was not dangerous anymore, so she lay there and let herself be carried away down the stairs and thought she could still hear the soft snoring of her only friend, Trin.

It must have been late because only the steps of her captors echoed on the stone floor and it seemed they would escape the castle without any challenge. The rough movement of being carried was making Nina feel sick, and it was hard enough to breathe with the hood and gag on, making it impossible to follow the conversation of her captors.

Dalwyn led the way out onto the sky path that linked the great crown wall of Acclaro city to the castle. He had the two newcomers and his thirty flame warriors trailing behind him. Up ahead a figure in a dark robe stood waiting as they struggled through the strong wind that tore at their clothes. One of the flame warriors carried Nina over his shoulder, the upstart child was still bound, blindfolded and gagged. They could not take the chance that Nina would relay any important information to Zacriel and spoil the carefully laid plans especially since they were now aware that Nina could access the astral plane.

As they neared the robe figure it turned to regard them with eyes that burned with a sickly yellow glare.

'You are Dalwyn,' asked the infernal in a rasping voice that seemed to have trouble articulating the words.

'I wouldn't be out here if I wasn't,' Dalwyn snapped back at him.

'Quail, Infernal lord of pestilence warned me of your insolence,' as Dalwyn began to retort the infernal held a hand up before him.

'I will not call your mounts if you insist on being difficult, and don't think that my lords will be terribly upset should they find your broken body in the city after you happened to take a tragic fall.'

Dalwyn leant in close to the figure who now was grinning at him.

'So you would be fine with staying here in this miserable world then spawn? I am the only chance you have of returning to the infernal lands beyond the gates, and in case you are not just stupid but also blind we outnumber you thirty to one. Do you really want trouble?'

The Infernal wasn't grinning anymore and turned away then began to bellow out words that Dalwyn couldn't understand. When the Infernal had stopped yelling it turned back to Dalwyn with a barely suppressed smirk that showed rows of sharp teeth that spilt from its lips.

'Well, call them spawn. I have no patience to wait up here like this for your mere amusement.'

'I am not amused at your being here Dalwyn, I am amused at what is to come for you and your followers.'

Dalwyn hardly heard the Infernals words. His gaze had been drawn from up behind it where the storm clouds were now roiling as if a maelstrom was forming, then the clouds appeared to coalesce into a mass of lunars that were unlike any Dalwyn had ever seen. These lunars had a touch of fury in them from the flame touched coloured bodies to the thick barbed bone that protruded from joints from which bled a steady sluice of gore as powerful wings propelled them through the storm. These fabled creatures were the steeds of perdition that the four infernal lords would send to carry the souls of those worthy mortals back to the Infernal lands. One of the flame warriors slipped on the treacherous iron floor as he turned to run and fell away and down out of view, his screams lost in the wind.

'Hold firm Flames, they will not harm us, they are our transport,' shouted Dalwyn. The lunars raced down on the devilish wind and their landing threw up sparks as the bone legs that jutted from the thorax struck into the iron path for purchase. The first lunar skittered and lunged forward as Dalwyn approached it which threw him of balance. He felt himself slipping towards the edge and in his peripheral vision the infernal stood roaring its laughter into the fey wind around them. A hand pulled him back to his feet easily, it was Flint, one of his flame warriors.

'Can't have you dying on us sir. These damned beasts would devour us without you to stop them. Dalwyn wiped the sluicing water from his brow as the infernal approached him.

'Mount up Lord Dalwyn, they won't stay for much longer. Already they are angry to be transporting such as yourselves when as far as they are concerned only infernal royalty should command them. Quail says they will take you as far as the Veiled lands, then you are on your own, and don't forget your promise because he hasn't.'

'I will need one of my men taken to Shelton's Crag for reinforcements.'

'Yes, I know of this and it has been planned for.'

As Dalwyn once again approached the unholy lunar before him it sunk lower to allow him to climb upon its back. His men followed his lead and Dalwyn bound Nina to himself with rope. He still had some use for her yet.

With a great sweep of wings Dalwyn's mount leapt from the skywalk into a dive that caused him to shut his eyes in fear as they plummeted then turned tightly to follow the curve of castle Acclaro before striking out over Arrowhead Lake. When his sense returned to him he saw Nina in front of him shaking with fear or was it cold, her blindfold had fallen down and the sack torn away with the fury of the storm. As they charged through the night Dalwyn promised himself never to leave his life in the hands of any of the infernal lords again.

Chapter 32

The house was quiet when Ishmael was chained back up inside the courtyard. He had expected there to be an ongoing argument between Diego and Fajira when he returned.

When Diego stepped out of the house into the courtyard he cradled his pipe in one hand and lit it with a burning piece of coal. Ishmael noticed that Diego's tunic had blood on it, which could have been from Lucinda. There was also blood caked on the monitor's knuckles and some spotted his face.

'What have you done to Fajira and Fausto?' asked Ishmael, unable to keep the tremor of worry out of his voice.

'Of what concern is it of yours, Yucca?' sniggered Diego as he squatted just out of reach of Ishmael. Diego took a deep draw of the pipe as he stared back at Ishmael.

'You talk as if they are your family, Yucca, not mine. I understand the mistake I made with you now and realize I was stupid to leave you here where you could fool my wife with your lies and turn my family against me. You see, I know what you have done. Fajira told me that you informed her of my meetings with Lucinda. You should never have done that Ishmael, now you may just have ruined everything I have strived for here and condemned yourself to death. I had hoped that events would not come to this, Yucca or should I call you Ishmael as my wife calls you? Does she lay with you too or have you been content just to turn my family against me?'

Ishmael grated his teeth in frustration. 'You are the one who has wronged me, and then you blame me for your marriage falling apart because you are too stupid to hide your affair. Everyone had heard about it, Diego, and have known for some time now. You don't deserve such a family as you have. Just release me from my debt and I will be gone from here. You can keep the coin owed me as I care not one little bit for tainted money. You can still save this marriage you know.'

Diego laughed ruefully. 'No, Yucca, there is nothing to save now.'

'What have you done to them, Diego? You didn't hurt them, did you?'

Diego just emptied his pipe.

'Yucca, there is only one more thing to take care of,' and with that he rose then stalked back into the house leaving Ishmael alone again.

Ishmael strained to see back into the house, but the dining room was empty as far as he could tell. If Fajira and young Fausto were dead, it was his fault that things had gone this way. Had it been it necessary to let Fajira know about Lucinda? These and many more questions were bombarding his thoughts as he stood there. He realized he had been holding his breath as he waited, straining to hear something.

He stepped away from the window and back into the yard near the middle where his chain was limp and waited. Diego would return to kill him, and Ishmael would be damned if he would go easy. His nerves felt jangled and his stomach upset while sweat sprouted across his face, he could taste his own fear. With a violent wrench Ishmael vomited then moved away from it, wiping his mouth with the shirt he wore. Now he had been ill he actually felt better, and when Diego returned Ishmael stood ready.

Diego came out with a chair that he sat facing Ishmael, then he retuned back inside to reappear soon after carrying Fajira, who appeared dazed, maybe unconscious.

Ishmael walked forwards, hoping but also knowing the chain that held him like an animal would never reach that far. Diego worked fast, using a rope to bind his wife to the chair thoroughly as she moaned. From where Ishmael was he could see a large red welt across her left cheek.

Diego gagged Fajira then squatted beside her to watch Ishmael again as he refilled his pipe with mixture.

'I think my wife needs to see what happens to those who betray me. It's funny, you see, Ishmael. I sought to keep this side of me away from my family, but the fact that you both plotted against me means she now will have to witness your death. I should have killed you the first day I crossed your miserable path,' Diego shrugged theatrically. 'Believe me when I tell you this. Killing you is one of the last things that will give me some happiness. As he took his time finishing the pipe, his narrowed eyes never left Ishmael, and they swelled with promised death.

When Diego finished his pipe and approached, Ishmael raised his hands up in front of him in a side-fighting stance. He found himself breathing heavily through his mouth, and then Diego attacked with a feint before driving a fist into Ishmael's side.

The blow was deflected as the arm that protected Ishmael's ribs took the brunt of the force. Ishmael retreated after a flurry of punches that changed levels between his head and abdomen as the monitor weaved around him, easily striking when he chose without letting Ishmael form any kind of defence. One blow caught Ishmael across the side of the head and he staggered.

Ishmael lunged out at Diego with his own attack but the blow was easily turned away. They disengaged with Ishmael breathing hard.

Diego just smiled then shook out his arms before advanced once again; Ishmael stepped in close blocking two blows on his arms and covering his face. He grabbed Diego by the shoulder, who twisted away from him then followed up with a hard blow to his cheek that sent Ishmael down on one knee.

Diego danced away again. He was smiling.

'Come on, monk, this is how to win your freedom. That is what you wanted, isn't it?'

Ishmael said nothing but rose again, and this time when Diego walked in he circled away from him. Diego cut him off from all angles until Ishmael was at the end of the chain, then he smashed a fist twice into his face with jabs before delivering a sharp blow under Ishmael's jaw, making him crumple.

As he lay there dazed. Ishmael saw Diego approach Fajira who was awake now, watching with frightened eyes. Diego was saying something, but Ishmael couldn't decipher the monitor's words as Diego backhanded Fajira across the face, knocking her and the chair onto the ground.

Ishmael tried to rise, but his balance was gone so he staggered to fall again on his side. Diego reached down and pulled Fajira back to a sitting position. Her gag had come loose with the blow, and her sobs came to Ishmael as he began recovering his senses.

'Diego, enough! This has got to stop; you are killing him!'

'That is exactly the point, my love,' said Diego, then he turned back to Ishmael and crashed three fast punches into his face.

When Ishmael came to, Diego stilled crouched over him, laughing.

'You really don't have the stomach for a fight, do you, Yucca?'

From behind them Fajira spoke again, and Ishmael only barely managed to hear her words.

'You always were a coward, Diego. Always willing to beat a woman or someone weaker than you.'

The monitor turned and moved away from Ishmael now.

'If you know what's good for you wife, you will be quiet.'

'Or what? You will hit me again? I have become accustomed to the brutality you share out to those you supposedly love.'

'Shut up, you stupid whore!'

'You know I never wanted to wed you, but my father convinced me it was needed for the honour of the Vorm family. He saw something in you, Diego, a shrewd businessman who knows the streets and all the tricks. Someone who could be a strong ally in the future and raise fine children for the continuation of our lineage. But I tell you this, my father never saw the coward behind all the bravado, for if he had you never would have been allowed to marry into the Vorm family.'

'I told you to be quiet.'

His voice had fallen almost to a whisper as he faced Fajira.

'I tried to love you, Diego but the hatred inside you has taken the man I briefly knew and twisted him into something unrecognizable. I was loyal when you shunned my bed each night to be with a whore because I still believed there was good in you, but now I know what you are. Fajira began to chuckle.

Diego hit her, snapping her head to the side.

'You find that funny, do you?'

Diego's fist rose again, but when a shadow fell across them from the house he paused to look up. It was Fausto, who stood there dressed in his sleep clothes; he had blood caked in his hair and leaking from his nose. He had dragged Ishmael's sword with him, which now was angled at Diego.

'Father, I promised to myself that there would be no more hitting us. You just won't stop until you kill us.'

'So, you plan to kill me, then, son?'

The sword blade wavered in the Fausto's grasp.

'If I have to, though you could just leave.'

'No, I will not leave what I have built here.' Diego walked slowly towards Fausto, who now had tears dripping down his chin to mingle with the blood there.

'You're weak, boy, like your mother. Must be most of her blood in you.'

Diego slapped aside the blade just as he reached it and grabbed Fausto by the tunic, dragging him forward. Fausto squealed, and Fajira began screaming.

'No, not my baby, not my baby, please, Diego.'

Ishmael rolled behind Diego, crashing into his legs and making them buckle. Father and son fell over next to him. He was rewarded with Diego's forehead crunching into his face. Fausto now lay beneath Diego who was strangling the boy.

When the boy went limp Diego let go of him then stood holding Ishmael's sword with it poised above Fausto.

A voice called out from the other side of the gate.

'Monitor Diego, it is the town guard; we have come to make you answerable to your crimes.'

'Go away! The allegations are false; this is a family issue and none of your business.'

The gate to the yard behind Ishmael swung open as a handful of guards rushed in, the foremost armed with a crossbow. Diego snarled then leapt towards them, the sword slicing down into the guard's shoulder. There was a loud twang as the bolt discharged. It hit Diego with a thud that sent him spinning him away from the guards, who now fanned out with bared blades.

'Desist your fight, monitor, you are hereby under arrest!'

When Diego turned back around, Ishmael thought the bolt had missed him, but then he saw the hole through Diego's sternum where the feathers of the bolt still protruded from the man's chest.

Diego staggered back against the courtyard wall where he slid to a seated position. He looked around at them with eyes that had become uncomprehending, then his head slowly slumped onto his chest.

Fausto stood there staring at his father then ran to his mother.

'Mother, are you all right?'

'I am, son. You were so brave. Now untie me.'

Chapter 33

Zahra stopped at a non-descript house amongst a cluster of similar homes squeezed together among the narrow, cobblestone roads and alleyways where the sun didn't make it to the ground but was closed out by the huge, patch work rooftops of tiny homes making the whole seem one. The house had a second story like the others that projected out from the ground floor, and this was mirrored by those on the opposite side of the street meaning they nearly met in the middle, forming a tunnel above where Zahra stood.

A polished timber sign showed the name 'Soul Forge' which had been crafted with iron and had a picture of a clog beneath it. Zahra tapped the rapper twice against the door which itself seemed brand new and out of sorts with the rest of the place except for the sign.

As Zahra waited she turned to check the road behind her to be sure no one was following her. The tunnel was empty but for the faint shuttered rays of sunlight that managed to reach the dank cobblestones like faint rays of hope.

Zahra turned back as the door opened, and an old lady with wispy, red hair tied back in a bun looked out at her, smiling. Her clothes were faded with holes and her hands were stained black except for the knuckles, which were swollen to an angry red, but her smile was warm and kind.

'Yes, lass? Can I be of assistance?'

'I'm looking for Marnie. A friend directed me here.'

'A friend, you say? I have many friends, but these days my head is all befuddled and I often forget who my friends are.'

'Klaus, priest of the death jester.'

The door started to close.

'His temple was in Whitman's Peak.'

The door stopped where it was and opened again. The woman stared at Zahra, her hands clenched tightly together.

'Did Klaus have a message for me by chance?'

'He did, he said I should tell you that he has found his peace. That you should know he is very thankful for knowing you.'

The old lady bought her hands to her mouth, and Zahra thought she would start sobbing, but instead she swallowed hard, exhaled loudly, and then waved Zahra into the warmth of a front room lit by candles with one wall adorned with high cupboards. Each cupboard had a thick padlock on it. The strange room piqued Zahra's curiosity and as if reading her mind, Marnie answered her unspoken question.

'They are for my guests to store any baggage outside their rooms. I assume you will be staying, but first I require your mark.'

'Mark? I'm not sure what you mean, Marnie.'

'When you take up the life of shadows you are marked, and if you truly are as you say, then I must see that mark or you will have to leave here.'

Zahra realized then that Marnie meant the clan tattoo she had received when she had joined the Kenzu. She lifted her shirts to show the raised scar symbol of the Kenzu upon her right ribs beneath the breast.

Marnie grunted then motioned for Zahra to cover up again.

'Now, warrior of the Kenzu, I will tell you the rules you must abide by here within this safe house. Oh my, I'm forgetting my manners.' Marnie yelled into the adjoining room: 'Jet, bring tea for two.' Then she guided Zahra over to a small table with two seats in the corner by a lamp.

There came no answer, but moments later a large man entered the room carrying a tray with tea for the two of them, and his huge hands made the tray look like a toy. He regarded Zahra with clear eyes and a look that told her he was much more than a tea servant.

'That will be all, Jet,' said Marnie, and after a long moment and questioning look from the old lady, he backed out of the room.

'Don't mind him, lass, he holds a strong distrust of strangers and worries too much for me.'

'Marnie, you should know I mean you no harm.'

Marnie smiled then and reached across the table to grasp Zahra's hand in hers.

'Firstly stop calling me Marnie. It is not my real name. Klaus was my son, and I believe that from the message you give me he has found his final peace. It gladdens me that someone like you was there alongside him when he died, and I will grieve his loss but not until after the business between you and me is finished. No weapons are tolerated in this house except within this room. You will be given access to a locker, and all your weapons, armour, or any other possessions you wish to store will stay here with access only granted once you walk outside this house. Violence is forbidden within these walls while talk of religion, contracts, or clans is also unacceptable. You pay when you leave, do you understand, lass?'

'Yes, I do.'

'You may call me Gladys, and you are?'

'I am known as Zahra.'

'Zahra… I like that, it's a strong name. Now you should be aware that I have one other rule, and that is we all dine together. I care not for your missions or plans, and I insist that all who stay beneath my roof dine with me. Lucky for you, dinner will be ready within a chime or two, so don't stray too far. Your room is up the stairs in the next room on the right, and here is your key,' she said handing Zahra a long brass key.

Zahra stowed her weapons within the cupboard that Gladys

opened for her then made her way through the pleasant room next door adorned with many flowers that gave off a sweet aroma, and brightly painted works of art. Her room upstairs was one of four, and she was childishly happy to see a large feather down bed, a vanity complete with mirror and beauty products laid out in an orderly fashion next to a chilled jug of water. Zahra went and sat at the table, admiring the room with wonder, when a soft knock came at the door. Zahra opened it to find the large man she had met down stairs.

'Sorry to interrupt,' he said in surprisingly light voice.

'Mother Gladys has told me to take you to the baths; she says you will be pleasantly surprised.'

The old lady was right, and soon Zahra sat soaking in a wooden tub filled with hot water, with oils and soaps at her disposal. Zahra turned to the maid who had brought her fresh towels.

'How is this hot water possible? I see no fire or boiling tubs and this bath is made of stone as if carved from the ground itself.'

'Yes, that is correct. A natural spring bubbles up beneath this place, and Gladys had a stone bath built around it. It is only one of three in the city, but I doubt many still living are aware of this one. Gladys would rather die than give up her heated baths.'

'How long have you served Gladys here?' Zahra asked the maid.

The girl laughed out loud and splashed water at Zahra playfully.

'I am not a maid or servant for Gladys. I am your sister, a fellow assassin, but I was relieved of my money in the city, and, well… let's just say it's not free to stay here, so I am a guest with a debt.'

Zahra lay back again now the other girl had finished soaping her back.

'Which clan are you from?'

'Uh uh uh said the girl, placing a finger to her lips, 'remember the rules here, Zahra. No clan talk. The walls have ears, and I actually believe that Gladys even though she plays the kindly old grandmother could hear any breach of these rules within this place. Now relax a while if you must, but I have other chores to attend to. What's your colour?'

'My colour, whatever do you mean?'

'Preferred colour of clothing. I will have an array of clothes brought to your room for dinner, but you may choose the main colouring and whether you prefer skirts or pants for you.'

'Green is my choice, and pants,' said Zahra, masking a yawn with the back of a hand.

'I could get used to this instead of being on the road. May I know your name before you go?'

'Just call me Tess. I will see you at dinner.' She winked then shut the door behind her.

Later after bathing, and now back at her room Zahra found a long box on the bed that held an emerald green undershirt with a white laced top to go over it, and light green pants with a darker, emerald sash. Her boots had been cleaned and polished while she was bathing as well.

The clean clothes were a welcome change, realized Zahra staring as she stared at her image in the mirror. Once she was more than happy to be in the field looking after Ishmael, but she now longed for some stability in her life, whatever that could be. A normal life of children and washing, cooking and being a slave to a man would never suit her, but to have her own remote place somewhere with the right person, well, that would be different altogether.

Pushing that fantasy from her mind, Zahra admired her outfit one last time then descended the stairs for dinner.

Zahra had always prided herself on the fact she was never late for any type of meeting or event. She liked to arrive, get her bearings, and then settle in for what was to come, also that meant that if something should happen to waylay her arrival then it usually was dealt with in time for her not to be late. She would be at the table before any other guests and have an advantage over them.

Zahra strode into the dining room before realizing she wasn't the first to arrive at all. There were four chairs and places set, and hers was the only one empty. *So much for being first*, she thought, trying to reclaim her demeanour.

The other guests had been sitting quietly, presumably waiting for her, and as she entered they all stood courteously. Gladys was at the head of the table dressed in a beige and silver dress complete with a jewelled necklace and set of earrings; she looked divine.

At the opposite end of the table sat a man with a long face, with hair fading to grey, his wide smile showing off a fine set of teeth. The last diner was the one that caught Zahra's attention the most. The woman looked just out of her teens, with bright eyes that danced with laughter on a freckled, alabaster face. Zahra knew this face, it was the girl who had head-butted her in the crowd earlier that day. Unlike the others, she was dressed plainly without adornments in her auburn, shoulder-length hair, and she wore a full sleeved mauve shirt with skirts of purple and white. She wasn't smiling. Standing off to one side of the table stood Tess, who nodded at Zahra; then, at a look from Gladys, she left.

If Gladys or the other diners had noticed the uncomfortable pause and stare between Zahra and the girl, they didn't show it. With a wave of her heavily ringed hand, Gladys motioned for them to be seated as she herself stood.

'Welcome to my table. I believe you are now familiar with my rules so let's get on with the introductions then. The man among us is Tale Longfoot, a true gentleman who as his name suggests can tell a wicked tale. This lass to my left is known only to me as Rue and has been a guest of mine for some time now,' Gladys patted Rue's hand as Tess returned with a bottle of wine.

'Finally, the newcomer is Zahra, a Brimmerlander if her skin is anything to go by, and a friend of my son's. Tess, some wine now, please.'

Tess poured a deep ruby coloured wine as a slender, young man moved slowly behind, her setting down a platter of spiced bread slathered in honey and another platter of sliced fruit.

Zahra ate slowly, relishing the food, and for a time the diners stayed quiet.

'The war may yet reach here to Soarnestia,' spoke Tale Longfoot, breaking the silence. Already refugees from Whitman's Peak and Glimmersedge have caused a raucous down on the road.' He dabbed at his mouth with a napkin. 'Did either of you ladies happen upon any trouble to do with that at all?'

Rue dipped a piece of pear into honey then munched it noisily. 'The impending war holds little interest to me personally, I have bigger fish to fry.'

'That hints at a selfish nature, Rue.' said Gladys with her fork stopped before her mouth. 'Do you think that events taking place outside your own little world won't creep in and envelop you as well?'

'My mother always said. "Look after yourself first, Rue, then worry about the rest of the world," said Rue.

Zahra realized all eyes were on her, now and she finished chewing with as much composure as she could then dabbed at the corners of her mouth with the napkin.

'I came through Acclaro. The capital now belongs to the infernals, and Whitman's Point was wiped out the following day. I was fortunate enough to escape along with the refugees from the Point.'

'Those poor people. No one deserves to see their homes destroyed and forced to flee for their own safety,' said Gladys, shaking her head slowly as she chewed.

'Is it a common thing for you to run away from things, Zahra?' asked Rue with her fork half raised to her mouth.

Zahra looked over at Rue, who stared back blankly.

'I'm not in the habit of running away from anything unless a situation offers me nothing but death. One day you might learn that lesson, if life is kind to you and you survive your youth.'

They matched stares a moment, then Tale broke the silence once again.

'Ah the follies of youth. I for one wish I could travel that path again. Rue, you can bet we are all envious in a way of you with your whole life ahead of you.'

'Not me,' said Gladys. 'My youth was full of pain and loss, and though everything that has happened to me has led me to this point in my life, there is no way I would go back and do it all again.'

Rue twirled her fork across her knuckles.' My purpose and my life are one and the same, and my actions are based on the wisdom of my elders who taught me how to live. There are no regrets or hopes, there just is the task I have and the service to my clan.'

Zahra wiped her mouth with a napkin. 'Well I guess that explains why you lack… ah what's the word, *substance*, then, Rue?'

The others laughed except Rue, who still sat poised with her fork half way to her mouth, the whitening of her hands around her utensils betraying her anger as she glared at Zahra.

The main was a grilled fish with buttered vegetables, gravy, and hot bread. Few words were spoken, which was testament enough to the taste of the meal. Zahra had rarely eaten this well during her life and enjoyed every bite. A mixed berry wine served by Tess completed the main beautifully.

Talk, when it resumed, turned to the inevitable subject: the return of magic.

Tale drained his wine and regarded them all. 'I had always thought I would never see magic in my lifetime, but if the rumours are to be believed then its return is imminent. I reckon I could die happy if just once I could see magic.'

'How so, Tale? For all we know this magic could be the worst thing to happen. If you ask me, our world is better off for it since people can't be trusted to use power wisely,' said Glady's, leaning forward on her elbows.

'It's man's nature, my dear.' Tale pulled a pipe from his jacket and a wooden container. 'Anyone care for a smoke or mind if I do?'

Rue sat twirling her fork across her knuckles. 'Some believe that if you control the magic you control the world. That this magic, if it does exist, was hidden by certain powers until they deemed it ready to return, yet I find that strange if true, because who gave them this right to choose for everybody?'

'Zahra leant back in her chair; the clothes she wore felt scratchy on her skin, and she felt flushed from the wine. 'Personally I don't believe it will ever return. If I held that choice, I would rather die than see it being abused all over again.'

Glady's nodded. 'Strange sightings have been reported from the city of dreams claiming that miracles have taken place, and of course many more unbelievably ridiculous claims have surfaced since. The thing that makes me think something is true about these rumours is the clamouring of worldly powers, is the manoeuvring of the infernals and all the nations.'

'It appears to me,' said Tale drawing deeply on his pipe, 'that the secret is out and finally someone knows what really happened to cause the Severing. The nations and rulers everywhere are fighting to be in the best position to gain from its return. By the Infernal hells, no one even exists who has experience with magic, so how will people react? Not well, I fear!'

'Well, someone sure knew what happened, Tale,' exclaimed Rue, putting the knife down on her plate. 'Otherwise we wouldn't be having this conversation.'

They all agreed on that, and Zahra wondered how much Rue knew and why she had assaulted Zahra earlier that day when they had been caught up in the crowd. Could she be a danger to Ishmael?

Over a decadent dessert of cherry pie with warm cream, conversation was steered to each of them by the shrewd lady of the place, Glady's.

'What I want to know is where each of you goes from here. Of course I understand there may be some things you won't be telling.' She smiled at Rue then. 'Please humour an old lady who doesn't get out much as a fitting end to a great meal and I will thank you now for gracing my table.'

'Well guess I will start then,' spoke Tale around his pipe.

'I don't get to be involved in clan business much these days or want to. I am heading for the Godhead sometime soon, and with the recent tidings of war most likely sooner. Then I plan to take to the oceans and sail off into the sunset to die.'

'A touch dramatic,' Zahra said with a laugh.

'Story of my life, Zahra. I would have stayed to win the heart of Gladys here, but she doesn't suffer fools. They tend to go missing.'

They all laughed at that and then regarded Zahra.

I'm looking for someone who thinks by being with them I am in danger. This is all I have now, and whatever comes will come, as they say. It has been so long since I did something normal like this, and once everything calms down I may just opt for more of the same.'

Rue smirked at Zahra as she spoke. 'I too search for someone who can change my world if I let them. I know I'm close now to achieving what I must regretfully do, and that realization is what spurs me on because it will lead to greater glory for my clan and my soul.'

Gladys smiled at each of them in turn. 'Well, I have little to live for now, I have received news of my only child's death, and the clans fight over whom I have allied with even though it's none of them. The time draws close for me to choose, they say, and so to me these words mean my time is nearly up but bugger if I will go quietly. I will fight like I have for every scrap in my life to help all our clans evenly and greet each day as a new blessing. I want you to know you are welcome while the blood still pumps through my body and to thank you for sharing a moment, however, brief with me.'

As they rose from the table, Tale strode over to take Zahra's arm in his.

'Allow me to escort you to your room, Zahra, there is a matter I wish to discuss with you.'

Zahra nodded, trying not to feel alarmed, and smiled at the man as he led her upstairs. When they got to her room he quickly checked the area for signs of intruders then turned to her. While he searched Zahra armed herself with the letter opener on the drawer and held it against her thigh out of sight.

'Now, Zahra, I am sure you are quite able to look after yourself and what I'm about to tell you is in breach of the rules Glady's sets here, but I'm an old man and no longer care for such stupidity. Rue is not who she seems. She is a heart blade, and they have been hired against the Kenzu.'

Zahra's mouth fell open. The heart blades were a select group of madmen who worshipped their sect with sacrifice, and should any of their operatives be defeated or the contract broken the sect made it a point of gathering to see the contract was fulfilled.

'My question to you, my dear girl, is why would the hearts be looking to go against the Kenzu?'

Zahra punched Tale in the shoulder and smiled. 'You know I can't tell you that, Tale unless of course you wish to be on the heart's hit list too.'

Tale shrugged then straightened out his jacket. 'If I was younger then I would join you, but my creaky old bones make stealth a thing of the past. Good luck, girl, and watch that back of yours.'

That night Zahra hardly slept even though the door and window were both locked and bolted. She doubted that Rue or anyone else would break the treaty within these walls, but there was always a first time for everything.

The night passed uneventfully, and when Zahra emerged from her room and went downstairs the dining room was empty. She saw a plate of pastries and bowl of fruit with a letter telling the guests to help themselves. Jet stood waiting to unlock her equipment, and after she had gathered it he held out a small scroll to her.

'This is from the girl Rue; she left it for you early this morning.'

Zahra opened it, expecting to see some 'holier than thou' letter denouncing her or the Kenzu clan as weak and a thing of the past. What she saw were the following words:

'See you at the Godhead, Zahra, I bet I can find Ishmael before you.'

It was signed, 'You're Death.'

Chapter 34

Ishmael rose from the kitchen stove where the broth bubbled nicely. He filled two bowls and loaded them onto a tray along with fresh bread he had bought that morning. Once inside the bedroom he pulled back the curtains revealing the sprawled bodies of Fajira and Fausto on the sleeping pallets.

They both complained loudly at the sudden light.

'What, you going to sleep all day then?'

Fajira climbed from the bed to squat beside him as he pushed the tray forwards.

'You both need to eat something,' he said.

Fajira took one of the bowls and passed it to Fausto, then got her own. As they ate in silence, Ishmael studied each in turn. He could still see bruising around Fajira's face while Fausto had quite a lump on his head that had required stitching. His own wounds still ached but were healing nicely. They appeared to be healing naturally and not from the accelerated healing from the Mother.

Fajira mopped the last of the broth with some bread before looking at Ishmael.

'You're leaving soon?'

He knew she meant it as a question, but it sounded oddly like an accusation.

'There are people that need me, Fajira, and something very important I need to discover first.'

'We will come with you.'

'You can't do that,' Ishmael said. There is no way I can guarantee your safety.'

'As far as the Godhead then?'

'You need to grieve, Fajira, and take the time to decide on what you will do now. There is the warehouse to run and your house here.'

Fausto had stopped eating to watch both of them, spoon in one hand.

'Don't tell me what I have to do, Ishmael, I have had enough of men like that. I lost Diego a long time ago. I will waste no more time grieving a man who beat his family. My house can stay, and I'm sure you can help recommend someone to manage the warehouse in my absence.'

'Why would you come with me after all this trouble?'

'There is nothing here for us now. My family live in the Godhead, and it is customary for a widow to return to her family's side. I know the road, and we can travel with plenty of coin while you spend time on your sojourn to petition Illume. Fausto has seen little of the road due to Diego's reluctance to let him out much.'

'To the Godhead, then we go our own ways?'

'Yes, then we go our own ways.'

Fajira moved to cuddle Fausto, who since the death of his father and the beatings he had endured had become silent and distracted. He was easily startled and became inconsolable unless Fajira was close by.

'You will finally see the road,' she crooned, kissing his face.

'Soon you will know what it is to be of the Vorm.'

Ishmael watched them both, hoping Fausto would recover from what he had endured at the hands of Diego. Ishmael needed to get the crystals from Fajira, needed to be sure they were still safe.

'Fajira?'

She looked over at him, strands of hair splayed across her face.

'I need to see my belongings.'

Fajira reached down to her throat, unclasped something there, then held it out to Ishmael; a key.

'It unlocks the chest in Diego's sun room at the front of the house,' she said, watching him closely.

Ishmael hurried to the room where Diego had enjoyed most of his free time at home. The chest was made from hard timber with brass hinges and clasps. Ishmael turned the key then pushed back the heavy lid. On the top a pile of papers listed all the necessary information on the business Diego had run along with details of customers' and potential trade ideas that might prove valuable to the future of the operation.

Beneath them he found the two crystals, which called to him with an insistent pull deep within his abdomen. There came an answering surge within him that momentarily took away his breath as the magic within him responded. Ishmael pulled out the deep-blue crystal first, which was cold to the touch; light danced along its edges as he held it up. Holding the blue crystal made Ishmael feel nauseous, and he found it difficult to focus on anything while holding it.

Ishmael placed the blue crystal on the ground in front of him then unwrapped the white one that the Harlequin had given him. Unlike the blue, when he touched this one a sense of peace came over him and he felt instantly invigorated. It was both strange yet exhilarating to have the crystals back in his possession, and now he was reunited with them he thought again about how the coterie still didn't know how to use these crystals to help return magic to the world.'

'Mother! What is Ishmael holding?'

Ishmael cursed silently then turned still holding the white crystal to see Fajira and Fausto behind him. The surge came again from his stomach, then palms, as a strange liquid light extended from Ishmael to form a shimmering oval that surrounded Ishmael.

Fausto and Fajira cringed away from the crystal and Ishmael.

Ishmael was aware of what he was doing but not how as he visualized a vortex opening and facing out of his abdomen, then he gently pulled the white light back inside himself and with a last flash it was gone, leaving the morning light the only source of illumination once again.

Both Fausto and Fajira stood eyes wide with mouths agape at what they had witnessed. Fajira was crying, but they seemed tears of wonder.

'That was the most beautiful thing. Did you see that, Fausto?'

'Yes, I did, but what was it?'

They both looked at Ishmael expectantly.

'I think you at least owe us an explanation, don't you Ishmael?' said Fajira from where she still stood in the doorway.

'I can't and won't lie to you anymore: it's magic! Now you know why I was in such a hurry, Fajira. I am one of the coterie of the heart, and I like my father and those before him have guarded the world's magic until it can return, which soon it will.'

There was an uncomfortable silence before Fajira spoke again, 'Ishmael, surely you jest with us?'

When he didn't answer, and Fajira realized he wasn't joking she squatted, shaking her head in amazement. 'From who do you guard it Ishmael?'

'There are those who would see magic returned to our world before the Mother is capable of receiving it. That time is coming soon, but first I must be reunited with the others like me, our coterie.'

'So why travel the road then, Ishmael? Why risk losing the crystals if they are so important?'

Ishmael stood and took Fajira's hands in his. 'I need to see with my own eyes whether the gods are alive or dead. I cannot continue until I know the fate of the lady of Illume.'

Ishmael looked at Fajira expecting to be mocked, but she simply smiled uncertainly then rose and left the room. 'I have many questions that I want answers to Ishmael. Can we talk about this later?'

'Yes we can Fajira. I just need some time.'

'Come, Fausto, let Ishmael have some time alone.'

'But, Ma, can I see it again? Do you really think its magic?'

'Maybe another time, Fausto now come along.'

She knows something, thought Ishmael when they had left. Fajira knew something about the gods.

It was another three days before they left the home of Fajira. Ishmael had advised her to take Seki on as the foreman for the warehouse, and the small man's shrewd mind would be an asset, and because of his good standing with the workers who in high regard by the workers who held him in high regard. The home was left empty for the new monitor who had yet to arrive. Fajira gave away most of the family's possessions as gifts or as a way of parting.

Ishmael was glad to be leaving this place that he now only associated with loss. He could feel the tentative pushing against his mind as one of the other coterie probed him but were kept out by his steady mental defence. Ishmael knew he couldn't hide from the coterie for much longer and maybe he could convince them of the need to do this however he suspected the others were not taking his absence well.

The cloud of dust rolled in and over the waiting platform whose occupants had now swelled to a large crowd. Ishmael hoisted Fausto onto his shoulders so the boy could see, and he laughed with Fajira at Fausto's exclamations of delight as the two large heads of the sand whips emerged from the dust snapping at each other.

'Look, Ma, the sand whips, they're huge, bigger than I ever thought possible.'

'What do you say Ishmael?' said Fajira, giving him a wink. 'Should we feed Fausto to the beasts? They look famished.'

'No, young boys cause them indigestion, or he will just get stuck in their teeth.'

They all laughed, then slowly the crowd began to creep forward to load up the carriages and finally Ishmael felt like he had returned to his quest for Shae the Lady of Illume.

Ishmael had expected they would travel within a carriage with others who were keen to make their way farther along the road towards the coast and away from the trouble brewing still around Acclaro. When they moved forwards at the front of the crowd, two guardsmen stepped forward to help pull the three of them out of the crowd.

'Our apologies, Lady Vorm, there has been a mix up with your location, but never mind, all is well now. Just this way, my lady.'

Ishmael followed along at the back as they climbed into a large carriage that was opened by a man with a topknot of dark hair and, a mouth of gold teeth which showed as he welcomed Fajira aboard. Unlike the other guards he had always seen, Ishmael noticed this man had an orange sash around his waist.

The carriage was decked out with heavy chairs clothed in furs, set around a long dining table that held all manner of foods, most of which Ishmael had never seen before. Fausto wasted no time and soon was sitting with a heaped plate before him eating noisily as Fajira moved to a decanter. The Sapphire wine within shimmered with white points looking as if someone had caught the very stars within that bottle. She poured two glasses and carried one over to Ishmael's side.

'Ishmael, drink with me. Tomorrow I will begin my formal grieving and all but water and fruits will be prohibited to me for ten days.'

Ishmael nodded his head in acceptance and swilled from the glass, feeling the fizz of it against his lips which then exploded into a subtle vanilla sweetness.

'Why are we travelling with all this fancy food, and why were we pulled from the crowd for this special treatment, Fajira?'

'Why? To keep up appearances, of course. I am a daughter of the Vorm family who lived these lands long before the Godhead was built and when the road was overgrown with nature and teemed with the souls of those trapped in its walls.'

'What do you mean? Said Ishmael as he drank.

'The magic of the road captured the souls of any who died upon it or were foolish enough to touch the one of those trapped within the walls of the road. If you touched one of the lost, you took its place. As you can imagine, some areas would have been chaos with the chorus of voices clamouring for help.'

'Why are you and your family the Vorm so revered in these parts?'

Fajira hesitated a while as if weighing up whether to speak; then she looked over at Ishmael as she finished the wine.

'The Vorm family were once no more than bandits that raided along the road, mainly through Brimmerland. As they grew wealthier the bandits became cockier and raided as far as Trystland. For many cycles the Vorm illegally taxed the road's pilgrims while evading the forces of the three great nations that border the road, causing strain to their coffers while murdering their soldiers.

The king of Trystland had long admired my family and how they ran their operation while staying ahead of the king's next move,' Fajira continued. 'He called a truce with the Vorm, to which my great grandfather three times removed acted warily. When they met to discuss terms, the two were like old friends that had been away from one another. So great was their mutual admiration of one another the king propositioned the Vorm family: to guard the road, making it safe for pilgrims on their way to the Godhead as well as other duties as the official guard of the Seekers Road.

'During the Severing the King of Trystland along with his family died, and to this day the nation is kingless and will stay that way until the gods return to take their place again. My family stepped up amongst the confusion and turned the people's despair to hope. The gods would come back, but only if their mortal followers continued to sacrifice for them. We found out the link was not broken but very weak, and slowly but surely my family learnt to converse with the gods again. You will see it's the truth when we get to the Godhead, Ishmael.'

With the town of Glimmersedge far behind them, Ishmael felt hope stir within him. On the morrow he would be able to pray directly to Shae the Lady of Illume. When he had been trapped in the astral, Ishmael had been shown much by way of vision but nothing at what the fate of the god's had been, which he felt was strange. The only way he would know for certain if the gods still walked among the living was to go to the one place where millions flocked and believed their deities still existed.

Ishmael spent the next chime in deep prayer, he would need to be clear with his intent as he approached this holiest of meetings, and he intended to be found not wanting when his goddess turned her gaze on him. With Illume's blessing then he could continue with the task of returning magic to this world now it had recovered from its damaged state.

Ishmael felt the urge to open contact with the coterie, even Raul if he was open to it. This was the right time to connect with them again. With his companions now sleeping Ishmael moved through the movements to open his energy vortices, then he sunk down into his chosen position and opened himself to the astral. Ishmael let his mind reach out for the others and recoiled as Jona reached back with such force it filled him with nausea.

'Ishmael, you're still alive! We have tried our hardest to get to you, but your walls were too well constructed. I'm so happy you are alive and well.'

Ishmael smiled despite himself. He had missed Jona; in fact he had missed all three of them in a strange way. They were like siblings due the burden of the power they all carried and the constant feeling of each other through the connection they shared.

'Jona, I'm okay. I ran into some trouble, but now am free from it and will be on my way to meet with you all as soon…'

'As soon as what?' spat Selene, her a voice full of spite. Clearly Selene wasn't impressed with him shutting them out.

'As soon as I stop at the Godhead to give worship to the Lady of Illume.'

'Oh, that's fine, Ishmael we are only being hunted across the known world and you would rather go pray. Anyhow, without magic the gods are dead, so why offer worship?'

'You can't conclude that the gods are dead, Selene. Nowhere in the vision did the Mother show me the death of the gods, did you?'

'Maybe you are right, Ishmael, but she also showed in the vision how the gods misused their power by meddling in mortal affairs, which I pretty darn sure we can say is one major reason why the great war started.'

'Enough, you two! This is important,' cut in Jona.

'We need to wait for Raul before we can continue discussing anything,' said Jona with a note of frustration in her voice.

'I'm already here, Jona, I slipped in while you were all distracted,' sighed Raul before continuing. 'Listen, all of you, I am on my way to the safe house; however we have run into a problem. Katerina, my sentinel, has fallen ill with fever and unless I know the location of the safe house I cannot continue onwards. All I know is the location is quite remote and Katerina says it is easily defended with easy access to food and water. Before falling ill Katerina said clan master Haakon was also on the way. How long before the rest of you arrive?'

'We have made good time so far and will be arriving sometime in the next one to two days depending on weather. All this land travel has being making me ill,' said Selene.

'What about you Jona?'

'Our progress is slow. We will arrive in around ten days' time. I figure there is no hurry if Ishmael is off on some quest to find himself.'

Ishmael groaned silently. 'I'm not going to repeat myself, so what you need to know about this trip to the Godhead is that it is a necessary task for me to complete. It will give us valuable insights into whether our gods are still with us and still hold the power over their followers.'

'Ishmael, what you need to do is travel here as soon as possible. Your absence from us puts us all in unnecessary danger. Our task is to return magic to the world, but currently you have two of the crystals with you while we have none. Share them with us and let us see where our task is leading,' pleaded Selene.

Ishmael roused himself from the bed to retrieve the two bundled crystals. First he unwrapped the white, which increased its steady glow, then he took out the blue one, being careful not to touch it with his skin yet. The blue crystal began to strobe softly drawing gasps from all including Ishmael.'

'What's it doing, Ishmael?' Selene asked.

'I can't say, because I really don't know,' Ishmael replied. 'This is the first time I have had the two crystals out together and they have done this. Maybe it's because we are all here in contact at once.'

Time seemed to slow down for Ishmael. The blue light had created a pulsating hole within the white illumination of the earth crystal and Ishmael felt his awareness drawn towards it. Before him was his astral form, and seeing this other body of his while conscious caused a strange buzzing in his ears. He willed his astral form up to the blue light. Was he supposed to step through? Was something beyond that he needed to see?

Ishmael stepped into the pulsing blue light as Raul's words came to him as if from a long distance away.

'Ishmael, can you hear us? I think he's lost it. Just our luck for this fool to find two of the crystals.'

Ishmael followed Raul's voice as the blue washed over him, and he stepped out of its safe glow into a field where a white wagon stood tied to a fence with a group of four cular lizards lazing over one another as they rested. It was afternoon with only a hint of Aspre above and a number of small campfires, around which huddled figures sharing food. At the closest wagon, two figures sat looking out from behind a cloth canopy. Ishmael stepped forward, noticing that he couldn't feel the long grass on his legs or the sigh of the wind that ruffled the leaves on nearby trees.

Even the deepening shadows of the day had a blue hue to it that allowed Ishmael to see further. Ishmael walked towards the wagon and the two figures. The first one sat near the fire, long, auburn hair splayed out around her. This must be Katerina, he realized before turning to regard Raul. The man was just as he appeared when in the astral. He sat tall and proud, looking capable and strong. He could faintly hear the voices of the others calling him.

'I am still here. It seems that using the two crystals together open a door,' replied Ishmael while marvelling that he was in two locations at once.

'A door to where?' asked Raul.

'Are you ready for this?' giggled Ishmael as a sudden euphoria settled over him? To the location of whoever is conversing with the bearer.'

'To us, you mean then?'

'Yes, that's right, Jona. I am looking at Raul.'

Ishmael watched as Raul opened his eyes then jumped up to look behind him.

'I don't see you Ishmael, you're lying!'

'If that is so, Raul, then who is the woman with the auburn hair sitting beside you in the wagon?' He felt Raul's presence torn from his and the scene around him began to fade as Raul stood fast looking behind him where Ishmael laughed at the game.

'Where are you monk? Trying to spy on me?'

Nearly gone now, Ishmael continued to watch as Raul called out to him, but he stayed quiet and pretended he couldn't be heard. The woman beside Raul had stood too and Raul turned to her.

'Cassandra, it seems our movements can be followed by Ishmael's use of the crystals.'

As he faded and came back to his own body, Ishmael saw the crystal's glow was nearly gone now as if their energy were depleted. He was so bothered by the whole incident with Raul but not sure why that he nearly ignored Jona and Selene. Raul had referred to his sentinel as Katerina and yet he had just witnessed him call this woman Cassandra, but why?

'It seems Raul doesn't want us to see what he is up to,' Ishmael said to them now that Raul had departed.

'He has never acted as if he wants anything to do with us, and your sudden reappearance has maybe pissed him off like the rest of us, Ishmael,' offered Selene in a voice thick with sarcasm.

'I know it means little, but I am sorry, Selene, and I hope one day I can explain my choices to you. I am drained now and tired. We will talk tomorrow.' Ishmael disconnected himself.

As he sat there packing away the two crystals his mind kept returning to Raul and why he would be worried about Ishmael or the others being able to watch him. Ishmael wrapped the crystals up and put them back into his pack. Then he arranged the pack as a pillow and lay back to sleep, unaware of Fajira regarding him intently from where she lay.

Chapter 35

They gathered at dawn outside the rusted gate to Tinselthwaine. It took four of them to pull the gate open and in doing so it fell from its brittle hinges, leaving the stone door built into the mountainside towering over them.

Latasha motioned for Haakon to pick her up, and he scooped her frail body into his arms.

'We require light as we move through the hollow citadel,' Latasha said. 'Nobody has walked these halls since the Severing that I know of. The moonstones that adorn my palanquin are perfect for retaining sunlight and should be used before fire itself once we are inside. To carry naked flames within the citadel was a crime in the past, and that rule must be maintained.'

Once the three large moonstones were pried from the palanquin, they were ready to continue.

'Don't suppose you have a key, Latasha?' asked Tek as he surveyed the doors once more.

'Tek, this door will not open for anything but magic. The door we are looking for is beneath your feet.'

They searched the area to find a loose stone in the paving, and when it finally was found it revealed a thick iron ring pull handle that needed some work freeing it of its home of dust and rust. They activated it, and a square of stone floor slid slowly back revealing a long staircase disappearing into darkness framed in thick spider webs.

'I don't like the look of that, reminds me of a tomb,' someone whispered behind Haakon and Latasha. With light from the moonstones they continued onwards with their movements disturbing dust and revealing a floor patterned with lines of silver, green, and red adding colour to this hidden place.

Faustus bent slowly tracing one of the patterns. 'I would guess that this is actual crushed gemstones in the floor. But why?'

'The crushed gems are protection wards. Once activated they could be used to protect the ancients and control access to the different areas accordingly. It was once a beautiful thing to walk amongst the gem trails when they lit up,' replied Latasha from up ahead.

The way onward was obscured by the dust cloud they had created, and many times when their route changed direction it added to the confusion they all felt as their direction sense was lost. The fear came then slowly winding up through each of them, stifling breath under the weight of the mountain.

'Soon we will reach the hollow that runs vertically through the citadel; it is there we can rest again with fresh air before we descend.' Latasha began to sing a soft melody about hope and life, and moment by moment it lightened the mood of the party.

The passage-way opened out to a circular chamber so wide that Haakon couldn't see its end. The pit they came to in the centre of the chamber was the hollow Latasha had spoken about, and they could see the dusky shadows on its opposite side too. As they moved forwards towards the edge the ground became littered with skeletons and remains of weapons and armour. In Haakon's arms Latasha wept, the gentle shuddering the only sign of her distress, and he faced away from the others until she could compose herself.

'These are the bones of my kin. I tried to convince them leave, but as you can see, they didn't treat the danger seriously and died here from starvation or by falling down the hollow.'

Faustus sat rubbing his ankles which had puffed up from the walking. 'So, what do we have that your kin didn't, and how will it get us down?'

'You have me, the last singer from the ancient order of sound.'

'So… you mean to sing a song that will lead out from this place?'

'No, I mean to summon the ancient beast that transported my people up and down the hollow citadel. It is the only safe way down.'

'Haakon placed Latasha in a sitting position against his pack and once comfortable she began to sing in a faint warbling tone that felt to Haakon as if it penetrated his body. The singing was in her language with its pauses and playful tones that caught the imagination and filled Haakon's head with images of nature.

Haakon couldn't tell how long Latasha sang, but when the silence took over they stayed quiet, lost in the moment. He found some water for Latasha in the pack.

'Is it finished now?'

They were interrupted by a shrill keening that echoed down to them from higher up the hollow.

Yasmin had an arrow nocked in a moment. 'It seems the summoning has attracted more than we wished for.'

'It has been so long since it has been summoned that it may take multiple attempts. The next song is a long one. Haakon, you must be sure I am not disturbed since we cannot afford for me to mess this up.'

'We will move Latasha to our center, then we defend her in a circle,' ordered Haakon, and they all hurried to their positions and waited.

Latasha sang again, louder, stronger and more forceful than before, the sound rolling around the room to disappear into the hollow. Haakon stood sword ready, glancing around at the others of his clan who were equally ready, even Faustus.

Scrabbling came from above them in the hollow, and a gust of air raised dust through which they came. The creatures were winged like birds or had talons and beaks. Tek was snatched away with a scream and then his attacker leapt back into the hollow with its prize.

An arrow from Yasmin winged one creature, leaving it flapping around screaming. Another creature skipped off the stone, half flying half running, and its talons tore at Haakon; his sword hilt smashed its beak in and sent it sliding away against the stone. Two more of Haakon's men fell on the wounded creature with swords until it lay still and they pushed it off the edge.

Faustus turned the last dead creature over, looking at its feathered back and arms. 'What are they? The bastards got Tek!'

The song continued and Latasha began to tire, but her eyes squinted with the effort and her hands clenched her thighs. They were ready when the next wave came with spears, and Haakon saw Faustus angle a discarded spear up into one creature's charge as it impaled itself. Lou was knocked from his feet by one feathered beast then snatched away by the second right behind it. Yasmin's arrows cut a deadly path through the attackers and when the remaining lost their nerve she was left with only two arrows.

They were down to six now, and as the song dwindled away the third wave came this time from the sides of the hollow. Haakon slashed around at the feathered form in front of him feeling his blade carve through it as something collided into his side and he fell into Kent whose strike went wide, hitting the stone and sending up sparks. Faustus struggled as one attacker gathered him with its wings, wrapping tightly over him, but Yasmin stabbed up through its armpit and it fell off the old physician. A beak raked across Haakon's shoulder, slashing leather as it swivelled for his face; Haakon held it away from himself with one arm as he severed one arm from its body with his blade. Covered with gore he brushed it from his eyes and turned for the next foe, but they were done.

A green pulsing light could be seen emitting from the hollow now.

Haakon looked to Latasha, who grinned weakly and grasped his arm.

'It's coming, Haakon. It's actually coming.'

Chapter 36

Ishmael was startled out of sleep by an excited Fausto.

'Ishmael, wake up! We are arriving at the Crag.'

Ishmael rubbed the sleep from his eyes. 'I thought we were going to Cabre. What's the Crag, Fausto?'

'Cabre is the capital of Soarnestia and the Crag is the castle, silly, come and look!'

They pulled one of the windows open then poked their heads out as the sand whips slowed to enter the opening portcullis ahead. Along the wall huddled figures clamoured over one another to surge towards the opening. Ishmael looked up at the castle that towered over the road stretching into the clouds. It was the ugliest castle he had seen.

'It's made from blocks of obsidian, Ishmael, can you believe that? It must have cost a fortune to build.'

The sound of yelling bought Ishmael's attention back to the crowd rushing the portcullis, where a group of soldiers had emerged. A soldier of rank yelled for the crowd to stop, but someone threw something that hit him in the face, knocking him down, and then the soldiers took to the crowd with clubs and the screaming began. Ishmael saw an elderly man stagger away, blood streaming from his head as nearby children huddled together crying. Some of the crowd ran straight back towards the sand whips, whose heads snapped forward at the unexpected meal. Then they were moving forward under the portcullis and past where soldiers still battered some men who were cowering against the wall.

'Stop, stop hitting them, this is terrible,' screamed Ishmael out the window.

Fausto was laughing then stopped when he saw Ishmael's face.

'What is it, Ishmael? They deserve it for trying to sneak into the city without following the rules.'

'No one deserves that, Fausto. They are people like you and me.'

'But they know it's not allowed to travel the road on foot and have broken the rules. My father used to say if everybody broke the rules there would be chaos.'

'I disagree, Fausto! These people are in need of food and shelter and breaking rules is wrong, but to attack a person for it is barbaric.'

Ishmael felt a hand on his shoulder; it was Fajira.

'Ishmael, come on now, these people out there are not our concern.'

'Fajira, nobody deserves what I just saw.'

'Maybe not, but there are two types of people, and one of those are victims.'

'So is that what you, Fausto, and I were in Glimmersedge?'

'That's not fair, Ishmael.'

'I'm just pointing out that we are all victims sometime, Fajira.'

'No, Ishmael, not the Vorm. We became the other type of people, victors.'

'There was no victory in what I just witnessed, for anybody involved,' Ishmael argued.

'It's not that simple, Ishmael. What separates them is their outlook in life. Victims see obstacles while victors see opportunities. You were right saying we are all sometimes victims, but everybody has the ability to emerge victorious.'

'That's a great little speech, Fajira, but how were those people to do that?'

'If I was amongst them I would have used the distraction to climb aboard one of the carriages. If people choose to succumb to life's struggles they will be blinded from what's possible, but if they truly open their eyes they may find a way to be victorious.'

'When I was a brother of Illume, we would go down into the city to help feed and clothe the poor. Yes, some of those people wallowed in their misery that they had bought upon themselves, but others could do nothing about their situation.'

The carriage door opened and five men who wore the orange sash came in to collect the baggage, bowing to Fajira as they entered.

'See, what I have learned, Fajira,' Ishmael continued, 'is that there is suffering in life for everyone without causing more. The Mother showed me visions of the Severing that I believe was a warning to all the people of our world to stop and take notice of what they were doing to her. The Severing wasn't supposed to just be a healing of our world but also a cleansing of old ways. The end of an old way of life necessary for creating a new world where people live in harmony with nature instead of wreaking destruction upon it.'

'Well good luck, if that is what must happen for you to decide when to bring back the magic, Ishmael. We create, we destroy, and then we die.'

'Do you worship one of the gods, Fajira?'

'In my family we are forbidden to worship them.'

'Forbidden, why?'

'Because we serve both the gods and the people of this world as a bridge between them, so to have a predilection to one of them would be wrong and would influence our neutrality in spiritual matters.'

'Fajira, that doesn't make sense. What about your soul?'

Fajira ignored Ishmael's question as she rose, ready to disembark. When they did, there was no sign of the fight between the soldiers and pilgrims except the bloodstains on the stone around the portcullis.

One of the guards stopped before them, bowing low. He wore the orange sash with a silver band through it.

'Fajira, your father is impatient for your arrival and has organised personal transport from here onwards.'

'Our transport was just fine,' said Fajira, and when the guard stayed where he was she sighed. 'What is this new transport you speak of?' 'It is just beyond the portcullis to the Trystland side of the Crag. There will be no need to travel like the commoners from here on, my lady.'

'Lead on, then.'

Ishmael hurried to catch up with Fajira and Fausto. 'Fajira, so why is it fine to travel the road any way you want to Glimmersedge and from Cabre onwards but not to Soarnestia?' Ishmael asked.

'The Soarnestians are paranoid warmongers mostly; they share a large border with the Veiled land and the monstrosities that dwell there so you can't blame them really? Recently pilgrims attacked the sand whips causing the deaths of hundreds not only from the creatures themselves but also from the riots that ensued and the violent reaction from the city guard so you can see some reason behind not just allowing anybody into their land in a time of war.'

After some words between the Vorm soldiers and the Soarnestian guards they were let through a smaller door in the portcullis onto the Seekers road where an open topped carriage stood harnessed to four magnificent horses.

'Oh they are so beautiful and regal, don't you think Ishmael?'

'I have little knowledge of such beasts, but yes they are fine looking animals.'

'I will teach you to ride them, Ishmael,' laughed Fausto. 'You are such a barbarian!'

'You are lucky your mother's soldiers are here or I would wring your flimsy neck, boy.' Ishmael mimed the action of strangling something and laughing.

Fausto jumped up onto the carriage. 'I'm sitting next to the driver,' he yelled back.

The trip took the better part of the day as they wound along through Trystland, for the most part unable to see the land because of the cliff faces that bordered the road. But when they were in sight of the tall towers in the coastal city of the Godhead the road rose out from the canyon walls and took a fairly steep incline which slowed their journey. At the top the delay proved to be worthwhile as the city which was larger than Ishmael could ever imagine sprawled out below them.

Fajira ordered the driver to halt so Ishmael and Fausto could have a moment to see the sight. Most of the structures had domed rooftops and those that didn't had rooftop gardens. The harbour on the far side of the city was swollen with ships, and in the center stood the one thing Ishmael had only ever seen sketches of, the Godhead itself. The gigantic head towered over everything else except the towers, and as they watched bells tolled to indicate the change of god as the face slid away to be replaced by Aeon, the god of time.

'How does the face change?' asked Ishmael turning to Fajira.

It isn't known, Ishmael. There is no way to enter the structure, which is totally carved from crystal. A door opens at the base, but that cannot be accessed without magic, though countless people have tried to find a way in.'

'It's glorious,' marvelled Ishmael shaking his head in amazement.

They carried on, and another larger group of soldiers riding horses joined them to help escort them into the metropolis. All sign of fatigue had vanished now as Ishmael drank in the sight of the glorious city, losing himself to his senses. Their escort led them to a large estate where a high tower rose from the middle of a large, rectangular building of white stone. On one side of the road neat rows of warriors drilled a pattern of swordplay in the dying light while on the other side women and children holding lanterns meandered through some type of orchid whose trees were laden with strange, swollen purple fruit. Ishmael could also see a huge market garden. The road led them to the front of the house where soldiers wearing all white except their orange sash stood with spears to attention beside the manor entrance.

Chapter 37

ajira placed a hand on Ishmael's arm. 'Don't speak until you are addressed and welcomed by my father. You cannot afford another debt of honour.'

He must have looked worried then because she squeezed his hand and smiled.

'Don't worry, just follow my lead and things will be fine.'

They climbed down from the carriage and waited as the doors to the manor swung open and a trail of servants flowed forth with bowls of water and short brushes and began sweeping the dust from their clothes. Fausto giggled as the man attending him tickled him with the brush.

Ishmael's own attendant indicated for him to extend his hands palm up and then washed them with sweet-smelling water. Finally a lady stepped up to him and with a small bowl that she said contained oils she anointed him with a tap on the forehead, throat, and eyelids.

'May your inner vison open to the gods, your voice be allowed to speak its truth, and your eyes drink in the wonders of our holy city.'

A short man with thinning, grey hair and wearing a maroon robe with the orange sash stepped forward, knelt, and then touched his forehead to the ground. He then rose and took Fajira in his arms.

'My Lady Fajira, it has been too long since this old man laid eyes on your beautiful visage. It is good that you are finally home once more.' He then beckoned Fausto forward and bent so they were of the same height. 'Master Fausto, finally you are free to visit us and learn of the heritage that separates you from the masses.'

Ishmael wondered at the strange words as the man turned to him.

'It is rare to have an outsider enter these walls. Your actions speak of great courage and a friend of Fajira's is a friend of mine. My name is Jenko. Please follow me, the lord Vorm awaits.'

As they followed Fajira explained that the man was the principle or head of the Vorm household, and in charge of running the estate. 'He looked after me since I was a toddler and regularly got us both into strife with his antics.'

The greeting hall was simply beautiful. The white stone floor and walls held sketched pictures of various people that Ishmael guessed were ancestors of the Vorm. Lanterns hung from pillars, softly illuminating the large room and designed to bathe the long table at the far end in more light than the rest of the greeting hall.

As they entered the hall two figures rose from the table and moved to meet them. The man hurried forward and buried Fajira in a great hug, sobbing as he did so and smothering Fajira in his huge, muscled arms. The iron-grey moustache and braided hair revealed his age, but Fajira's father was a warrior and still trained hard by the look of his physique. A large scimitar was strapped to his waist, holstered in a bejewelled scabbard.

'My Fajira, how can you ever forgive your idiot father who made you marry that pig Diego, who I thought was a better man?'

'I tried Father, I really did but having relations with other women is something I will never allow to tarnish my honour.'

The woman beside Lord Vorm then took Fajira in her arms. 'Welcome home, daughter. I need no longer worry for you now you have returned to us.' She had the fine features that Fajira had and moved with the light ease of dancer.

'Mother, Father this is my son, who as you can see has grown since you saw him at his birth. By right you should have had a larger role up to this point in his life, but due to Diego's whims he refused to let our son visit with you. Fausto, come greet your grandparents.'

Fausto shuffled forwards and bowed low.

'I am very pleased to finally meet you,' he said with a slight waiver in his voice.

Lord Vorm knelt so he was at the boy's level. 'No need to be afraid, boy, only our enemies need fear us, but never you, the son of a Vorm woman. Now come and hug your grandmother. She has waited for this moment for too long.'

Fajira's mother was weeping as she took Fausto in her arms.

'It will be fine now young one, you are with family now. I bet you are hungry? See that lady there by the door. She is Kirsten, my personal servant who will take you for a snack and show you around the house before dinner.'

With a shy smile and look back at Fajira and Ishmael, Fausto followed the servant out of the hall. Lord Vorm and his wife turned to face Ishmael. Ishmael bowed low and waited.

'Please rise, Ishmael. Fajira has told us only a little about you from our courier hawks but I believe we owe you a debt of gratitude for saving Fajira's and Fausto's lives. That is something we shall get to later. I am Kalis Vorm and this beautiful being here is my wife, Thalia. We know you must be tired, but it is our wish you dine with our family this night so we may repay a tiny sliver of the debt the Vorm family owe you.'

'Lord and Lady Vorm, it is a true privilege to meet you, and I look forward to getting to know you better while I am here in the Godhead, and just so you know, I consider there to be no debt. If not for Fajira I wouldn't even be here to meet you.'

While Fajira and her parents became reacquainted with each other, Jenko escorted Ishmael to his room.

'Jenko, is it possible that I might attend the dawn prayers in the morning, I wish to offer prayer within this most holy of places?'

'You are a priest?'

'Not a priest, Jenko, but a brother of Illume.'

'Right, one of Shail's children, I will have you escorted to prayer square before dawn and also taken to meet the priest of Illume at Shail's temple.'

'I won't need an escort, Jenko, from the trip here I know where the square is and I'm sure if I need directions someone will be happy to oblige.'

'That may be so Ishmael, but I have been told to provide an armed escort for you here at my master's home and within the city. I'm sure once you have been here a few days there will be no need for the escort. It is my master's way of making sure you remain unharmed.'

Ishmael doubted that and knew that even though it seemed he had freedom, he was by all rights still a prisoner in a different prison. He could however see the reasoning that Fajira had bought a stranger to her father's home and this was just a precaution.

The room he had been given was clean and spacious with its own bath chamber; a servant filled the bath for him and offered to wash him, but he sent her away preferring his own space. Finally he was here and could get the answers he needed from Shail, whose advice would ultimately decide his next move. He managed a brief sleep before the loud banging on his door and Fausto's laughter awoke him for dinner.

Ishmael had expected a lavish affair with many guests but he found he wasn't in the mood for gatherings or pointless conversation to fill the time. He was therefore pleasantly surprised when he was ushered into Lord Vorm's personal chambers, which opened out to the serene gardens at the rear of the manor. Fajira and the lady and lord Vorm awaited there among a thick blanket layered with many dishes and bowls of food. They made room for Ishmael and Fausto then filled their cups from the honeyed wine and toasted.

'To family reunited and special friends,' said Lord Kalis before emptying his cup and refilling it.

At his side Lady Thalia elbowed her husband, who faked injury at the blow as they all laughed.

'Dear husband, please don't overindulge while we are among friends?'

'Oh, Thalia, what am I to do? My only daughter has returned to us with the saviour of her life, and you wish me not to celebrate?'

'No, I didn't mean it like that, dear one.'

'Enough! Tonight I celebrate my own daughter and my grandson's arrival. I will hear no more of this, woman.' He passed Ishmael another cup of wine. 'Drink, my friend!'

The wine went straight to Ishmael's head and as fast as he drank one cup another was passed by Kalis. Luckily there was food to layer his stomach. The food was spiced meats with thin bread and dips and a thin milky, cake soaked in rum.

From somewhere a trio of musicians had arrived and begun playing soft music that had Fausto up and dancing a slow, heel-toe tapping dance as they all clapped on. As Ishmael sat sipping wine he looked about him at Fajira's family laughing and eating and felt at once blessed to be invited to join her family as well as sad that this was no longer an option for his family.

The night wore on until everyone, but Kalis and Ishmael had retired to their rooms and the candles had burnt out. Holding a flagon in one hand Lord Kalis stood with Ishmael gazing upon the beauty of the city around them.

'It is not what I expected,' slurred Ishmael.

'Does that mean you are disappointed with our city then?'

'No, no not disappointed at all, Kalis. I expected it to be chaotic and dirty because of all the pilgrims.'

'There is a reason for that, you know, Ishmael. Priesthoods are a fastidious lot and prefer a clean place to pray. It seems that the saying; "A clean uncluttered home gives a clean uncluttered mind" has something to it. The priesthoods decided together to create the city in an orderly layout that would be easy for newcomers to find their way around while making an evacuation easier in the case of an emergency or disaster. Any beggars or homeless people are quickly given food and shelter in return for assisting in keeping the city clean.'

'At dawn I will go to pray. Jenko informed me I need an armed escort to go with me. Is this truly necessary?'

'Ishmael, what you need to understand is that we have no concerns regarding you, but we do have concerns regarding your safety while in our city. I have many enemies who wish to do me harm, and if they cannot get at me directly then they may target or use those who are close to me to hurt me.'

More like you want to keep an eye on me, thought Ishmael, but here under the influence of too much wine was not the time to argue it further. If he must, then he would take an escort.

❧

Chapter 38

The summoning and the bale-green glow from down in the hollow sent the creatures that had attacked them into a frenzy, and they attacked again using their speed to get close to Haakon and his men.

'Latasha, what are these creatures?'

The worried shake of her head said it all. 'Never in my life have I seen such beings. They must have made this their home since we deserted it.'

As the green light grew brighter it brought with it a deep hum. Resting from the latest attack, Haakon could see the remains of their party were struggling to keep a calm, organised defence. He bade Faustus remove three torches from the pack behind Latasha and light them. It seemed like an eternity as Haakon waited for his old friend, but before the next wave came three of them held the burning torches before them to ward off their enemies.

The beast Latasha had summoned took up the whole circumference of the hollow. Its skin was grey and looked ribbed in places. Many tiny holes opened and closed upon the skin, emitting that green light as it seemed to float just above the floor like a cloak or blanket. What appeared to be two eyes regarded them as they chased away the latest foes.

'Take me to it, Haakon, so it may know me again.'

Haakon and the others moved Latasha and the packs onto the beast, which appeared solid enough to stand upon. They stood waving the burning brands above them to keep away any more attacks as Latasha lay her hands to the skin of the creature she had summoned with her ancient song.

'I had thought you dead, but you heeded my call even after so long. I have need of you, Eldra. Guide us down to the lake of stars.'

The Eldra didn't answer, if it even could, but it seemed to shiver at Latasha's words and touch. They descended slowly, the attacks increased in ferocity, and they were all called upon to fight as screaming figures dove upon their party again and again once the torches had burned out. The small party managed to hold their own until the hollow widened. Below them the lake could be seen from the pin pricks of light that flickered on and off in its waters.

Now the attacks came in a frenzy from all sides. Faustus knocked one away with his spear then fell to a knee with his hand on his chest, grimacing, but Haakon had no time to check his friend as one winged beast grabbed Latasha, dragging her towards the edge.

Haakon fell on it, stabbing wildly until it ceased moving, and when he regained his feet he saw the true extent of the damage they had suffered from the constant attacks. Not one of his men had been left unhurt: they had clothes and skin torn from the claws and beaks of their winged enemies. Besides Latasha, who now was seeing to Faustus along with Yasmin, there was only Liam left. The others had been torn away in the descent.

The Eldra skimmed above the water and stopped at a white sand beach. From overhead the cavern continued outwards, and far behind the beach a path wound up and away. Latasha stayed on the Eldra with her palms down on its skin for a time, and Haakon imagined she was thanking the strange beast.

Haakon wanted nothing more than to collapse into a deep sleep, but they were wet, exhausted, and all had sustained injuries that needed seeing to. He forced himself up and began collecting driftwood to make a fire.

When Liam saw what he was doing, he joined Haakon.

'Liam, you need to rest; that wound to the arm looks bad.'

'Am I hearing you correctly, clan lord? When you rest, so shall I; meanwhile, I won't bleed out from this,' said Liam indicating the arm curled against his chest that was obviously broken.

Latasha used her healing skills to aid them all, stitching and applying salves or bandages and shaking with the effort in using her weakened arms. Faustus lay close by breathing evenly now as he slept. *This is no place for him now* thought Haakon. *He has served me and the Kenzu well. After all this settles down its high time he was left at the clan house.* Except now they didn't have a clan house and this safe house would become their home for a time until he could get the coterie of the heart together. He cooked a simple meal of vegetables in broth, adding a powdered root to his and Liam's that would take away some of the effects of exhaustion. The rest he let sleep after their meal, and he sat beside the crackling fire.

'What I want to know, Haakon is why the winged demons stopped attacking us. They could have finished us off easily,' Liam said.

'Something scared them away when we got close to the water, but what it was I'm not sure. We still need to be watchful, 'Haakon replied.

With no other option, they waited and drank hot tea.

According to my knowledge of geography, we should be close to Karnock Forest, or what remains of it. Is it far from here to the safe house?' asked Liam.

'The forest that surrounds the lake is known as The Untouched and becomes Karnock Forest, which we must pass through. It should take only a few days at most.'

Haakon started to doze, and so they agreed to wake Yasmin and Latasha to take their watch. He was out to the world the moment his head hit the bedroll.

Chapter 39

It was the bitter cold on his skin that dragged Haakon out of his exhausted sleep. A chill wind blew off the lake, causing a flurry of smoke to waft into Haakon's face, and he coughed. He felt around for the water skin and drank the remains. The other blankets about the fire were all empty, and down on the sand along the lake edge Haakon spied three figures, one holding a burning torch.

'What does it say?' The voice of Yasmin floated back through the dark, and Haakon pulled on his boots and grabbed his sword heading in their direction.

'It says for us to leave or suffer a similar fate. I wish somehow we could make sure Haakon doesn't see this,' replied Latasha.

'See what?'

Haakon walked from the gloom to stand beside Yasmin who held Latasha in her arms.

Latasha didn't speak just held Haakon's gaze then directed it with her own to a figure on the ground, tied to a sitting position with the aid of branches and vines. It was Faustus, his old face was locked in a grimace, and his chest had a large hole through it. The missing heart now lay in his cupped hands that had been tied together. Strange words had been carved across his forehead.

'Haakon knelt before his old friend and began weeping quietly as he cut his friend free. Then with the others in tow Haakon carried Faustus back to their camp and began digging a grave. Yasmin stood with an arrow knocked to her bow as she stood watch.

Haakon paused in the digging, turning to Latasha who sat on the sand in front of him.

'What happened?'

'I was sitting watch alongside Yasmin, neither of us making any noise. We heard and saw nothing, but on our next round were surprised to see that Faustus was missing and had decided to go relieve himself. When he didn't come back we decided to look and then discovered him as you have seen. It was a warning to leave.'

'So I heard you telling Yasmin, but from whom?'

'From my kin.'

'Can you be sure?'

'The writing was in my language which few can say they know. It is the use of nature to decorate the corpse of Faustus that disturbs me so deeply.'

'That appeared just a reflection of madness to me,' said Yasmin.

'Yes, there is most definitely a touch of madness, Yasmin, but it is more than that. My people were the custodians of the Mother, and our duty was and still is sacrosanct and was always our first care. To see nature made such a mockery of doesn't bode well for us.'

Haakon paused in his digging; he had wiped a hand across his brow at some point and left a dirty mark smeared there.

'We will approach them as if going to war. To kill one of us in an act of cowardice is a debt I shall not let go unpunished, even if I must destroy them all.'

'It must not come to that, Haakon. Here they have the advantage, and we can't afford to dally long. The coterie need us.'

They finished burying Faustus then rested until dawn, when they broke camp and began the slow trek along the lake edge to the half circle of light that was the natural entrance to the cavern. When they reached the entrance it opened out below them to Karnock Forest, thick and twisted. The trees were a sickly white colour, and their branches and trunks showed lesions that wept a greenish sap, leaves hung listlessly from where they sprouted.

The ground was hard and cracked, which being so close to the underground lake shouldn't have been the case, thought Haakon as they watched from their vantage point. A playful wind crept over them, twirling the limp vegetation interspersed around the rocky decline before them. They began the slow descent, and the rocky slope crumbled easily beneath their feet, sending a wave of debris sliding down before them. If not for them holding onto each other they also would have ended up in a heap at the bottom.

None of them talked, and it seemed as if the dismal place was sapping any positive emotion right from them. Haakon felt empty and angry. He should never have allowed Faustus to come on this trek. Maybe if he had of insisted his old friend stay with the rest of the clan he would still be alive.

'Cutting through Karnock will reduce our travel time by at least a day. We should be at the safe house in two more days,' said Latasha

'This place is sick, like an open wound on the earth,' said Liam as he chewed on some dried meat.

'It is one of the original wounds the Mother suffered, and even after three hundred cycles you can see this place has never healed from the damage that magic has caused,' answered Latasha.

They continued on now into the forest, it was mid-morning and even the sun refused to shine on this dismal place.

Haakon paused to get a better grip on Latasha, who lay in his arms. He nodded to the sky where iron clouds gathered in the direction they were headed.

'Rain's going to catch us unless we can find shelter,' he said.

They picked up the pace and began to notice the sign of someone living in this place. Ornaments hung from the trees here in such a way as to provide a path forward. Wind chimes made from copper and iron strips were prominently displayed in the trees gave off an ever-increasing din, and the smell of burning timber was in the air. Liam kicked a fallen log alongside the path, and when it collapsed in on itself they could see it was hollow. Plump, yellow and black ants swarmed up at the intrusion and a mottled, brown fox with mangy fur broke from where it hid in the bushes to run past them. Up ahead Haakon could see a clearing where the trail ended. They stopped at its edge looking on with both horror and wonder.

Chapter 40

The pre-dawn chill misted from each exhaling breath as Ishmael and his Vorm escort walked towards prayer square. Hooded lanterns hung from the lamp posts, making this daily journey easier for all who were inclined to attend the early sessions. Not all of the religions held prayers at dawn, but Illume and the light of Shail's time was dawn when her light bathes the world in hope that comes from the new day.

The square was still busy with pilgrims besides those whose faith decreed they pray at dawn, and it took a while for Ishmael to find Illume's other worshippers. The dance of creation was just beginning when Ishmael found them, and he quickly added himself to their graceful ranks. Great bundles of incense sticks burnt around the square, their orange glow burning brightly. Streaks of red brightened the sky as the dance reached its climax, and the followers of Illume all adopted a kneeling position for meditation.

Behind them a soft wailing started that turned into a chant, and a slow tolling of bells announced the first morning chime. Focusing on his breath until the noise around him faded, Ishmael allowed himself to stay clear and allow his thoughts to drift by without grasping for them. When the bells tolled a second time, Ishmael opened his eyes and grinned. All about him and around the square worshippers paid homage to their gods. *They must be alive*, he thought, *otherwise why would so many people still pray to them?* They couldn't all be wrong?

From the square the Godhead towered over the worshippers, and though he had seen it from a distance nothing could truly describe the effect it had on him up so close. The visage of Aeon, god of time from yesterday had shifted to that of Sayed, the holder of knowledge.

Ishmael turned to his escort, who still wore the serious scowl from this morning.

'How many faces does the Godhead have?'

The warrior look surprised to be addressed.

'How many faces does a god have?' the warrior replied.

'Excuse me?' said Ishmael.

'Young sir, how many faces does a god have?'

'Well, just one, I suppose.'

'That is where you are wrong, if I may say so. You see, on the Godhead now is Sayed, the holder of knowledge, but he is also known to other cultures as Quill, the sacred recorder; Dale, lord of the tomes; and Calithe, maiden of learning.'

'So what you're telling me is that you don't know. Does anyone?'

'Once again, who can say whether the gods are all represented with their own visage? It is commonly thought that as a god loses his followers to disappear into obscurity then the chance of his visage appearing isn't possible, while that of a god rising in power and followers has more chance of gracing that most spiritual structure.'

'Would you mind if I look at the Godhead? I have heard about it for many cycles and to finally be here is something I never dreamed would happen.'

'That would be fine; take all the time you wish. I am at your service, young sir.'

Ishmael approached the Godhead, running one hand over its surface where it met the ground. It was cold to the touch, and like Fajira had said it was made from crystal, possibly even linked with the Jaldurial structures he was familiar with from Illume. If so, did it also have a spirit within it that could open the entrance no one had been able to do?

'Beautiful, isn't it?'

Turning to the figure that now stood next to him, Ishmael saw a young man with wavy, blonde hair and a freckled face gazing up at the Godhead.

'Yes, it is. It's the first time I have seen it. Are you here on pilgrimage too?'

'Oh not at all, I am Wynne and currently organize the followers of Illume and lady Shail within the city with regards to festivals and offerings. Our temple is down there further on Temple Street. If you need anything at all or just wish to come pray, then you are welcome.'

Ishmael smiled back at Wynne as the man strode away. He wasn't used to such kindness from strangers, and he looked around at the many faiths represented in the square that not only seemed to tolerate each other but live in harmony together. The thought was awe-inspiring for Ishmael.

It was mid-morning before Ishmael returned to the Vorm manor. The trip back was slow, with teeming crowds gripped in the fever of the festival only a day away. He was tired now from the late night of drinking then the early prayers and returned to his chamber to rest. When he got there Kalis was sitting in a chair looking out the window of the room.

'Ishmael, how was the morning with your goddess?'

'It was a morning I will never forget, Kalis. This city is truly magnificent, and I feel blessed to be able to experience the upcoming festival. I didn't expect to find you here, is something wrong?'

'No, my friend, you get the wrong idea from my visit. I was fortunate enough to spend the morning with my grandson, and Fausto mentioned something that piqued my curiosity, so I thought to ask you about it.'

Ishmael rinsed his face in a side basin filled with scented water. He didn't like where this was going and suddenly felt on guard but tried to relax. The last thing he wanted to do was appear defensive.

'Just ask, Kalis, and if I can help you I will.'

'Since the Severing my family have watched over Trystland and the road of Seekers. We have given everything to ensure peace is kept amongst those who seek to approach the divine, and we have mediated between the gods and their followers. Such a sacrifice no other family has ever known, but we swore to continue our duty until the gods return with the magic that is inherent to our beautiful world.

'Now this morning as I played with Fausto and we tried to outdo each other with boasts of our lives, I learnt that he had seen something truly remarkable or simply a lie to outdo his grandfather. Can you think what he boasted to me of?'

'Yes, Kalis, I know what you speak of.'

'Then I would like to hear you say it, my friend.'

'Why, Kalis, it has nothing to do with you.'

Kalis stood, walked to window, and rubbed his hands together.

'If I was to believe my grandson then you carry with you the very thing that could point to the imminent return of the gods, and yet while you are here in the holiest of cities in the home of one who has dedicated his life to the wellbeing of the divines' children you dare not to tell me of this miracle? I thought I could call you friend especially after what you have done for my daughter; however, friends don't withhold from each other.'

'Kalis, I have only just met you and your family, so forgive me if I don't regard you as a friend yet. What I am trying to do has greater consequences for more than just us two. I have a sacred duty that I have carried my entire life, and it's something that needs to be kept secret.'

Kalis strode over to Ishmael and grabbed the lapel of his jacket before Ishmael could defend himself.

'You would hide the fact that you carry magic and items of power when nothing like that has been seen for three hundred cycles?'

'Yes, I would, because I don't know you and I am alone and trying desperately to find my way. I come here to see if Shail can guide me before I resume my task, and I was hoping you might see it in your heart to help me further while I am your guest. Or am I now a prisoner?'

'Bah, if you were a prisoner you would be chained in the dungeon,' said Kalis, twisting away from Ishmael and sitting on the bed.

'Fausto told me of two crystals but said they are not the magic. You can tell me about them or not, but know this, Ishmael: our trust is made or broken here, now.'

Ishmael sighed. 'My tale will take time, and I would feel better knowing we are somewhere safe from prying ears.'

'We shall talk in my chambers then.'

Ishmael grabbed his backpack as they went. He felt sick to the stomach about what Fausto had told Kalis, but now was too late to beat himself up for his own stupidity.

Ishmael told Kalis everything even though he had decided not to. Once he started the tale of how the magic came to him he found he just couldn't stop and didn't want to. After so long without being able to openly talk about this burden, Ishmael found it cathartic to share it all until finally he finished and slumped back in his chair feeling empty. He understood the risk of telling Kalis so much but he needed Kalis to trust and help him while here where he knew no one besides the Vorm.

Two servants whisked into the room at a sign form Kalis and began removing the remnants of the meal the two of them had shared as Ishmael spoke.

Ishmael drained his glass and sat back watching Kalis, who in turn regarded him thoughtfully.

'If you and the others of this coterie carry the magic within you, then what significance do these crystals have?'

'That is one thing I cannot answer. The Mother communicates with me in dreams and has yet to show me what significance the crystals have.'

'Your story is an incredible tale, Ishmael, one that many would find hard to believe.' Kalis held a hand up stopping Ishmael as he went to speak. 'I am not saying I don't believe you, Ishmael, but, it would be easier to do so with some actual proof. Maybe a demonstration or a look at these crystals would put my mind at ease?'

Chapter 41

Ishmael removed the two wrapped crystals from his backpack. What harm could it do to just show them to Kalis? The magic was within him not the crystals. He removed them gently and sat them before Kalis on the blanket. The crystals sat there looking like the rocks they were until Kalis reached for the blue one, which then began to give off its blue light.

He snatched his hand away, looking startled.

'Can I touch them?' Kalis asked, looking over at Ishmael.'

'I am not sure if that's a good idea, Kalis, no one besides me has done so.'

Kalis reached forward anyway and picked up the white crystal. At first nothing happened and he turned it over in his hands inspecting it closely then it began to give off its white light, which grew more intense until it hurt to look upon. As Ishmael looked on Kalis stiffened and his eyes went wide and the crystals glow enveloped his form.

'Let go of it, Kalis,' said Ishmael, noticing his voice sounded young and panicked.

Kalis hung on and drool started dribbling down his chin, then he began to weep. Ishmael wanted to help but didn't know what would happen if he touched Kalis; maybe it would injure him or send him crazy. Ishmael inwardly cursed himself for allowing Kalis to touch the crystal.

Kalis began to shake, and then with a cry he slumped forward, knocking over wine and food, and the crystal dropped from his hands.

Ishmael scooped the two crystals up, wrapped them, and stashed them in the backpack before attending to Kalis. The Vorm lord was just coming to as Ishmael turned him over. With a cloth Ishmael wiped away the food from the face of Kalis as the man looked up at him uncomprehendingly.

'Kalis, it's Ishmael, can you remember what happened?'

Ishmael pulled Kalis up to a sitting position and poured water for him.

'Are you hurt Kalis?'

Kalis began to scream in a hoarse voice then the screams turned to sobbing. After a moment Kalis composed himself, and finished the water then he turned to Ishmael, hands shaking.

Someone was banging on the door from outside the room now which they both ignored.

'I saw things, terrible things. I saw the return of magic and what would happen when it's done. It must not be allowed to happen,' said Kalis, grasping Ishmael's shoulders tightly, then he collapsed and his eyes rolled back showing the whites.

Ishmael laid Kalis on his side so the man didn't choke, and then he unlocked the door.

The guards rushed in, nearly knocking Ishmael over and when they saw their lord lying prone amongst the food and wine. They trained their weapons on Ishmael.

'He's murdered Lord Vorm,' said one, holding the point of his sword against the hollow in Ishmael's throat.

Two guards crouched over their lord. 'He is still breathing. Get him up into that chair there.'

Ishmael stood motionless; one movement and he knew this guard would spit him without another thought. He quickly searched for a solution and then he heard Fajira.

'Let me through! What has happened to my father?'

'The man you bought with you has attacked Lord Vorm while they shared food. He is alive but unwell.'

Fajira turned, and her eyes flashed her anger towards Ishmael. 'Take him to the dungeon and chain him until he is questioned.

As they marched Ishmael past Fajira, Ishmael turned to her.

'I would never hurt your family, Fajira, you know that, don't you?'

'If you have, Ishmael, then nothing will compare to the pain you will endure.'

'But don't you want to know what happened?' Ishmael asked.

'I do, Ishmael, and you will get your chance to speak. Take him away!'

Ishmael spent the remainder of that day in the cold, stone cell. Now he was in a difficult situation again and separated from the crystals once again. He tried to meditate and stay calm, but his mind refused to cooperate and he imagined missing the festival and being forgotten to rot here in the dungeon when he had been so close to getting answers from his god. He would fail again like he almost had before the Mother had saved him.

When Fajira came, Ishmael could not hide his relief. She dismissed the guards who needed telling twice before they left her alone with him. They regarded one another through the bars of the cell.

'Fajira,' he began, but she cut him off.

'You attack my father, who welcomed you into his home, and make me out to be a fool. How do you think that looks, Ishmael?'

Ishmael held his tongue as he watched Fajira pace in front of him, her clenched hands telling him there was more to come. He must be careful not to anger her further.

'I know I owe you a debt for saving us from Diego, but then you do this, and if he dies I can promise you will die very slowly.'

'He knows about the magic, Fajira, and touched one of the crystals.'

Fajira paused then turned to him. 'How would he know such a thing I haven't told anyone else?'

'Fausto told him while playing a game with Kalis. Then he confronted me and demanded I tell him and show him everything.'

'I want to believe you, but my father has not woken up and he may never again. What you have said doesn't explain his condition.'

'The crystal did something to him, Fajira. He picked up the earth crystal, and then the light engulfed him and he began convulsing, and next thing I know he's babbling gibberish and collapsed in front of me. I swear that I never laid a hand on your father.'

Fajira turned away from Ishmael, and he saw she was weeping. He let her continue uninterrupted and waited for her to compose herself again.

'I hope for the sake of your soul that he awakens,' she said letting her words trail off, and then she left without saying another word.

❧

Chapter 42

It was night when they came for him again. Jenko unlocked the cell with a set of heavy keys, and two Vorm warriors escorted Ishmael to see Kalis in his chambers. The Lord of the Vorm was in his bed looking weak, but colour had returned to his skin and his eyes were clear and alert. Fajira stood with her mother, Thalia, who glared openly at Ishmael when they entered the room.

'Leave us but wait outside,' said Kalis, dismissing his men.

When the four of them were alone Thalia walked slowly over to Ishmael, unclasping a knife from her belt and holding it in front of her.

'If you dare think to hurt my family I will cut the heart from your body and feed your manhood to the dogs while you watch.'

Ishmael raised his hands before him defensively, looking to Fajira for help, but there was none coming and she refused to meet his gaze.

'Forgive my wife, Ishmael, she has had quite a scare, and it appears she and my daughter have strong feelings for me. Thalia, leave him alone. He is not to blame. I already have told you it's my fault.'

Thalia put away her knife then sat on the bed beside Kalis, still regarding Ishmael with a hostile look.

'Kalis, we need to speak in private.'

Fajira and Thalia began to object, but a look from Kalis they turned and left the room.

'Can you remember what happened before you passed out, Kalis?'

'No, I have no recollection after you pulled the crystals out to show me, then the next thing I remember is waking up here. Tell me what happened.'

'When you held one of the crystals you began convulsing. You told me that the return of magic to this world must never happen and that nature would turn against the races.'

Kalis lay back and closed his eyes. 'I remember none of that, Ishmael, and I am sorry you were apprehended by my men who thought you had murdered me.'

'The last thing I wanted was to bring trouble for your family; if you want I can leave here.'

'That would be a terrible thing, Ishmael. You are our guest, and the Vorm don't treat guests that way. Of course if you leave the household one of my men will still accompany you, for safety reasons of course.'

'When your men seized me they took my backpack with the crystals. Can I have it back please?'

'I'm sure they have it somewhere safe, and I will find out where so it can be returned to you. Now I feel weary and will rest. We will talk more soon, my friend.'

Ishmael wanted to talk more now but didn't want to trouble Kalis. As he left he couldn't help feeling that Kalis was lying to him.

Ishmael headed back to his room and encountered Jenko on the way. The clean-cut old man bowed low to him with a smile.

'Ishmael, the day of Giving begins tomorrow; I have taken the liberty of giving you an escort to attend the festivities. Tithes are expected at the temples, then the ceremony begins at noon.'

With everything that had been happening, Ishmael had forgotten the festival, and it would be a timely distraction.

'Thank you, Jenko, for being so thoughtful. I will make sure I'm ready to leave when the escort comes.'

Back at his room Ishmael hoped to see his backpack, but it wasn't there, so where was it? It was late now, so he would have to wait for the morning when he was clear headed.

Ishmael stood gazing at the amber ocean around him as it rippled and a warm wind blew around him, getting stronger. Maybe a storm was coming, he thought and when something faintly touched his shoulder he turned. The earth tree towered over him, branches creaking and swaying in the strong wind. A thin branch brushed again along his shoulder as if trying to get his attention. The touch from the tree was reassuring, and he felt his fears melt away as a nurturing feeling washed everything else away.

His mind filled with the image of the coterie standing back to back with fire around them and screaming as infernals attacked them, and he felt the despair of Raul, Jona, and Selene as they were overwhelmed by enemies. The scene vanished, leaving Ishmael standing again before the tree through which a lithe figure stepped. She walked up to Ishmael and gently cupped his face in hands that ended in leaves at the end of her fingers. Then she pulled his head down towards her gently, and he noticed the stars in her eyes as if he gazed upon a cloudless night, and her hair was a flutter of butterflies that shimmered with colour. She kissed him on the lips, and he felt himself stir in his loins and his heart beat faster with the love he felt for the Mother. Then she released her hold on him and began walking backwards and disappeared into the tree leaving him alone and scared. A voice whispered into his mind.

'Come home to us, we need you here.'

Ishmael woke with the dream fresh in his mind. It had seemed more than a dream, though, and he found sleep was the last place he wanted to go. He rose and began meditating, making sure he kept his walls up to stop the coterie breaking through. They despised him, maybe hated him now he had gone his own way again instead of heading to the safe house. Why couldn't they just understand he needed to do this? Ishmael knew he was different to the other coterie members, a pariah cast out to wander alone in the hope of finding redemption and answers. He would get these both from Shail of Illume.

❧ ❧

Chapter 43

The clearing was mostly filled with a cottage crafted from iron and other metals twisted together and rusted in some places to form a crude home. There was no sign of wood or stone, and green smoke wafted from a rusty chimney giving off an astringent smell that made them cough. On the porch near the front entrance sat an iron chair made to resemble a throne in the shape of a tree; spread branches loomed over the seat whose backing had been crafted to resemble the angry visage of a woman's face.

Latasha gasped and covered her mouth to stifle another cry.

'They have forged a home of metal, the one thing we use only to make war. It is forbidden to decorate our homes with any metals, but it seems my kin have forgotten that.'

'We have forgotten nothing!'

They pivoted to find a figure kneeling on the path behind them. A metal mask covered the figures face, and it wore white leather and chainmail armour. Haakon saw that to their right up in the branches a bowman stood ready to fire.

The figure advanced slowly, and Haakon could see long, dirty, silver hair tied back behind the mask. Was this Latasha's kin, the ones who murdered Faustus?

'Drop all your weapons into a pile then walk into the clearing with arms raised, do it now!'

Haakon gently placed Latasha on the ground then turned and stood his ground with one hand on his sword hilt.

'Or what, will you murder another of my companions?'

'That was no murder. It was a kindness to relieve him of his suffering, nothing more.'

Haakon slid the blade out enough to show its keen edge.

'He was my friend and mentor, and you killed him. Whether he lived or died is not your choice to make.'

'The old man would have died in the night from his wounds anyway. I merely performed the duty you were too weak to perform for your friend. Why have you come here?'

The ancient in the chainmail stepped forward again, and at Haakon's nod Liam and Yasmin drew weapons and formed a triangle around Latasha to protect her.

As if seeing Latasha for the first time, the ancient stopped and removed his mask.

'Is this some sick jest you play, bringing one who is an impostor to our kin?'

Latasha's voice rang out true and strong. 'I am no impostor. I am the sacred voice, the opener of doors, summoner of guardians. I am Latasha Meldoriel, last of the star tower, and it sorrows me to see my kin like this.'

The bowman emerged from behind a tree to stop twenty feet away, staring at Latasha curiously while another figure also armed with a bow showed itself from atop the roof of the house.

'We don't know that name. The Severing killed all our people but our small family here. You must be an impostor!'

A long, shrill whistle came from the house. 'La-Dre, go see to Cor-Ru.

'What, why me Bael? The old fool is useless! He most likely wants food again.'

'Now, La-Dre, or do I have to go myself?'

Lowering his bow, the one called La-Dre looked them all up and down then stalked off to the house and disappeared inside.

Yasmin nudged Haakon with her shoulder. 'Haakon this isn't good. We don't know who is in there.'

An arrow embedded itself in the earth near Yasmin's leg, causing them all to jump. 'The next of you to speak dies.'

The door swung open again with a screech of metal as the ancient who had gone inside emerged, leading a wizened figure who moved slowly and looked ready to topple over at any moment. He was led to the chair on the porch and hoisted up so he sat facing them all.

'My boys think I'm an old nuisance. They forget I was there when we ruled this world. Let the one who dare call herself Latasha Meldoriel come forward.'

'Stay here, Latasha. They can't be trusted.'

'Haakon, I must go so the elder can identify me, otherwise we all die.'

'Then I will come too,' he began, but Latasha was already shaking her head.

'No! We talked about this already, and I must do this alone.'

Haakon sheathed his blade and lifted Latasha, then he walked forwards to stop at the edge of the porch and placed her there on the ground.

'What has befallen you that you need assistance to move around?'

'The nerves in my legs no longer work and have been damaged beyond repair.'

A wheezing laugh came from Cor-Ru, whose pale skin was spoiled with blotches and with silver hair matted by what Haakon now realized was blood.

'I know what being feeble feels like too. Our magic would once have cured us of these frailties we suffer, but that is no longer an issue, is it, Singer?'

'You know me then?'

'Cor-Ru knows all our people, and until this very moment we believed we were the sole survivors of the ancients. You are alone?'

'Yes, alone since the Severing until I find you, my kin here.'

An angry cry came from the ancient on the path who strode around them to stand facing Latasha from the side of the old one.

'You dare call us kin. Prove it.'

'Bael-Mal, enough of this!'

With an outraged look at the seated elder, Bael-Mal threw his hands up in disgust.

'Can you vouch for her, Cor-Ru? He sneered, and the old one shrunk away from him.

'It's obvious who's really in charge here,' whispered Haakon to the others. 'Attack him first if all hell breaks loose.'

'I knew one who went by that name. Meldoriel is a family proven for magi and sacred singers. There is but one way you can prove your lineage.'

Before he could say more Latasha began to sing softly, and it struck Haakon in that way a stirring song reaches the heart, bringing a lump to his throat as Latasha sung about loss and broken trust and the demise of the ancients and their broken vow.

He was startled to feel tears on his cheeks and more so when he saw Liam and Yasmin similarly affected. The old ancient wept openly when Latasha stopped. Looking from him to Latasha, the one called Bael-Mal stepped forward then slapped Latasha across the face.

'What have you done to him!' he roared, drawing a sickle blade from his belt.

Haakon surged forward, his blade sweeping down where the ancient stood and slamming into the metal porch floor as Latasha's assailant skipped easily away. In that short time, Haakon saw the ancient behind them had disarmed Liam, who lay twisted in pain, and Yasmin, snarling with a sword to her throat.

'One move by any of you and I will give the order for your death.'

'*Chul tal rom Koeh*,' shouted Latasha.

'Bael, she knows the old words, stop this now!' The old ancient said.

This time it was the old one whom Bael struck with his mailed glove, knocking Cor-Ru to the ground. Then he turned to Latasha and Haakon.

'If you value your lives then surrender now.'

'And if we don't?'

'Then you are fools whose deaths will mean little.'

Latasha looked up at Bael-Mal. 'Knight of war, is this how you treat your people and the Mother?'

He ignored Latasha. 'Dre, Nim collect their blades. Tonight there will be a reckoning.'

At Latasha's imploring look Haakon surrendered his blade and let himself be searched. He was content that they missed one of his weapons.

Latasha stood tall through all this, never wavering and keeping her gaze on Bael-Mal.

'Under the law of reckoning I make my one demand allowed as the defender of honour.'

'You surely jest, Lady Meldoriel. You're at out mercy, and the only good grace I can offer you is that I can guarantee your safety through this night. That is all the good grace I will offer you.'

Latasha ignored Bael then turned to Cor-Ru, showing nothing but disdain for the younger of the ancients. 'Venerable Cor-Ru, it seems to me that Bael-Mal, no longer recognizes the wisdom of your cycles. He appears to think he now leads the ancients.'

Cor-Ru sat straighter and had a firm resolve to his look as he stared at the younger ancient Bael. 'While blood still flows through my veins and my cycles name me elder, I will respect your demand if I can, singer.'

'My one demand is that this false reckoning is conducted here on the very flesh of the Mother whose heartbeat still reverberates through our bodies.'

'Madness! I reject that request.'

Defying his age, the elder stood and pointed at Bael. 'You have no authority to reject the laws that have stood for centuries. We may have fallen far from the graces of the Mother, but without our laws we are nothing. Latasha Meldoriel, last fair lady of the ancients, I acknowledge and accept this demand under the old laws, so let it be done.'

※

Chapter 44

Under the watchful guard of the warrior Bael, Haakon and his small band rested in the clearing. The twin ancients retreated inside the metal home with Cor-Ru to prepare for the reckoning as Bael stood guard over them rather than prepare for the evening.

It seemed to Haakon that the full moon of Aspre was a fitting accompaniment for this strange trial especially with no sign of the red moon Tamul.

'At least that's a positive omen,' snorted Yasmin who paced restlessly around them. Liam sat eating and Haakon was amazed at the man's ability to be calm under any circumstances. Did he realize that if Latasha lost this reckoning whatever that was, they would all likely die here tonight?

Bael had taken time to mark out four squares in the soil, then he placed something in each of them. One he filled with flowers that grew around the clearing, in the next he placed a metal bowl filled with water. Then one was marked with a burning torch at each corner, and the last he adorned with a pole off which hung wind chimes.

They sat and waited under Bael's watch, and Haakon dealt out what little food they still had. When Latasha touched his wrist telling him it was time, he could see no reason to indicate anything was different, but then the metal door screeched open and Cor-Ru was carried out into the clearing by the twins, who placed him opposite the four squares then sat flanking their elder. Bael moved to join them, his arrogance showing in his movements.

When everything was quiet, Cor-Ru began.

'Since the dawn of time our people have judged one another by the use of a reckoning. This is the first one in over three hundred cycles and could well be the last for our people. We stand her under the holy moon to judge one of our own. One thought lost to us and whose leadership was sorely missed since the Severing nearly destroyed us. Latasha Meldoriel, tonight you stand as defendant of this reckoning, to be judged by the four elements of the Mother who will also bear witness to this event. Address us if you will and choose the first element.'

Haakon watched Latasha meet the gaze of each of her kin then she turned to him and squeezed his hand in a manner meant to be reassuring, but it wasn't.

'Never in all my long cycles did I think I would be the focus of a reckoning. I am here freely of my own will and accept the judgement handed down to me as Aspre is my witness. Let us begin. I choose water.'

Haakon carried Latasha to the square with the bucket in it. She sat straight and proud but couldn't hide the tremors that racked her body from him. He placed her down then retreated.

The twin they called Drey stood and approached Latasha.

'Latasha Meldoriel, do you acknowledge that you had access to the wisdom of all our race, living or deceased?'

'That is right. A magi has the ability to access the knowledge our ancestors had discovered and is given the freedom to learn from any living ancient regardless of position or family.'

'Then why with this extraordinary power at your disposal did you fail to use that knowledge is such a way as to inform your people to the danger they were in? A sacred singer illuminates the way for their people through music and magic, and you did nothing. I further propose that the breakdown of your family relationship was due to them voting against you in attaining the role of high magi. You retained the role of sacred singer by accepting a position on the council of nations without the consent of your people. It could be said that you feared the loss of power that you had been sated with and wished to make sure nobody else could take that away from you. You excluded your own people in the council's dealings instead, saying they lacked the cohesion and maturity needed for such a role. In assisting the Severing you acted heartlessly with total disregard for your own people. How do you plead?'

Haakon let out a long breath. He could see Latasha struggling to compose herself through the accusations and wiped the tears from her cheeks before speaking.

'I acknowledge your claims, water bearer, now hear my truth. As high magi of the ancients and sacred singer, it was my role to teach my kin of the past, guide them in the present, and lead with the future in mind so our race would flourish forever more while serving the Mother. When I first took my role as sacred singer, I was devoted beyond all else, and my efforts to educate what was happening to our Mother were ignored by most who had fallen prey to weakness from the other races and chosen instead to play at war and seek riches for themselves. The amphitheatre of echoes where I conducted my lectures was mostly empty even after pleading with our leaders for help. Our society had fractured under the weight of its obligation, and people looked elsewhere for self-gratification. Can this be blamed on me, one individual? I think not!

'I caused so much upheaval trying to get our people to listen to the signs the Mother had given us that certain factions turned on me, one being my father. He was under pressure from other influential families to reign in his upstart daughter or there would be consequences. A silent vote was held and I was evicted from the sacred assembly to be stripped of the role of high Magika.

'The council of nations approached me at this time as a suitable candidate and with no other duties and acting on the disturbing dreams straight from the Mother I chose to join them when no other ancient would represent us. I refute the claim that I fear the loss of my power. I never chose that power, and I was freely elected by our kin at a time when I thought that role still meant something to our people. Now I know it was all just for show. Nobody really wanted change, upheaval, they just wanted to be left alone to do as they pleased while our duty, our purpose faltered, until we fell from grace.

'The council of nations was created to bring awareness to all our leaders that we had a larger problem than our petty wars. We had to save our world. I agree on only one thing you said, water bearer. Yes, I was rewarded for joining this council of nations who was made up of the most powerful magi across our world. The reward, if you could call it that, was to lay my soul and body bare to raw magic and take upon me many enchantments to enhance my abilities so we could cast the spell that brought on the Severing. I nearly lost my mind to the things that dwell in that raw power and desire to influence those trying to wield it. Most of us died from that power, but I was one of the lucky ones. It turned out I wasn't lucky at all. To wield the weapon that destroyed nations and, lives, and caused the fall of gods was the hardest thing I have ever done. If I had to go back, I would choose to die instead.'

Drey turned to face his kin. 'Fellow elemental bearers you have heard the trial of water, how do you judge?'

Haakon noticed the ancients all had a flower and a dagger placed before them on the ground. As he watched they approached one by one to stick the dagger or the flower in the earth before Latasha. Haakon leaned in to Liam. 'What do they mean?'

'The flower signifies life, the dagger death,' Liam replied.

'Death!' Haakon started to rise, but Yasmin pushed him back down.

'Stop it, Haakon, now is not the time.'

'I never thought this could mean Latasha's death.' He shrugged from Yasmin's grasp and stood. All eyes turned to him.

'Sit down, Haakon, my love, the trial has begun and we must see it through.'

Haakon saw it then, how he had been tricked by her. 'You never told me you die if you lose this trial, Latasha.'

'It is our way, Haakon, and nothing is decided yet. You heard what you wanted to hear. What other type of trial could this be?'

He let himself be pulled back down as the four ancients voted.

The twins placed flowers in the soil and became shy when Latasha gifted them with a wide smile. The elder Cor-Ru placed a dagger without looking at her. Lastly Bael walked slowly over, giving the twins a long hard stare and spitting in the ground before them. 'Cowards!' He placed a dagger before Latasha.

'I choose fire,' said Latasha and Haakon picked her up and carried her to the square with torches. 'Latasha, you don't have to do this foolish trial.'

'I can't run from this, Haakon, and I fear once again that what happens here will affect the coterie of the heart and all our world. There is still hope and my people can survive.'

Bael approached Latasha, shaking his head slowly as he did so.

'Latasha Meldoriel, I want to know how it felt.'

Latasha looked confused. 'How what felt?'

'To have all that power. To wind your way through all our race's memories as sacred singer, bearing witness to our great accomplishments and failures. To have access to the most terrible artefacts of war and power at your disposal. To be endowed with countless powers that would make you godlike as you hold the world's fate in your hand. I believe that you fell to the corruption that power leads many to. You were caught up in the heady social elite and their games, losing the trust of the people with only your high and mighty outbursts bringing attention to the issue of the Mother. You say you tried but did you really? I doubt it that one who says she took her position and its promise so seriously would give up so easily on her kin and the races of the world. While you conducted petty squabbles, the world lay dying and your kin lost, and yet you come here speaking to us of duty when we all know you failed in yours! How do you plead?'

Each harsh word seemed to beat Latasha down that bit more until she cowered under the accusation. Haakon was happy to see the grim set of her jaw and the determination in her eyes as she sat straight again.

'Fire bearer, I acknowledge your accusations, now hear my truth.

'It was a great honour to be named sacred singer. I dove into the memories of our race with gusto and abandonment, believing now I could make the change that I, like all us ancients, knew deep down at the core of our being needed to happen. Long before my duty as singer or high Magika were anything but dreams I was aware of the Mother dying. As a child I spent so much time in the sacred places of our world at the heart of nature that only us ancients knew of and were allowed to disturb. The Mother came in dreams that frightened me with visions of death and destruction if change did not happen. I was a child, doted upon by all, and when I voiced these dreams they were merely seen as the cute imagination of a child. Nobody believed me, but that did not deter me from my purpose as I visited the sacred places, learning what I could and how we could save the Mother. I learnt to choose whom I approached, choosing those who would know of what I spoke. Like me there were many, but they also had been turned from, sometimes punished, for their efforts to bring the struggle our world faced out of the shadows.

'The one thing I learnt from the past of our race is that time changes everything. Gone were the days when our people were solely devoted to the Mother. Where once every ritual meant something and told a story of this world and us, its guardians. We stayed away from cities and other races not because we thought ourselves superior to them but so our motives would remain pure. That all changed when our race chose to court the races and teach them of our connection to the Mother, or Earth as they call it. Some listened and change bought hope for a while, but the humans spread like a virus. This aggressive race never rests and must always seek to evolve. Without the long term vision of our extended lives to see the possibilities of their actions, humans tore down forests, polluted rivers, and dug deep into our Mother, digging out her secrets all in the name of greed, and this they passed on to our people. I must be honest, fire bearer, it was exhilarating to be full of power and know that you can crush your enemies or bring a loved one back from death. However, I was no novice to the arcane arts even before the Severing, and I know the terrible cost of having such power. A cost many would never be able to pay. To use it for anything but good was and is impossible, because I am not made that way.

They voted three flowers to one dagger with the dagger being placed again by Bael.

Latasha chose earth next. La-Nim sauntered over to sit cross-legged outside the Earth sphere opposite Latasha.

'Latasha Meldoriel you speak often of being the caretaker of the Mother but rarely how all our people, the ancients, are caretakers. Becoming lost in the favour of followers and self-importance of the lofty station you achieved, you neglected to share what the council had proposed because to you our opinions did not matter, and you looked down on those around you as lesser and unable to make a difference. You should have told all of us.

'Our proud race was here at the dawn of time; we were strong, devoted, and noble. Beyond all else we protected one another and we flourished. You swore to fight for us and the noble truth in any moment. You swore to uncover deception and fight evil alongside us and you did, for a while. Then you turned your back to us, you pushed your kin away, and nearly destroyed the very ones you swore to serve! How do you plead?'

'Earth bearer, I acknowledge these accusations, now hear my truth. I never looked down on our people. I adored them, but they were taught to fear me. Fed lies so they refused to hear me, and your leaders ignored the warning from the Mother. We all were warned, every one of us. Our connection with the Mother had grown weak until her cry for help only filtered through to the few, but it was too late and we failed her. We all failed her individually. You say I serve you, my people, and I say you are wrong and if you have fallen so far as to have forgotten why the ancients were created then we are in dire times indeed. I never served you, I serve the Mother!'

The vote was three daggers to one flower from one of the twins, which meant the total vote was now six flowers to six daggers. The strain was showing on Latasha now. Haakon carried her to the last square he could feel her weariness. He leant in to whisper.

'Latasha, if you lose this vote they will kill you. I won't let this happen.'

'Don't do this to me now, Haakon. I am not your bauble that you cannot afford to lose. These are my people, and whether you think our ways are strange and barbaric sometimes is not on trial here, I am.'

'If you think that after all you have put me through I will stand by and watch you killed then you don't know me at all.'

'Haakon! This has nothing to do with you. Now put me down.'

Haakon placed Latasha down then moved back to Liam and Yasmin. 'If they find her guilty then be ready to fight.'

The last trial was air and the elder Cor-Ru was carried forward.

'Lady Meldoriel, I couldn't help overhear the concern of your friend, and you are right that this has nothing to do with anybody but us ancients. What is at the core of our people?'

'The Mother is at our core. We are her caregivers charged with protecting her.'

'No, Latasha I mean before the Mother, deeper than that sacred connection to her.'

'Venerable One, there is nothing deeper than that connection and duty.'

'Sacred Singer, you are wrong! The thing at our core is and always has been magic. It could be said that even without magic the races of our world have flourished while the Mother heals from the damage she suffered. The one race that didn't flourish is the ancients. Can you tell me why?'

Latasha had begun to weep, and it took all Haakon's strength not to rush over to silence these fools.

When Latasha continued weeping, Cor-Ru's hands were clenched into fists, and he seemed stronger now when filled with anger.

'The time for weeping is over, singer. Tell us why magic is so important to our race. Tell us!'

'Because without it our race will die.'

'And why is that, singer?'

'Why do you punish me this way when you know this already?' shouted Latasha.

'I do this so all here may see that you have confused your sacred duty with the survival of our kin. Now, why will we die without magic?'

'Because we need magic to procreate.'

'I see you do indeed realize the significance then of the choice you made for all of us and how the fall of our race and its near extinction can be blamed on you. You chose the Mother over your kin when you had no need to choose either. Together we could have retreated from mortal affairs and waited this out in seclusion. Together we could have brought magic back and all been here to see the world change. You thought you were alone, but you never knew about us survivors even after three hundred cycles passed. Instead our people were caught up in the devastation of the Severing to die in the thousands as the sky cities fell to earth. The races turned on our people, blaming us for the Severing since we named ourselves the caregivers of the Mother. We were hunted down and blamed for the chaos that followed. I have lived for over nine hundred cycles and seen our race at the pinnacle of its age. Look around, singer, at your kin. With you we are five, and you are our last living breeder. The power of our race was in your hands, and this is what you have built for us.'

He spat on the ground then went silent.

'Air bearer, I hear your accusations, now hear my truth. My kin refused to hear my plea, so I turned to the only people who did, my fellow magi who formed the council of nations. It was decided by us, the representatives of the races, to save the Mother, for without her we have no world. You may be think even the sacred ancients are above the Mother, but sadly you are misguided. We had our chance to serve, and we broke our vows by choosing to be as the other races. To even suggest I serve you before the Mother is insulting and something that was first taught to our children. I wanted it to be different, I wanted time to forge an understanding so we could face this problem together, but time ran out and I was forced to act. If you think I did what I did without knowing the consequences then you are wrong. Every day I live knowing it was my decision that could wipe our race out, and it was with surprise I have found my people again. The truth is, Cor-Ru, we are still here and now we can make a difference if you are all able to put aside your petty differences, put aside the need to place blame at the feet of others than yourselves.'

The twins voted first with one flower and one dagger. Haakon watched intently as Cor-Ru the elder lay a dagger at Latasha's feet.

'The decision you were forced to make was no easy thing, and I acknowledge you did your best in trying to help your people and the Mother. In choosing the Mother you removed the one tool that truly would have made this necessary transition easier. You removed us, your people and chose to take the burden for yourself. Singer, you were wrong.'

The clearing was silent as all eyes turned to Bael-Mal, the knight who had been openly hostile since they arrived. Haakon watched the arrogant ancient take his time to wander over to Latasha.

He turned to Liam and Yasmin. 'Be ready; since you have been disarmed, go for the daggers and be ready to defend Latasha.'

Bael circled Latasha as he spoke. 'Time changes everything, singer of lost songs. We have changed since you stole our birthright and doomed our race to this.' He gestured at the other ancients. 'We had no way of comprehending what was happening when the Severing began. Numb from the horrors of watching my closest kin die, I huddled in the mountains with those I could find and save, and in time we met up with more of our own people. News filtered through, confirming that not only had our magic been lost but it had been caused by our very own sacred singer, a past high magi and daughter from a noble family. Until this day I never knew why you chose the Mother over us, your own flesh and blood. We could have changed and stopped the damage to the Mother if we truly had been made aware of her perilous condition. Instead the Mother turned against us just like you did. Slowly our numbers dwindled as more and more of us fell into melancholia. When we encountered others they attacked to get what little provisions we had and with our reliance on magic for so long our survival skills were piteous. The world, including nature, had turned against us, and in turn we turned against it. The Mother might still be everything to you, but to us she means nothing now.'

'Is that why you have taken to living in that monstrosity?' said Latasha, pointing at the metal house. 'You made your home from the one thing we use only to make war and that was forbidden to use n our dwellings.'

'You don't get it, do you, Latasha? You and the Mother no longer matter to us anymore. We are a different people, and I'm our future.' Then Bael thrust his dagger into the ground at Latasha's feet with a laugh before turning to face everyone. 'The reckoning is complete. Latasha Meldoriel, we find you guilty and condemn you to die for the transgressions against your people.'

Chapter 45

'Now,' shouted Haakon, rushing forward with Liam and Yasmin.

Bael was faster than all of them though and caught Yasmin with a kick to the chest sending her flying back into Haakon. By then Liam was locked into a grapple with the ancient, who pulled the man into a hug with a growl then smashed his forehead into the assassin's face.

As Liam crumpled Haakon stepped past him to confront Bael, who taunted him. 'I hope you fight better than your warriors.'

Haakon's jab took the ancient in the throat then he was in the dance with Bael as each threw a series of strikes. He caught Bael again with a punch that split the skin under his left eye. 'That's for Faustus.'

Bael's stance was too narrow, and Haakon's momentum kept him off balance as he sought to repel the deadly strikes. Then he was through Bael's defence and landed two hard strikes to the chin. Bael collapsed.

Haakon went to Latasha while keeping his gaze on Bael, who was attempting to stand. 'Latasha, are you okay?'

'Yes, I am, but this changes nothing. I have been judged and found guilty.'

'There must be another way. You can't throw your life away at a time when your knowledge is needed. You can still save your people, but without you they can't breed. If you die now then that will end any hope for the future of your people.'

'There is another way,' called out Cor-Ru.

They all turned to the elder; even Bael as he wiped blood from his face.

'Your companion is correct. Without you, we perish. You abandoned us once, and this cannot be allowed to happen again. The alternative I offer as the elder is this; you stay with us, your kin, and together we find a way to move forward and prepare the world for the return of magic. If ever the ancients needed their sacred singer it is now.'

'What of my friends?'

'They are free to leave here. I can promise that no harm will befall them.'

'Wrong again,' said Haakon. 'If you think I will leave her with you then you are even madder than I thought.'

Bael chose that moment to lunge at Cor-Ru and embrace the elder, who shuddered. This was no embrace, Haakon realized. Bael had stabbed Cor-Ru.

'I can't and won't promise anyone's safety,' said Bael as he tore the dagger out of the elder. 'Latasha will become our slave until we can breed, but first your friends will die.'

Haakon began moving, forward but now the twins had their bows again ready to kill. Their weapons were trained on Bael. The arrows struck Bael simultaneously. He stood mouth gaping, then with a look of disbelief he fell.

The two brothers dropped their bows then ran to Cor-Ru.

'Elder, are you hurt?'

'I am dying. I felt death's hand on my shoulder and the turning of shadows to say my time has come.'

Latasha pulled herself forward until she was before the elder and the twins.

'Can you find it in your golden heart to forgive me, old one?

I have failed our people,' said Latasha, laying her head before him.

'No, singer, you have not failed us; I realize that now. You were one who had pure intent and you stuck to your duty even when your own kin refused to believe your warnings. The consequences of what you did were indeed terrible, and yet if you had of not acted with the council the Mother would have died. Instead, thanks to your courage and foresight, our world and our people have a second chance, a chance to make things right.'

Haakon saw Latasha start weeping now as the ancient patted her back softly.

'Shhhh, child you are with kin now, shhhhhhh.'

'I'm weeping because I have just found my people again after three hundred cycles and one is dead while you lay here dying, and there is nothing I can do.'

Liam nudged Haakon. 'We can bandage him, Haakon. We have enough supplies to keep him alive. Let me check the wound.'

Latasha called Liam forward. He washed his hands with fresh water from a canteen and peeled back the old ancient's shirt where a nasty wound wept blood down his waist and groin.

Liam examined the wound and then spoke to the elder directly.

'Old one, you have had your bowel perforated by the dagger, and the slow trickle of blood loss will see you live two to three days.'

'We can clean it and poultice it. He will live, won't he?' asked Latasha, her voice filled with hope.

Liam kept silent a moment before answering Latasha's question.

'The blood loss could be stopped, but that is not going to be the cause of death. Sepsis and septic shock will be. His bowel will leak bacteria throughout his system.'

Haakon recruited Liam and Yasmin to help him build a shelter. The trees around that clearing were rotten like the forest they had passed through, and the three of them had to walk for half a chime before finding healthy timber, cut it, and drag it back. When they returned the two brothers were digging four body-sized holes looking like graves. Latasha sat before the elder and had made a small mound of the cracked dry earth with a hole in the top of it.

Latasha pulled her necklace out from her tunic and opened the clasp to the pendant that hung there. Inside lay a small green seed. 'This seed is from the garden of senses, the last one, and from it our culture and race shall begin again.'

She tipped the seed into the small hole, patted the earth down around it, and then sprinkled water over its surface. 'As you die, old one, this new plant will grow from the nutrients of your body and so you return to the Mother.'

The elder shuddered and grimaced.

'I have lived along life and now I know our people have hope of survival I can pass from this world content.'

Haakon constructed the shelter to cast shade over the four trenches as Latasha lay in the center, singing to the seed she had planted. This went on all night, and the twins joined their voices to hers as Haakon, Liam, and Yasmin cooked a broth for themselves since the ancients wouldn't eat during ritual. They slept away from the ancients that first night, and Haakon guarded over the two remaining clansmen that had accompanied him and Latasha. He found he couldn't sleep anyway after all that had happened that day, and he felt buoyed by the fact that Latasha had been reunited with her surviving kin. He didn't know how long they would stay here but guessed it would be until the elder died.

Soon he would be with the coterie of the heart and know they were safe. They would need his protection in the coming cycles, and once again he would need to form a plan to keep them safe. With Latasha he could provide them with a link to the Mother and some insight on how to perform their duty when the time came.

The second day Cor-Ru was lost to the mutterings of fever, and Latasha stayed by his side singing to him.

One of twins came up to Haakon as he sat watching Latasha and smiled shyly at the assassin.

'She call his spirit and keeps it here until the seed sprouts. Her music also calls to the spirit of the seed, urging it to survive and flourish, and in the next two days we will see if her work is successful.'

That day was one of complete rest and the mood was a sombre one where they sat reflecting on their lives and what would come next. As dusk approached on the second day, the twins carried Cor-Ru and placed his fragile form on its back, then they gently covered him up to his neck in soil. Then Latasha buried both the twins in the same fashion, which left one spot for her. When she turned to him, Haakon was already by her side.

Her eyes were swollen red from all the weeping, and her skin was pallid and pale. Haakon made her drink water, then he held her to him allowing her to draw some measure of comfort from him since that was all he had to offer her. She pulled back eventually and kissed him hard. 'Bury me like I did the others, then leave us alone. We will be in this state until Cor-Ru passes from this world, he and the twins will reconnect with the Mother, and if all goes well you may witness a miracle.'

Haakon did as requested, then he built a small fire to warm the three of them as they guarded the ancients.

'What are they doing, Haakon?' asked Yasmin that night.

He shrugged. 'All Latasha said was that they were reconnecting with the Mother.'

'The brothers told me what they would do,' said Liam. 'They are recapitulating, and since they are the caretakers of the Mother they bury themselves to be a part of her. The technique is for retrieving and healing your energy and prevents further energetic losses due to past experiences. Ancients perform this at every change of their lives.'

Chapter 46

Ishmael stood on Temple Street waiting to enter the temple of Illume. The street was filled to bursting with people of all cultures and beliefs come to deliver their tithes to the god they worshipped for the day of giving. The man in front of Ishmael and his escort dragged a chest along the ground with the help of a teenage boy, and others in line seemed likewise weighted down with wealth. Ishmael looked about, but nowhere could he see the poor that every city had. Vorm soldiers patrolled through the crowds and stood at the entry of every temple to be sure the event went smoothly.

He turned to his escort, whom he had noticed earlier was a different man to his last escort. It seemed Lord Vorm would change them each time. Was it him he mistrusted, or his men? Ishmael knew he was wasting his time following such lines of thought, because there was only one answer.

'It's a strange thing, this city.'

The guard grunted and spat. 'Why do you say that?'

'Well each city I have ever been in has many poor who live there. They may be kept away from public places, but are still there lurking in quiet alleyways or hidden out of sight in abandoned buildings to come out at night. This is the only city I have ever visited that seems to have no poor people.'

'We pride ourselves in Trystland for looking after the poor. We clothe, feed them, and use them to help us keep the city clean. They are a valued part of our nation and are treated as well as any other.'

'Then where are they?'

'To keep them from falling foul to their base desires of greed, they are persuaded to avoid the festivals.'

'Persuaded? Are you seriously saying that the poor are kept from their divine right to commune with their deities, all so pilgrims to this great nation and city can avoid seeing them beg for money and food or steal from its citizens?'

'The poor that work for our city can pray all they like, but not on festival days within certain times. The agreement we hold with them is that we provide food, shelter, and employment in return for them leaving the millions of pilgrims that flock here every cycle alone.'

'That is a gross imbalance of how you treat the people of Trystland.'

'Name me a city that has a fairer way to treat the unforgotten, as we call them.'

Ishmael thought for a while but found he couldn't, and if he looked at Illume where the poor were locked up or chased below the mountain, then maybe Trystland had the right way of dealing with their poor and destitute.

Ishmael climbed the stairs that formed the entrance to the temple of Shail, goddess of Illume. A priestess swinging an incense censer twirled around him gracefully, covering his form in the sweet smoke as a priest intoned a prayer of welcome.

'Step into the womb of the goddess and know that Shail watches over you. Shail brings hope with the new day. Shail warms our hearts against evil. Shail calls our souls when they are separated from our bodies. Shail illuminates all who follow.'

Ishmael was then anointed with the oil of myrrh, which aided contemplation and meditation and creates peace. He made his way down into the temple center where the glass roof allowed the sun's rays to penetrate down and reflect off what seemed to be gold tiles. A priest wearing a robe of silver stood playing a man-size harp, plucking beautiful notes that lifted the heart with its yearning voice promising the divine.

Before Ishmael a tall statue of Shail stood resplendent with precious metals. At her feet lay the altars of acceptance, and it was here that pilgrims heaped their tithes and offerings to Shail. From his pockets Ishmael pulled a coin purse of gold cetas, and then one of silver ketches which he placed reverently on the nearest altar.

Ishmael began intoning the ritual words. 'As you have illuminated our lives from the beginning of time, I freely give you my riches so you may once again notice us, your children, and bathe us in your holy rays to keep evil from our doors.'

Ishmael began to walk off behind the altars then follow the other pilgrims out the back of the temple when a priest stepped forward and placed a hand on his shoulder.

'Son of Shail, I couldn't help but notice that the offering you so kindly gave was somewhat less than expected of such an influential man.'

Ishmael couldn't believe what the man was saying and began to turn away but the priest wasn't having it and instead gripped him harder.

'If we truly want Shail to appear here tonight then our tributes must outweigh all the other faiths. Shail thanks you for what you give, but more is needed. Child, can you offer more?'

Rather than answer, Ishmael pulled his pendant of Illume from under his shirt that indicated he was one of her holy brothers, and the man scowled more, pulling Ishmael close to whisper in his ear.

'Brother, I would expect more of Shail's chosen!'

'There are enough riches to fund a kingdom, and you want more? Careful, priest, or is it that perhaps a fair amount of this wealth finds its way to your door?' Then Ishmael pulled free from the priest's grip and stalked off. He glanced about carefully as he waited to leave the temple and watched as piles of precious stones, gold ceta's, and jewellery stacked to overflowing the altars and tables all around.

Ahead stood Wynne, whom he had spoken to while looking at the Godhead, and the man beamed his contagious smile before embracing Ishmael.

'I was hoping you made it, Ishmael. By the look of the tributes we have a great chance of attracting Shail here tonight and stealing the show from the other gods.'

Ishmael felt sickened at the priest's words and felt the sudden need for fresh air. He clasped Wynne's hands in his before staggering out of the temple to find his guard waiting for him.

'That's where you got to. I thought you weren't to let me from your sight?'

'No weapons allowed in temples, Master Ishmael and a Vorm soldier shall never remove his sword when on duty.'

'So what happens with the tributes, and when are they weighed?'

'At two chimes before sunset the tithing stops and the scales of splendour is wheeled into position, then the temple's offerings are compared until one faith is determined to have given the most.'

'So once all the tributes are weighed, where does it go?'

'I cannot divulge any more on the subject, Master Ishmael. It would be proper for you to ask one of the Vorm family if you want to know more.'

Tired and still shocked at the wealth he just seen from his walk down Temple Street, Ishmael indicated he wished to return to the manor as he tried to comprehend what all the wealth that was being amassed would end up. The Vorm, temples, or was it some other use that the average person like him wasn't privy to?

As Ishmael and his escort entered the manor, Fajira approached him. 'Ishmael, come; my father wants to see you.'

'Fajira, I just want to relax, it has been a long morning.'

'Please, Ishmael my father won't take no for an answer.'

The last thing Ishmael wanted to do was see Kalis. He wanted to pray alone, not in a temple but alone to his god. His belongings still had not been returned, and he no longer trusted himself not to say something in anger to Kalis.'

Ishmael turned and spoke quietly to Fajira.

'Fajira, the truth is that I feel a prisoner here and think everybody blames me for what happened to your father, who insisted he pick up the crystals. I am forced to take an escort whenever I leave the manor and feel that even though I am treated respectfully I am not trusted or wanted here. I think it's better if I just say my goodbyes and leave.'

'No, Ishmael, don't go. We can talk to Father, and I know how much this festival means to you, so stay until it is finished and then go on your way. Please,' begged Fajira.

'This is the last thing I ask of you. Fausto would be distraught if he didn't get a chance to say goodbye.'

'Fine, but in two days when the festival ends I will take my leave.'

Ishmael lunched with Kalis, and though the incident with the crystals was gone, its echoes still haunted the meal.

Kalis dabbed his mouth with a napkin.

'Ishmael, I have decided that since you are a newcomer here and this is your first festival in Trystland that we will accompany you for the weighing of tributes this afternoon.'

'Your presence will be most welcome, Kalis. My time in this wonderful city of yours comes to a close, and I can think of no better way than to spend it in your gracious presence.'

Chapter 47

Zacriel sat at the long, official, dining table laden with enough for a large family. Zacriel didn't know what half of the dishes were, and already he had eaten his fill. Six servants stood spaced around the table while three of his elite stood guard behind him at the entrance to the royal dining room, and yet Zacriel felt lonely. It was a new emotion for him brought about by days of running Acclaro while keeping the horde of Infernals happy enough that they didn't totally destroy the city.

There was so much official nonsense that came with being a ruler that he hadn't anticipated, and Zacriel refused to delegate any of his duties to others who he just didn't trust. He longed for the life of a normality again where he only had to worry about himself, but that was no longer possible and hadn't been since he took the first step on the infernal road. Now Zacriel was the bone lord and the final of the four infernal lords with nobody to dine with and a group of emissaries waiting to see him with the demands of their leaders. Soon the other three infernal lords would be on their way to Acclaro to greet their new brother or, as Zacriel expected, more like to put him in his place. He had destroyed the lady of Whispers, and now the others would be watchful and even band together to do away with him or control him.

There was one person who he wished could have been here dining with him bringing excitement, laughter and happiness to this dining room of gloom. Nina. He missed Nina.

Zacriel beckoned for a guard and wiped his mouth.

'Fetch Nina from her room, I desire her company.'

'Zacriel, it is almost midnight, the girl will be asleep.'

'No, she won't, trust me, and do as I ask. Can you manage that? Good. Now go; I don't want to be kept waiting all night.'

The guard hurried off, and Zacriel motioned for more wine to a serving girl whose pretty hands were shaking so badly the wine slopped onto the table as well as the goblet. Zacriel grabbed her hand, and the girl yelped.

'It's okay, I won't hurt you, but leave the wine I will pour it myself.' though he tried to not let it anger him, he could feel his temper rising and once he would have revelled in the servant's fear but tonight her fearful reaction bothered him.

'I'm truly sorry for my clumsiness, Lord Zacriel, I will do better next time,' said the girl, mopping up the wine with her apron.

'Leave me. You may all retire for the night and clean this tomorrow.'

He watched the servants file out of the dining room before emptying his goblet in a long swallow and refilling it right away. He finished another before the guard returned with a girl that wasn't Nina.

'Lord Zacriel, this girl was in Nina's chambers, but Nina is nowhere to be found.'

'Well, the guards of her chambers would know if she had gone somewhere.'

'Lord, there were no guards outside her chambers. It was guarded by Dalwyn's men, not ours.'

'I don't care whose men they were, just find Nina and Dalwyn! Turn this castle upside down until they are found.'

That left Zacriel alone with this red-haired girl who was struggling not to stare at the food and didn't seem frightened at all.

'What's your name, girl?'

'Trin, I am Nina's friend, and thank you for letting me move into her chamber with her. Now we are sisters.'

'I have a problem, Trin. I have all this food and already my belly is full and I was hoping Nina would help me eat it, but she is not here so I think her sister should eat instead.'

'Really? Oh no, I can't, Lord Zacriel. I am only a servant and I will be beaten if I eat from the royal table.'

'Trin, I am the king, and what I say is what happens. Sit and eat. You may never have another chance to dine at a king's table again, and it would make Nina happy to know you were doing so.'

Trin sat and soon had a plate heaped with food in front of her that she began to eat with the silver utensils but didn't know how.

'Trin, when I eat I use my hands, and so can you. Nobody will ever know.' He winked at the girl and waited until she had eaten her fill before talking again.

'Trin, where has Nina gone?'

'I really don't know, Lord Zacriel. I woke to the slamming of the tower door and Nina was gone, which was strange because all of her belongings except her books are still in the tower.'

'Did anybody come in tonight to see Nina?'

'No, but I was sleeping, so they might have stolen her away. Do you think she will be okay?'

'I hope so, Trin, I really hope so.'

'Nina was right about you.'

'Right about what?'

'That you are not as horrible as you pretend to be.'

The guards returned, and Zacriel ordered one to take Trin back to the servant's quarters with a message that if the girl had any sign of a beating or poor treatment then Zacriel would tear the offender apart.'

'Goodnight, lord Zacriel. Please find Nina.'

'Lord Zacriel, the chambers are empty, and so are Dalwyn's. There are no sign of him, the two visitors, or Dalwyn's men.'

'Damn him, I should have killed him when I had the chance.' Zacriel stood and swept the dishes from the table then began throwing plates at the walls while the guards stood stone faced.

Zacriel retired to his room and the balcony with a fresh wineskin as his infernals continued to search.

Dalwyn had been a noticeable absentee lately since the two visitors arrived. He knew the girl Kaitlin but had refused to say from where, and Dalwyn had said the man was the answer to his and Zacriel's dilemma and would lead them to the coterie of the heart. Yet that didn't explain why Nina was missing too or why Dalwyn would take the girl whom he detested with him… unless she knew something that Dalwyn wanted kept secret.

A chime passed, and Zacriel was still waiting for the search to conclude as he watched his lunar fly circles playfully around the balcony and him.

When Rapture stomped onto the balcony and dropped to one knee, Zacriel had consumed enough wine to slur his speech.

'Any sign of Nina or Dalwyn, Rapture?'

'Not a sign, Zacriel; they are not in this castle. The guards at the phoenix gate were seen letting someone leave the city though and are under question now.

'There is another matter, bone lord.'

'What now?'

'You have guests waiting for you in the throne room, and I took the liberty of having fresh food cooked and fresh drink opened.'

'Who are these guests who can partake of my hospitality so easily then?'

'The infernal lords, sire.'

Zacriel turned to gape at Rapture. 'They weren't due for days or so, and you say they are here now?'

'Sorry, Lord Zacriel, I could hardly see them turned away from our gates.'

Zacriel, leant against the balcony, unstoppered the wine skin, and took a long slug.

'Rapture, I am in no state to meet them tonight, and I am of a mind not to entertain them on their terms. Kindly relay this message on my behalf that I am immersed in matters too important at the moment and regretfully have been surprised by their arrival. Arriving at the scheduled time would have allowed me sufficient time to make sure all their comforts were organized.

I shall see them in the morning, and they are welcome to break their fast with me in my dining chamber.'

'I'm not sure they will react well to that news, lord.'

'I don't care what they want, and it will do them good to wait since they thought turning up at my castle in the dead of night, days before our scheduled meeting would give them the advantage over me. I won't let them have it, Rapture, and they are to only keep a personal guard of three each while in the castle proper. The rest can billet with the pigs for all I care.'

Rapture departed, and Zacriel went to drink more wine then thought better of it and instead tossed it from the balcony. He blew the whistle, watching as Midnight returned to him, allowing its master to stroke his soft wings. Zacriel knew he could leave now on Midnight and disappear. Nobody would be able to find him, and he could go far away from Acclaro and the self-important infernal lords, forget about the coterie, and just wait like the rest of the world for the return of magic instead of trying to rush it.

He could also turn his back on Nina since she was gone now, but he wouldn't do such a thing. *She would still need him to guide her in the coming days to make her stronger.* Then he thought, do I need her?

He realized that, no, he didn't need Nina, but he wanted her to be near him. He wanted to protect her innocence, to provide her with the things he never had until his journey down the dark path had gone too far. Nina was gone, and Dalwyn had taken the one thing he cared about away from him.

Forcing himself to put Nina out of his mind, Zacriel turned his thoughts to his new guests, the infernal lords, and how he would placate them while maintain the respect they would demand. He was not looking forward to the morning and would need his wits about him to stay free of their machinations. Briefly he entertained the idea of killing the three remaining lords like he had the Lady of Whispers.

Chapter 48

The next morning it began to rain, so Haakon, Yasmin, and Liam put aside their troubles to get soaked through then chase each other through the puddles that formed. It rained like the land here had finally been freed from the sickness that had infected it, and for a time it seemed to Haakon that life had regained some of its normalcy. The sun rose to reveal signs of change in the clearing around where the four ancients communed with the Mother. Tufts of grass now poked through the hard soil in a carpet of bright green and ever so small but still visible was a sprout protruding from where the seed had been planted. Haakon knew it wouldn't be long before Cor-Ru died, his heartbeat was slow and weak now. That evening as they sat around telling tales, Cor-Ru gave an almighty cry, then his body bucked twice before he sank back down into the earth with his head lolling lifelessly to the side. There was no pulse: he was gone.

When Latasha emerged from the earth along with the twins, they were changed and seemed at peace with the elder's death. They appeared renewed with such vigour that brought a simple joy to their actions. The three linked hands then sat around the seedling, singing through the night until one by one they fell silent and collapsed from exhaustion.

Haakon later awoke ensnared in the tangle of Latasha's hair and long arms. Content to lie there a while, he absently traced his fingers over her skin and the raised scars there. Everyone else was asleep when Haakon got up to brew hot char, which he placed on the smouldering coals from last night's fire before going to empty his bladder. As he peed he turned then nearly covered his leg with his own piss at the sight of the waist-high plant that had grown from the sprout. The plant was a thick vibrant green with rich, dark soil. Cor-Ru's corpse seemed to have sunk down into the earth out of sight. Haakon stood there gaping as he scratched his ass, wondering out loud. 'Plants don't grow that fast.'

A chuckle came behind Haakon and he found Latasha had dragged her body over to him. He picked her up, and she wrapped soil-stained hands around his neck then planted soft kisses along his chest and shoulders. 'That is no ordinary tree, Haakon. You have gazed upon the Mother in the astral, but never have you seen her physical body that had died long ago. This is the Mother's new body on the material plane, and it being here will change this barren land to one of teeming life. That it even grows is a sign from the Mother that she has decided to forgive us our transgressions. Soon the Mother will prepare herself to take back the magic that belongs to her.'

Later that day they all worked together to pull apart the metal home that the Ancients had built under Bael's guidance as a protest against the Mother. The tree had almost doubled in size now, and the vegetation around was spreading like the fine hair of a new baby. This horrible place would soon become a place of beauty again.

Latasha outlined her plans to them all as they ate. 'Now the Mother has seeded, this area will become a stronghold of nature. We must hurry now to the coterie who are in need of our guidance and protection,' she said, turning to Haakon.

Haakon looked forward to seeing the safe house; the newly built manor was still under construction to turn it into a fortress. It stood within Auxil's border and lay nestled against the back of the Tiariacs in a valley large enough for thick, rich paddocks bursting with vegetables and fruit to grow complete with herds of livestock.

A small colony of malformed people lived close the safe house. They called themselves the warped ones due to mutations they suffered when the world was devastated in the Great War.

'We must continue with caution,' Haakon warned the others. 'I cannot access the astral realm, so very little communication exists between the coterie and me. Tonight Latasha will attempt to enter the astral and make the coterie aware of our pending arrival. Until then rest up, because we leave at first light and the twins come with us.'

'Awww, come on, Haakon,' said Yasmin. 'It's bad enough looking after Latasha. With the twins our job is nigh impossible, and they're not even handsome or clever.'

The twins had easily fit in to the small band and were slowly escaping their fear of the Mother and nature as they learned how to live again after cycles of torment under Bael's rule.

⸎

Chapter 49

Haakon chose an easy pace that allowed the group to forage as they went and now out of Karnock forest there was an abundance of game and berries. In the distance the ancient fortress where the Severing had been cast loomed over the landscape, a strong reminder for future generations of how things had gone terribly wrong. At the border of Auxil they came to a town known as the Mix.

'In this place we must be careful, this is a lawless town and there is no way of knowing who is here at any given time,' Haakon told them.

The winding road moved through some fields of twisted, thornlike plants with crimson flowers. Strange, hooded, misshaped forms moved through the field snipping cuttings as they went and stopped to stare back at Haakon's group with curiosity.

'What is that stuff growing, Latasha?' asked Haakon.

'Wraith flower, which is a crop that is harvested for its flowers. Smoking the flowers allows users to enter the astral world which seems to be the new thing for people to try. The astral is no game, it has many dangers and many people become trapped there or die when the effects of the drug are still taking place. You cannot leave until it wears off, so if such dangers like storms happen then the only way is to ride it through to the end, which as far as I know has never been done.'

Farther ahead they were met with four riders who hailed them with a wave as they approached on the backs of sleek hounds that easily stood as high as a man. The strange beasts were silent and watchful but never appeared aggressive.

'Good day to you. My friends and I are just passing through; we have no desire to stay and we mean no danger to your people,' said Latasha.

'We trust nothing that comes from the twisted remains of Karnock Forest where for many cycles pale-skinned warriors stole our livestock or murdered our people.'

'Those responsible are dead now, and Karnock is healing,' said Haakon to the nearest man.

One of the riders cleared his throat and then spat down at Latasha. 'And yet here among you are three of those tainted ancients whose kind have proven to be our enemies.' Haakon moved to her side, his hand on sword hilt now.

'Easy, friend we mean no harm and want no trouble. What the lady says is true. These ancients by my side have removed what was stopping the land here from healing and now are leaving.'

'We have lived here our whole lives and suffered the effects from the Severing, but we survived, even flourished, here on the edge of Auxil where few dare to go. You expect us to believe whatever you say after just wandering into our midst?'

Haakon raised his palms as he tried to calm the man.

'You can see we mean no harm and have kept our blades sheathed. Whether or not you believe what the ancients tell you is nothing to do with us. Once their warnings went unheeded and the Severing followed. Now they tell you news that should lighten your hearts since it will help you, it is not to be scoffed at.'

The man nimbly leapt off the huge hound to stand before them. 'My forefathers were here when the Great War devastated this land, and through it all nobody came to help us. We were forgotten while everything we loved was torn down by war. Never before today has an ancient come to speak with me or my kin about the land.'

'It wasn't possible up until now,' said Latasha. 'Time has healed our world so the Mother is nearly ready to bring magic back. We have all lived in fear as the world fell apart, but now is a time for healing.'

'Will this heal?' One of the riders tore off his head covering, and they saw his skin was blotched and bulbous with growths. One eye was half covered with thick, swollen boils. 'Or how about my daughter here?' He grabbed one of the riders who shrank away but was pulled off her mount anyway.

'Father, no, don't show them, just let me be!'

'Shut up! It is important that we let outsiders know of the terrible things we endure. We shall no longer hide from outsiders what we are.' He pulled the girl forward then tugged down her dress to reveal her back while the girl sobbed. Her skin was raised in places like extra bone growth, and a blue-green fungus covered most of her skin. The places free from the fungus were red and scabby as if she constantly scratched.

'Put your head down, girl; they need to see it.'

'Father, no,' pleaded the girl, but the heart had gone out of her now, and she fell to her knees, bowing her head forwards. Her father held her long, grimy, blonde hair to the side, revealing a circular wound from which a small, black twig-like thing protruded from the skin with black lines spreading out over her shoulders to the front of her body.

Latasha moved forward gingerly. 'Oh, child, I have never seen anything like this and don't know what I am seeing.'

'She got stuck while working the fields of wraith, went against my words and refused to wear protective clothes.' The father spat and roughly pulled the girl's dress back up. 'One of the farm lads decided she was ripe for rutting, and when she refused, he pushed her into the wraith crop. We thought we removed all the thorns, but as you can see we were wrong. Now she wanders through her nights usually unaware of her surroundings and by first dark is asleep until sun up. There is nothing we haven't tried to keep her awake at these times.'

Latasha touched the girl on the arm making her jump away as if the contact would harm her.

'Don't touch me, it's contagious.'

'No, child. I don't know what they have been telling you but it isn't contagious. Latasha turned the girl around and carefully pulled her hood away from her face. 'The black webbing, does it stop here above your breasts?'

'It continues on down over the left one and stops there where my heart is. When I sleep there are things that call to me, and then I'm looking down on my sleeping body with a cord connecting to my chest that is filled with a dark fluid flowing out of me to somewhere, I know not where. There are many of us caught in that world, and when I'm there they light up in my mind like lanterns. All paths lead me to this one place, and it's a prison of sorts with walls thousands of feet tall where those like me gather to attempt to bring the wall down while whatever waits on the other side encourages us with promises of anything we want. I don't want to go there, and yet by daylight I'm exhausted after chimes of attempting to claw holes in the wall or climb it.'

'Listen to me, child, this is very important. You are at one of the gates to either the Celestial realm or Infernal realm. The creatures on the other side long for the portal to be opened, and those like you affected by the wraith root are attracted like moths to the gates where subconsciously you know a way back to your body exists. If you wander aimlessly in the astral for long enough, something will take you for its own.'

'I can't stop going there, and as much as I try to avoid the place it is where I always find myself.'

'You have become a part of the wraith plant, mired in the astral without control. Until you trace what holds you there at that wall and destroy it, you will continue to jump between worlds until the astral absorbs you entirely or you get swept away in a storm. You must leave this place and get as far away from the wraith fields as possible so it's hold is weakened.'

'You think we can just uproot ourselves and our lives just like that? This is our livelihood,' said the father, crossing his arms over his chest.

'Then you have a choice to make: your precious crops or your daughter's life,' snapped Latasha, turning on the father.

They left the man and his daughter arguing after that and entered the border town where large areas of stacked wraith root sat drying in the sun as people darted around it snipping and bagging certain pieces. It was hard to ignore all the misshapen figures at work. It was a small town, and in the centre square stood a monument of a hard woman holding a bunch of wraith root high over her head.

At the far end of the small town they came to a Brimmerland outpost of soldiers that watched the border into Auxil.

'Here stops Brimmerland. Over that rise and you're into the lands of Auxil and whatever roams through the storms; best head that way into Brimmerland and the safety we provide,' muttered the soldier as if really not interested.

'Wish that we could, but we have business in Auxil a day's ride from here,' replied Haakon.

The hard stares of the soldiers only became stonier, and they all made the sign against evil as Haakon and his party continued past.

Auxil had been also known as the veiled lands since the Severing. Storms rampaged across the land, making the surface almost unliveable at times, which had driven the people underground or into the mountains. The lower lands of farms were tucked into a half ring of mountains that protected it from the worst of them. The farms here provided produce for the communities sheltered in the mountains and did a roaring trade in fresh food and meat. The safe house they headed to had been taken by the Kenzu after its owner failed to pay them for the protection they had provided him in the early cycles of his business. Eventually they accepted this land as payment, and it had been a great addition to the coffers of the clan as well as a prime location to rebuild the clan house.

Within a chime the party was soaked through with the heavy rain and chilled by the strong wind. They were stuck out in the open now as they approached the safe house. The sentries would be alerted to their presence soon if not already, and Haakon, Liam, and Yasmin donned their clan colours before they advanced towards the safe house where the coterie and their sentinels awaited them.

A group of riders approached in the next chime on beasts that blended in perfectly with the bursting fields they had passes, which made them only visible when they were within twenty feet of them and they blocked the road.

The large warrior at their front had a shock of snowy hair and moustaches down to his chest.'

'Ox, you great lump of shit, are you going to keep your master waiting all day?'

'Haakon, I apologize, it's just that I had forgotten what an ugly cur of a mutt you are.' He dismounted the chameleon lizard mount, which hissed at him, and was rewarded with a punch to its snout. 'See, even the beasts find the sight of you distasteful, Haakon.'

The two men embraced heartily and then the warrior knelt before Latasha.

'Lady, It is a fine sight to see you again, and I feared we would never recover the loss of your wisdom and beauty when I heard you were at the gates of death. Lucky you are alive, because we all would suffer the backlash of Lord Kenzu's grumpiness otherwise.'

'Don't bend to me, Ox. You never have to abase yourself to me, come here.'

The big man embraced Latasha awkwardly so as not to harm the petite ancient.

'That's enough, my lady. If we hold any longer Haakon going to lose his smile and get jealous. He always was jealous of my fine looks and intelligence.'

Haakon rolled his eyes. 'We travel half way across the continent to be met with this unhospitable mutt. Lead on like a good hound, Ox, I am in dire need of a drink.'

The safe house had high stone walls that allowed defenders to stand on the ramparts and fight off attackers, and it left a sizable courtyard near the stables for mustering soldiers and storing supplies and grains. The second level of the house which was still being built looked out over the four fields that spread out around it. Two were vegetable fields and the other two had livestock breeding on them, and in the middle of each stood a lookout tower and another one at each corner of the house's defensive wall.

'It's starting to look more like a fortress than a safe house,' said Latasha.

'Yes, I gave the men here notice some time ago that this would be the future clan house, and I was hoping for it to be complete when we came,' Haakon replied. 'However as you can see, things are moving ahead well and it's a good place for the coterie to hide where we can protect them.'

The place was teeming with Kenzu people, and they had to stop several times as respected members of the clan came to pay Haakon homage.

Chapter 50

A feast was in full swing by the time Haakon and Latasha finally made it down to the table, but when they entered the dining room everybody fell silent.

'You would feast without your leader?' Haakon spoke.

'We left you both alone to make up for lost time, old friend,' said the Ox, holding out a mug of ale to Haakon.

'Tonight I am not your clan leader. Tonight we celebrate what it is to be Kenzu as brothers; now let's drink. That's my last order.'

There was a clashing of mugs on the table as Haakon drained his ale and belched, then laughter when Latasha pushed him away from her.

'Go and be with your men, you barbarian.'

The drink flowed and friendships were strengthened as Haakon made his way around the table making sure to spend time with everybody. He got to his sentinels Benjani Dotoolo and, Ansar Pel who embraced him warmly. They were like children to him, his best warriors, and it was good to see two of them again.

'Where are Zahra and Kaitlin?'

'Raul, Kaitlin's charge, turned up at the gate alone two days ago, causing quite a stir. He was injured and said Kaitlin and he were victims of an ambush on the way here. Kaitlin diverted the attackers away from Raul saying she would meet him here, but so far she has not shown up and may well be dead.'

'Did you send out trackers?'

'Yes, Haakon, we have done all we could. The trackers found no indication of an ambush or any indication of Kaitlin at all. It is a very strange situation.'

'Tomorrow I will question Raul. What of Zahra?'

'There has been a rift developing within the coterie. Zahra led her charge, Ishmael, first to Acclaro where they both very nearly died when the city was taken by the Infernals. Now they have gone off again on their own, this time to the Godhead by the Seekers road so Ishmael could reaffirm his faith in his god.'

'That doesn't sound like Zahra to go wandering around when she knows the importance of this mission.'

'We tried the astral, but it's too dangerous with the storms becoming more regular. The last Jona heard was when Ishmael was travelling the Seekers road with two of the crystals, the earth and air. We have the water and fire crystals here, which leaves one more, spirit.'

Two women came forward and curtsied to Haakon. The shorter one smiled and put her hand on his arm. 'I am Jona, and it's good to finally meet you, clan lord.'

Then Selene stepped forward. 'I have never been so glad to see someone arrive as you, clan lord. Long days we have waited here far from my native oceans, unable to get a decent drink anywhere. Your men run a tight operation, Haakon, but at least this night we drink.' She raised her mug and swilled down the contents along with Haakon then poured them both more.

'Benjani tells me you fought with Ishmael, Selene.'

'It was nothing really, Haakon. Ishmael warned us when Brianna was attacked, and he knows more than any of us, which is why we need him here with us now.'

'Have you tried to contact him again astrally?'

'Ishmael, like the rest of us has learnt how to erect mental walls to defend against attacks or unwanted communication and he shut us out. We only know he is in Trystland and has two of the crystals.'

'Was Zahra with him, his sentinel?'

'I'm not sure since he didn't mention anything about her. It's as if he doesn't trust us.'

Haakon wanted to continue the conversation but was whisked away into a dance as the hall fell to clapping and hooting at the stomping dances of the men in the hall. A group of ladies had surrounded Latasha, exclaiming over her hair and waiting on her, and when he tried to go to her he was met with curses and threats that if he came any closer he would be lord of nothing. As much as Haakon was enjoying himself, he couldn't shake the feeling that this celebration was somewhat premature since still one of the coterie was absent.

⚜

Chapter 51

Ishmael waited expectantly as a man took to the stage where a huge conch shell sat that would enhance his voice for the crowd. 'Greetings, spiritual warriors, and welcome to the day of tributes. Now as it is customary, the tributes will be weighed.'

One by one the priesthoods carried out their tributes on carts dragged by the priests themselves, and under the guidance of the high priests they were then unloaded onto the huge scales. It was a long, laborious process broken up well by a series of performers telling the story of each religion. In this case the first tribute was by Irdalar, the goddess of water, whose beautiful priestesses wiggled scantily clad bodies to flutes and harps as the story of the blue woman being stolen from the ocean was told.

Ishmael watched the story unfold as Irdalar was trained as a slave to the king of Scuttle whose land was beset by drought. The slaves were treated so well by the king of Scuttle and were more like family than slaves. When the drought beset his kingdom he suspected a curse and set about creating a generous offering to Irdalar for help. The king of Scuttle was shocked later that night when the locked door to his chamber swung open, revealing Irdalar, skin now an ocean blue and eyes swirling with energy. The king pleaded for Irdalar's help to protect his people from the famine, and she walked the streets purifying water from despoiled wells, and finding as she went a fey magic designed to deprive the kingdom of Scuttle from its valuable water sources. Irdalar cancelled out the curse, and as the story went, Irdalar, who had always loved the king became his wife. Ishmael was mesmerised by the whole scene, even laughing when Fajira elbowed him in the ribs as he goggled at the dancing ladies swinging their hips before the Vorm lord and them.

The afternoon wound on, and the heat of the day began to take its toll as people in the crowd collapsed from exhaustion. Unlike the crowd, Ishmael and the Vorm family were steadily provided with drinks and food as well as given room to relax or move around. The crowd was packed so thick that Ishmael feared people would be crushed. As he watched he saw a woman collapse and was amazed when the people around her lifted the stricken woman above their heads to pass her to safety.

'Kalis, why do these people insist on staying out in such heat waiting? It's so dangerous.'

'It is something I have tried to stop happening, but pilgrims have brought with them a touch of the fanatical. It is now seen as bad luck to leave before the final tribute is weighed.'

Throughout the long afternoon, Ishmael was constantly surprised at how the crowd looked out for one another while singing and dancing. As each tribute was weighed it was compared with the others, and the top ten tributes were marked on a vertical pole by the religious symbol that represented each religion. When the temple of Illume was called, Ishmael cheered so hard he nearly fell from the platform they were on. Currently the temple of the Jade, lady of prosperity, sat at the top of the listings, and Ishmael wondered whether that was correct since it stank of corruption; it was widely known that those of noble birth worshipped her.

No matter how many times Ishmael witnessed the dance of creation and the birth of Lady Shail it still made him teary and he stood proud watching her story woven from the incredible dancing of the priests and priestesses. The last of the tribute was lifted onto the scales, then a hush fell on the crowd.

Arman stood beside the conch shell again as anticipation grew. 'It looks like the lady has plenty of offerings on this holy day. Let me hear you cheer if you call the lady your saviour!' The cheering rang out from around them, delighting Ishmael that Shail was so well represented. The emblem of the sun rising over the horizon began to climb the pole to the cheers of the crowd. Illumes faithful roared their approval as it rose higher still past Irdalar and the death jester and past Jade, the lady of prosperity, to sit at the summit. Ishmael turned to Fajira, who had just moved up beside him on the platform.

'Look, Ishmael, that's your goddess. She has climbed to the top of the tributes, a great achievement.'

'What happens to the winner, Fajira?'

'They get to commune directly with their god,' Fajira replied.

'But, how does that work?' Ishmael asked.

'Whichever god wins the tribute then manifests directly inside the Godhead and is able to address their followers.'

'So all the riches here are merely to get the attention of our gods so they talk to us?'

'Ah, in a sense yes, that's right,' said Fajira. 'Why do you ask?'

'It's just amazing to me how much wealth is on display today, and when the gods have little or no use for monetary gain, then why is this the way it is conducted?'

'We don't make the decisions, Ishmael, the gods do. All we do is carry out their divine instructions.'

'So what happens to all this wealth? It doesn't mysteriously disappear once this festival is finished.'

From his other side Thalia tapped Ishmael on the shoulder and leaned in to speak with him.

'Why are you so worried about the riches gathered, Ishmael?'

'I think you misunderstand me, Thalia. I'm not worried, it just seems plausible that this wealth will find its way somewhere and to someone, and I for one would feel better knowing it goes to a good cause and not to factions that have no interest in spiritual matters.'

'Let me put your mind at ease, Ishmael. Only the winning temple is exempt from tithing of the tributes. The tributes from all the others are used in keeping the road safe and making Trystland a sustainable land to bear the burden of these constant pilgrimages. The money also go towards paying for the many needs of Trystland.'

Ishmael said he understood, but that was far from the truth. Today he had seen more riches than a nation would need, so someone was getting very rich, maybe the Vorm.

There was one final tribute to be weighed, which was now being loaded onto the scales from the temple of Cinder, lord of might and war. A troupe of dancers emerged from the crowd then began a dizzying routine of rolls and somersaults as they told the story of Cinder and how he defeated every warrior who chose to meet him in battle. There came a series of bangs that had people ducking and looking around in alarm before the sky above lit up with orange and red explosions and the fireworks went off to whooping yells and screams of excitement.

Then a massive man strode out to the middle of the dancers with a sword resting across his shoulders. He roared and tore the shirt from his torso, revealing a ridiculously muscled abdomen and chest. It was Cinder, and when he waved his hand silence fell. 'Gods, surely you mock me by sending weakling warriors to fight me. There is nobody who can match my skill, and maybe even the gods fear me in battle.'

From somewhere laughter began and the dancers fled, leaving Cinder alone as a tall, lithe figure approached him. 'I am Rill, god of war and I accept your challenge, foolish mortal.'

With a scream of fury Cinder attacked. The fight choreography was well planned, and the flexibility and skills of the two warriors breathtaking. As the story told, Cinder struck Rill a glancing blow that spun the god to the ground; then he stepped up and cut his throat announcing, 'I am Cinder, god of war, lord of might.' And so the performance ended with Cinder ascending to godhood still undefeated in battle.

When the applause had died down again the tribute flag began to rise as the crowd watched in excitement. When it stopped level with the Illume flag, Ishmael thought they had drawn, but then it climbed higher to stop above the lady of Illume. The crowd erupted in cheers, and Ishmael saw fights begin as warriors took the excitement too far and spilt blood in the name of Cinder. The priests of Cinder filed out in front of the scales; they were dressed for battle and carried above them on a palanquin the head priest of Cinder, a muscled older man with grey hair and beard.

He stood then threw his arms in the air.

'The might of Cinder has spoken, and soon he will commune with us as is our reward. Praise be the day soon when he returns to lead us in our coming battles.'

Ishmael saw a commotion off to the side and moved to the back of the platform so he could make out what was happening. He chose to ignore Kalis as the Vorm lord turned to follow his gaze. A man in a black, hooded robe was being hastily escorted by a ring of Vorm soldiers, who used the hilts of their swords to knock anybody aside that got in their way. They disappeared behind the godhead, and then Ishmael couldn't see what happened to them after that. He turned back to the tribute where Arman was trying to quiet the crowd.

'It is fitting that with war maybe soon on the horizon that Cinder, god of war, lord of might, wins the tribute. As it is the holy custom of Cinder, blood must be spilt in his name. Bring them forward.'

Kalis moved over to stand by Ishmael. 'What did you see that caught your attention, Ishmael?'

'The robed figure being escorted by your men, who was that?'

'One of the high priests. We afford them every possible protection, which is the least we can do for them.'

'Your family was chosen well to perform the role that you do. I can hardly imagine the difficulty in managing that; it must be a nightmare,' said Ishmael though he didn't believe what Kalis had said.

'Actually you are right, Ishmael, and that is why we have so many people working for us. To make what you have seen of our city work smoothly takes a massive coordinated effort behind the scenes, and we do it well. Now if you pay attention you will see a more negative side of our beloved city and religion.'

Arman was calling for quiet. When most of the noise stopped he pointed out five people that the Vorm guards had lined up. Out of the five, one of them was a woman who collapsed with a cry then broke into wailing. She was dragged to her feet by a soldier who slapped her hard to get her to cooperate.

Arman continued. 'These five people that you see are pilgrims to our holy city, and not only have they broken our laws and disrespected our customs, they have stolen from the tributes. Watch carefully and see how we treat such criminals in Trystland.'

The head priest of Cinder had climbed down from the palanquin and now hefted a heavy axe.

'Cinder, to you we devote this blood offering and eagerly await your return.' With a shout he swung the axe, which cut through the first man between his neck and shoulder. It took two strikes to kill the man; the second man must have weighed up his chances and lunged for the high priest, who simply smashed the axe handle into his face then hacked through his side, nearly tearing the body in two as the crowd roared, watching on.

Ishmael had seen enough and turned away. His eyes met Kalis, but he no longer cared if the Lord Vorm disapproved of his actions or not. That is when he noticed the woman in the crowd staring up at him. Her fixed stare reminded Ishmael of a predator and startled him which he tried to hide. The woman smiled but continued to stare, so he turned away. Did he know her? Ishmael was sure he had never seen the woman, and when he looked again she had gone. When Fausto jumped out at him he almost cried out, and though he was annoyed with the boy he found himself laughing, the strange woman forgotten.

Servants brought them trays of food and refreshments as the bodies were dragged away and the blood washed from the cobblestones.

Fajira offered Ishmael a goblet of wine, which he refused, and she leaned in to him. 'Ishmael, I know what you are thinking. They were criminals, and if my father let anyone get away with stealing from the tributes to the gods it would be chaos.'

Thinking it better to say nothing, Ishmael stayed silent but smiled as Fajira took him by the hand and led him into the celebrations that carried on into the night. The drinks flowed and barrels of wine were rolled into the square where beneath the severed heads of five criminals, the city celebrated.

Zahra meandered through the revelry, hardly noticing the music or crowd when they jostled against her. How much longer could she stay here in the hope Ishmael would appear? For all she knew he could be dead now. Zahra had searched for Ishmael for the better part of a month since leaving Glady's house in Soarnestia. She had adopted the roles of three people since arriving here before deciding to settle on one, an acolyte of Dusk, the hidden goddess of secrets. Beneath the indigo robe Zahra had her normal garb on complete with a full assortment of daggers to go with Moonbite. At times Zahra had wanted to give up, to get angry at the fool man whose life she was meant to protect and would if he just stopped running from her. In a way she mused who could blame him after Zahra had neglected to make herself known as she watched over him at the monastery at Illume. Maybe she didn't know Ishmael as well as she thought she did.

Ignoring the pleas to stop and drink or partake in a dance, Zahra watched the crowd. Earlier there had been some commotion atop one of the platforms where the wealthy sat but she couldn't find out what had happened. Resigning herself that the night was wasted, Zahra decided to go for the fried duck that was served with sautéed vegetable from one of the street stalls. She paid a silver ketch and took a bite of the spicy duck as she walked away behind two men.

They staggered arm in arm with a child and two women trailing behind them under a heavy escort of Vorm soldiers.

When Zahra heard the name Ishmael, she looked up to see who had spoken. As Zahra moved closer to see who was under escort, one of the guards elbowed her roughly in the ribs then waved her away when she ventured too close.

'Look where you're going, acolyte; this is one group you should avoid.' He edged his sword out of its hilt, and now other Vorm guards slowed as they took note of the confrontation.

'My apologies soldier, the drink has just gone to my head is all,' said Zahra, raising her hands in apology and backing off.

One of the other guards turned to look at her as they continued on. It was Rue, and she looked at Zahra then smiled blankly before turning away.

Chapter 52

They staggered into the Vorm household at an ungodly time with Ishmael holding Kalis up between him and Fausto as Fajira danced along behind them, singing. Thalia directed them to lay Kalis in their chamber, and as Ishmael did so he spied his pack and could see the earth crystal inside. With the help of Fausto, they got Kalis out of his coat and shoes then into the huge bed. Ishmael glanced again at his pack before turning to leave and nearly bumped into Thalia.

'You do realize that he will never let you leave with the crystals, Ishmael.'

'Thalia, I have no choice but to take them with me, and I will fight or die until you give me back what is rightfully mine.'

Thalia turned to Fausto and Fajira. 'Leave me a moment; I would speak with Ishmael alone.'

Once alone, Thalia took Ishmael by the hand and led him over to a seat indicating he should be comfortable.

'My husband has always been greedy and driven by power. When we married I thought it was something I could change, but it is so deeply bred into him and all the Vorm males. These days he spends more time with the high priests organizing their damn festivals than with me, his wife. We had children early, as you know, and I thought Kalis would mellow alongside me as a father and husband. I was wrong.

'Now he is older and the stress of running the city and the Seekers road has taken its toll. A full moon ago Kalis began training our oldest son to take over at least some of his responsibilities, and I was overjoyed. Finally I would have time with the love of my life and we could enjoy our grandchildren. Then news came from Fajira that Diego was dead and she was returning home to us with Fausto. She mentioned this strange man from the Rothair mountain city of Illume who had saved her and Fausto from Diego's abuse, and we were and still are very thankful. I should have been happy knowing my only daughter returns home with my grandson, and I was happy until you showed Kalis those damn crystals.'

'Thalia, I…'

'Let me finish, Ishmael. When Fausto told Kalis about the crystals and magic I knew he would never be able to rest until he had seen them himself, and I wasn't worried because magic was dead and never coming back- as far as I was concerned, anyway. Whatever that damn crystal you brought into my home did to Kalis, it has forever changed him.'

'Thalia, I never…'

'Do you know he now has visions that wash over him showing devastation and slavery of all the races in a world where nature has become dangerous, aggressive, even turning against people? What is it he is seeing, Ishmael?'

'It's the Mother showing him what lies ahead for us all unless the magic can be returned by the coterie of the heart in the most favourable circumstances.'

'But why does my Kalis have to see these things when I was just settling him down, Ishmael? He is acting strange and no longer the man I know. Why didn't you stop him if you knew what could happen?'

'That's not the way it was, Thalia. You know what Kalis is like, he wouldn't take no for an answer, and I had no way of knowing what would happen should he pick up the crystals. He is lucky he didn't go mad.'

'I think maybe he is right now. Take those damn crystals and go far away from us,' Thalia said forcefully. I thank you for what you did for Fajira and Fausto, but it is not good for us to be near you.'

Thalia carried over his pack and shoved it against his chest. 'It's not safe for you here, Ishmael, so leave while you still can.'

Ishmael wondered briefly if that was a threat, but looking at Thalia now he saw it was said in frustration with deep weariness.

'Can I say my goodbyes to Fausto and Fajira then?'

'I think it would be best if you just left now. Seeing them will just upset them both.'

Ishmael wanted to argue that goodbyes are always better but thought it just easier to go.

He checked through the pack, making sure both crystals and his money were there, then headed through the house to the yard and the estate exit. He had just made it to the road when he heard shouting behind him. It was Fajira.

'Ishmael, wait, are you really leaving now?' She reached him out of breath and with eyes full of tears. From the house Ishmael heard Thalia calling her back.

He took Fajira's hands in his. 'Fajira, I wish you all the best. This is not how I wanted our goodbyes to be, and I have grown to care deeply about you and Fausto.'

Fajira grabbed Ishmael's chin and stared into his eyes. 'You are a good man, always trying to help people. There is so much I owe you for what you have done for us, so please tell me what I can do for you.'

'I don't need anything. I will attend the festival tomorrow and be on my way. Please just say goodbye to Fausto for me.'

'I will, I promise. If things had been different maybe we could have grown to have something special between us… Now go, Ishmael, my mother sent you away but didn't tell you that the Vorm guard have been asked to keep you under watch.' Fajira reached up and kissed him deeply, catching Ishmael by surprise, then she playfully swatted his face, shooing him away.

Chapter 53

At a loss of what to do now, Zahra pondered her choices. Follow Rue into the Vorm household and risk getting found out by the heart warrior or the Vorm guards, or wait here to monitor who entered and left the estate. Opting for the latter, Zahra took a spot down the road from the Vorm estate at a gaming house where she found a clear view by the road and could lose some coins playing cards.

Rue had made it clear that she was going after Ishmael and had left her a challenge as to who would find Ishmael first. What could it mean if Rue was here now with the Vorm, and did she know something Zahra did not? Hopefully her disguise had fooled the girl.

Not even a chime later, a robed figure carrying a pack came hurrying down the road from the Vorm estate, catching Zahra by surprise since she had become deeply immersed in the card game. She rose to follow the figure when the man opposite her grabbed her wrist.

'Just where you think you going, priestess, it's the middle of the game.'

'I'm out,' she said pushing a silver ketch into the middle and moving to scoop up the rest of her winnings.

'No, you don't,' said another man smoking a pipe, a sailor with beefy forearms and tattoos of sea monsters across his chest and arms. 'Sit and finish the game so we can win back a little of what you so skilfully removed from us.'

'Here take the lot,' said Zahra, slapping down the gold on the centre of the table. 'Split it between you. I need to go.'

Ishmael decided to retrace his way to the Godhead before finding a place to stay the night. He knew he should leave the city entirely now he had the crystals; however tomorrow he would hear a real live god speak and learn if Lady Shail of Illume lived.

He had been walking a while and was getting close to the square when he had the feeling someone was following him. When he turned, nobody was there. He stood watching and then laughing at his own silliness and continued on until the hairs on his neck stood tall and he could feel the anxiety in his shallow breathing. He stopped again at the corner of a building, peering back along the lantern lit road.

A Vorm guard came into view moving quietly through the shadows trying to stay hidden. As Ishmael watched, the guard stopped to check tracks and took off the helmet. He recognized the girl from the festival earlier in the day who had looked at him with such hatred it had bothered him deeply.

Ishmael ran. Whoever this was did not have his best interests in mind. Was she one of Dalwyn's people or the Infernal Zacriel's hireling? When he reached the square it was empty from all the festivities except two guards smoking near the stage. Ishmael angled away from them towards the Godhead. When he turned to check behind him he nearly yelled. The girl dressed as a Vorm warrior was only twenty feet away- how did she get so close so fast?

She looked pleased with herself and raised an instrument to her mouth like a flute. Something shot out at him, bouncing off his pack that he used to shield himself. The second projectile struck his left thigh, making Ishmael gasp. It was a dart, and as Ishmael tore it free from his flesh he could see the dart had been coated with a greenish fluid, most likely poison. Ishmael turned and stumbled away. Glancing over his shoulder he saw the girl calmly put away her weapon then continue walking towards him again.

What would Zahra do? Thought Ishmael and instantly knew to keep some distance between him and his attacker while looking for somewhere to hide. Ignoring the pain shooting through his thigh, he sprinted across the square toward the only thing he could see that offered cover, the Godhead. A shout came from the stage as one of the guards saw him or his pursuer. Stopping, he turned back and waited. The two guards were holding their swords out in front of them, ready for fighting. They edged towards a heavily shadowed area from which the woman emerged, smiling and holding her hands out in front of her to show she was unarmed.

Good, a diversion. Not waiting to see what transpired, Ishmael turned to run, and one of his legs gave way beneath him. On one knee Ishmael fought to ride the waves of nausea and heaviness that suddenly affected his muscles. He staggered onwards, reaching the great crystal Godhead, and leant up against its cool surface hoping the effects of the poison would subside. Ishmael panicked as the heat rushed up his body and his arms and legs got pins and needles. He was going to pass out.

When Zahra managed to slide out of the establishment, she had lost sight of the figure. She hurried off into the square and could hear the steps of someone running but couldn't see anyone until a challenge was shouted out in the darkness.

'Halt and show yourself!' Then more running followed by screaming and the sound of two weapons striking each other.

Zahra armed herself with a dagger ready up each sleeve then crept closer, finding two guards crumpled by the side of the stage, one still moaning. A slight rustle sent Zahra spinning away from where she stood as a blade that would have sliced through her neck rang off the cobblestones, sending sparks flying. Zahra slid out her two daggers using one straight away to deflect the next sword strike.

Rue kept pressing Zahra as she danced in and out with deadly strikes. Whistles sounded and the sound of boots running towards them alerted Zahra to a new problem. She kicked out, striking Rue near the inside of an ankle, knocking her off balance; then she kicked the inside of the girl's opposite knee hard, turning away from Rue as her knee gave away and the sword's arc barely missed her.

'You two stop fighting now!'

Zahra ran, cursing at the heavy robe that hindered easy movement; she was close to the stage and rolled under the supports that held it in place. On her stomach she wiggled across under the stage then emerged to slink away in the darkness with shouting back behind her. It was too dangerous to keep looking for Ishmael now, if that was who had hurried past her at all. Rue would most likely hunt her now that she had exposed herself.

It was too busy now to stay in the square, so Zahra returned to the room she had rented from a sailor. It was only then that Zahra realized she was injured and bleeding from a cut to the back of her left arm, the weaker one. Well at least her fighting would not be hampered by the injury. It was too hard to sew the wound herself, and so she decided to bandage it and have it sewed in the morning.

Zahra kept replaying the sight of the hooded man hurrying through the night and if it had been Ishmael. The more time she spent thinking about this made her believe that the figure had indeed been Ishmael. Why else would have Rue been seen in the guise of one of the Vorm following the figure like Zahra had?

The next day of the festival was on everybody's lips, and being the final day it also would be when Cinder, the god who won the tributes, would speak to the masses. This event was the most attended religious ceremony across the world, according to a sailor deep in his cups. In the morning she would be ready for Rue and anything else that would come her way. If Ishmael was close by like she expected, then Zahra would need to be at her best, and for that she needed to rest.

The infernal staff had laboured through the night to prepare a breakfast befitting the visiting lords, and they had done their best to appeal to their specific demands. Now the table was laden with trays of uncooked flesh, blood gravy along with many unsavoury versions of regular foods that disgusted Zacriel, who never ate uncooked flesh. Taking his seat at the head of the table, Zacriel motioned for his ring of elite warriors to allow the infernal lords into the chamber.

The three infernal lords were not what Zacriel expected at all. The first one through the door was easily seven feet tall with soulless eyes and sharp features that culminated in a hooked beak. The Infernal lord's torso and arms were covered in bright scales that appeared to be moving, and on closer inspection Zacriel could see they writhed with vermin. Zacriel had heard of this one; he was called Quail, the eater of souls.

Next came an obese man wearing a mask of bone that looked to hook into his face; down his bare arms tiny mouths gibbered madly and a smaller set of arms that ended in claws protruded from below his ribs out the side of his torso. The mask turned towards, him and Zacriel knew fear not of something purely evil but more like complete madness that ate away at one's sanity. The creature's thousand mouths were laughing, whispering, and jibbering.

Zacriel motioned Rapture forward. 'Who is this?' he asked loudly while trying to appear like he wasn't doing so.

'The Unseeing lord whose true face delivers those who see it to madness and often suicide.'

Then the third entered, and Zacriel's body thrilled with lust as the lithe woman with insipid skin entered the chamber. She was naked, and only the long, grey hair that flowed down past her knees covered her sexual organs. Her steps left a trail of blood across the cobblestones and onto the floor rug that had been invaluable and now was worthless. This was Lilith, mother of demons. Each stopped and bowed or curtsied low then took a seat and sat.

Then twenty servants, looking terrified, filed into the room ready to serve, and Zacriel pitied them for he knew what was coming. With a look and a nod to Rapture, the doors were bolted shut from the outside. The three infernal lords turned to Zacriel expectantly.

'Welcome, fellow lords, please take what is mine and feast.'

Quail struck out with his beak, tearing into a serving man. The unseeing lord grabbed a teenage girl by the hair and dragged her over to a wall then pushing up against her let its mask rise. The screams were hideous, and the girl had some sort of seizure as she collapsed to the floor where the unseeing lord began to eat her.

Lilith had two men mesmerized. She whispered in one man's ear then the other and sat back with a wink for Zacriel, picking up a glass of wine. The two men went at each other like wild animals, tearing at each other with unrestrained hatred. One of them seized a long serving fork and smashed his opponent with it twice over the side of the head then stabbed the fork down his throat with a roar of victory. Lilith beckoned him close with a bent finger, and he dropped the fork then ambled forward towards her into her waiting arms.

Zacriel watched as Lilith tore the shirt from the man's body and loosened his belt. His trousers fell to the ground, leaving him standing before her swollen with need; she opened her thighs and dragged him forward and the two began thrusting wildly. It didn't last long. The man gave a long cry as he orgasmed, and Lilith tore his throat out, with her long lacquered nails. She turned to Zacriel.

'You want some, handsome?'

He grimaced but shook his head even as his body responded with excitement. What he saw next he would never forget, and it would often make him awaken with a fright. Lilith's belly began to swell, she was panting hard and tearing into the bloody gobbets of meat on the table. Within a short time her belly was big enough to burst as it squirmed with its contents. As he watched in horror and fascination, Lilith gave birth right there to twins. The first one came out screaming, and she put it on one rosy nipple while the second one hung limp and dead on her belly. One pink lacquered nail sliced through the umbilical cord, and Lilith tossed the dead baby to Quail.

The deaths became crueller after the infernal lords had initially sated their hunger and then they seemed to thrive on how much they could make their victims suffer.

When the slaughter was complete the guests and Zacriel retired to change out of their bloodstained clothes and then meet for drinks on the royal balcony where the real confrontation would begin. Zacriel called Rapture over, whose barely restrained bloodlust at the sight of the butchery was quite an achievement.

'Rapture, see that what we discussed earlier is done. Everything will hinge on you completing this task.'

'Yes, bone lord, it will be completed.'

❧❦❧

Chapter 55

When Ishmael awoke he was laying on a bed of cushions in a strange chamber surrounded by glittering lights. At first he thought he was looking up at the stars, then he realized they were candles as his mind cleared. A jug sat on a table beside him, and he checked it was water before drinking. His trousers had been removed and the wound on his thigh bandaged where the dart had hit him. The last thing Ishmael remembered was being chased through the square by that woman posing as a Vorm guard.

With his head still foggy, Ishmael began to look through the cushions and surroundings for his pack where the crystals were stashed. A collection of books covered a long table in oddly stacked piles that looked ready to fall at any moment, and a ladder at the side of the chamber descended through the floor as well as up through the ceiling, presumably to another level. This chamber seemed just for sleeping and relaxing.

'Hello?' he called then began to climb down the ladder, which led to another sizable chamber with an eating area and a corner where chamber pots, lanterns, boxes of candles, and other assortments lay stacked on shelves. Ishmael could easily see the outline of a door here in the wall, but there were no handles or grip to open it. The other side of the chamber held a cell of some kind with iron bars. A prison maybe but for whom?

When he finished searching the two chambers he slowly climbed up to the third one, which from all appearances was a living area with a circular table covered in maps and art materials. A pile of parchment painted with portraits lay scattered on the floor, which was made of dark crystal like the walls.

In the middle of the chamber, encased in metal straps, sat a strange black gem pulsing like a heart. The crystal wall to his left was clear in two large oval shapes through which Ishmael could see down into darkness where some shapes gathered. Between these clear viewing areas a metal tube sloped down to a comfortable-looking throne-like seat, and connected to its end was a huge conch shell covered with material. It looked like a long musical horn and seemed similar to the one Arman had used to speak on the stage the day before.

'Have you worked out where you are yet?'

Ishmael almost fell over at the voice that came from his side. He turned to see a man maybe thirty or so cycles old drinking from a bottle and munching on a pastry. Instinctively he reached for his sword, but it wasn't there anymore.

'The Godhead,' said the man, wiping his mouth with his napkin.

'What?' asked Ishmael feeling confused. 'What about the godhead?'

'You are in it.'

'Impossible! They said it hasn't been opened since the Severing. Why would I trust you, whoever you are?'

'We have gotten off on the wrong foot, wouldn't you say, Ishmael?'

'You know my name, how?'

'If you give me a chance, Ishmael, I will explain.'

Ishmael took a deep breath and exhaled slowly. Okay, explain then.'

'You are in the famed Godhead, and I'm guessing it was someone of the Vorm household or one of the priesthoods who told you it's impossible to enter it. Do you want some food? No, well, okay I will continue. I am called Aeon. You might also know me as Father Tyme, Gourd the life devourer, or Roselle the unraveller amongst other names.'

'Is this some sort of sick joke? If you're Aeon, then I'm Shail of Illume.'

'Oh, who's jesting now then Ishmael? Shail is most beautiful and never takes the form of a man.'

Ishmael felt faint. He looked at the obsidian crystal that was shimmering now, not pulsing, and a deep voice carried through the chamber.

'Is this him, one of the sacred?'

'Yes, Onyx, this is Ishmael, and he is having a horrid time believing where we are and who I am.'

'I can imagine it's been quite a shock for Ishmael,' said the crystal that Aeon had called Onyx.

'You are the first Jaldurial house spirit I have seen outside of Illume,' said Ishmael.

'I will excuse your naivety this time because we have just met. None of us are Jaldurial house crystals, we are harlequin even if we have no material body but our heart. Now if you don't believe this man is Aeon there is one easy way to establish it. Just look into his eyes. You do remember the stories, don't you, Ishmael?'

'The legends say Aeon, god of time, has one eye dark as night while the other is light as day, and they change each day.'

'Come here and do what Onyx says, Ishmael, I won't bite.'

Ishmael moved over to sit by the man who called himself a god then looked into his eyes, and sure enough one was dark while the other was light.

'How can it be?' Ishmael asked.

Aeon poured two goblets of wine for the both of them. 'Drink, my friend, you are about to hear a lot of things you won't want to.'

'This is the Godhead we are in, and those clear areas are the eyes of the god at any one time. If Onyx chooses to he can clear the whole structure so from inside it's like the walls aren't even there.'

'How did you know my name?'

The man stared at Ishmael for a long moment. 'Do you need more evidence I am Aeon?'

'The eyes could just be some sort of trick.'

'I dream about moments and can see every possibility for every action that a soul takes. In the time of magic I could walk those moments and paths through anybody's life. Pause it or stop it completely. I wielded the power I had for my own needs and my ego controlled me, otherwise I would have listened to the warnings the Mother sent. Even gods forget that the Mother rules over us too.

'Sorry to digress… now I can only dream, and for the first time since the Severing I dreamt of the Mother and my vision opened. The Mother showed me what happened at the Severing and how the coterie of the heart was created with the Kenzu assassins as their sentinels. Finally she showed me the coming together of the coterie and how you have separated yourself from them, cast yourself out. To bring about such change as the return of magic the coterie must be together, trust one another, and be solely focused on the outcome.'

'There was something I needed to do,' Ishmael said, 'and as you say, we must be solely focused, which I am not. So what choice do I have but to get myself into that state?'

'The Mother rules all else, Ishmael, and there is nothing more important than listening to her. I failed in this and lost most of my power; don't do the same.'

'I needed to come here and see for myself if the gods live, and so far all I have found is greed, brutality, and a fool who claims to be the god of time.'

'I am the only living god.'

'What did you say?'

'I am the only living god, Ishmael, and your lady Shail of Illume as you know her is gone forever.'

'Then why didn't you die like the other gods?' asked Ishmael, feeling flustered.

'I can't die. Just like you can't take away the magic you can't take away time, and so here I am.'

'What, a prisoner to the Vorm?'

'No, not a prisoner, I choose to be here. The Vorm look after me well and bring the rarest of delicacies with their fine gifts. Everything I need they get for me, and I also stay because the harpies are my only memories of the other gods, my kin.'

'Who are these harpies?'

'They are treated like kings and queens and kept segregated from anyone else as they undergo strict training in such arts as acting, languages, and lore so they can imitate the gods perfectly. On festival days the harpie representing the god who won tribute day is escorted here from the Vorm estate so they remain hidden from the public.'

'Why would someone even bother to do such a thing?'

'To fool all the believers, of course. People want something to believe in so they feel safe, they want to know things will be okay when they die and that they will go to some great place without any more pain. Religion has become about greed, Ishmael, as you said earlier. Let the people think they are actually communing with their gods and you will become richer than you could imagine as those believers load the gods with their prayers and tributes. Someone has gotten terribly wealthy out of this scam. Can you guess who?'

'It's the Vorm, isn't it? They created this trickery.'

'Yes, but with the help of the priesthoods.'

Ishmael sat down. He was finding it hard to breathe, like suddenly his chest was filled with sand, and his palms felt clammy.

'It will be okay, Ishmael. Your foundations have been rocked, and that is not an easy thing to take, but it will pass.'

'Aeon, you are telling me that the Vorm bring these harpies here who are specially trained to imitate the voices and mannerisms of the gods in a bid to deceive the masses into believing the gods are still alive so they keep donating riches?'

Aeon clapped.

'Now you see what is happening.'

'They must be stopped, their scam exposed.'

'Ishmael, you must leave here to meet the coterie before more of you die. It is the Mother's will, and you have ignored her attempts to sway you. Now being here you are in unnecessary danger that affects not just you but also the rest of the coterie of the heart.'

'How do you know about the coterie?'

'I am also able to commune with the Mother, which is how I knew you would come here to the Godhead. I just didn't know when, and so I have waited for you to make your appearance.'

Aeon walked over to Onyx, the harlequin crystal. 'Onyx, clear the walls so we can see outside.

The walls cleared, and Ishmael could see into the square where Vorm soldiers had gathered.

'They won't stop searching for you, Ishmael. What you are attempting to do in bringing back magic threatens the empire that the Vorm have created.'

'I will leave here, Aeon, but first I will expose this lie at the festival tomorrow.'

Aeon poured another goblet of wine, passed it to Ishmael, and they clinked goblets together. 'I was hoping you would say that, Ishmael. My life has become way too droll of late and in need of some excitement.'

Ishmael finally managed to doze for a few chimes until morning. He was outraged at the trick the Vorm performed on the pilgrims. When he realized no more sleep would be possible, he rose to help come up with a plan with the help of Aeon that would expose the Vorm and priesthoods. It was after dawn when they finished with their planning and outside already fully robed priests with acolytes scurried about as regular patrols of Vorm guards patrolled the square.

When a knocking came from below, Onyx spoke.

'The harpie is here. Hide yourself, Ishmael, before I open the tunnel door.'

Ishmael hurried to the second level, which was Aeon's personal chamber where the harpies and Vorm were forbidden to enter. His heart was thudding in his chest as he waited, listening.

Aeon came and got him when the Vorm had left, and Ishmael could feel the excitement building. They were really going to do this.

'Where is the harpie, Aeon?'

'In the cage where he is meant to be until the theatrics begin. Then they are usually taken upstairs and chained before the shell, but today that won't be happening. I have drugged his food with dreamfever powder so he will sleep like a baby. Now we are free to move onto the next step,' said Aeon with a smile.

━━━ ❧ ━━━

Chapter 56

Sipping from a bottle of pure children's tears mixed with blood wine, Zacriel sat with the three lords that had ruled the Infernal lands even before the Severing just like the Lady of Whispers had.

Lilith sat facing Zacriel making sure at all times he could see a generous amount of flesh, and most likely trying to distract him from the important matters at hand. He turned his chair so it faced the other two lords and not Lilith directly. As much as he tried to ignore it, he could see in his mind the birth of the child earlier that morning, which she now held tight to her chest. It was told that Lilith had an army of thousands of her own children, and after seeing that it took less than a chime for them to be born he believed she must have an incredible force at her disposal.

The Unseeing lord sat regarding Ishmael. 'You don't seem so happy to see us, Bone lord. You look distracted, and I must wonder whether you want us here at all.'

'There is no reason why I would be happy to meet any of you, let alone all three of you at once. You arrived in my city deliberately ahead of schedule with the aim to undermine my authority. I realize you must have been wondering who this upstart lord is that would dare take the place of the Lady of Whispers. Well, do I meet up to your expectations?'

'You could never be compared to any of us three, Zacriel. You act like you have strolled the fields of slaughter or traversed the dread river when we all know you are nothing but an unknown pup without any clue how the game of power is played,' growled the Unseeing lord.

'I couldn't care less for your games of power. You can hide behind your mask, Unseeing lord, and pretend that I don't give you cause for concern. The Lady of Whispers also neglected to take me seriously, which was a terrible decision as you can see.'

Quail regarded Zacriel with glittering eyes then clacked his beak in annoyance. We won't make the same mistakes our sister made, Zacriel; however don't sit here and threaten us when you are like a spider to a child who rips the legs off it…'

Quail would have continued talking, but Zacriel talked over him. 'The problem with the Lady of Whispers and you three lords is that you still believe deep down in your souls that you can't be killed, and yet here I am wearing the rose, carrying the sceptre. You should be careful; because news of one of the dread infernal lord's demise has spread fast, and now others must be eying your lofty positions, wondering just how vulnerable you are. Here in my world you are no more able to survive death than any mortal, and I know that like myself you won't enter the astral since our presence there causes incredible astral storms that would kill us.'

Quail tipped his head on an angle looking exactly like a bird would. 'We would know of your motivations, Zacriel. For hundreds of cycles we had, let's say, an uneasy alliance between the four of us when the lady was still alive. Now you have usurped her and thrown all our plans awry.'

'My only purpose is to see magic returned to this world so we may all return home to our rightful place in the Infernal lands.'

Even as he said this Zacriel was questioning his sincerity and wondering if the three lords would see through him and know he wasn't sure what he wanted anymore. This was all he had now that Nina was lost to him because of Dalwyn's betrayal. Holding the rank of an infernal lord was way above his expectations and his dream of ascension that he had been moulded to fulfil by his master was upon him. He had the rank and now just needed the gates to open between the planes to see his dream become reality.

'I apologize for my indignation, my lords, I expected you to come here baying for blood and wanting to put my head on a spike. Now I see that all four of us can achieve more together. Yes, I am new to this but with your guidance and trust we can together return to the home you so desire to see again. As I sit talking with you I have realized that my only way forward is beside you and not against you. I have nothing else since I have already lost it, but I will not be treated like an imbecile or have all I have built here in Acclaro ripped away from me. Here in my city that I won fairly you are my guests, and any attempt to undermine me will not end well for you.'

Lilith laughed as she changed her baby to the other breast, and Ishmael could see the blood trickle from the nipple where it had suckled.

'Zacriel, we understand you. This is your city and your rules. Power is gathering around Acclaro, and this place will be very important in the coming battles. The last time I noticed a convergence of power was as the Severing was happening. So mark my words all of you, this place is important to hold.'

'Not just important to hold, but if done well and with all the infernals at our disposal we could carve out an empire here that will stand even after the gates open back up and magic has returned,' added the Unseeing lord.

Zacriel rose and stood at the balcony looking over his city. 'It is imperative that we use this time to marshal our army and clarify our goals. Forces gather at the edge of Thantos. Culchar has closed its border and have aligned themselves with the king of Scuttle who hold the path to Cavere with their own armies as those of Cavere are gathering in the north east to fight the gathering barbarian hordes. It is only a matter of time until they come against us, my lords, so it is time to do what we do best. Sow the seeds of despair and make examples of our enemies for all to see. There is nothing to be gained by sitting here locked away in the capital while our army combusts among itself. Our warriors want blood, so let's give it and more to them.'

Lilith looked Zacriel up and down admiringly, then she traced a nail down his thigh, laughing as he twisted away from her touch and sultry laugh.

'I have already taken Wilhelm's point with my legions, but Brimmerland has a force gathered along the road near the town of Glimmersedge while Soarnestia has sent squads of raven warriors to raid the Point and reinforce Glimmersedge, who have caused much damage to our troops,' said Zacriel regarding the three infernal lords.

Lilith giggled like a teenager and clapped her hands together. 'This will be fun, but we must turn Acclaro into a terrible place to behold and litter the Glyph grasslands with trophies of our enemies so that any enemy forces are met with a sight that will strike fear to their heart and break them. I want the Glyph to be utter desolation.'

'There is the situation with the coterie of the heart. I nearly had one in my grasp when the city fell, but he escaped. It is imperative that they are found. I could always…'

'That won't be necessary, Zacriel, replied Lilith. 'Dalwyn has assured us he can take care of the situation.'

'Dalwyn, how do you know of him?'

'Lilith's baby was sleeping now and as it snored with its little mouth open he could see rows of teeth disappearing deeper into its mouth. He looked up into the gaze of Lilith, who was smirking at him suggestively.

'Of course we know of him, Zacriel. Did you honestly think he had just contacted you about the coterie and the crystals? We sent him to you. Dalwyn has taken our leave to pursue the coterie and return with them here for this is where the final reckoning will take place.'

'That was how Dalwyn got out of the city, wasn't it?'

'We had him let him out when he knew of our impending arrival. For the four of us here, we cannot allow complacency to turn us away from our task, and you were far too distracted by the human child to be focused on what we need you to be.'

'If you or anyone else has hurt Nina I will see to it that you suffer until death is the only gift you want.'

It was meant to be a threat, but the three infernal lords burst into laughter.

'Oh, the folly of youth. Zacriel, we care not for what idle threats you throw at us or what bad blood is between you and Dalwyn. While we await Dalwyn's return, you will raid the growing armies to destabilize their forces while we plan for the coming defence of Acclaro.'

'That won't be happening, my lords. This city is my domain, and your authority here is second only to me.' Movement came from the chamber inside as the doors opened and the heads of nine Infernals were dumped before the four lords in a woven basket.

'If you don't recognize these, they belonged to the personal guard you had in my chambers while we talked here. Now you are truly vulnerable, and I believe like the Lady of Whispers you are addled in thinking you cannot die or won't be killed.'

The balcony entrance was filling with infernals loyal to Zacriel, and Rapture stood ready to give the command should it be needed.

'Think carefully, my lords. I am sure Rapture here would love the opportunity to take the place of one of you. Now this is what is going to happen. You, Quail, will take your forces south to Wilhelm's point and take command there. It must be defended so the armies of the roadside nations have no easy way to attack us from that direction. Unseeing lord, you will take your invisibles and harass the armies of Scuttle and Cavere. Lilith, your succubi, will infiltrate Culchar and assassinate the five thus robbing them of leadership, then you will cause havoc in the city causing as much damage as possible. Your considerable amount of children will scour the land around Acclaro for slaves to return here.

'If you thought that I would do all the hard work and just let you meander in to take charge, then think again whether your life means anything at all to you and if you wish to see the Infernal realms again.'

Zacriel's Infernals drew their blades as they waited for the lords to choose.

The blood had drained from Lilith's face, and she held her baby so tightly it began crying until it stopped as suddenly as it started and its head fell limp. Lilith dropped the baby to the ground and turned to Zacriel.

'We will do as you say Bone lord, not just because your plan makes sense but also because you offer us no other alternative. I for one will remember this slight. This is not over.'

'No Lilith, it's not over; in fact, it is just beginning. You could say it is merely foreplay, which I would have thought you enjoyed considering your reputation.'

'I love foreplay, Zacriel, but I would prefer to be the one not being fucked.'

Chapter 57

Ishmael sat with Aeon, watching the spectacle around them as they dined on a thing Aeon referred to as chocolate that was like nothing Ishmael had ever eaten and after too much made him feel ill.

'How will I know when to speak?' Ishmael asked Aeon.

'I will cue you when to get in place. Don't worry; there will be much fanfare before you do your bit.'

'What if things go wrong?'

'If you follow my plan exactly then there is little danger of anything happening to you.'

'And your dreams showed you that?' Ishmael asked.

'In a way, yes, but that doesn't mean a different outcome is impossible. You are what I would call a catalyst, as are the others of your coterie, and that is why you were all chosen to hold the magic. Because you are configured differently on an energetic level, you cause change wherever you go, and in you here now in Trystland I see endings and completeness.'

'What about you when all this changes everything; where will you go?'

'I find it sweet that you even care,' Aeon said. 'Don't worry, just fulfil your destiny and I will be somewhere applauding your gallant efforts.'

'Sometimes I just shake my head and think I can't do this,' said Ishmael. 'Everything is happening too fast, Aeon, and I feel like I'm running out of time. I don't want to put anybody else in danger.'

'Ishmael, you can't take the blame for your father's death. He should have prepared you earlier but didn't, which left you without the guidance of a sentinel up until recently.'

Ishmael raised an eyebrow. 'One of your dreams?'

'Yes, Ishmael. Don't be so hard on yourself; you have been through a lot and lost your family, now your faith too. There is nothing left to do but complete the sacred task given to your family long ago.'

Mid-morning came and the festival was in full swing again. The square was full of warriors and priests of Cinder. Decorations for the god of war had been hastily erected early that morning, lending the square a crimson look of fluttering flags to accompany the loud war drums being battered by shirtless warriors with bulging muscles and war chants. Already, Ishmael had spotted fights breaking out among the revellers as the crowd grew.

'Kalis told me they run a secure city and the laws are mostly obeyed, but this could get ugly out there, and the Vorm guards hardly seem interested,' Ishmael commented.

Aeon turned to look at him. 'He was right then. The exception is festivals, especially when one of the gods is going to speak. This time it is Cinder god of war, lord of might, and so as their beliefs dictate there will be fighting, battle, and blood, and this will attract a crowd willing to participate in this while others of a more, let's say, *gentle nature* will stay in their homes to avoid the overflow of the festival.'

That knowledge soured Ishmael's mood further as he realized he was going to shatter the beliefs of a horde of blood-fuelled warriors and killers.

'It could be worse Ishmael. If the Jester had of won, then the body count would be extreme even by this early chime of the day.'

A blare of trumpets rang out above the din, and the drums fell silent. A procession was slowly winding its way through the throng, and Ishmael could easily see the orange-sashed guards escorting Arman to the stage. Near the front of the crowd a man sprang forward, bellowing, and charged the escort. He smashed a Vorm guard aside before being skewered by the blades of two others.

The fallen guard was dragged into the crowd, who fell upon him like animals, and Arman was quickly pushed up onto the stage while the other Vorm elite formed a barrier down along the front between the stage and the crowd.

Ishmael watched with a hand over his mouth in shock. 'By the light of Illume, was that truly necessary?'

'You will see worse before the day is out, my friend.'

Arman waved his arms for quiet, and so it happened.

'Greetings on this festive day, my friends. A red day for sure and ripe for war, fighting, blood, drinking, and one more thing; can you guess what it is?'

'Sacrifice!' screamed thousands of voices back at Arman.

A woman was pushed forward from the crowd and lifted onto the stage. Her hands were bound behind her back, and she wore the traditional blue robes of a collator with white sleeves to show she studied the races and cultures. She pushed herself to her feet and stood proudly glaring back at the insults hurled at her. Her slightly wrinkled face put her somewhere in middle age and her tight grimace told that she was well aware this could be her last moment.

Arman hushed the crowd again.

'This is Muriel, a collector and collator who had everything she could want given to her on a plate for the service she provides Trystland. Like many, she sought to rise above her station and attempt to cause rebellion by sprouting lies aimed to hurt not just the citizens of our great nation but anybody who would put their faith in the gods. Muriel wants us to believe the gods are dead.'

There was such outrage at that comment that the crowd surged forward and the Vorm only managed to barely push them back as Muriel stood unflinching. The drums began a low beat as Arman sidled up beside Muriel and placed his arm around her shoulders; she tried to push him away, but he was too strong. The crowd began chanting two words: 'Kill her!'

Arman struck the woman in the face then clasped both hands around her throat as she fell to her knees. Ishmael watched him squeeze the life from her body and felt disassociated from what he was seeing, as if his mind had decided it was better to focus on something other than the horror in front of them.

Beside him Aeon was weeping. 'Now you know why I will help you, Ishmael. Nobody deserves to hold this power over people. If the true Cinder were here then you would see a slaughter of all these wretched creatures. He supports bravery and skill over outright murder.'

When Ishmael looked again things were worse. Arman had sliced the woman open to hold up the heart for the crowd to see. He painted his face red with her blood then carefully placed the heart in a burning brazier before meticulously washing the gore from his hands and arms with the help of an acolyte of Cinder.

'So has the offering been accepted by the god of war? Look upon the godhead and tell me, children of the gods, and chosen of Cinder.

'Turn the godhead red and make it shimmer, Onyx,' yelled Aeon to the harlequin spirit.

'Doing it now, Aeon.'

There came a collective gasp by the crowd and roars of approval as the Godhead turned crimson.

'Now it takes time for the gods to be able to communicate with us, so while you wait for my signal, drink, fight, and celebrate. When we return you will be able to tell your children you were there the day Cinder spoke to the masses.'

'Ready yourself, Ishmael; you are next. They usually wait a chime before the god speaks, but be ready.'

Ishmael felt relaxed. He could feel his eyes growing heavy, and he dozed. The Mother was there beside him. She smiled and reached forward to kiss his cheek, the tiny twigs through her hair scratching his face as she did so. 'The time is coming now, Ishmael. Witness.'

Then he was above the Glyph grasslands where a tower of crystal reached four arms into the heavens, surrounded by armies. He could still hear the Mother's whispering in his ears.

'Find this tower and you find your coterie.'

Ishmael continued to watch and his view zoomed in to see someone handing a dark harlequin something. He saw infernals flow out of Acclaro in a winged horde and a group with their backs to him weeping over a fresh grave. He realized he was crying and with one bark-covered hand the Mother turned his face towards hers. She was no longer smiling. 'You should have been with the coterie by now, Ishmael, but have chosen your own path, which will have repercussions. Now you know what you must do and where to go. Don't fail in this.'

Ishmael awakened as if no time had passed. Aeon walked in and handed him a water skin. 'I have put another with your pack for when you leave.'

'What will happen to you and Onyx, Aeon?'

'We will accompany you, of course. Onyx has been separated from his kind for over four hundred cycles, so the kind thing to do would be for us to return him to them, the harlequin. As for me, I need to be a witness when you return the magic.

With the dream still fresh in his mind, Ishmael was now sure his choices had angered the Mother. There had been a sinister edge to the dream, and Ishmael had a fleeting thought about whether the Mother truly was so helpless or if she just manipulated people to achieve her ends. This was quickly followed by a feeling of shame at how he had let the coterie and the Mother down. It seemed now a sure thing that he was no longer trusted by the Mother, who might decide to guide him with a firmer hand.

Any further examination of his dream was forgotten as Arman appeared back on the stage.

'Children of the gods, put aside your rivalries, hate, and differences to behold Cinder, who has come amongst us from the Celestial realms to prove as we do each cycle that the gods live.'

The crowd roared, screamed, laughed; and Ishmael watched thinking the world had gone mad. Aeon nudged him.

Ishmael grasped the end of the tube that was the mouth piece to the great conch shell and brought it to his lips.

Chapter 58

Zahra took the role of runner for the stage after paying gold to the girl who had the job, and was more than happy to give it away.

'That Arman is a cruel man; be careful of him,' she said as she took the gold and left.

One of the other runners hurried over to Zahra. 'You, follow me we need someone else to help with the speaker's requirements, now off you go.'

'Where do I go? Sorry, I'm new and was just told to stay on the side of the stage.'

'New, you say? I can't keep up with the changes in faces around here. I will take you there myself, come on.'

Zahra was led to a tent where the two Vorm guards parted to let them through. In a basket there was a large hamper of food and beverages. 'That basket, grab that, we haven't much time.'

They hurried back to the stage where off to the side Zahra helped erect a table then loaded it with jugs of water, wine, and ale; with loaves of bread, cheese, skewers of meat, and fruit.

'And don't be thinking to help your stinking self to any of that meant for the speaker or it's the death for all of us.'

Time was passing by painfully slowly and Zahra sat guarding the buffet from daring children who became bolder as the morning awakened the city. As the heat arrived early, Zahra, now bored silly, hungry and parched, found it increasingly harder to ignore the table of cold drinks and fine foods. Her two constant companions throughout the morning looked as bad as she felt. They were huge even for Vorm elite, and their bare arms displayed tattoos of bright ink that Zahra had never seen before.

'Those are beautiful- the ink I mean, not your big, muscled arms, although they are nice,' said Zahra to the closest one, who turned to eyeball her suspiciously.

'What! You never had a girl talk to you before?'

'It's bad enough having to stand here all day without listening to you talk nonsense, girl.'

Zahra turned to the second guard, who was blessed with many stomach rolls and very chubby cheeks like a child in a giant's body.

'Is he always like this? I bet you didn't think that when you signed up to be one of the Vorm elite that you would have to spend so much time with someone so exciting, did you?'

The second guard said nothing.

'Since neither of you are willing to talk with me, then I will do all the talking. It's not the company or the heat that bothers me as much as all this drink and food right there while we try our best to ignore it.

'I bet your both as thirsty as I am. Can you imagine?'

'Nobody but the speaker is touching anything,' said the muscled brute.

'Yes, okay, grumpy, we already established that, but just imagine sliding out one of those cold skins of wine or even water. That cold liquid gushing down our dry throats.'

The second guard smiled slowly with his eyes half shut.

Zahra sidled up next to the second guard. 'You can almost taste it, can't you?'

The big man nodded, then his eyes flinched open as the other guard struck his chest.

'Ignore her, you idiot.'

'I bet you are hungry too, hey, big guy? Never enough to fill you up in the barracks? Or maybe because the others who pretend to be your friends purposely feed you less- for your own health of course.'

'I'm not fat,' said the big guard, glaring at her now.

'I know you aren't, but I bet you are hungry.'

'Yes, I am, but so what? If I eat that there it's my last meal; now shut up or you will be replaced.'

'Oh my, well, fine then, just trying to pass the time.' She turned back to the first guard. 'I thought you were bad, but he's much worse.'

This bought a chuckle from them both, which they quickly hid and stood taller as if more alert.

'Can I tell you both something?'

'No!' said the first guard.

'Yes!' said the second guard.

'I will take that as a yes then. You sure you both aren't related?

'Anyway I just wanted to say this is my first time here and that's why I'm talking so much, because I am nervous. I don't really know what's expected of me.'

'Serve the speaker what he desires from the table and have a basin of clean water with fresh towelling ready for him to wash.'

'Whatever does he need a basin for?'

'You certainly are new here. Today there will be bloodshed in Cinder's name. Arman will perform sacrifices.'

'Who are the poor bastards then?'

At that moment a young man carrying a heaped tray of food passed close by, and Zahra intercepted him.

'Where is this platter going?'

The man looked at her, unsure what to do.

'Tell me, then, I don't have all day, and it won't do to send double the order, will it,' she snapped.

'It's, ummm, for the nobles on platform three. I still have three others to collect.'

'Let me help you then. I will take up this one while you get the other two.'

'Really, you will do that? Thank you. I haven't seen you here doing this before.'

'I used to do this cycles ago, but today is my first time back. It's all very exciting, now off you go.'

Zahra took the heavy platter and, scooped off three pieces of everything, which she shoved into a bowl in the sack under the table. The two guards kept stealing glances her way.

'Wait here both of you. I will only be a moment to deliver this. She hurried to platform three where the Lord Vorm, Kalis sat upon a chair being fanned with wide, green leaves. A striking older lady in a red gown sat consoling a young boy, who was weeping against her chest.

'Come on, Fausto, enough now things will be fine.'

'Yes Ma, but I will never see Ishmael again! He left without saying goodbye like he promised.'

So Ishmael had been with Kalis and his family.

As Zahra climbed up the ramp onto the platform, a guard blocked her way. 'Put it on that table there, will you.'

Zahra did as requested, overhearing a guard talking with Lord Vorm.

'Two dead soldiers this morning in the square and one missing.'

'Was it the work of our missing guest?'

The lord Vorm glanced at Zahra, and then they fell silent until she was heading down the ramp again. The child must have been speaking about her Ishmael. She didn't know, but the possibility he was here seemed more likely since this is what he had wanted to see. Or was she just hoping for miracles? Back at the table the two guards looked like they hadn't even moved.

'Since you two are so disciplined, I am going to reward you for your steadfastness. I have food for us all, and before you get all righteous there, grumpy, it wasn't from the speaker's table.'

They ate in bursts, avoiding bringing attention to themselves but nobody seemed to care anyway. Soon the three of them were left satisfied and the guards seemed to look at her with less suspicion now. *Amazing how men will come around when food is available*, she thought.

A commotion had begun in the crowd. The blare of trumpets rang out above the din, and the drums fell silent. Zahra could see Arman being escorted towards them from the crowd. She watched a man charge the escort and die for nothing and saw a guard torn apart by the crowd before Arman made it to safety.

He strode over to the table, beckoning Zahra forwards. 'Water, chilled, and melon, but hurry.'

As she fetched this she was aware of his stare following her.

'Here, speaker.'

'You must be new here, girl, I would have surely noticed a pretty thing like you. Later I will require your service, so be sure to stay ready for my every whim.'

I bet he wants my service, thought Zahra smiling back at him.

'It will be my pleasure, speaker.'

Arman took the stage, and Zahra began to scan the crowd for either Ishmael or Rue. The assassin would be close, and it was most likely that she had murdered the guards last night. As the time approached for Cinder to address the crowded square, Zahra began to get nervous. The crowd was so fired up that the littlest thing could set them off into a riot.

⁓

Chapter 59

'Children of the gods, put aside your rivalries, hate, and differences to behold Cinder, who has come amongst us from the Celestial realms to prove as we do each cycle that the gods live.'

The square fell silent.

Then deep laughter filled with contempt carried through the square.

'You have all come here for selfish reasons, don't try and deny it. Look at the ones who stand beside you; you are no different to them. Filled with petty concerns, here you are, desperate to be told the gods live and everything will be okay with the world.'

Zahra was confused, and so were the guards beside her. Even Arman, who gestured one of the Vorm guards over to him.

'By the Infernal hells, what is going on?'

'I don't know, speaker, we are trying to find the problem now.'

'The gods don't hold the power you think they do. They became like us when the Severing cut us from our true essence, magic. And like us they can and have died… all except one, the god of time, who can only die when time ends.'

The crowd were jeering now, throwing drinks and worse at the stage.

'Let me repeat that for all of you. All but the god of time are dead or missing. The time of the gods was gone the moment they defied theirs and our creator, the Mother. See, look around you and watch how the Vorm guards scurry to stop me broadcasting this message. I am not Cinder, I am a man of flesh and blood who has been shown a great lie that I have chosen to reveal to you all. The Vorm and the priesthoods would have you believe the gods are not dead because without the tributes they have no wealth. They have made themselves filthy rich by robbing you blind.'

Zahra watched a group of priests break away and hurriedly leave the square as fresh fights broke out and parts of the crowd began chanting. ' Lies, lies' over and over.

Once again laughter carried across the square.

'Do you want proof of this scandalous lie you have been fed?'

There was only a scattering of calls for proof, then the voice repeated itself.

'Do you want proof?'

After the fifth time the crowd was roaring yes, Arman had moved back onto the stage trying to quieten the crowd, but he was drowned out. Zahra saw a commotion near the platforms and saw Kalis gesturing angrily as guards swarmed away from him. What was he so concerned about?

'And so, people of the world, now you shall see truly.'

Like everyone else Zahra craned her neck to see what was happening. From behind the stage the Godhead, which was bathed in crimson, faded to become clear crystal, easily seen through, and standing there were two people.

One of them was Ishmael holding a tube to his lips. Zahra was so happy to see him alive that her concentration slipped as she stared open-mouthed like thousands of others.

'See, I am just a man, not a god. You have lost yourself in the lies of religion when there really is one above the gods, the Mother. Only she is worthy of your worship. If anybody this day should incur your wrath it is the priesthoods and the Vorm, not those who like you have been fooled while the priests grow richer.'

Then the world around Zahra fell apart. The fat guard Zahra

had made friends with plucked up Arman then hurled him into the crowd, grabbed a loaf of bread and wineskin, then walked off.

The Vorm soldiers around the stage had drawn steel and were cutting down those at the front of the crowd who were being pushed forward by those behind them. Cries of terror and dying turned the day into a scene of hell.

Chapter 60

Ishmael stood looking down on the spectacle below him with Aeon, who clapped him on the back. 'That's done it, then Ishmael.'

From where the platforms sat that the nobles used, Ishmael could see Lord Kalis staring across at him; he held something and raised it along his head, a bow.

The words, 'Get down, Aeon! Were barely out his mouth when an arrow whistled in and lodged itself in the crystal close to where they stood. For a moment Ishmael was confused as to why Kalis fired since the crystal would stop the arrows, then he realized the area in front of them could be used as a door opened. Kalis had used a arrow that interfered with Onyx's control of the structure and would stop Onyx closing any entrances. The second arrow struck Aeon in the chest, knocking him down.

'Aeon?'

'I'm fine, Ishmael. The wound will hurt for a damn long time while it heals, but it can't kill me. Get that arrow out from the wall.'

Another two arrows ricocheted past Ishmael. He leant out the opening, grasped the arrow, trying to pull it free. Behind him Aeon had torn the arrow from his chest.

'The lower level, Ishmael, quickly! I can manually lock the door there.'

'Bring back rope if you have any, Aeon, we might need it to climb down.'

I will get some,' said the god disappearing to the lower level.

Ishmael turned back and began twisting the arrow again, trying to pull it from the crystal without much luck. Down on the stage he saw a familiar face. Zahra.

Zahra was there on the stage, which had now been swarmed by the crowd. She was waving her arms at him as she struggled closer to the Godhead. He tried yelling to her, but the noise was terrible and loud bells were ringing through the city.

Aeon returned with the rope, and Ishmael tied it off then dropped it down to the stage where Zahra began to shimmy up it. 'Zahra, my sentinel, is here,' said Ishmael at Aeon's curious look.

Now more arrows were slicing down around Ishmael and Aeon, and they were forced to retreat farther into the structure. He risked a look to see how Zahra was doing and saw there was a girl below her on the rope.

'Zahra, watch out below you!' he yelled, not sure if Zahra had heard his warning.

Ishmael was relieved as Zahra made the entrance; he helped pull her up to him as arrows continued to angle in from the Vorm platform. They ducked back under shelter, which allowed the strange girl to climb up too. She grinned then slipped a half crescent blade from her belt, twirling it through her fingers easily.

'Nowhere else to run now, but I will give you a choice, Kenzu. Give me the boy and you live.'

Ishmael and Aeon watched on as Zahra drew her crystal sword, tilting the blade so the sunlight glinted along its keen edge and reflected into the other girl's eyes, forcing the attacker to turn away.

Then Zahra struck, managing a quick hit to her enemy's arm where a crimson line appeared, Zahra's blade then slammed down against the girl's crescent blade. It fell from fingers down to the stage below. The next slice would have decapitated the girl, but she merely leant back to let the blade slice past then struck Zahra's sword arm with both hands, jolting the sword free. Zahra fell away into Aeon, and they both went sprawling down with the attacker close behind, so Ishmael stepped between them, kicking out to keep the girl away.

'So you're the one who all this trouble is over, then? You could make things easy for us all and come with me. You are valuable and won't be hurt, but my employer wants what you have.'

Arrows continued to ping around them.

'What is to come cannot be forced, and I will walk my own path to that moment,' said Ishmael, punching out as the girl darted towards him and batting aside the weak punch.

She slammed a fist into Ishmael's chest, knocking him backwards. Zahra then tackled the girl, and they grappled on the crystal floor fighting for the upper position.

'Aeon, help her, she's my sentinel.'

Aeon just stood watching and raised his hands helplessly, 'I can't interfere Ishmael.'

The girl had Zahra below her now and had straddled her torso. She smashed an elbow into Zahra's head making Zahra turn away to avoid it striking her face, but Zahra couldn't avoid the next three that slammed her head against the crystal floor.

Ishmael cried out Zahra's name, and the girl looked over at him.

'You had your chance; now she dies thanks to you.

A volley of arrows rained in, forcing them all to take cover, and Ishmael felt a pain in his forearm where an arrow grazed him. The attacker lay slumped on Zahra, her back and neck riddled with arrows. She was breathing in a strange rattling sigh.

'Ishmael, help get her off me; I can't breathe.'

He rolled the girl off Zahra and even then she began reaching for the curved blade near her.

'Why won't you just die? Ishmael yelled at the girl then grabbed her shirt and shoved her body off the edge into the crowd below them.

With the help of Aeon they removed the arrow from the crystal then slumped down thankfully as the crystal began pulsing; then the doorway closed and the strange voice of Onyx could be heard.

'Those damn arrows will be the death of us. I'm sorry I nearly let you down, Aeon.'

'Don't be a fool, Onyx, you know as well as I this might happen.'

'We have to leave,' said Ishmael.

'It's too dangerous, Ishmael,' said Zahra. 'If we go out there while the crowd is in this frenzy we will be lucky to live.' She bandaged Ishmael's injured arm.

'Then what can we do, Zahra?'

'Is there another way out of here?'

'Yes, there is a tunnel through to the Vorm household,' said Aeon. 'It's how they get the harpies here who pretend to be gods.'

'Then what are we waiting for? Let's go,' said Ishmael getting to his feet.

'Not so fast, Ishmael,' said Aeon.

'This calls for caution. Kalis will expect us to use the tunnel to escape, but that would be a big mistake.'

'How do you know that?'

'A dream. I saw it in a dream.'

'You expect us to risk our lives according to your dreams? Who are you anyway,' asked Zahra.

'There is no time for that conversation, but you need to trust me.'

'Zahra, I know I gave you no reason to ever trust me again, but if he says he dreamt it then it will happen. Just hear him out. I can explain him later.'

'So what do we do then?'

'We stay here in the safety of the Godhead,' said Aeon, and the three of them sat in the middle of madness with nothing to do but watch the ugliness that man could cause one another unfold around them.

Soon they had all lost interest in watching the horrors outside their crystal haven and asked Onyx to return the surface to its original black so they wouldn't have to see anymore.

Chapter 61

Much later when the banging started, it was Onyx who knew what was happening.

'They are in the tunnel trying to force their way in here,' said the harlequin spirit.

'It must be Kalis. He will want revenge for what I have done to his family and operation,' Aeon said. 'Can he get in, Onyx?'

'They can force their way in, but it will take chimes, maybe even days, unless they have more of those interrupter arrows.'

Zahra came over to Aeon. 'We need weapons. What do you have here that can help us defend that tunnel?'

They were happy to keep busy and compiled quite a supply of usable weapons. Lamp oil was poured into bottles with rags stuffed in the necks ready for throwing. Honey was smeared at the opening of the tunnel where enemies would have to climb up a ladder then into the Godhead, then broken glass was layered in the sticky surface, which would slow the attackers. Knives, broomsticks, anything that could be wielded in combat were stacked on each level near the ladders, and on the top level the heavy lounge chair was dragged close to the ladder hole ready to cover it.

They got the harpy out of the cage, and soon the man was babbling away like they were old friends. He was named Kito from the island nation Delve, and he had a deep voice that Ishmael realized was perfect to use as the voice for Cinder. Onyx cleared the walls regularly for them to see what happened around them, and now there was a ring of Vorm guards around the Godhead. Another ring faced out and fought off anyone that came too close. Bodies were everywhere, the wounded cried out for help, and still the fighting continued. Ishmael couldn't see what happened outside the square, but a series of explosions said something was happening deeper in the city.

Now ready, they stopped to rest and enjoy some food to keep the nerves away and their strength up. The four of them were watching the sunset when they were interrupted by Onyx's voice.

'They are coming along the tunnel. Eight of them; seven I know by their step, one I don't. Lord Vorm is with them, and I won't be much help in this matter Aeon, I'm sorry.'

'They have an interrupter, don't they?'

'Yes, they do. I would just like to say that I hope when I am able to communicate again that it is your faces I see. It's getting dark now… so dark.' Then Onyx fell silent.

Ishmael held out a hand to help Zahra rise, which she ignored and brushed past him.

'Zahra.'

'Not now, Ishmael. Once everything is finished here then we will talk.'

Aeon practically beamed with amusement as he got up. 'Good luck with that, Ishmael.'

It was still slow going for the attackers, who first had to remove a lot of furniture stacked above the entry. When the last was pushed away, they were met with the spear thrusts of Kito and Zahra; they made a vicious team up until Kito was shot in the stomach with a crossbow and curled into a ball screaming.

'Aeon, come on, step up and help,' called out Zahra.

'He can't, Zahra, it will interrupt events.'

'I don't know what that means, but if he doesn't interrupt this event coming our way then none of this will matter.'

Ishmael grabbed the fallen spear and stood beside Zahra.

'Sharp thrusts, Ishmael. If they grab our weapons we will lose the level quickly.'

Ishmael stabbed down at the next man trying to come up the ladder, the spear point skewered through his cheek then down into his neck, making him fall away. Another bolt flew past both of them, and Zahra reached for a bottle of oil that Ishmael lit. Zahra tossed it down the ladder hole. There came a breaking of glass followed by a gush of flames, then screaming and that terrible smell.

'Quickly get up the second level,' Zahra yelled at him. Aeon had already carried Kito up the ladder and was wiping the sweat from the man's face as he held his hand.

'Am I going to live? I want to live, not die, and I want Serena, my daughter, to have a good life.'

Aeon leant forward to give the man some wine. 'Here drink, soon the pain will be all over.'

'But, my family, please tell me they will have a good life, please.'

'Your Serena will live with your wife until she is sixteen, then one of her drawings will garner such attention as to give her a position as a mediator between greater powers. Kito, your daughter will save countless lives with her guidance and will forever remember you.' Aeon held Kito against him as the man sobbed.

The Vorm attacked with crossbows first, then up they came. Zahra smashed the first one's head into the glass and honey until he fell unconscious and knocked over those below him on the ladder.

'Ishmael. It's Kalis. 'Let's stop this madness. We need to talk.'

'The madness is in you, Kalis. The crystals are in my care, not yours. If you expect me to believe you will forgive me for destroying your scam, then you disappoint me. There is no need for talking now since you have shown your true intent towards my task.'

'I won't be letting you get away, Ishmael, but how about your companions? Don't you want them to live? And where is Aeon, the last god? He is awfully quiet.'

'I am here, Kalis. I told Ishmael everything.'

'What will you gain from doing that?'

'Not having to watch you take advantage of our people while you tarnish the gods names with your lies and sacrifices will be a nice change. The time of your family is over, Kalis. Now the only thing that remains is whether you help Ishmael perform his sacred duty or kill him and take the crystals for yourself. Do you remember what you saw? Is that what you want to have happen to this world, Kalis, because unless Ishmael and the coterie are allowed to do this the right way this could be the end for all of us.'

'That was different. Ishmael did something to me, drugged me, and I had hallucinations.'

'You know that isn't true, Kalis. The Mother spoke to you and showed you what would happen if the crystals were not used the correct way in returning magic to our world.'

'I will not stand by while you destroy everything I have worked so hard to build!' yelled Kalis. 'All I have given for the great nation of Trystland and the millions of pilgrims who travelled the road under my care, and now you seek to tear away the very foundations of our lives? I don't think so!'

They attacked again; this time one had a spear that they drove up through the ladder hole while a second fired their crossbow, forcing the defenders away. 'To the second level, now,' said Zahra. She stood guard while the others retreated up the ladder.

Ishmael looked for Kito, but there was no sign of him, and he turned to Aeon. The left side of the god's face was smeared with Kito's blood, leaving one red cheek and one clear white side. 'He didn't make it, did he, 'said Ishmael.

'No, he didn't, and that is one more reason why you must survive. His death must be remembered and avenged.'

Ishmael grabbed a new spear and stood beside Zahra to help her defend.

'I don't think we can defend it like this, Ishmael.'

'Why do you say that?'

We are trapping ourselves if we go up, and that gives Kalis time to keep sending in his men until the job is done and we lie dead as traitors.'

'So you think we should attack now?'

'Yes, I do. Onyx said there were eight, and so far we have put five out of action, so it's even and we won't get a better advantage than now.'

Ishmael nodded his agreement.

Chapter 62

When the next attack came they drew the fire from the crossbowman, then down they went with Zahra leading the way. She jumped over a slashing sword and landed on the man's bent leg.

He fell screaming with bone jutting from his thigh. The second guard, who was just coming up from the bottom level, ducked his head back down, and Zahra's sword struck the ladder. When his head popped up again, Ishmael's spear took the man in the neck, and as he fell the shaft of the spear snapped.

There came a cry from below as someone was hit by the falling body. With no other option since Zahra was behind him, Ishmael descended the next ladder to see two men attempting to climb to their feet, one a Vorm guard. The other's grey moustaches and braided hair gave him away instantly; it was Kalis the Vorm lord himself.

Ishmael screamed his fury and jabbed the broken spear into the guard's side; as he fell he grabbed Ishmael's legs and dragged him down too.

Zahra kicked Kalis in the face, and he went down again. Ishmael struggled against the guard, who was strong and was now close to getting him in a choke. The spear was still jutting from the man's side, and Ishmael grabbed it and pushed it deeper until the man squealed and tried to slither away from Ishmael, who put all his weight behind the next stab.

Ishmael left the man to die and looked over at Zahra, who was facing off against Kalis. Kalis held his hands ready to fight like a boxer and had taken a low stance. Kalis danced in delivering two punches to Zahra's body, striking her on the arms, but he knew they would have hurt her anyway. A moment later he did it again, this time a fast jab that rocked back Zahra's head. She just managed to turn out of the way of the following sharp hook that would have taken her head off. In came Kalis, again and though Ishmael was aware Zahra was a much more superior fighter than him, he wanted to get in there to take her place. Zahra lashed out with a kick to the inside of the Vorm lords knee then struck him across the shoulder with her knife. Kalis head-butted Zahra but was off balance and caught her to the side of her head. Ishmael had waited for an opening, and as Zahra fell away from the head-butt he stepped in, delivering a straight punch that Kalis had no way of seeing, and as he fell his head cracked against the stone floor.

Zahra glared at Ishmael, who shrugged and was shaking his hand. 'I think my hands broken. What, I got him, didn't I?'

'I don't need you to save me! Well, at least we can bargain our way out of here.'

Zahra tied the arms of Kalis behind him then gagged him too, and when they slapped Kalis awake all he could do was walk.

Chapter 63

They used Kalis as a shield as they cautiously moved down the tunnel before them. They took a tight left then continued for a long time to another ladder with a closed hatch. It led to the private garden of Kalis, where brightly coloured plants occupied huge pots around a square courtyard of cobblestones layered in moss. A wooden trellis formed a roof that was run over with bright green vines bursting with white flowers. The location made total sense, realized Ishmael. Kalis would be the only one besides the harpies and the elite who knew about the tunnel or the scam that the Vorm had created.

Ishmael knew where they were now and led them through another yard set up for duelling with a weapon wall holding all manner of melee weapons and two rows of seats faced the duelling lane. Zahra took the lead, merging with shadows and slinking her way along; when she was at the midpoint of the duelling lane three guards rounded the corner running.

They scrambled out their weapons as Ishmael held a knife against the Vorm lord's throat. The first two guards moved opposite in a semi-circle to try and get behind them, but if they just held their nerve, there would be no room to do so. The third one lowered his blade and put up a hand. 'Stop, they have Kalis as a hostage.'

The other two guards backed away at his order.

'What are you thinking now, the three of you? You can't just march out of here alive,' said Kalis whose gag had somehow come loose.

'That's where you are wrong, Kalis because that is exactly what we are going to do, and then you will live to see the sunrise,' Ishmael said.

'I can't and won't let you leave.'

'Quiet, Kalis, I have no patience left for you.' He turned to the guards. Get Fajira or her mother. I will discuss this with them and no other. Do it now or Kalis is going to lose something.'

They kept walking slowly through the house with a growing group of guards following them through a long kitchen. The smell of food made Ishmael feel sick and they passed it then into a large coatroom and out into the entrance hall. Fajira waited with another five soldiers.

'Ishmael, I was totally surprised when I found out it was you in the Godhead. I had believed you would be smart enough to flee the city.'

'That is what I am trying to do, Fajira. Your father wanted me dead, and I would have been if Aeon had not saved me.' He gestured to the god who stood silently behind Ishmael. 'The scam your family has run has affected too many lives to count. Aeon showed me the true horror, and once I knew, there was no other choice but to uncover it for the masses. The fact that you knew about all this disgusts me, Fajira; you seemed such a gentle person.'

'You could have just left it all alone, Ishmael. Yes, we trick the masses, and yet we run the road in such a fashion that pilgrims were safe for centuries. We gave the people hope, and even if it was just one person who had their life turned around because of the greatest trick in the history of man, then who can argue that it wasn't worth it? Without the belief in the gods our society would crumble and chaos would result.'

When Aeon spoke, his voice was clear and loud and full of retribution. 'We were to blame as much as any and thought ourselves above the Mother, and when she found only few to aid her cause she shook us, the parasites, off her. The gods just never thought they were in danger too, me included. The Severing was supposed to also be a reset where man and the other races of the world could start again with respect for the Mother and learn to live in harmony with her. Man and the other races are malleable, and yes, they survived without that true feeling of connectedness, of being separate and alone. We gods were never alone, but we just filled our life with such trivialities as riches and vanities that drowned out that connection and glutted us in hate and greed.'

Fajira let Aeon finish and shook her head sadly. 'I challenge you to tell me, who could have run the Seekers road better than the Vorm? Even after all that is happening now, it is just a hole in the road that needs repairing, and then when the common people of this world get over the knowledge of what the Vorm have done slowly they will continue to worship something as they look for peace and meaning through ritual. New gods will be born in the thoughts of mortals, and new legends will be created. Aeon, you know this to be true.'

'Yes, I believe you are right, Fajira, but for one thing. This time when magic is returned by those like Ishmael chosen by the Mother herself, things will be different. We had the chance to play nicely, but I guess instead we broke our toys like a naughty child who has no idea about the repercussions of their actions. Ishmael and the coterie have the chance to repair the damage that still lingers from the Severing. They are the heralds of a new age where power is freely returned to our world, and if anything should go wrong or the coterie is destroyed then I believe we shall truly see the might of the Mother once again.'

At that moment Thalia arrived with more soldiers. She cried out when she saw Kalis tied with visible swelling and bruising of the side of his face.

'Kalis, my love, what have they done to you?'

Ishmael stepped forward. 'Thalia, see us safely out of the city and your husband lives. I never wished for this to happen, but now it's come down to this there is no turning back. I must see my sacred duty done, and it will mean only loss for you if the Vorm try to stop me now. You saw what the crystals did to Kalis, and I am the only one here that can handle them.'

'You have signed the deaths of my family, Ishmael, and delivered us our greatest treasure just before tearing our lives apart,' said Thalia as she stood beside Fajira.

'Your family is strong and will find another way to rip people off. You are bandits and I think that's in your blood and can never be bred out. By letting us go, not only do you keep a husband and father but you take the first step in healing that is needed to bring peace and harmony back to our world.'

Thalia turned her attention to Aeon. 'Aeon, you are leaving us after being cared for by my family since the Severing, and now you turn your back on us too after all we have done for you,' said Thalia pointing an accusing finger at Aeon.

'I would have survived anyway, Fajira. You just gave me such comforts as to make my stay more comfortable, and for that I am eternally grateful. I have a new path, now and where once I trained your harpies for you in how to act like the gods, now my task has changed and I must assist to see the balance restored to this world.'

'Then go, Aeon, and you too, Ishmael, who came to us with tooth and claw hidden and earned our trust. We are the Vorm, and we will recover. I give you my word as the lady of Vorm that you will not be harmed this day but should our paths cross on the morrow or any day there after I will not and cannot guarantee your safety.'

Chapter 64

They were given an escort of ten men who led them to the closest city exit and navigated the rioters that now fought in the streets and were destroying anything they could. Some attacked the group and were brutally stopped, giving the predators who roamed the city reason to seek easier targets elsewhere.

'We head north to the border of Soarnestia where we may be able to gain passage with the raven warriors,' said Aeon.

'I am wanted in Soarnestia,' said Zahra. 'I was blamed for many deaths after I needed to escape the authorities, who would have stopped me from continuing my search for Ishmael. I would offer the options of skirting Soarnestia and crossing Auxil or heading to the docks and sail west passed the wall of Sulk to climb the teeth up to the Sulk highlands.'

'They would never help us, Zahra,' Ishmael countered. 'The Sulk retreated from the world of man long before the Severing and might not look so fondly on our trespassing on their lands.'

'Even if that's true, we have you and the crystals, and if the Sulk are as intelligent as it is told then they wouldn't stop you from passing through their lands.'

The party agreed on travelling to the Sulk lands and they spent the rest of the day making their way to the coast. After finding a small houseboat hidden amongst a graveyard of derelict boats, they stopped for the night in the glow of fires that still raged in the Godhead. Aeon lit a small fire and after finding a stocked pantry began to cook while Ishmael and Zahra kept watch.

'This is good, Aeon,' Ishmael said around a mouthful of food.' I would never have suspected a god to be able to cook.'

It only took me three hundred cycles to master the arts of cooking,' Aeon replied. My life had been kind of quiet since then.'

Ishmael took the final guard and was woken up at midnight. The moons were obscured by cloud, and still the crimson glare of Tamul showed through, filtered like watery blood as if in response to the blood spilt below in the Godhead. Ishmael climbed up onto a nearby boat and shimmied up the mast to get a good view around them. Back towards the dock a crowd had gathered and was sharing food among themselves. The harbour was choked with fleeing vessels that had become entwined at one point, and a battle was playing out in the water.

When Ishmael was sure of his surroundings, he climbed back down and sat against the hull of the boat the others slept in. Growing tired, he felt his head droop, making him fall to the side and come awake to find a figure standing before him. At first Ishmael thought it was Zahra, but the person's hair was light brown and their clothes that at first had seemed dark were in fact stained from blood. Arrow tips protruded from one of their arms. It was the girl that Zahra had called Rue.

Rue kicked Ishmael in the chest, and he fell forward, coughing. She looped an arm behind his neck and dragged him upright. A query came from the boat.

'Ishmael?

'Ishmael, are you there?'

Ishmael was still struggling for breath and saw Aeon climb down from the boat and jump down to the ground.

'Ishmael, what are you doing?'

Rue tossed something on the fire, and a series of fizzes and bangs went off, lighting up the night and blinding Ishmael. He could feel himself being dragged, and he struggled. He heard Zahra shout something in the night, which was answered by Aeon, but the choke hold was making him light headed and the voices sounded far away.

A hand clamped over his mouth and he managed to bite down; it was removed with a quiet curse, and Ishmael had some air again.

'Zahra, over here,' he managed to get out, then something hit the back of his skull and he was thrown to the side as a figure came running out of the darkness. It was Aeon, and as Rue was standing to face the new threat Aeon collided with her, striking her in the waist, and his momentum knocked Rue off her feet and onto the small fire.

Rue cried out and managed to grab hold of a charred log and struck Aeon to the side of his head, he just pulled her close and pushed her back down into the flames, which caught her hair and her clothes. Aeon backed away to stand between Rue and Ishmael. Rue tried to rise and windmilled around in a silent scream before collapsing.

Zahra had arrived now, and she thrust Moonbite through the Rue's chest, putting the girl out of her misery.

'That will stop rue for good. Are you okay, Ishmael?'

'Aeon, you saved me, but you said you cannot interfere with things otherwise there are terrible consequences.'

'I spoke the truth, Ishmael, and made a conscious choice to intervene this time because if you had of been kidnapped there was very little chance of our world surviving. There will be a backlash to my interference. I have only interfered once before, and it caused thousands of deaths in the land of Scuttle from a dormant volcano.

'I have seen the flow on effects of this action when I attacked Rue, and it is too late to change now.'

'What will happen, Aeon?'

'That I refuse to share with you and is something I shall carry with me always, along with the deaths that will follow.'

No longer able to think of sleep, the three of them steered the boat slowly across the harbour to the far side of Trystland. It took three chimes to get there without running into any more trouble. When they landed, they were at the base of the Teeth, which was the rough, rock staircase that wound up the huge cliff face bordering the west side of the Seekers road near the Godhead.

'Come on, Ishmael, we have a long climb in front of us, and if we can make the top before noon there is time to rest,' said Aeon trying to motivate Ishmael.

Ishmael just nodded. He was exhausted and needed sleep but somehow they carried on and helped each other up the winding stairs from where the view would have been magnificent if not for the billowing smoke from the city.

'Wherever I go there is death and smoke and destruction,' Ishmael said to Aeon as they walked.

'That is because you are bringing about change, and the old structures fight against that change, they are desperate to stop it from happening. The Vorm would never sit by idly watching the centuries of hard work destroyed in one night of madness, but it has happened anyway, and you were the key to that change. Your other coterie members would be causing change wherever they go too.'

Now Ishmael's thoughts had been drawn to the coterie, he felt the pressure of his guilt press in. They were a team, and he had shut them out so he could follow his own selfish goals. Now he must put all that had happened behind him and reach out to them, which meant lowering his mental walls.

They stopped to eat and sat on the wooden planking that ran along the narrow path. With their backs to the wall the three sat and shared water and food. In a few chimes they would make the summit and then would be in Sulk territory. Who knew what sort of welcome they would get if any at all.

Now finished eating, Ishmael noticed Zahra watching him.

'You need to contact the coterie, Ishmael, so they know where we are and that soon we can join them. The other sentinels have already gathered at the safe house and wait for us.'

Ishmael exhaled; he felt suddenly nervous, and if the coterie rejected his attempt to make contact, what then? He had hardly done what he needed to help the coterie.

'It's time, isn't it, Zahra?'

'Yes. You have travelled to find out your family has forsaken you and now your faith has been lost and you know the gods except Aeon are dead. These two losses can be approached by the path of loss and self-depreciation and blame, or you can see this as having the chains that they caused now broken, thus setting you free on a new path where you get to choose.'

Chapter 65

Ishmael made himself as comfortable as he could and began breathing deeply. He let his walls fall away and reached out for Jona with his mind, seeking to connect with her. The connection was quick, too quick, and as Ishmael took Jona's vision he at first thought something was wrong with her eyes before realizing he was seeing from a prone position on the ground.

'Ishmael, they found us, and we will die horribly like Brianna did.'

Ishmael saw Jona's hand wipe her nose, and it came away bloody. In front of Jona, Ishmael saw two soldiers bearing the crest of a flame dragging a woman by the hair who was cursing loudly. It was Selene, and a man charged into view slicing through one of the guards to stand over Selene protectively. It was her sentinel, realized Ishmael as a circle of warriors closed in on the man. He fought bravely, taking two guards with him before being knocked down. Selene was distraught and went wild, biting, scratching, and screaming like a banshee as Jona lay half dazed to her surroundings.

'Jona, you need to get out of here. Get up and move.'

'Betrayed, Ishmael, can you believe that? Raul betrayed us. We are supposed to achieve our task together, and yet we are more separate than ever.'

A guard came into view and hauled Jona up then backhanded her across the face before dumping her alongside Selene.

The old bastard Dalwyn Trevlon appeared.

'Tie them up in the middle of the main room. Later we can have some fun with them both.'

Raul jumped in between the two women and Dalwyn.

'You promised not to harm them, Dalwyn.'

'No, Raul, I promised not to kill them. This is no time for weakness. You are as much a part of this as me. I never asked you to betray your friends.'

Raul waded forward and slammed a meaty fist into Dalwyn's grin, but the old man stood his ground and jammed his fingers into Raul's windpipe then raked his eyes with his fingers. Raul pushed away from Dalwyn to create space and stood regarding him, and a woman who stepped to Dalwyn's side with a drawn sword.

'You and Dalwyn said no harm would come to us, Katerina. You are my sentinel and supposed to protect me.'

'Katerina scoffed and spat on the ground. 'I was never your sentinel Raul. I killed her and took her place. You were too lost in lust to see through my lies. Anyway, I had no choice, and Dalwyn pays top coin.'

One of the last four prisoners were an ancient and even though Ishmael had never seen one he had seen plenty of art depicting the strange folk. The ancient was being carried by a rugged older man who looked dangerous and moved with total ease as if unconcerned by what was happening around him. The ancient he carried had wasted, thin legs and was tall with a waterfall of silver hair. She was staring at him, and he knew her. It was the thing in the cocoon that had been connected to the earth tree. She just nodded then turned away, and her look said what a thousand words couldn't. *Why you aren't here? Without you the coterie is weak.*

Zahra sat beside Ishmael with Aeon waiting as he mumbled quietly in a trance state. Then without warning he stood screaming and lurched forward towards the cliff edge. Zahra managed to grasp his shirt and pull him back with Aeon's help.

'Ishmael, what happened?' asked Zahra, holding him by the shoulders when they managed to settle Ishmael down.

'He has them, all three of them, and it's my fault.'

'Who has them, Ishmael, who?'

Ishmael's eyes cleared, and Zahra saw him recognize her and where he was again.

'Dalwyn Trevlon. They are in great danger now while I am here chasing my own selfish motives. I forced them to wait too long, and now it's caused their capture. We are undone!'

This book is dedicated to my daughter Lily Church who brings so much joy to my life that I sometimes feel as if my heart may burst with happiness.

If you enjoyed reading my novel Pariah please take the time to go to amazon or my face book author page and leave a review.

Thank you from the bottom of my heart for reading my book.

Troy Church.

www.ingramcontent.com/pod-product-compliance
Lightning Source LLC
Chambersburg PA
CBHW071146100726
47908CB00002B/271